WARLOCK GRIMOIRE IV

KOBOLD Press

CREDITS

Designers: Lou Anders, Wolfgang Baur, HH Carlan, Robert Fairbanks, Basheer Ghouse, Richard Green, Tim Hitchcock, Jeremy Hochhalter, Victoria Jaczko, Rajan Khanna, Sarah Madsen, Ben McFarland, Jonathan Miley, Kelly Pawlik, Sebastian Rombach, Adam W. Roy, Paul Scofield, Amber Stewart, Brian Suskind, Mike Welham

Developer & Editor: Scott Gable

Additional Editor: Kenny Webb

Art Director & Graphic Designer: Marc Radle

Cover Artist: Marcel Mercado

Interior Artists: Tony DiTerlizzi, Justine Jones, William McAusland, Pedro Potier, Dean Spencer, Phil Stone, Karl Waller

Publisher: Wolfgang Baur

TABLE OF CONTENTS

Tony DiTerlizzi

BEYOND THE LEAVES OF THE WORLD TREE

by Scott Gable

No, there is another…!

A fourth *Warlock Grimoire* to rule them all—and to mark the First Age of Warlock. Let us celebrate:

- **Warlock Lairs:** 79 lairs + the hardcover volume *Warlock Lairs: Into the Wilds*
- **Warlock Zine:** 37 + *Warlock Guide to the Shadow Realm, Warlock Guide to Liminal Magic,* and *Warlock Guide to the Planes*
- **Warlock Grimoires:** 4 hardcover volumes

And so, after such a wondrous run, it is with these current pages, the ones you're holding right now, that we lower the curtain on this chapter of Warlock. You have given us the privilege of guiding you through Midgard. Together, we've traveled throughout its many lands and even beyond the leaves of Yggdrasil—catching a glimpse of the multiverse looming ever just past the horizon. With your love of the setting to guide us, we have filled its history books to bursting.

"But are we never to see the glory of Warlock again?" you ask. To which I can say most exuberantly, all the stars, all the entrails, and all the tea leaves unanimously agree: "Ask again later."

Meanwhile, in these pages, we explore the lives of Zobeckers and discuss the priesthood throughout the Crossroads. We meet with the kobolds of Lillefor and Melana and with the elves, including firsthand accounts of the windrunner elves and historical context for the lost courts. And speaking of things lost, there is much on sunken Ankeshel and its long reach through the ages. Plus, we uncover details on many of the threats, both monsters and void cultists, that you might find throughout the multiverse, for your safety and ours, and we take you to the wonder that is the elemental planes. There are even some specious lies about Baba Yaga!

We've collected here everything from *Warlock 29–37* and added new, never-before-seen pieces on the hive of villainy that is Misto Cherno, on the strange gnomes of the Wastes, and on organized crime in the Southlands. There are even a couple Tony DiTerlizzi illustrations for you to stumble across in awe.

This is 5th Edition content from the amazing kobold artists and designers you've come to love. This is magic—and now it's yours to explore and to spin into something greater. We proudly deliver unto you *Warlock Grimoire 4*, the final secrets of the multiverse that we uncovered for you, our otherworldly patrons. None of this could have happened without you, and it has been my sincerest pleasure to serve as your guide. Thank you, from all of us at Kobold Press.

Yrs of the Dark and Fantastical,
Scott Gable
Editor, Kobold Press

LORE AND STORYTELLING

MYSTERIES OF THE LOST ELVEN COURTS

by Sarah Madsen

The elven courts once spanned much of Midgard, shining and elegant in their splendor. With the passing of the Great Retreat, many of these once-grand courts were left abandoned, slowly relenting to the passing of time and decay. Some of these courts still house residents of one type or another, whether Arbonesse exiles that refused to leave their homes, servants who were abandoned when the Last Horn sounded, or unnamed entities that have moved into the abandoned halls like hermit crabs into an empty shell.

The elves built their cities in wild and beautiful places. With access to the fey roads, few elves worried about passage overland, so courts that were tricky to reach during their heyday are practically impossible to approach now. These forests are filled with deadly and terrifying threats, and the roads are choked by centuries of undergrowth. The elves' lands have been reclaimed by nature, by the unquiet dead, or by their own descendants. Mysteries abound within these lost courts, and rumors spin ever wilder tales of what lies within the ruined grandeur of the elven holdings.

For more on elven courts, see *Warlock 7: Fey Courts.*

CLOUD DRAGON COURT (TOMIERRAN FOREST)

To the east of the Arbonesse lies the Tomierran Forest. Once the home of not one but two elven courts, the Tomierran now hides more secrets than it gives answers. Nearest to the Greater Duchy of Morgau, the forest's proximity to the undead empire means it sees more than its fair share of incursions, but its stewardship under Saintmistress Rowanmantle keeps the undead from encroaching too far.

Overshadowed by the infamous ruins of Thorn, the remnants of the Cloud Dragon Court are far less flashy. Paired with its seclusion deep in the forest, it has seen far fewer tomb raiders and adventurers than the former elven capital. Even those that know of the court's existence are hesitant to make the journey—the risks of delving into the Tomierran are great indeed, and the rewards are unknown.

Triple Spires. During its height, the Cloud Dragon Court held three main spires. These thin towers stretched ever upward, reaching far past the tops of the trees, a marvel of elven construction and magic. The three spires were called the Star Spire, the Moon Spire, and the Sun Spire, and they formed a perfect triangle at the center of the city.

Each of these spires contained dozens of small chambers and a long spiral staircase that terminated at an open cupola with a domed cap. Here it was possible to look out over the entirety of the Tomierran. On a clear day, one could glimpse the Nieder Straits to the north past the twisting branches of Holda's Tree.

The spires were connected by the three long sides of the Hastate Conservatory, a soaring glass spire atop a triangular white-stone courtyard. Elves moved through these hallways in quiet contemplation or picnicked in the courtyard with the Dreamer's Cloud hovering between the spires far above.

The day the elves left the halls of the Cloud Dragon Court and took their magic with them, the spires collapsed to the earth far below them, shattering stone and glass alike. All that now remains of the fallen towers is a forest of debris and three jagged stumps of white stone.

FORGOTTEN SCHOOL: DREAM MAGIC

The arcane practitioners of the Cloud Dragon Court were the progenitors of a lost school of elven high magic: dream magic. Dream magic allowed the elves to use dreams for a multitude of purposes: divination through *oneiromancy*, research and espionage through *dreamstride*, or even using a *phantasm* to assassinate an enemy from a distance while they lie dreaming.

Given elves' non-slumbering nature, dream magic was incredibly difficult to master, and many elven mages thought it folly to dedicate so much time and study to an art that may well be out of the reach of their kind. Others thought it a passing fad or a fringe offshoot of liminal magic that would be absorbed into other spellcraft or eventually fade away. Indeed, the elves of the Cloud Dragon Court may never have created, practiced, or mastered dream magic without the aid of a particularly powerful ally: Kalikamorea, the Dreamer.

Few artifacts or records remain of dream magic, but a scroll or book may be found within the broken ruins of the Cloud Dragon Court.

DREAM MAGIC SPELLS

Dream magic uses the malleability of dreams to harness and channel arcane power.

DREAMSTRIDE

3rd-Level Illusion (Dream, Ritual Only) | Druid, Wizard

Casting Time: 10 minutes
Range: Self
Components: V, S
Duration: Concentration, up to 10 minutes

You reach out with your consciousness and step into the dreams of another creature in order to view a memory or gather information. The creature must be on the same plane of existence as you and have a minimum Intelligence score of 7. If the target is not asleep or in meditation (in the case of elves or similar races) when the spell is cast, the spell fails. This spell has no effect on constructs or undead.

When you cast the spell, you enter your target's dream, and you view the events as an invisible third party. The creature is unaware of your presence, and you cannot interact with the dream in any way other than the method listed below.

As an action, you can reach out your consciousness and attempt to influence the course of the dream. For example, you may cause something new to appear or cause the tone of the dream to change to a nightmare (or vice-versa) or influence a "character" in the dream other than the target to act a certain way. When you attempt to influence the dream, your target must succeed on a Wisdom saving throw against your spell save DC. On a failed save, your attempt to alter the dream is successful. On a successful save, you are immediately ejected from the dream as the dreamer awakens.

For the duration of the spell, your body lies in repose in the location you cast the spell. You are blind and deaf to your body's surroundings, though you can feel and are aware if you take damage. If your body is moved, the spell ends. If your target is awakened, the spell ends.

ONEIROMANCY

1st-Level Divination (Dream, Ritual Only) | Cleric, Druid, Wizard

Casting Time: 10 minutes
Range: Touch
Components: V, S, M (a bit of mushroom)
Duration: Concentration, 4 or 6 hours (see below)

Dreams can be gateways to understanding, and you can induce such prophetic and insightful dreams in yourself and others. You touch a willing creature of your choice. The creature immediately falls into an enchanted dream state and remains for an entire long rest (4 or 6 hours, depending on their race) unless awakened or if they choose to end the spell early. During this long rest, they experience dreams and visions centering around an event or question of their choice, specified at the casting of the spell. The dreams may be literal, or they may be wrapped in symbolism, omens, and metaphor and left to the dreamer to interpret. This dream state counts as sleep or meditation for the purposes of a long rest.

If the target's sleep is interrupted, the dreams induced by this spell end. The target may still complete a long rest and gain its benefits, but they do not return to their previous dreams.

Elves and other creatures with immunity to magical sleep choose whether or not to be affected by this spell.

This spell has no effect on constructs or undead.

PHANTASM

6th-Level Illusion (Dream, Ritual Only) | Sorcerer, Warlock, Wizard

Casting Time: 10 minutes
Range: Self
Components: V, S, M (an item from the target, a pinch of grave dirt, and 5,000 gp worth of powdered sapphire, which the spell consumes)
Duration: Concentration, up to 1 minute

You reach out with your consciousness and influence the dreams of another creature. The

creature must be on the same plane of existence as you and have a minimum Intelligence score of 7. If the target is not asleep or in meditation (in the case of elves or similar races) when the spell is cast, the spell fails. This spell has no effect on constructs or undead.

Your target must succeed on a Wisdom saving throw against your spell save DC. On a failure, their dream becomes a nightmare, and they take 4d10 psychic damage. On a success, they take half as much damage, the spell ends, and you take the same amount of psychic damage as you are shoved from the dream. At the start of each of their turns, the target repeats the saving throw, taking an additional 4d10 damage on a failed save. Once the target succeeds on their saving throw, they are immune to this spell for the next 7 days. The target cannot wake themselves, but if they are awakened by an outside force or if they fall to 0 hit points, the spell ends.

If the target succeeds on their saving throw, they may attempt a DC 20 Wisdom (Insight) check. On a success, if they are familiar with you, they recognize you as the attacker. If they are unfamiliar with you, they do not recognize you, though you may seem strangely familiar if the two of you meet at a later time, and you may even evoke feelings of unease.

For the duration of the spell, your body lies in repose in the location you cast the spell. You are blind and deaf to your body's surroundings, though you can feel and are aware if you take damage. If your body is moved, the spell ends. If your target is awakened, the spell ends.

At Higher Levels. When you cast this spell at 7th level or higher, you deal an additional 1d10 psychic damage per spell slot above 6th (5d10 at 7th level, 6d10 at 8th level, 7d10 at 9th level).

KALIKAMOREA, THE DREAMER

Between the Triple Spires hovered a cloud over a mile in diameter, its hazy edges just out of reach of the cupolas at their tops. The cloud's appearance, whether fluffy and white or dark and stormy, depended entirely on the mood of its inhabitant: an ancient cloud dragon known as Kalikamorea, the Dreamer.

Kalikamorea was already ancient when she came to the Tomierran, and history is unclear if she made her home there and the elves built their city around her or if the elves had already established their home within the Tomierran when she arrived. Whatever the case, the cloud dragon and the court beneath her existed in harmony for ages.

Kalikamorea rarely left her cloud. Those who wished an audience would climb to the apex of one of the spires to petition the dragon. If she were in a welcoming mood or if the elf was one of her favorites (and make no mistake, she had her favorites), Kalikamorea would initiate a telepathic bond between the two. Conversations with the Dreamer could last for hours or even days, and often the elf involved would meditate far longer than necessary once they descended the spire, their exhausted mind struggling to process everything they had learned from the dragon.

When the elves left for the Summer Lands and the Triple Spires collapsed, Kalikamorea's cloud dispersed, and she disappeared. Some claim she was invited to accompany the elves on their exodus, some believe she fled across the lands to the east, and still others whisper that perhaps she never existed in the first place—merely a collective dream of the elves.

Tears of the Dreamer. Scattered throughout the ruins of the Cloud Dragon Court are strange crystals. About the size of a man's palm, these pear-shaped gems are cold to the touch and faceted as if cut and polished, though they've never felt the bite of a grindstone. The gemstones are usually found in shades of blue, green, or white, though reds, oranges, and yellows have also been discovered. There is only one black stone known in existence. The jewels are of pristine clarity and flawless in every aspect.

These crystals are known as the Tears of the Dreamer and hold memories and magical essence within them. The jewels can be ground

into a fine gem dust and used in place of spell components.

Additionally, if a PC studies the depths of one, they gain access to a memory locked within. Glimpsed in fleeting images, half-heard words, and vague emotional impressions, the memory is from one of the former residents of the Cloud Dragon Court, typically an elf (though it's not unheard of to glimpse the memory of a servant). Each holds at least one memory, though some have been found with multiple related memories.

Experiencing a particularly vivid memory can convey knowledge to the viewer, and in some cases, the viewer has temporarily gained a particular skill, though the working knowledge fades fairly quickly.

So far, none have been found to hold a memory from Kalikamorea, though scholars and treasure hunters alike hold out hope to one day find such a stone.

TEARS OF THE DREAMER

d100	GEM COLOR	RARITY	SKILL	VALUE
1–20	Blue	Rare	Perception or Investigation	5,000 gp
21–40	Green	Rare	Insight or Deception	5,000 gp
41–60	White	Rare	Medicine or Nature	5,000 gp
61–69	Yellow	Very Rare	Sleight of Hand, Acrobatics, or Forgery Kit	10,000 gp
70–78	Orange	Very Rare	Alchemists Tools, Arcana, Martial Ranged Weapons	10,000 gp
79–87	Red	Very Rare	Thieves' Tools, Stealth, Medium Armor	10,000 gp
88–96	Purple	Very Rare	Navigator's Tools, Survival, Martial Melee Weapons	10,000 gp
97–100	Black	Legendary	Any three proficiencies (player's choice)	50,000 gp

Summer Gardens (Gennecka Forest)

The Summer Gardens, also known as Osilessidra after its queen, lie hidden deep within the Gennecka Forest. Travel to the city during its height was daunting for those not skilled in the arcane. The only reliable way to reach the city was via fey roads, and traveling the trails through the forest was a feat only undertaken by the most determined. This was by design, for while Queen Osilessi did not outright ban those not of elven blood from her realm, she looked for more subtle ways to discourage them from entering her borders unless specifically invited.

Once a retreat for the elves of Midgard, Osilessidra was a city of pristine gardens, greenhouses, and conservatories of all types, filled with carefully cultivated (and heavily protected) plants from the Summer Lands themselves, offering respite to those homesick for the Elflands. The city also boasted vast libraries, filled with magical and mundane tomes of all sorts. Making the trek to Osilessidra was dangerous, but many scholars deemed the quest worth the risk for even the barest of glimpses of the vast knowledge held within its marbled halls. Study was popular here, not just of literature but of the arts of all kinds, and it was not uncommon for elven bards to spend several seasons wandering the halls and gardens in the process of honing their craft or to find luminaries reclining on elegant cushions, sketching the blossoms and each other.

Now, the Summer Gardens are but a wild and crumbling shadow of what they once were. Much of the grounds have fallen to time and have been reclaimed by the forest, save for the few chambers still tended to by the Steadfast.

Alabaster Libraries. Maintained by the Steadfast, the Alabaster Libraries are housed in the west wing of the queen's palace. The rooms themselves are kept locked, opened once a day when the gnomes enter to dust shelves, polish furniture, and tend to the tomes that line the walls. The gnomes that work the Alabaster Libraries know exactly what books reside within, their precise location, and their condition, and notice immediately if something is out of place or otherwise amiss.

Alongside the treasures of knowledge, the Alabaster Libraries contain multitudes of trinkets and treasures in the form of paintings, sculptures, ancient maps, bookends, and priceless tchotchkes displayed upon the shelves. Any one of these could fetch a high price to the right collector, but retrieving it out from under the nose of the protective Steadfast and getting back out of the Gennecka unscathed would be a challenge indeed.

Gardens. Many of the carefully tended flora from the Summer Lands have long since withered to dust, but rumors persist in certain circles that rare and wondrous plants can be found in the ruins of the Summer Gardens. Rumors also claim that monstrous carnivorous plants roam the grounds and are happy to make

TEARS OF THE DREAMER
Wondrous Item,
Rarity Varies by Color

This tear-shaped gemstone is roughly the size of an adult human's palm. Though cold to the touch, it hums with mystical vitality, and fleeting images can be glimpsed along its surface.

A creature may spend a short rest meditating on the images within. During their meditation, they experience a memory held within the Tear, as determined by the GM. When they complete the meditation, the creature gains one proficiency, as noted in the Tears of the Dreamer table. This benefit lasts for eight hours. Only one creature may gain this benefit at a time, and the item cannot be used in this way again until the next dawn.

Additionally, a Tear can be ground into a fine gem dust that can be used in place of the spell components of equivalent monetary value. Doing so destroys the Tear. The worth of the gem dust is noted in the chart below. If the spell consumes the spell components, it instead consumes the equivalent value of dust.

a meal of any wayward traveler. Nonetheless, some botanists and alchemists are willing to pay a hefty amount of coin to adventurers willing to brave the risks to bring back cuttings or live plants.

Within the gardens is an elaborate hedge maze of rose bushes that has somehow remained pristine despite the passing of centuries, a twin to the Prickling Maze of the Court of Roses in the Arbonesse. Unlike the roses found in the Prickling Maze though, the roses here are not sentient, nor do they speak. They do, however, give off a heady fragrance that can bewilder and charm those not of elven blood. Any creature who enters the maze may find themselves lost, not just confounded by the twists and turns of the pathway but beguiled by the roses themselves.

Though the Blood Duke Rüzgar, ruler of the nearby province of Zaldiri, is keen on the forest, an annual tribute of rare mushroom elixirs from the Steadfast to sooth the ancient cave dragon's old battle scars—along with the arrows and spells of the Gennecka's other inhabitants—keep the morza satisfied for now.

Treasury. Servants and their children were not the only things left behind by the elves when they left Midgard. In many cases, anything too difficult to transport was abandoned—including vast treasures. It is rumored that, hidden somewhere on the grounds of the Summer Gardens, is the treasury, still full of all the priceless art and treasures the residents were forced to abandoned. But the elves built their locks to last, and their traps were deadly.

THE STEADFAST

When the Last Horn sounded and the Great Retreat began, the elves left much behind, including their gnomish and halfling servitors. Many of these servants ventured out into the wide world beyond, embracing new opportunities, but a few remained behind to maintain what they could of their former homes in case the elves ever returned. Even many of these departed the empty estates after some time, realizing the futility of serving masters that had long since abandoned them.

Though generations have passed since the elves left Midgard, the descendants of gnomish servants still remain within the Summer Gardens. They call themselves the Steadfast, clinging to their duties and loyalties in a way they see as honorable and dedicated. Despite their determination and the occasional addition to their ranks, the numbers of Steadfast have dwindled over the centuries. Currently, they only have enough manpower to maintain a few of the gardens' chambers, and they focus their attentions on the Alabaster Libraries, the throne room, and the queen's chambers. Everything else has fallen into disrepair.

WILLOW COURT OF THE WINEWOOD

A relatively small court, the halls of the Willow Court rested in the southeastern portion of the Winewood in Rumela. Nestled up against the protective wall formed by the Griffoncrags, the Willow Court enjoyed the fruits of the forest and the mountains alike. Orchards were cultivated within the Winewood. Terraced vineyards were built up the steep slopes of the Griffoncrags while precious metals were pulled from mines at the base of the mountains and griffons roosted in their peaks. While the bounty from their trees didn't quite match the harvests in the Summer Gardens, their wines never quite lived up to those created in Dornig, and their griffons were never quite as grand as the ones found in the Margreve, the Willow Court nonetheless carved out their own name.

When the Mharoti claimed Rumela for themselves, the borders of the Winewood shrank inward as the dragonkin felled the trees along the edges for their new construction. Still, the depths of the forest remain mostly untouched and unexplored, save for the druids who make their homes within. But even they avoid the ruins of the Willow Court, concerning themselves more with the dragonkin at their eastern and southern borders.

GRIFFONS OF THE WILLOW COURT

The Griffoncrags are aptly named. In the warmer months, it is not unusual to see young griffons wheeling and playing amidst the thermal updrafts or to spot a solitary adult or pair hunting far afield. The golden griffons of the Griffoncrags are smaller and faster than the breeds found in the Margreve or Zobeck.

The ruins of the Willow Court hold the remains of stables and rookeries, now empty of anything but dust and mold. The griffon riders of the Willow Court often traveled to the Griffon Court to train and then returned to train others. The griffons of the Willow Court were kept more for sport and pleasure than for protection though. While remnants of griffon barding and polearms for griffon-mounted combat can be found, the majority of the saddles and bridals that remain are sleeker and more ornate, crafted for comfort and prestige rather than battle.

WILLOW COURT WINE

Made from the grapes grown on the western slopes of the Griffoncrags and fermented in clear mountain spring water, Willow Court wine was once enjoyed by the elves of the Winewood in vast amounts. One of the few exports from the city, it was enjoyed even as far as the Griffon Court in the Margreve Forest (though many of the Griffon Court preferred the sweeter wine made in Thorn). The vintners of the Willow Court each had their own enchantments that they wove into their fermentation vats and aging barrels, trade secrets that maintained proper temperature, pressure, and sugar levels to create the perfect wine.

When the Great Retreat occurred, much of the wine was left behind, either in barrels in the warehouses tucked at the base of the Griffoncrags or in bottles in the wine cellars throughout the households of the Willow Court. Though much of this wine has been plundered

already, finding a forgotten bottle or a hidden cask might still be possible. A bottle of such recovered wine would make a fine gift to an elf of any sufficient age and memory or to a noble of discerning taste.

Wild Fermentation. Sometime after the Great Retreat, some of the enchanted fermentation vats and aging barrels were destroyed when the roof of the building they were stored in collapsed. The enchantments seeped from the shattered wood along with the liquid within, permeating the soil and water and releasing their spores into the air. The circle of druids who now reside within the Winewood (see *Warlock 7: Fey Courts*) utilize the forest's unique environment to their advantage, but outsiders may find the atmosphere (not to mention the smell) off-putting. Additionally, foodstuffs brought within the Winewood, especially fresh fruits, quickly go sour and become inedible unless magically protected.

LOST ARBONESSE

Unlike the other lost elven courts, Lost Arbonesse was not abandoned but destroyed. The tales tell that more than 400 years ago, the great beast Isonade rose from the depths of the Uttermost Sea and dragged the northwestern portion of the Arbonesse into the sea. Now, the ruins of the court lie beneath the waves as the stumps of the great trees and shattered remnants of its structures dot the coastline.

But what waits within the drowned elven city is a mystery to most. Sailing the waters is hazardous at best, for the hidden ruins can pierce the hull of even the most cautious ship. Spirits of the unquiet dead and strange creatures from the depths haunt the coastline and the waters themselves, quickly stymying any attempted excursions.

The few elves in Midgard that remember Lost Arbonesse before it fell to the sea refuse to speak of it, whether out of fear or sorrow, and seem uninterested in making any major efforts to explore the ruins. Better to let the ghosts (and their memories) rest.

DROWNED TRINKETS

Strange treasures often turn up on the coastline where Lost Arbonesse sank. Shattered pieces of furniture, broken trinkets, and crumpled odds and ends all make their way to the sand even now, centuries after the city's destruction.

The strangest, and possibly saddest though, are the bits of sea glass that roll onto the shore, revealed each day by the receding tide. This glass—not just blues and greens but vivid reds, purples, yellows, and oranges—are the remnants of the elaborate stained-glass windows that once resided in the city's grand halls, and they glitter and gleam in the sand all along the coast. However, these beautiful, almost organic-looking baubles are shunned by the locals. It's considered bad luck to take them from the shore. More than one story circulates of an elf or elfmarked that collected a piece of the tumbled glass as a memento to a lost loved one and was later driven mad by haunted whisperings or found drowned by saltwater in their own bed, nowhere near the ocean.

BEACON FOR THE UNDEAD

The destruction of Lost Arbonesse was an act so terrible, so tragic, it sent shockwaves through the region and fundamentally altered the land and its arcane underpinnings. Countless undead were created that day, not only from the citizens and visitors that drowned beneath the waves but by a massive influx of pain, sorrow, and rage. The coastline and sunken city teem with ghosts, zombies, and other undead, both those that were created there and those that have been drawn to the region like moths to a flame.

Some of these undead are much like the others any adventurer would find at all points of the map. Some, however, bear unique features that have only been seen in the area of Lost Arbonesse.

Water Wights and Brinemaidens. Many of the undead found in Lost Arbonesse display similarities to the more intelligent undead found throughout Midgard, but they have an unnerving affinity for the water in and around the ruins of the elven city. They bear elven features, and some even wear scraps of armor said to bear the crest of the houses lost beneath the sea.

WATER WIGHT

An undead elf, draped in the rotting trappings of a long-lost civilization, shambles toward you through the surf.

Similar in disposition and behavior to common wights, the water wight is nonetheless unique to Lost Arbonesse. Wielding rusted and rotting weapons of the lost elvish culture, the water wight is a vengeful and unforgiving foe.

Lost Honor. The water wights were once soldiers of the great elvish houses of what is now Lost Arbonesse. They rage against their helplessness at the fate of their city and their loved ones, and seethe at the injustice. They continue to mindlessly protect their houses and lands, with little regard to the fact that they—and everyone they knew—are dead. They cannot be reasoned with, unable to face the truth of their tragic end.

Undead Nature. A water wight doesn't require air, food, drink, or sleep.

WATER WIGHT

Medium Undead, Neutral Evil
Armor Class 14 (studded leather)
Hit Points 45 (6d8 + 18)
Speed 30 ft., swim 30 ft.

STR	DEX	CON	INT	WIS	CHA
16 (+3)	13 (+1)	16 (+3)	10 (+0)	13 (+1)	15 (+2)

Saving Throws Con +5
Skills Perception +3, Stealth +3
Damage Resistances necrotic; bludgeoning, piercing, and slashing from nonmagical attacks
Senses darkvision 60 ft., passive Perception 13
Languages the languages it knew in life
Challenge 3 (700 XP)   **Proficiency Bonus** +2

Aversion to Dry Ground. When the water wight is on dry ground, it has disadvantage on attack rolls.

ACTIONS

Multiattack. The water wight makes two Longsword attacks. It can use Drown in place of one of these attacks.

Longsword. *Melee Weapon Attack*: +5 to hit, reach 5 ft., one target. *Hit*: 7 (1d8 + 3) slashing damage or 8 (1d10 + 3) slashing damage if used with two hands.

Drown. The water wight locks eyes with its enemy, conjuring within its target the raging waters of the sea. The target must make a DC 14 Wisdom saving throw. On a failure, salt water fills the target's mouth, throat, and lungs, and the target has no breath left and immediately begins to drown. The target may repeat the saving throw at the end of their turn. On a success, the effect ends. The effect ends if the target or the water wight is reduced to 0 hit points. A target that dies in this fashion rises 24 hours later as a **zombie** under the water wight's control. The wight can have no more than six zombies under its control at one time.

BRINEMAIDEN

A ghostly figure of an elven woman floats toward you through the water, its empty eye sockets fixed on yours, its mouth open impossibly wide in an unearthly wail.

Cousin to banshees and drowned maidens, the brinemaiden is the lost spirit of an elven woman drowned within Lost Arbonesse. She floats along the coastline and even through the submerged ruins, retracing steps she took often in life. A brinemaiden is an angry and frightened spirit, lashing out at any nearby living creature in her confusion.

Bound to Baubles. A brinemaiden need not be confined to the place of her death and may be bound instead to an item from her life. A trinket, a piece of jewelry, or even the last thing she saw as she drowned can be the tether for her rage-filled soul. Many brinemaidens are bound to bits of Lost Arbonesse sea glass, as the shattered remnants of stained-glass windows filled the swirling waters around them as they drowned. Individuals that wander away from the ruins of Lost Arbonesse with one of these prizes often inadvertently brings a brinemaiden with them.

Undead Nature. A brinemaiden doesn't require air, food, drink, or sleep.

BRINEMAIDEN

Medium Undead, Chaotic Evil

Armor Class 12
Hit Points 58 (13d8)
Speed 0 ft., fly 40 ft. (hover), swim 40 ft.

STR	DEX	CON	INT	WIS	CHA
1 (−5)	14 (+2)	10 (+0)	12 (+1)	11 (+0)	17 (+3)

Saving Throws Wis +2, Cha +5
Damage Resistances acid, fire, lightning, thunder; bludgeoning, piercing, and slashing from nonmagical weapons
Damage Immunities cold, necrotic, poison
Condition Immunities charmed, exhaustion, frightened, grappled, paralyzed, petrified, poisoned, prone, restrained
Senses darkvision 60 ft., passive Perception 12
Languages the languages she knew in life.
Challenge 4 (1,100 XP)   **Proficiency Bonus** +2

Detect Life. The brinemaiden can magically sense the presence of creatures up to 5 miles away that aren't undead or constructs. She knows the general direction they're in but not exact locations.

Incorporeal Movement. The brinemaiden can move through other creatures and objects as if they were difficult terrain. It takes 5 (1d10) force damage if it ends its turn inside an object.

ACTIONS

Corrupting Touch. *Melee Spell Attack:* +4 to hit, reach 5 ft., one target. *Hit:* 12 (3d6 + 2) necrotic damage.

Calls of the Lost. Each creature within 60 feet of the brinemaiden must succeed on a DC 13 Wisdom saving throw. On a failed save, they must use all of their movement and must take the dash action to move directly toward and into the nearest body of water, as the haunting wails of the drowned call out to them. The creature may take no other actions, bonus actions, or reactions. The target may repeat the saving throw at the end of their turn. A creature who reaches the water while under these effects swims (or walks, if they cannot swim) their full speed directly away from the shore until the effect ends. If there is no water nearby, the creature spends their turn wracked with mournful sobs.

Wail (1/Day). The banshee releases a mournful wail, provided that she isn't in sunlight. This wail has no effect on constructs and undead. All other creatures within 30 feet of her that can hear her must make a DC 13 Constitution saving throw. On a failure, the creature drops to 0 hit points. On a success, a creature takes 10 (3d6) psychic damage.

DRIFTING PIECES: THE REMNANTS OF ANKESHEL

by HH Carlan and Ben McFarland

Ankeshel lingers on the edge of awareness for most Midlander sages as a distant memory of a forerunner civilization that fought the aboleth to a mutual destruction. The once-great city remains a lost empire, sunk beneath the waves in the chilly waters off the coast of Cassadega. The current inhabitants stand upon the bones of its Ankeshelian predecessor, whose name is lost to time and the Isonade's fury. It is the source of strange coil rifles, brilliant orichalcum, unusual magics, and the esoteric element of vril, bottled in batteries of brine, glass, and metal. The people of the Western Wastes seek this dead culture's legacy with an insatiable thirst and undoubtedly reckless abandon. Their efforts have borne fruit, especially in the years following the discovery of Thalassos IV's tomb complex and the partial unlocking of the Ankeshelian language. The following text offers up a few of the more notable findings, the strange behaviors of those who have now spent decades searching, and the new wonders they have rescued from the remnants of Ankeshel.

Floating Observatory of Watered Glass

The island of Motun drifts on the currents of the Western Sea, occasionally wandering as far south as Barsella but never far from the coastline—unless nudged by the passage of the Isonade. Roughly circular and about 2,500 feet across, it sports rough beaches of mostly loose gravel and a little sand. The island's interior slopes upward 30 feet to a broad, flat-topped hill of exposed bedrock, comprising the innermost 1,000 feet and hosting the observatory grounds. Just beyond the high-water mark, a band of foliage approximately 200 feet thick rings Motun, mostly concealing a ruined Ankeshelian structure. Beyond this barrier forest is a ring road of broad, paved causeways, spiraling into the deeper island interior.

Once a site of astronomical divination during the war against the aboleth, Motun became unmoored and began drifting after a massive battle against the aberrations and their armies. A few pirates can confirm its existence, but they only use the island to resupply and haven't attempted establishing a settlement there. An orichalcum dragon (see below) lairs in one of the ruined temples, and its various guardians have ensured no trespassers survive for long. But some visitors have landed, wandered about, and quickly left, spreading tales of the island's splendor and rich construction among Midgard's western port taverns.

A temple complex stands atop the hill at its center, more than a dozen structures surrounding a broad, rectangular pool hewn from the rock and filled with crystal-clear water. It was once called the Reflecting Glass. A short, marble wall lines the perimeter while an unblemished bronze statue of Priest-King Dhyzhaan III rises over the mirrored surface of the water on a pediment of blackest stone, bearing an Ankeshelian glyph inscription. A claw-footed and animated observation tower stands mutely and would obey the bearer of a missing bracelet, but those able to speak with objects may convince it to maneuver about the observatory's edge. Those who use the pool to read the stars' positions while casting a ritual divination do not suffer cumulative penalties for multiple divinations. When used for scrying, the target has disadvantage on the saving throw and makes the save as if the caster was both familiar with the target and had a body part or lock of hair.

Many shrines and monuments litter the areas immediately adjacent to the Reflecting Glass and temples. For one such sculpture, placing a stone up to the size of a human head inside its abstract orichalcum form for a short period makes it as malleable as clay until the next sunrise when it becomes solid rock again while retaining its new shape. Another votive shrine holds a wide-mouthed bowl of dark metal, perpetually filled with purple flame. On specific stellar conjunctions, anyone may use the pool's scrying function after sacrificing an object of deep personal value to the votive flames, regardless of spell slots or other spellcasting ability. After a fiery sacrifice, a petitioner gains a small mote of free-floating purple flame, which cannot burn them, hovering over their forehead until they complete two long rests. Using the observatory's scrying power causes the mote to immediately disappear.

In another temple alcove floats the image of a sleeping Ankeshelian encased in a massive shard of crystal. The translucent form, still bearing a mote of purple flame on their brow, is projected from a person trapped in a vault hidden somewhere on the island. The dragon knows of this individual but hasn't truly attempted to find them. It's unclear what might happen if the individual is released from their slumber.

Iccasakti and the Remnants of Ankeshel

Modern Cassadega is unable to match the advanced, sophisticated civilization of Ankeshel, working only from the often-broken fragments discovered in submerged ruins. From the use of orichalcum and the creation of their unique weapons, the Ankeshelians were resourceful and brilliant—unsurpassed by any other civilizations of the time. As such, there was a need to create, produce, and protect these treasures. At least one guild of Ankeshelian technocrafters maintained a regular cooperative retreat on Motun, and they frequently stored incomplete and partial projects for later study or completion. Other crafters, when present and available, collaborated with one another. The success of one technocrafter advanced all Ankeshel, encouraging a communal atmosphere of mutual prosperity between the creators and drawing them away from the secretive attitudes of the aboleth. The cavern repositories on Motun hide shelves full of drafts, plans, raw materials, and half-sketched thoughts from decades of work. After the fall of Ankeshel and the mutual destruction of the aboleth, the orichalcum dragon Iccasakti sought refuge in the forgotten forest of Motun and discovered the cavern workshop complex used by the technocrafters.

Iccasakti's lair consists of a series of caverns, drilled out by Ankeshelian automatons who maintained the island during the creation of the retreat, also overseeing the propagation of the islanders' favored plant—the winwydden. Several of the automatons remained on the island to assist as needed, and when Iccasakti sought safety in the cavern, the automatons offered aid and safety to the creature. Thus began a centuries-long relationship between the sentient creatures of Motun. The automatons ensured the protection of their lair by creating

intricate traps throughout the caverns and limiting light sources. The caverns are dark, narrow, and frequently treacherous. The winwydden is able to notify the automatons—and the inhabitants of the cavern—of activity on the island. If adventurers interact with the winwydden in any capacity, then there is no way to enter Iccasakti's lair without the dragon learning of the intrusion.

A system of mirrors creates ambient sunlight within the cavern throughout daylight hours, charging crystal illuminators that carry a soft glow through the night and serving as a greenhouse at the heart of the lair to nurture the winwydden and a variety of other species that Iccasakti has tended to for centuries. The greenhouse thrives, even deep within the wandering island, through the sheer determination of its keepers. The seeds from the flowers shine with pearlescent pastel hues, and Iccasakti keeps all of them in jars. If examined by adventurers, they will discover names of the dead Ankeshelian technocrafters. While Iccasakti thinks the names are naturally occurring through the magic of the island and their sentimental memories for the dead, the automatons secretly continue to etch the names of their dead friends into the seeds. This has gone on for centuries as the automatons developed a warmth for Iccasakti and its belief in magic.

Within the galleries and chambers of the cavern system, each crafter had their own space to explore and experiment with Ankeshelian magitech, and in the centuries since the Ankeshelians disappeared, those ideas were brought into the light and reviewed by Iccasakti. The forgotten, half-finished creations of the technocrafters were eventually fixed by the automatons and Iccasakti. Through their combined intelligence, they tinkered, assembling the fragments until they created unique constructs, thus fulfilling the original goals of the Ankeshelian crafters. These creatures are made of metals and gemstones and lack advanced sentience. However, when the automatons need additional support or strength, they utilize the constructs on the island. Iccasakti has taught them how to play card games, and they continue conducting daily matches. The constructs also create their own oddly inspired toys out of the discarded devices and construction materials stockpiled in the caverns. The cycle of creation never ceases on Motun.

While the island appears quiet from the passing of time, within its caverns there is a vibrant culture full of mirth. Accustomed to their solitude and fearful of the people of Cassadega, the island's reclusive inhabitants prefer to live this way.

STORY SEEDS

Legend of Iccasakti. Legend has it, within the island of Motun, a cavern lies hidden behind acres of lush, emerald vines. The vines stretch across every available surface, waiting on any unknowing stranger to walk into its deadly trap. Those brave enough to fight through the vines discover a vast cavern filled with the secret fortune of an ancient orichalcum dragon. Rumors swirl throughout Bemmea's ports about the mysterious dragon, boasting a lair full of glittering, priceless treasures, but no explorer can confirm its existence. If it once existed, the ancient beast has certainly long since perished, per the legend.

What Stares Back. Arriving on Motun, the adventurers discover the Reflecting Glass, activating its scrying power. However, the glass appears to be focused on Baba Yaga's hut, and Grandmother seems aware of the PCs' attention through the magical sensor of the pool and unamused by the intrusion. In a fit of anger, she sends a powerful elemental to attack. The resulting tempest and battle blow the floating island somewhere remote in the Western Sea but near another island—possibly the Isonade. Strange creatures wander the far shoreline. Will the group risk disembarking, or see where the ocean currents bring Motun next?

Ankeshelian Fauna and Flora

Like most of central Midgard, the creatures once found on the fringes of the Ankeshelian Empire were not unlike the rest of the Midlands. In fact, some blooms from Carnessa or strange rarities of the swamps near Tintager began as projects of the arcane experimenters of Ankeshel, always pushing natural boundaries. The following creatures represent especially uncommon examples, truly only observed in remote and unplundered Ankeshelian sites.

WINWYDDEN

With such rich, abundant vines and leaves, opening toward the sky, each one glistens in the morning light as if beckoning us to sit with the vines and see the universe as it does—with open wonder and humble welcoming.

—"Winwydden" entry in
The Endless Lamina

Adapting Growth. Pleased with the solitude on the island, the winwydden continues to grow both across the surface of the island and in the caverns beneath. Every new sprout carries with it the deadly slime used to trap and destroy anything that crosses its twisting vines. Given the plant reaches across the island, covering old structures and disguising the accessories and bones of the dead, the nutrients absorbed on the farthest reaches of it travel back to the main plant living in the darkness of a dragon's lair, growing out from a shrine. The winwydden thrives on the desiccated remains of whatever it touches. And it does not distinguish between the humans, boats, or birds that cross into its space—simply eating everything.

The winwydden has not been found on other Ankeshelian islands and appears currently confined to this single location.

Ooze. There is a distinct ooze on the tops of the leaves across all the vines, which looks slick and unassuming, but it will poison any creature not from Motun as it attempts to breakdown their flesh for nutrients. The winwydden is not biased in selecting targets, and it will happily consume any creature who encounters it, either through ooze or strangulation.

WINWYDDEN

Large (Plant), Unaligned
Armor Class 13 (natural armor)
Hit Points 51 (6d10 + 18)
Speed 20 ft., climb 20 ft.

STR	DEX	CON	INT	WIS	CHA
14 (+2)	13 (+1)	16 (+3)	10 (+0)	8 (−1)	8 (−1)

Saving Throws Dex +7
Skills Nature +4, Perception +4, Stealth +7
Damage Resistances cold, fire
Damage Immunities lightning
Condition Immunities blinded, deafened, exhaustion
Senses blindsight 30 ft, passive Perception 9
Languages Draconic
Challenge 5 (1,800 XP)   **Proficiency Bonus** +3

Death Burst. When the winwydden drops to 0 hit points, it explodes. A creature within 20 feet must succeed on a DC 14 Constitution saving throw or take 14 (4d6) poison damage.

Lightning Absorption. Whenever the winwydden is subjected to lightning damage, it takes no damage and instead regains a number of hit points equal to the lightning damage dealt.

Spanning Consciousness. The winwydden is one organism that appears to be made up of several. It knows what is happening simultaneously across all its vines and can act accordingly.

ACTIONS

Multiattack. The winwydden can make one Vine attack and one Engulf attack.

Vine. *Melee Weapon Attack:* +4 to hit, reach 30 ft., one creature. *Hit:* 13 (2d8 + 4) piercing damage, and the target is grappled (escape DC 13). The target must make a DC 13 Constitution saving throw. On a failed save, the target takes 14 (4d6) poison damage and is poisoned until the end of its next turn. On a successful save, the target takes half as much damage and suffers no additional effects.

Engulf. The winwydden makes a Vine attack against a grappled target. On a hit, the target is engulfed. Engulfed creatures are blinded and restrained, and they must succeed a DC 14 Constitution saving throw or take 13 (2d8 + 4) bludgeoning damage at the start of the winwydden's turn. The winwydden can engulf only one creature at a time.

ORICHALCUM DRAGON

It emerged from the ruins, catlike and precise. We froze in place and watched it stalk between shattered pillars before leaping into the sky like a watchman's flare.

> —Roland, Bemmean treasure-seeker

Rare Hermit. Unusually reclusive even compared to other metallic dragons, the orichalcum dragon remains the subject of legends. Most believe them to be merely tall tales or misidentified bronze or gold dragons.

ORICHALCUM DRAGON

Large Dragon, Usually Neutral Good
Armor Class 18 (natural armor)
Hit Points 142 (15d10 + 60)
Speed 40 ft., fly 80 ft., swim 40 ft.

STR	DEX	CON	INT	WIS	CHA
20 (+5)	20 (+5)	19 (+4)	14 (+2)	12 (+1)	18 (+4)

Saving Throws Cha +7, Con +7, Dex +8, Wis +4
Skills Arcana +5, Perception +4, Stealth +8
Damage Immunities force
Senses blindsight 30 ft., darkvision 120 ft., passive Perception 14
Languages Ankeshelian, Aquan, Common, Draconic
Challenge 8 (3,900 XP)   **Proficiency Bonus** +3

Amphibious. The dragon can breathe air and water.

ACTIONS

Multiattack. The dragon makes either two Claw attacks and one Bite attack or one Breath Weapon attack and one Claw attack.

Bite. *Melee Weapon Attack:* +8 to hit, reach 10 ft., one creature. *Hit:* 12 (2d10 + 5) piercing damage.

Claw. *Melee Weapon Attack:* +8 to hit, reach 5 ft., one creature. *Hit:* 12 (2d6 + 5) slashing damage.

Breath Weapons (Recharge 5–6). The dragon uses one of the following breath weapons.

Dreams and Nightmares. The dragon exhales a heliotrope wisp of dreamstuff, which it fashions according to its whims. The breath can take the form of a wall of fire, stone, or ice, or even a massive, disembodied claw. The dreamstuff walls are 10 feet high and may be a 50-foot-long wall or a 20-foot-diameter circle or a 15-foot-diameter, 10-foot-high dome. Those within 5 feet of either side of the fire or ice walls must make a DC 15 Dexterity saving throw, taking 27 (6d8) fire or cold damage (as appropriate) on a failed save or half as much damage on a successful one. Passing through the wall of fire requires a single saving throw. The 5-foot segments of the stone and ice walls have AC 18 and can suffer 50 or 35 hit points, respectively, of damage before they burst. Walls last until the dragon uses their breath weapon again.

If the dragon creates a Medium disembodied claw (AC 18; 50 hp), it may use a bonus action each round to direct the claw to attack a target within 120 feet, or to grapple the target.

It has the dragon's Strength and Dexterity and does not fill its space. On a successful claw attack, the target takes 27 (6d8) force damage and is pushed 5 feet. The claw may attempt to grapple a Huge or smaller creature within 5 feet of it. If the target is Medium or smaller, it has advantage on the check. While the claw is grappling a target, the dragon can use a bonus action to have the claw crush it for 12 (2d6 + 5) bludgeoning damage.

Telekinetic Hum. The dragon exhales, generating a telekinetic force that pummels all targets within a 5-foot radius of a targeted point. Targeted creatures must make a DC 15 Strength saving throw, taking 45 (10d8) force damage and being pushed 15 feet on a failed save or taking half as much damage and suffering no additional effects on a successful one. If something prevents a target from moving the full distance, it takes 4 (1d8) additional damage per 5 feet it was prevented from moving. Alternatively, the dragon may target a single Huge or smaller creature, and that creature must make a DC 15 Strength saving throw, taking 27 (6d8) force damage

and being flung 45 feet in a direction selected by the dragon on a failed save or taking half as much damage and suffering no additional effects on a successful one.

Change Shape. The dragon magically transforms into a humanoid or beast (with a challenge rating no higher than its own) or back to its true form. Otherwise, other than size, their statistics are the same in each form. Equipment may be merged with their new form at their choice. They revert to their dragon form if they die.

AN ORICHALCUM DRAGON'S LAIR

These dragons live in caverns, ruined temples, and other secluded structures, decorated with recovered artwork and statuary.

On initiative count 20 (losing initiative ties), the dragon takes a lair action to generate one of the following effects. The dragon can't use the same effect 2 rounds in a row:

- The dragon sees into the future and, until the start of the next round, either increases the DC of its breath weapon by 2 or gains advantage on any attacks it makes.

- The dragon is magically accelerated, gaining +2 AC, advantage on Dexterity saves, and an additional Attack, Dash, Disengage, Hide, or Use an Object action until the start of the next round.

- The dragon may choose to absorb the next spell cast on it as a reaction and may either heal for 1d10 hit points per level of the spell absorbed or immediately recharge its breath weapon.

- The dragon unleashes a psionic scream that pierces the minds of all enemy creatures within 60 feet. Each creature must make a successful DC 15 Wisdom saving throw, taking 16 (3d10) psychic damage and being frightened on a failed save or taking half as much damage and suffering no additional effects on a successful one. A frightened creature may make a Wisdom saving throw at the end of their turn, and on a successful save, they are no longer frightened.

Ankeshelian Magic

Salvagers often discover the spells of the sunken empire inscribed—or even grown—on the surface of curled shells, equivalent to contemporary scrolls, which crumble after being cast or transcribed.

ICY PRISON

3rd-Level Conjuration | Sorcerer, Warlock, Wizard

Casting Time: 1 action
Range: 120 feet
Components: V, S
Duration: Instantaneous

You target a Huge or smaller creature within range. A spiked iron maiden fashioned out of ice forms around the target. The target may make a Dexterity saving throw, taking 7 (2d6) piercing damage, 7 (2d6) cold damage, and being restrained on a failed save or taking half as much damage and suffering no additional effects on a successful save. If the target is submerged or standing in water at least a foot deep, they have disadvantage on the saving throw.

While restrained, the target must make a Strength saving throw. On a successful save, they are no longer restrained. On a failed save, they take 3 (1d6) cold damage and 3 (1d6) piercing damage. The icy cage (AC 14; 30 hp) lasts for 1 hour or until the target breaks free. The cage is vulnerable to fire damage. Half of any damage inflicted on the cage is also inflicted upon the restrained target.

At Higher Levels. If you cast this spell using a slot of 4th level or higher, you may either increase the DC of the Strength saving throw by 2 or increase either the piercing or cold damage by 1d6. The DC may not be increased more than twice.

MEMORY SEEDS

2nd-Level Necromancy | Druid, Sorcerer, Warlock, Wizard

Casting Time: 1 bonus action
Range: 120 feet
Components: V, S, M (a small see, see description)
Duration: Instantaneous

Upon planting a seed found in the lair of Iccasakti, the orichalcum dragon of Motun, you target an enemy you can see. Evoking the magic of Ankeshel and the dead who suffered in its destruction, the seed seeks vengeance. The ooze from the winwydden (see above) combines with dirt and the corpses beneath the plant to create an Ankeshelian zombie (reducing hp to 10 and removing damage and condition immunities). The seed is consumed by the vines as the winwydden violently thrashes, lifting bones and sifting dirt as the ooze infuses the desiccated remains. The zombie is created at the conclusion of the round.

The zombie will attack the identified enemy. Once that enemy is vanquished, the zombie will fall into the winwydden and be consumed by the vines.

The seeds will not germinate away from the Island of Motun unless the winwydden is propagated.

At Higher Levels. If you cast this spell using a slot of 3rd level or higher, you may plant multiple seeds and create additional zombies at the GM's discretion.

VRIL AEGIS

2nd-Level Abjuration | Sorcerer, Warlock, Wizard

Casting Time: 1 bonus action or reaction, which you take when the target is hit by an attack
Range: 30 feet
Components: V, S
Duration: Instantaneous

A shimmering field of force surrounds the target, only visible when struck. You can target yourself or another creature, and until the end of your next turn, the target has a +2 bonus to AC, including against the triggering attack.

Additionally, the target has advantage on saving throws that would impose the restrained or paralyzed conditions. If they gain or already suffer those conditions, they may immediately make a saving throw to end the conditions.

At Higher Levels. If you cast this spell using a slot of 3rd level or higher, you may either increase the bonus to AC by 1 or extend the duration by 1 round for each level above 2nd.

Ankeshelian Relics

Within the lair of Iccasakti, the dragon has forged their own items from orichalcum—created to one day be used by the rightful heirs to the Ankeshelian empire.

ANKESHELIAN ORICHALCUM YOKE

Wondrous Item, Legendary (Requires Attunement)

This harness of mithril cable is attached to an orichalcum belt, collar, and manacles. You can activate or deactivate the yoke as an action, and while activated, you have an AC of 20 or a +2 bonus to your AC, whichever is greater. You also gain a force blast attack that targets one creature or object within 40 feet and deals 2d6 force damage. You can use an action to hold your blast, charging it for an additional 1d6 damage per round held (to a maximum of 5d6). While holding your charge, you have advantage on saving throws against spells targeting you. In addition, you are immune to force damage and resistant to all nonmagical damage.

For each minute the yoke is activated, you must succeed a DC 15 Constitution saving throw or gain a level of exhaustion. The DC for each successive save increases by +1 until you finish a long rest.

DRAGON GAUNTLET

Wondrous Item, Very Rare (Requires Attunement)

An otherwise unassuming copper gauntlet, it is etched with the image of a dragon roaring into the sky—an image never seen in Ankeshelian contexts outside of Motun's caverns. Once worn, the gauntlet attaches to your wrist, piercing skin and grafting to tendon. As an action, you can utter the command word to summon flexible orichalcum plates, outfitting you magitech armor. The armor is considered plate mail and is anchored to the gauntlet. While equipped, the armor provides resistance to all bludgeoning, piercing, and slashing damage, and you can speak Draconic. You can dismiss the armor as a bonus action.

The *dragon gauntlet* can only be removed with a *greater restoration* spell or by severing your arm.

GLYPH TILES

Wondrous Item, Very Rare

You can activate a tile as an action, and it will fly up to 60 feet to a creature, exploding in a burst of magical energy that consumes the tile. Choose one of the following effects when you use the tile.

- *Disorienting Teleport*. The target must succeed on a DC 15 Wisdom saving throw or be teleported up to 100 feet in the direction of your choice, appearing in the nearest available empty space, and targeted by a *confusion* spell.
- *Dispel Magic*. Any active spell of 5th level or lower on the target ends.
- *Water Breathing*. The target creature can breathe underwater for 8 hour and gains 20 temporary hit points.

Background: Ankeshelian Scavenger

Descendants from Ankeshel who reside in Cassadega have learned to keep their lineage private. Inappropriate interest and inquiry from strangers—ranging from unceasing questions to crass jokes about the aboleth to flagrant bigotry—have created a culture of fear among

TALES OF THE YOKE

It is thought that devices like the *Ankeshelian orichalcum yoke* once numbered in the thousands, though some were more potent than others, allowing the Imperial Cerulean Vanguards to strike deep into aboleth waters. Members of Linnorm House in the Northlands claim a sorcerer discovered one but disappeared on the Isle of Loki. Drunken sailors in Barsella tell of a skeleton lying pinned under a rock, wearing one, in the treacherous bay of a small nearby island. A broken yoke exists in the Academie Arcana in Bemmea, hanging unrecognized in a museum display. They are out there to be found, but it'll take some effort.

the descendants of the defunct civilization. However, observing an Ankeshelian in the water removes all doubt as to their ancestry. Their ease in the water, even in times of distress, is unlike that of others.

Skill Proficiencies: Investigation, Stealth.

Languages: One of your choice.

Tool Proficiency: One type of artisan's tools.

Equipment: A crowbar, a lucky trinket you found, an incomplete but suggestive treasure map, and a belt pouch containing 15gp.

d8	PERSONALITY TRAIT
1	I seek out only the most challenging of salvage jobs.
2	I never want to discard junk or old items if I think I can possibly trade or sell them.
3	I can tell you where I found every item I own and the circumstances around its acquisition.
4	Everything is treasure to someone.
5	You can sell anything. You just have to be willing to wait for the right buyer.
6	I never pass up the chance to nose around ruins or wreckage for something worthwhile.
7	I won't be swindled on the value of my salvage. I know what it's worth.
8	Sometimes you take a loss on the first bit of salvage to build a relationship and profit long-term.

d6	IDEAL
1	*Orderly*. There is a code regarding where and when you salvage. (Lawful)
2	*Perception*. People hide things in the same way, no matter the culture. You just need to look. (Any)
3	*Ingenuity*. If someone made it by hand, I can open it by hand. (Any)
4	*Legacy*. I bring the past back to the present and rescue its memory. (Good)
5	*Curiosity*. There are so many interesting lost things in the world! (Chaotic)
6	*Greed*. As long as it has value to me, I'll keep it around. As soon as it doesn't... (Evil)

d6	BOND
1	I revere the lost culture I rescue from beneath the waves and loathe those who would disrespect it.
2	I ensure another generation knows not only what came before but also its value.
3	Do you want to see what's important to a person? See how they bargain for something sentimental.
4	People who simply exploit the past for gain in the present are culturally bankrupt.
5	A rival scavenger snatched an important piece of salvage from me and sold it to a merchant. I'll recover it one day.
6	Someone important to me died in a salvage operation, and all my jobs are for their memory.

d6	FLAW
1	Anytime someone throws something away, I check it for value.
2	Sometimes, I can't give up what I salvaged, even if I really need to.
3	Someone willing to steal from the group salvage is no one I can ever trust.
4	I love a good storm and never run from one. It means there's going to be something to salvage!
5	I don't pay much attention to the monetary value of objects as much as the object's immediate utility.
6	I hate it when people call my salvage junk. Don't presume to know what I value.

FEATURE: ONE PERSON'S TRASH...

Devoid of meaningful family connections or emotional ties to your homeland, you wander the world on the lookout for things missed by others. You scavenge throughout your travels—not as a pest but as a connoisseur of forgotten treasures, misplaced lore, and hidden gems. You can walk into any establishment or ruin and see what is plainly missed by others. With a ready eye, you have a knack for guessing where people might conceal valuable objects. When considering found items, you can always determine the mundane items with the most value and accurately determine if a sale or trade is equitable. You have advantage on Intelligence (Investigation) checks to find hidden objects.

SUGGESTED CHARACTERISTICS

Finding the lost wealth of others is practically the definition of an adventurer, though most find themselves embroiled in far more violence than scavengers usually prefer.

Tales of Drowned Legacies

There are many ways you might incorporate Ankeshelian elements into your Midgard game, and they need not be limited to underwater adventures. The passing centuries have scattered the empire's inheritance across the world.

Endless Acumen. The Reflecting Glass of Motun has provided the orichalcum dragon's only glimpse of the outside world since the destruction of Ankeshel. Fearful of the aboleth

civilization that destroyed their homeland, the dragon uses the pool's magic to learn about the world beyond and its people. Satisfied to observe society moving on, the dragon doesn't resent the isolation. Instead, they use their time to learn and etch their memories in the cave.

The young daughter of the Lord Speaker of Barsella's Founders Council, Lula Anthor, seeks to hire adventurers. Lula used a small reflective glass to communicate with her pen pal, only to discover they are a dragon. Lula will pay for someone to take her to the island to meet her friend in person, and she won't take no for an answer. Before anyone asks, she is armed and unafraid. After all, her best friend is a dragon.

It Belongs in a Museum! A local scavenger recently arrived at the party's usual fence and amateur scholar with a sack of Ankeshelian coins, several glyph stones, a functioning vril battery, and a strange crown. Unaware of what they possessed, they sold the salvage for cheap. The fence has tipped off the party that a cache of potent relics must be somewhere nearby: they just need to either buy the location, trail the scavenger, or otherwise acquire the stash to learn what baubles lie waiting. Unfortunately, the last salvage visit activated a **winwydden** (see above), which now menaces the area. They'll need to deal with the aggressive beast before they can search for more loot.

Researcher's Endeavor. An ancient Ankeshelian botanical tome, titled *The Endless Lamina*, highlights the mystery of the **winwydden** (see above) growing from a particular cave on Motun. With recent rumors of a nearby unmoored island, the botanists want to hire a team to escort them to this suspicious locale—and potential fragment of Ankeshel. If correct, and this is Motun, then this is an opportunity to find and study the plant in its native habitat. However, its deadly nature remains undocumented since no one has survived an encounter to share their experience. Professor Druell Rafferty of the High Order of Geomancers in Barsella posted a call for unafraid adventurers willing to venture into the unknown for an unprecedented, princely amount of coin.

BABA YAGA: A TANGLE OF MISTRUTHS

by Lou Anders

"How do I know that this story is true? Why, one who was there told it to me."
—unknown

Much has been said and yet still little is truly known of the one they call Baba Yaga. She is the most terrifying of beldams, yet on occasion, she is also a dispenser of wisdom and a granter of favors. The Wild Old Woman is known to enjoy dining on young humanoids and has a special fondness for nibbling on gnome. And she is not above eating the tougher meat of, well, anyone else. Yet despite her well-documented appetites, there are those desperate enough to petition her for aid. Even so, the witch's boons frequently come at costs higher than that which drove these unfortunates to solicit her in the first place.

What follows are some of the many strange and often contradictory bits of folklore—but also some scholarly efforts—that are devoted to Grandmother. Good luck gleaning any truths from them. They're most likely fictions and misunderstandings, or at best half-truths, but you never know what small portion of detail may save your life at some point. (You can read more about Baba Yaga in *Midgard Worldbook* and *Warlock Grimoire 2*.)

Where on Midgard. Merely locating the Feywitch is no simple task. However, it is said that the truly despairing can *always* find their way to Grandmother. She enjoys striking bargains, after all, and Bony Legs, as she is sometimes known, never gives up a chance to add to her store of secrets, hidden knowledge being her favorite commodity. The rarer the secret one holds, the greater chance there is of stumbling upon Grandmother or even being sought out by her. But should someone be brave or foolish enough to look for her, then know that when she is not riding through the woods on the back of an enormous sow or flying through the air in her iron mortar, steering her way with a pestle and covering her tracks with a broom, Baba Yaga can most often be found dwelling in the heart of the Margreve Forest or upon a lonely stretch of the Rothenian Plain.

Baba Yaga's dwelling is not hard to miss. Leaving the hut aside for a moment, the surrounding grounds are also distinctive. They are usually marked by a wooden fence capped at intervals by humanoid skulls, each lit from lanterns within so that the light shines out of the eye sockets. As unnerving as this might be, it is made doubly so by the claims of those who have visited the hut and returned to tell the tale that there are always just enough empty posts awaiting new skulls to account precisely for the heads of those visiting. More so, the lanterns flicker, winking on and off as if in response to the presence of visitors. On occasion, the skulls have even been known to speak. But as remarkable as the fencing is, what it contains is far stranger.

The "dancing hut" of Baba Yaga stands on two enormous chicken legs and often struts around the yard. Above the giant fowl parts, reports of the hut's appearance are varied. At times, the hut presents as a simple peasant's hut, constructed of wooden logs and with no windows and featuring only a single door. At other times, it is a more elaborate cabin with a porch and several stories. Most chilling are the tales that swear that the hut is made not of wood but of humanoid bones. The illusionist Xaldri Lamblewomple—formerly of the Arcane Collegium until his mysterious disappearance of a year ago—in his ambitious and ill-considered treatise on Grandmother's domicile, points out that the hut is reminiscent of a certain traditional Krakovan building that is constructed on a stump and used to bury the dead. Its lack of windows and its single door are to discourage both the living from disturbing the dead and the dead from disturbing the living. Lamblewomple argues that Grandmother takes on the symbolic role of a priestess who leads the cremation rites, suggesting there may be deep mythic significance in her proclivity to roast people in her ovens. Unfortunately, Lamblewomple is not available to expound further on his theories since the wizard's current whereabouts are unknown.

But logs or bones, hut or resting place for the dead, all accounts agree that the dancing hut will turn away from intruders, refusing them entry, unless they address it properly. One wishing to enter the hut must say, "Turn your back to the forest, your front to me." If these words are spoken, and it must be stressed that they should be spoken *politely*, the hut will face the speaker and kneel, settling upon the ground. Access isn't guaranteed by this though. There's an even chance the door will be locked, and the door's keyhole is a mouth full of razor-sharp teeth. But presuming the door is unlocked or the lock is picked without the loss of too many fingers, intruders who enter generally find themselves in the kitchen. The keyword is *generally*, for rooms do shift around in the interdimensional space within the hut— bigger on the inside than the outside—and the total number of rooms in undocumented. (For more specifics on Baba Yaga's hut, see *Warlock Grimoire 2*.)

Entertaining Guests. Should Grandmother be at home, she is frequently reclined atop the freestanding stove for warmth. Sometimes she appears larger than an average woman, up to 15 feet tall when standing, and if encountered in this form, her legs may stretch from one side of the kitchen to the other. It should be pointed out, lest one be taken by surprise at the sight and give offense, that her nickname Bony Legs is not a reference to having skinny limbs. Rather, on occasion, one or both of Grandmother's legs appears skeletal, either actual raw bone or skin stretched so tight as to depict the bones clearly. Should the bony leg (or legs) be on display, visitors are advised to ignore it and never call attention to it under any circumstances whatsoever.

Straight away, Baba Yaga will attempt to gain the upper hand in any ensuing conversation. She can unerringly smell what country a visitor hails from, and she usually points this out at the start to unsettle them with her knowledge. She frequently asks next, "Are you doing a deed or fleeing a deed? Are you here of your own will or by compulsion?" What she makes of the answers to these questions is inconsistent and unpredictable. One should be cautioned that, while Baba Yaga enjoys bantering with her guests, she will frequently threaten to eat the overly curious. This may have something to do with the rumor that the Witch of the East ages an entire year whenever someone asks her a question. If that is so, then she is balancing her love of secrets and enthusiasm for haggling with her desire to not age overly. At any rate, she has a ravenous appetite, and all conversations with her are likely to include some mention of her appetites and her estimations of how well or poorly a visitor might taste.

Should Grandmother indeed decide to eat someone, it can be hard to dissuade her. However, Myrieem Yulan-Rhal, a Kariv herbalist and fortune teller, maintains that the Great Crone can be distracted if one can find and blow her magical horn, the *Tripple Horn of Baba Yaga*. This item is comprised of three horns of different lengths and with differently sized bell flares, bound together into one instrument. Yulan-Rhal instructs that one must blow the first horn softly, the second one louder, and the third louder still. Sounding the horns in the correct order summons ravens that surround and harry Baba Yaga, distracting her, and a firebird, which will emit a blinding ray of light to further facilitate the horn blower's escape. None of this, it should be noted, has been verified by anyone else. And why would she keep such an item just lying around? It would certainly need to be useful to her otherwise.

Should the horn prove unavailable or insufficient, would-be meals are occasionally said to find aid from the many servants of Baba Yaga that dwell in and about the hut, including an awakened cat and several dining and cooking utensils, among others. The utensils are believed to be polymorphed beings who have offended Baba Yaga in the past. The witch's own dentures, the famous iron teeth of Baba Yaga, have even been known to be at odds with their mistress a time or two. Baba Yaga also keeps and breeds horses. The equines are the least potentially helpful of her servants, but they are worth noting as it is said they are so fast as to be able to cross the world in a day.

Friends of Grandmother. Of course, Grandmother has allies too, though some are unwilling and others unwitting. First among these are her horsemen, known as Bright Day,

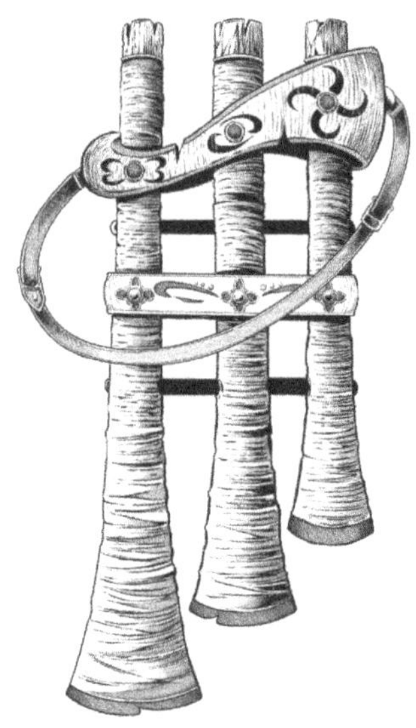

Red Sun, and Black Knight—or as Baba Yaga refers to them, "My Bright Dawn, my Red Sun, and my Dark Midnight"—and they are never seen together outside the confines of her property. Indeed, through some strange cosmological conjuring on Grandmother's part, the horsemen are each connected to a specific period of time, as measured by the sun. Bright Day is bound to and governs dawn to mid-day, Red Sun from mid-day to sundown, and Black Night from sundown until daybreak. As such, only one can exist on the material plane at a time. Whether the horsemen were at some point ordinary humanoids who came under the witch's sway, or whether they are actual personifications of the day, is unclear. (See also **Baba Yaga's horsemen** in *Tome of Beasts*.)

The lich-like being known as Koschei the Deathless is another of Grandmother's favored servants. Once king of a long-forgotten land, Koschei feared death so much that he turned to bizarre rituals to sustain himself. Extracting his soul, he placed it in a pin which was placed inside an egg, itself inside a duck swallowed by a rabbit in the belly of a goat. Or some tales say that rabbit is sealed instead within an iron chest buried on Buyan, the mythical isle of the dead. Either way, so long as his soul resides in its home away from home, Koschei cannot ever truly die.

Koschei also rides an incredibly swift horse, and it is believed only Baba Yaga's steeds are fast enough to catch him, but surely that is insufficient to explain her power over him. The nature of Grandmother's hold over the immortal king isn't clear. It's possible she gifted him his horse. It's also possible she possesses his soul's receptable—or at least knows where it is and how to claim his hidden soul. It is just as likely that she has merely allowed Koschei to *think* she knows. Whatever the case, Koschei serves Baba Yaga on occasion, though he is never overly enamored with being her servant.

The most numerous of Baba Yaga's servants are the hundreds of **vila** (see also *Tome of Beasts* and "Grandmother's Daughters: Secrets of the Vila" later in this issue of *Warlock*) that tend to congregate in the Margreve but can be found most anywhere. Baba Yaga refers to these fierce forest protectors as her daughters, though this is unlikely. Regardless, she treats them with a tenderness no other creature receives. For their part, the vila are generally willing to do her bidding, though at times individual vila have aided mortals in their attempts to escape Grandmother's appetites.

Price of a Deal. But should someone succeed in reaching Baba Yaga, in escaping both her stewpot and her minions, and in bargaining with the Queen of Hags, what does Baba Yaga want? What price does she set upon her knowledge or her gifts? If the petitioner knows something Grandmother doesn't, that will most assuredly be the cost for her aid. Otherwise, she is liable to ask for something seemingly innocuous, like a fingernail clipping or the memory of a lost love, but these things invariably serve to aid her in her twisting schemes. She might ask that someone deliver an apple to a young girl living alone in the forest or take a golden brooch to the River King or present a silver mirror to King Lucan of the Blood Kingdom. Grandmother loves to

set tasks that seem innocent enough but prove nigh impossible. She might ask for someone to clean her kitchen, only to have it grow to enormous size or for its oven to belch out an avalanche of soot. She might request that her herd be corralled, only for the equines to gallop halfway across the world. On more than one occasion, Baba Yaga has insisted someone marry one of her daughters and then instructed her servants to murder the spouse-to-be the night before the wedding. (See also "Misto Ellel: The Thundering Town" and "Niemheim: Notes on Gnomish Diabolism" later in this issue of *Warlock* for more on those who have dealt with Baba Yaga and that remain in her constant orbit.)

There are also rare reports that a mystic named Jezibaba, sometimes called Granny Witch, is connected to Baba Yaga, perhaps even by ties of blood, but this remains all folklore, of course. Jezibaba lives in a hut similar to Baba Yaga's, but it is never made of bones, and it is typically found on the shores of a tranquil lake. Far gentler than Grandmother, Jezibaba is generally helpful to those who treat her with kindness and respect. The greatest of all herbalists, Jezibaba is often sought by those struggling with fertility and healing. She has been known to take on apprentices, teaching them about the magical properties of plants. Jezibaba is usually accompanied by her children, the Jezinky, all of whom are djinn.

The Nature of Grandmother. As much as is known about the Feywitch, so little is understood about what exactly Baba Yaga *is*. Some believe Grandmother is a forgotten goddess of the Underworld. Others that she is a being from another world entirely, who only came to Midgard after millennia spent in other lands. Stranger yet is the assertion that Baba Yaga is not one but three separate beings, all named Baba Yaga. This supposition is supported by accounts of Baba Yaga appearing in multiple locations at the same time and by the rare visitor that believes they have encountered her and her two "sisters." Whether these are actual sisters, doppelgangers, or the same person transposed in time is not clear. A horrible possibility must be entertained that the three Grandmothers might even be a dark mask of the Norns—or the Norns might be a more benevolent mask of Grandmother.

A seldom-told tale from the gnomes of Niemheim offers one possible glimpse at Grandmother's origin. The story details how a powerful arch-devil sought to distill the essence of evil by cooking the twelve most wicked women in Midgard in a caldron. As the horrible concoction boiled, the devil absentmindedly spat in the mixture. Unfortunately, in so doing, he inadvertently added a bit of his own soul. This empowered the foul soup, and out hopped Grandmother. She slew and ate the devil immediately, and then the witch stole a mortar and pestle from the devil's kitchen and flew away. While this tale is considered apocryphal by most, the idea of Baba Yaga entering the world fully formed rings true. After all, while she may have sisters and daughters aplenty, it is hard to conceive of Grandmother ever having had a mother herself—or indeed being anything other than the terrible crone she is now. But take all matters pertaining to the Hag of Hags with more than a pinch of salt, and think on it again on the morrow, for as Baba Yaga herself is fond of saying, "There is more wisdom in the morning than in the evening." The night walks the same road as dream. And if you have a dream of Baba Yaga, it is sure to be nightmare.

At Grandmother's House

You are very likely to find something strange at Grandmother's house.

BABA YAGA'S CAT

Tiny Beast, Chaotic Neutral

Armor Class 12
Hit Points 10 (4d4)
Speed 40 ft., climb 40 ft.

STR	DEX	CON	INT	WIS	CHA
3 (−4)	15 (+2)	10 (+0)	10 (+0)	14 (+2)	12 (+1)

Skills Perception +4, Stealth +4
Senses passive Perception 14
Languages Common, Sylvan; telepathy (see below)
Challenge 0 (10 XP) **Proficiency Bonus** +2

Feline Telepathy. Within the confines of Baba Yaga's property, the cat can magically command any beast within 60 feet of it, using its limited telepathy.

Keen Smell. The cat has advantage on Wisdom (Perception) checks that rely on smell.

ACTIONS

Claws. *Melee Weapon Attack:* +0 to hit, reach 5 ft., one target. *Hit:* 1 slashing damage.

NIEMHEIM: NOTES ON GNOMISH DIABOLISM

by Wolfgang Baur

The gnomes of Niemheim are not the only gnomes of Midgard, but they are by far the best known. Mostly, this is because they are particularly dangerous and entirely willing to kidnap, murder, and steal as needed to protect their strange woodland realm.

These evil gnomes are justly infamous for their troubles with Baba Yaga and their tightly entwined relationship with the hells. And they are closely allied with the one they call the Master of Knives—better known elsewhere as the arch-devil Parzelon, the Lord of Secrets.

Recent Gnomish History

While most know the story that a gnomish prince named Vander Steingau broke a sworn blood oath to Baba Yaga 200 years ago, rather fewer know that Prince Steingau did so in order to steal magical power from Baba Yaga to fuel his own ambitions. He stole two items: one being the *Ebony Star*, a magical gemstone said to contain the soul of Baba Yaga's grandchild, and the other being a book of her secrets, sometimes called *Grandmother's Grimoire* or the *Oxtail Libram*, after the oxtail that the tanner left on the book's leather cover. Neither item is well known outside of gnomish arcanist circles.

To recover them, Baba Yaga sent her ala hags and strigoi, her vila, her psoglav, and her ravens to capture and question and destroy gnomes to punish them for Steingau's betrayal. The prince took the book and black gem to the Eleven Hells where Baba Yaga couldn't find him—and Niemheim suffered until King Redbeard made his pact with **Parzelon** (see *Creature Codex*).

IN SERVICE TO THE LORD OF SECRETS

Because Parzelon is the Lord of Secrets, he prizes secret knowledge highly and always seeks to acquire more, stealing them so that they are no one's but his. Thus, when Steingau raised such ire from Baba Yaga and made off with prized treasures, well, the possibility of protecting a few gnomes and gaining priceless information from Baba Yaga was rather irresistible.

As a result, Parzelon has expanded his cult widely among the Niemheim gnomes, though his name is not known to those who do not traffic in diabolism. The Lord of Secrets granted the gnomes spells to summon allies and to hide gnomish travel and activities from others. At the same time, Parzelon is cautious of devoting too much attention to Niemheim: he has rivals in Chernobog and Mammon, and each seeks the gnomes' devotion for themselves. And while the gnomes are fearful, they are also clever, and their king seeks to end their reliance on infernal aid.

In practical terms, Parzelon sends various fiends to Niemheim (**spree demons**, see

Creature Codex, **bearded devils**, and others) to protect the gnomes, and in return, the gnomes provide a steady supply of sacrifices and learn all the secrets they can with spies, arcane scrying, and outright theft from humans, undead, and Baba Yaga's allies—all while keeping his own name hidden insofar as possible. Most gnomes, even members of the Eleven Knives and affiliated tinkers and scouts, simply refer to him as Our Patron, the Master of Knives, King of the Eleven Havens, and similar circumlocutions. Their gratitude is quite real though, and stories tell of the "lost generation" of gnomish children, thousands and thousands of them, taken into Grandmother's stewpots and never seen again.

CULT OF CHERNOBOG AND THE DARK FIVE

The older faith among the gnomes included worship of Yarila and Porevit as well as Hecate and Rava—with some attention paid to Lada as gnomish goddess of healing, light, and luck. All of that worship though (except for Lada) is long gone, referred to as the Ancient Five but rarely. Lada alone retains some minor attention in temples otherwise given over to Chernobog, the Goat of the Woods, Mammon, Marena, and Parzelon: the Five Dark Protectors.

The faith of Chernobog, the god of night and murder, was always part of the darkness under the deep shade of the Wormwood Forest, but in times past, it was rooted out and extinguished by brave gnomish heroes. At best, it was a cult for bandits and necromancers. For 200 years though, it has served as a cloak of darkness over the gnomes of Niemheim, for Chernobog was the gnomes' first protector—before the bargain with Parzelon was struck.

Now, there is a high priest of Chernobog in the city of Königsheim, with his hellspur cavaliers to carry out his orders, and his priesthood is in every village, ready to blind the eyes of Baba Yaga's servants—or indeed the eyes of the undead of Morgau or the centaurs of the Rothenian Plain. Unlike Parzelon, the priests of Chernobog require far less blood and sacrifice, only fervent prayers and the annual soul of a young gnome or human brought to the Black Spire of Chernobog in Königsheim at midwinter.

GNOMISH TINKER SCOUTS

The gnomes of Niemheim send out scouts, posed as bards, tinkers, pilgrims, cloth and leather merchants, and other generally beneficial persons, visiting Morgau, Zobeck, Vidim, Perunalia, and the Magdar Kingdom with goods to trade. What they are really seeking are sacrifices for Parzelon though, and most have a small wagon used to carry off abducted victims to the nearest forest grove for dispatch from this mortal world (see sidebar).

GNOMISH TINKER SCOUT

Small Humanoid (Gnome), Any Evil
Armor Class 13 (leather)
Hit Points 32 (5d6 + 15)
Speed 30 ft.

STR	DEX	CON	INT	WIS	CHA
8 (−1)	14 (+2)	16 (+3)	11 (+0)	12 (+1)	17 (+3)

Skills Deception +5, Perception +3, Persuasion +5, Stealth +4
Senses darkvision 60 ft., passive Perception 13
Languages Abyssal, Common, Gnomish
Challenge 1/2 (100 XP) **Proficiency Bonus** +2

Knife Familiar. The tinker scout has a knife familiar (see below).

ACTIONS

Ritual Knife. *Melee Weapon Attack:* +4 to hit, reach 5 ft., one target. *Hit:* 4 (1d4 + 2) slashing damage plus 7 (2d6) poison damage.

Spellcasting. The tinker scout casts one of the following spells, using Charisma as the spellcasting ability (spell save DC 13):

At will: *avert the eye*, horn of Parzelon*, spider climb*
3/day each: *bless, hat trick**
1/day: *haste*
(*) see below

NINE SWORDS OF NIEMHEIM

The nine cities and towns of Niemheim are said to be linked to nine swords of the gnomish princes of old, blades forged by the finest gnomish bladesmiths, long before the pact of Redbeard and Parzelon and the corruption of the gnomes. Some say the blades were gifts of the elves, later corrupted by Parzelon, the Hunter, the Black Goat of the Woods, and other dark gods. A few believe that recovering these swords might grant the gnomes the favor of Mavros, the war god, and allow them to defend themselves, rather than relying on the hells for their protection. Certainly, King Redbeard thinks so and has sought to recover them.

KNIFE FAMILIAR

Tiny Construct, Unaligned
Armor Class 18 (natural)
Hit Points 14 (4d6)
Speed 0 ft., fly 40 ft. (hover)

STR	DEX	CON	INT	WIS	CHA
8 (−1)	18 (+ 4)	10 (+ 0)	1 (−5)	5 (−3)	1 (−5)

Saving Throws Dex +6
Damage Immunities poison, psychic
Condition Immunities blinded, charmed, deafened, frightened, paralyzed, petrified, poisoned
Senses blindsight 60 ft. (blind beyond this radius), passive Perception 7
Languages one language that its master knows; telepathy (with master only)
Challenge 1/4 (50 XP) **Proficiency Bonus** +2

Antimagic Susceptibility. The knife familiar is incapacitated while in the area of an antimagic field. If targeted by *dispel magic*, the knife familiar must succeed on a Constitution saving throw against the caster's spell save DC or fall unconscious for 1 minute.

False Appearance. While the knife familiar remains motionless and isn't flying, it is indistinguishable from a normal knife.

Telepathy. A knife familiar can speak telepathically to its master and tell them everything it has seen or done within roughly a one-week period. Its memory is fleeting, and it can't remember events more than a week ago.

ACTIONS

Diabolical Knife. *Melee Weapon Attack:* +6 to hit, reach 5 ft., one target. *Hit:* 6 (1d4 + 4) slashing damage.

Cult of Eleven Knives

The Eleven Knives is a cult of gnomes devoted to maintaining, strengthening, and expanding the deal made with Parzelon. Their public face is the charming blade and bon vivant Corvin Hallowell (LE **gnomish knife cultist**, see *Creature Codex*), their director and demon summoner is the slovenly but talented young Magda Venyn (LE gnome **mage**), and their ally and liaison to the hells is one Frexxis (**bearded devil**). Between the three of them, the cult is quiet and effective.

Working with dozens or hundreds of gnomish tinker scouts, the members of the cult find victims and sacrifice them to Parzelon with remarkable and bloodthirsty efficiency. **Bearded devils, spree demons** (see *Creature Codex*), and the occasional pair of twin gnomish **assassins** all keep the Eleven Knives on a bloody road. In exchange, the devils keep working to protect every gnomish village and town from all enemies.

BLOOD MAGIC & BLOOD FEEDERS

The Eleven Knives counts among its members one of the greatest blood mages in Midgard—the mother of blades herself, the Hand of Marena and the scourge of the faithless, Churaya Heart's Desire (LE gnome **blood mage**, see *Creature Codex*). She is said to forge many of the cult's best blades, and she enchants them with blood magic to make *blood feeder weapons* (see below), which cause wounds to continue bleeding—most of which are in the hands of the Eleven Knives.

Spells such as *blood armor, blood tide,* and *bloody smite* (see *Deep Magic* for these spells) are common tools among members of the knife cult.

BLOOD FEEDER WEAPON

Weapon (Any Piercing or Slashing), Very Rare

Damage from this weapon causes wounds that continue to bleed. When a creature takes damage from this magic weapon, it takes additional damage at the start of its next turn, equal to half the original damage inflicted. If the creature receives any amount of healing or makes a DC 15 Wisdom (Medicine) check before its next turn, it does not take this additional damage.

In addition, if you score a critical hit with this weapon, you heal a number of hit points equal to the damage dealt.

Gnomish Spellwork

These following spells are best known among the gnomes of Niemheim. A few have made their way into other hands or are known among

PROPER SACRIFICES

The sacrifices sought by the spawn of Parzelon and their master in exchange for protection from Baba Yaga are steep but far less so than the decimation wrought by Baba Yaga when her cauldron was filled hourly with gnomish flesh, especially that of young gnomes. The sacrifices to Parzelon seem like a bargain in comparison: each month, 12 black goats, a handful of humans, and whatever vila, vampires, and darakhul the Eleven Knives and their tinker scouts can capture, trick, and bind as an offering. The offerings are kept out of sight of the general population of Niemheim, who lead their lives in willful ignorance.

Each such sacrifice is made under the dark forest branches (ideally in the Wormwood itself but any grove will do) with a quick cut, leaving the victim's blood to seep out into the earth or onto a large stone, sometimes with a candle. Having the blessing of a gnomish scout or priest always helps, as does the assistance of an infernal familiar (see *find diabolical familiar* spell below) or an actual devil or **spawn of Parzelon** (see **Parzelon** in *Creature Codex*).

tieflings and diabolists with ties to Chernobog, Parzelon, or the Eleven Hells.

AVERT THE EYE

Illusion Cantrip | Bard, Druid, Sorcerer, Warlock, Wizard

Casting Time: 1 action
Range: Self
Components: V, S, M (a glass eye or marble)
Duration: Concentration, up to 3 rounds

By wrapping your hand around a small eyelike object, you become invisible until the spell ends. Anything you are wearing or carrying is invisible as long as it is on your person. The spell ends if you attack or cast another spell.

At Higher Levels. When you cast this spell using a spell slot of 1st level or higher, you can extend the duration by 1 round for each slot level (2 rounds at 1st and 3 rounds at 2nd).

CLOAK OF CHERNOBOG

3rd-Level Evocation | Cleric, Sorcerer, Warlock, Wizard

Casting Time: 1 action
Range: 120 feet
Components: V, M (a hat of black bear fur, worn during casting)
Duration: Concentration, up to 1 hour

Magical darkness spreads from a point you choose within range to fill a 60-foot-radius sphere for the duration. The darkness spreads around corners. A creature with darkvision can't see through this darkness, and nonmagical light can't illuminate it. However, gnomes can see in this darkness normally. This spell is typically cast on the cloak of a priest of Chernobog leading an expedition.

If the point you choose is on an object you are holding or one that isn't being worn or carried, the darkness emanates from the object and moves with it.

If any of this spell's area overlaps an area of light created by a spell of 3rd level or lower, the spell that created the light is dispelled.

FIND DIABOLICAL FAMILIAR

2nd-Level Conjuration (Ritual) | Wizard

Casting Time: 1 hour
Range: 10 feet
Components: V, S, M (100 gp worth of charcoal, rich incense, and a written contract that must be consumed by fire in an iron brazier)
Duration: Instantaneous

This spell is identical to the *find familiar* spell, but it is used only by diabolists to summon fiendish, corrupted, or undead familiars. Instead of the usual spirits, you gain the services of one of the following:

d20	RESULT	CR
1–6	Lemure	0
7	Stirge	1/8
8	Dretch	1/4
9	Ghoul Bat (TOB2)	1/4
10	Kalke (TOB)	1/4
11	Corrupted Pixie (TOB2)	1/2
12	Fire Imp (CC)	1/2
13	Skin Bat (TOB)	1/2
14	Gumienniki (CC)	1
15	Imp	1
16	Quasit	1
17	Ink Devil (TOB)	2
18	Kuunganisha (CC)	2
19	Wind Demon (CC)	2
20	Bearded Devil	3

(CC) see *Creature Codex*, (TOB) see *Tome of Beasts*, (TOB2) see *Tome of Beasts 2*

Appearing in an unoccupied space within range, the familiar has its typical statistics. Your familiar acts independently of you, and it chooses whether or not to obey your commands—a spiteful familiar may work against you.

GNOMISH TONGUE

1st-Level Transmutation | Bard, Cleric, Druid, Sorcerer

Casting Time: 1 action
Range: Touch
Components: V, S, M (a bit of fox fur)
Duration: Concentration, up to 1 hour

You have advantage on Deception and Persuasion checks and on saving throws against spells that do psychic damage or affect the mind, provided they have a verbal component.

HAT TRICK

1st-Level Transmutation | Wizard

Casting Time: 1 action
Range: Touch
Components: V, S, M (a hat and a small silver triangle with hinges worth 50 gp)
Duration: 1 hour

You touch a hat and create an invisible entrance within it that opens to an extradimensional space that lasts until the spell ends. The extradimensional space can be reached by reaching into the hat. The space can hold one Medium or smaller creature and its carried goods, or up to 100 pounds of unliving material. The hat always weighs about 1 pound, regardless of its contents.

The hat cannot be pulled into itself. Attacks and spells can't cross through the entrance into or out of the extradimensional space, but a creature inside can see out of it through a small slit as wide as the hat. Anything inside the extradimensional space drops out when the spell ends or when the hat is destroyed.

Gnomish casters often crawl into their own hat to avoid detection or to be carried safely from town to town.

At Higher Levels. When you cast this spell using a spell slot greater than 1st, you extend the duration by 1 hour for each additional level, and the extradimensional space can hold one additional creature, or an additional 100 pounds.

HORN OF PARZELON

1st-Level Evocation | Bard, Cleric, Sorcerer, Warlock, Wizard

Casting Time: 1 action
Range: Self (10-foot radius)
Components: V, S, M (a hunting horn worth 200 gp, not consumed in the casting)
Duration: Instantaneous

You blow a hunting horn, creating a burst of noise that can be heard at a distance up to 3 miles away in open air or up to 900 feet in caverns or tunnels. Each creature in a 10-foot-radius sphere centered on you must make a Constitution saving throw, taking 1d8 thunder damage on a failed save or half as much damage on a successful one.

Gnomes and evil-aligned creatures hearing the horn know that they are called by the arch-devil or his servants. They know the location and direction of the horn's casting and move toward it with preternatural speed. One or more creatures arrive at the caster's location within 2d6 rounds. The exact nature of the creature depends on the area where the spell was cast.

At Higher Levels. When you cast this spell using a spell slot of 2nd level or higher, the damage increases by 1d8 for each slot level above 1st, and the distance increases by 1 mile, or 300 feet underground, per level.

LION OF PARZELON

5th-Level Conjuration | Cleric, Wizard

Casting Time: 1 minute
Range: 90 feet
Components: V, S, M (blood and a knife)
Duration: Concentration, up to 1 hour

You call forth a **spree demon** (as per *Creature Codex*). Choose a space within range, and the demon appears in an unoccupied space within 10 feet of it. The demon disappears when it drops to 0 hit points or when the spell ends. The demon is friendly to you and your companions for the duration. Roll initiative for the demon, which has its own turns. It obeys

any verbal commands that you issue to it (no action required by you).

If you don't issue any commands to the demon, it attacks the nearest living creatures, including members of your party. If your concentration is broken, the demon doesn't disappear. Instead, you lose control of the demon, it becomes hostile toward you personally, and it might attack. An uncontrolled demon can't be dismissed by you, and it disappears 1 hour after you summoned it. The GM has the spree demon's statistics.

SUMMON SPAWN OF CHERNOBOG

4th-Level Conjuration | Cleric, Wizard
Casting Time: 1 minute
Range: 90 feet
Components: V, S, M (charcoal and a knife)
Duration: Concentration, up to 1 hour

You call forth a **spawn of Chernobog** (see *Creature Codex*). Choose a space within range, and the spawn appears in an unoccupied space within 10 feet of it. The spawn disappears when it drops to 0 hit points or when the spell ends. The spawn is friendly to you and your companions for the duration. Roll initiative for the spawn, which has its own turns. It obeys any verbal commands that you issue to it (no action required by you).

If you don't issue any commands to the spawn, it attacks the nearest living creatures if in darkness or twilight or disappears 1 round later if in sunlight or bright light. If your concentration is broken, the spawn doesn't disappear. Instead, you lose control of the spawn, it becomes hostile toward you personally, and it might attack. An uncontrolled spawn of Chernobog can't be dismissed by you, and it disappears 1 hour after you summoned it. The GM has the spawn of Chernobog's statistics.

WORD OF PARZELON

2nd-Level Divination (Ritual) | Cleric
Casting Time: 1 minute
Range: Self
Components: V, S, M (blood from a bird)
Duration: Instantaneous

By splattering blood on a stone or in dust, you may receive a single-word answer from the arch-devil Parzelon about a specific person, place, or object within 5 miles or about a specific action you plan to take within the next 30 minutes. Roll on the following table, using your spellcasting modifier:

d20	RESULT
1	No response
2–6	Garbled word in a language not known to the caster
7–10	Answer is vague and potentially misleading
11–16	Answer is accurate, punny, or clever but not helpful
17–19	Answer is accurate and clear
20+	A precise and helpful answer

A SHINING CITY IN THE DEEP DARK: MYSTERIES OF LILLEFOR

by Wolfgang Baur

*(with HH Carlan, Odd Items of Kobold Traders and Kobold Delicacies tables,
and Victoria Jaczko, Report from the Ghetto and Kobold Tools)*

The kobold city of Lillefor lies deep in the underworld, far below the northern Margreve Forest and southern Morgau. Its walls and rushing waters shine like a jewel, glittering with the light of a hundred lantern beetles and dragonettes. While it is more than a week's travel from the surface, Lillefor's fame among kobolds is celebrated in countless songs and riddles. With a huge population to draw from, the scaled folk are strong enough to mine, build, trap, and tunnel far afield. Some consider it the first sign of a renewed kobold independence, a minor scaly kingdom in the Crossroads.

While most surface kobolds know of Lillefor, few will speak of it other than in the broadest terms—it is a sanctuary for them, a place of pilgrimage and safety, and the only city-state ruled entirely by kobolds. Indeed, in kobold tales and gossip, talespinners rarely mention it by name where any non-kobold might overhear. Instead, kobolds talk about Lillefor using circumlocutions such as "our little place" or "the shining city" or even "the floating town."

Most kobolds rightly fear that if dwarves or humans found out about Lillefor's size and prosperity, they might strive to conquer it and oppress its people, as happened in Zobeck. The mines of Zobeck still exist, they say, but their wealth flows only to humans, dwarves, and the fey. Not so with Lillefor.

A Brief History

The underworld city of Lillefor began as a mine, founded during the same period of kobold wealth and independence that unlocked the Great Silver Galleries under the Argental and that lead to the founding of Zobeck as a surface mining camp. Miners from that period followed thin veins to the north, and they soon created a small but thriving colony devoted to silver mining with occasional strikes of mithral and veins of valuable gemstones.

The original founder's name is lost to history. The kobolds say a bandit king made the law at first, or possibly it was a darakhul lieutenant who led the kobolds to Lillefor's silver trove. Either way, that first human or darakhul was slain by an ambitious kobold warrior named Uluk Sama, who then claimed the mines and warrens in his own name. King Uluk the First is considered the first rightful king of Lillefor with his twin bride-queens, Dre-locca and Lyn-far, who served as the mine captain and watch captain, respectively. The trio ruled for an astonishing 20 years, until Uluk was ambushed and slain by a darakhul assassin.

Some believe the first cavern was named Little Fort, and over time, this was shortened to Lillefor. More likely, the name derives from *lillesh*, meaning "silver" in Draconic. It certainly was a fortification at first, as derro, goblins, and even purple worms are cited as creatures "trapped and defeated" in its early days. Purple worm tunnels may have contributed to the growing city's connections to the surface. The Purple Tunnel is still the main route to the surface today, though it is considered uncomfortably narrow for humans and dwarves.

Regardless of its early history, Lillefor has retained its independence and a certain level of secrecy. The camp's access to an underground river and a thriving mushroom forest, bat colonies, and cave goat herds all helped it grow, despite its quite narrow passages and frequent attacks by purple worms. The kobold kings and queens of Lillefor are as numerous as those elsewhere, and their reigns are brief, typically only three to eight years long, occasionally a decade. Two historical royals are of particular note: Queen Alokka Lyn III and King Junmo VII.

Queen Alokka allowed the construction of the Gambling Temple of Azuran and thus brought the Dragon Gods to the deep dark. This in turn led to the interest and guardianship of the mated cave dragons Hargo the Pale and Yuukfaad, who seized the temple, incorporating it into their nest, and adopted the city and its queen as their own minions and friends.

In later years, King Junmo decreed that derro and goblins would be allowed to settle in Lillefor, among the previously entirely kobold citizenry, in return for providing warriors to fight purple worms and protect the city's livestock. These include **derro shadow antipaladins** (see *Tome of Beasts*) and **goblin mooncatchers** (see *Book of Ebon Tides*), some of them directly under kobold command, others called up by king and queen in time of need. The allied smaller races have often proven their worth against darakhul, dwarves, humans, and other foes over and over again—and the kobolds are delighted that they don't have to do all the fighting themselves.

Through the City

Lillefor is vertically built on both sides of the Lillet River, a small but steady waterway that runs through the middle of the city-cavern. The kobold warrens are above river level, and inhabitants reach their entryways, balconies, and small ledges using a few large, public ladders and dozens of paths that are merely damp, stone handholds. The ladders can be easily removed in times of threat, and the handholds are difficult to climb without claws and daring—their spacing is best for Small creatures, and awkward for Medium and larger ones.

Terraces for growing mushrooms indicate the wealthiest inhabitants, and the king and queen live at the top of the cliff, surrounded by nobles and favored heirs in the Dragon Courts. The royal terraces are often the site of music, archery contests, and other festivals—and on occasion, the royals throw coins down the cliff to the poor.

KOBOLD WARRENS

The kobold homes each extend into the cliff, dug through the hard stone by pickaxe and stubborn kobold toil. Each entry tunnel branches into a warren with passages 3–4 feet tall, linking living chambers, natural grottos, goat caverns, and mining tunnels.

In addition, each warren entrance is protected by a trap or two, as is kobold tradition. Some traps are little more than rattling bones strung on twine or leather, and others are set only when the owner is away—and they can be quite deadly. "Dead at the doorway" is a common enough cause of death. Enough so that kobolds typically shrug and say, "They should have checked the tunnel first."

TOO-TALL GHETTO

Because of Lillefor's small tunnels and caverns, few tall races enjoy visiting. A short-term "touring token" can be purchased at the entrances to town for 5 gp or more, and these permit a human, dragonborn, or other "too-tall" to visit the Lillefor Trade Quarter—a polite name for a damp, noisy ghetto of caves and huts built riverside. The trade quarter is often referred to as the Pack-Lizard Pen, though technically the tall-ceilinged caves are separate from the pack-lizard corrals. Nevertheless, many human, dragonborn, and dwarven visitors must first eject a lizard from their quarters before moving in themselves.

Learning to ignore the ripe stench of the corrals takes some doing.

CITY GUARDIANS: DRAGONS AND BULETTE

The kobolds of Lillefor benefit from Scout-Captain Filloburta's penchant for bringing monsters home to the city. The cave dragons at the royal court have been vital allies against darakhul and derro, the lantern dragonettes that nest on the river cliffs give the city light and character, and the bulette that dig in the hardest stone mines make it possible for kobold miners to extract far more silver and mithral than one might expect.

While the bulette are technically the property of the Lillefor army, in practical terms it is the Elder Miner and Chief Alchemist Jango Rikanrekko who trains, breeds, and controls them using soothing potions, verbal commands, and carefully controlled feedings.

His apprentice, the young and shy Rikansweldor, is learning all there is to know about bulette, for one of the city's great fears is a repeat of the Days of Trampling some decades before Jango's time, when the trainer and apprentice were both slaughtered by demons summoned in an unfortunate bit of royal sorcery. While that disaster led to the founding of the new dynasty under Kekarrac the Elder (also Kekarrac the Lucky or Kekarrac XIII), it also led to the more regimented training of bulette and their more methodical use in both mining and defense.

Floating Pods and Floating Temple

While much of the city is hidden in its warrens and tiny tunnels, humans and other visitors can all see the floating black pods that serve as helpful transport between the levels of the city. Also called puffbags or black floaters, these magical mushrooms are more-or-less flat and buoyant with a few tendrils drifting below them, somewhat like a jellyfish might have.

TRAVEL BY PUFFBAG

Boarding a puffbag to be lifted up the cliffside costs 1 sp for any kobold, 2 sp for larger creatures such as humans, and 4 sp for a pack lizard, and travel down to the river from the heights is free.

Each puffbag can carry its minder (usually an elderly kobold alchemist or a young mushroomfolk), plus 16 Small, eight Medium, or two Large creatures. Putting a Huge creature aboard a puffbag is not allowed and generally results in a catastrophic fungal explosion.

Each black floater is trained to rise and sink on command, and they take just a minute or two to go from the riverbed up to the heights of the Court of Dragons. Striking the puffbag or injuring it in any way results in a loud, booming noise, and the immediate attention of the city watch. Most often a fine of 200 gp or more is levied for anyone injuring, threatening, or mistreating a puffbag.

FUNGI OF AZURAN

The city puffbags are protected and fed by the priests of the Floating Shrine of Azuran, which itself sits on the back of one such floating pod. Its high priest, the rather unruly Kekel-Trekel, discovered the secret of these floating pods somewhere in the deep underworld, and he personally oversees their growth and care.

Each floating pod seems to live for one to two years before sinking permanently to the riverbanks and spawning hundreds of small puffbags. The spawning of the pods is usually a holiday for kobold children and parents alike, and the puffbags are perfect for games, puff races, and gambling.

After each spawning, the priests of Azuran collect the fastest, strongest, and toughest puffbags to grow into the next enormous floating pods of Lillefor via a secret process of feeding and enchantments. Queen Dre'Ssatoc herself is said to provide crucial binding enchantments for the harnessing and control of the pods, together with a myconid druid named Whitecap.

Ruler and Allies

King Kekarrac XIV and Queen Dre'Ssatoc are confident, sly rulers who have produced nearly two dozen heirs who vie with one another to be most favored. Many of them come and go as explorers and adventurers. They seek to buy the favor of family and the city's dragons and people with gifts, magic, and new wonders to entertain and feed the masses.

FLOATING PUFFBAG

Treat all puffbags as **boomer fungi** (see *Tome of Beasts 2*) with 140 hp and a flying speed of 20 feet vertically, or 5 feet horizontally. The kobolds do use their booming as a form of signal when the city is threatened, and puffbags make excellent platforms for spellcasters, archers, and slingers when the city is under attack.

COURT OF DRAGONS

The work of ruling the fractious city, its laws and justice, is done in the Court of Dragons, a palatial cave-warren large enough to house the royal cave dragons, powerful kobold royalty, plus a few dragonborn advisers, a flock of lantern dragonettes, and the best of Lillefor's families as squires, pages, secretaries, trapsmiths, scribes, and cooks. It is the largest warren of the city with more than 390 inhabitants, half of them of some noble blood.

The tunnels of the court themselves display kobold wealth and security, using wide-open space—which is a thing both terrifying yet status-enhancing to kobolds. Of particular note in large-form architecture is the Tenclaw Audience Chamber, a single cavern that serves as a throne room with the royal seats roughly 20 feet off the ground in a balcony, looking down at visitors below. The balcony itself resembles a dragon's head with ten large claws below it.

Royal audiences are not like those in most surface palaces. For instance, the court's cave dragon wyrmlings are often fed a goat or two during an audience with the king and queen (visitors find this distracting, which is probably the point). Lantern dragonettes and lantern beetles provide strong light from niches in the walls or small nests atop stalagmites while pixie's umbrella fungi float about the chamber, making for a chaotic and somehow strangely enchanted space.

Rumors claim that sometimes Hargo the Pale and Yuukfaad magically assume the form of the kobold king and queen and rule in their stead. Others claim that Hargo and Yuukfaad are kobold heroes who have ascended directly into semi-divine, draconic form.

LILLEFOR, THE HIDDEN CITY

Symbol: A white shield with an eight-pointed blue star and a wavy blue border

Rulers: King Kekarrac XIV (LE **kobold king**, see *Creature Codex*) and Queen Dre'Ssatoc the Fair (LN kobold **archmage**)

Heirs & Nobles: 23 acknowledged heirs (treat as **kobold chieftains**, see *Tome of Beasts*), including the 10 princes (Crindos, Kekarrac the Younger, Lukki, Mallerac, Mandos-Ka, Pandos, Simorlac, Thorstan the White, Torban, and Yktra-Yelesh) and the 13 princesses (Azuranka, Bullanka, Dre-Baal, Dre-Clarsa, Dre-Kazba, Dre-Talla, Dre-Urkle, Marek-Tolla, Ninuye, Passye, Shaye, Umberla, and Xinka)

Important Personages: Elder Merchant Jiro (LN kobold **thief lord**, see *Creature Codex*); Elder Miner and Chief Alchemist Jango Rikanrekko (LE **kobold spellclerk**, see *Tome of Beasts 2*); Hargo the Pale and Yuukfaad (adult **cave dragons**, see *Tome of Beasts*) and their 12 dozen (young **cave dragons**, see *Tome of Beasts*); High Priest of Azuran Kekel-Trekel the Gambler (CN kobold **first servant** of Azuran, see *Southlands Worldbook*); High Priestess of Baal Rezmal Truespark (NE kobold **first servant** of Baal, see *Southlands Worldbook*); Keeper of the Gates General Zuka the Bully (LE kobold **bandit lord**); Scout-Captain Filloburta Teranella (NG kobold **swolbold**, see *Creature Codex*); True Lantern Keeper Peepo Toddek (LN kobold **druid**)

Population: 48,000 (39,000 kobolds, 4,100 goblins, 3,000 derro, 900 dark folk, 900 myconids, 500 dragonborn, 400 lantern dragonettes, 200 shadow fey, and 15 cave dragons)

Strongholds & Temples: Cavern of the Bulette (kobold troops and heavy miners), Fiery Forge of Baal, Floating Temple of Azuran, Great Stalagmite Tower (bat rider stables), and Rava's Mill-Temple

Great Gods: Khespotan (patron), Azuran, Baal, Charun, Rava

Trade Goods: Silver ingots, cave salt, everlit lanterns, beetle armor, bulette shields, jasper and garnets, potions, puffbags, and mushroom bread (in order of importance)

Report from the Ghetto

Good evening, my glorious kin of the Zobeck Ghetto! This week's issue is brought to you by Creeli's Emporium of Legitimate Lockpicking Apparatuses and by the personal winnings of yours truly from . . . working, just from my regular wages. Anyway! On with the scuttlebutt skittering through our warrens.

MAYOR OLLECK HUNTING SMUGGLERS!

It's been brought to our attention that undercover members of the city watch have been spied on the northeast side of the ghetto along the Derry, looking for smugglers taking advantage of our chain bridges to evade taxes! We should, as good citizens, mind our own business and leave them to do their work, and do not, under any circumstances, distract them by scuttling across the street in the shadows and setting enormous rat traps for them to investigate while some other enterprising young kobolds hook up additional bridges to the north and south.

WORKSHOP EXPLOSION UNDER INVESTIGATION!

In the late pre-dawn hours of last Torsday, a multi-colored explosion rocked the warrens north of the royal workshops. Preliminary investigation revealed none of the workshops themselves are damaged, but a suspicious crater among the homes across from the apothecary has some locals asking questions. Timrod the Mighty, a young kobold recognized for his colorful robes, specialty goggles, and a persistent odor of sulfur, insists the crater has been there since before the reign of Kuromak VII, but his neighbors have refuted this on the basis that, "Timrod is an idiot alchemist who ate too many of his own concoctions." Also, "Look, he burned down half my wall while I was making a late-morning rat on a stick."

The investigation continues, but inquiry suggests questioning has turned away from whether Timrod the Mighty actually blew up his home and has focused more on what ingredients it took to make the explosion bright pink and green.

REWARD OFFERED FOR LOST TREASURE!

Aggreta Darkscales has offered a reward of 27 cp and a vial of an unknown substance that is, "Either a potion of healing or an experimental cleaning solution. I can't remember which," for the return of her favorite broom, which has the names of her ancestors etched into the handle. Aggreta says it should be easily recognizable by the petrified mouse nailed to the top of the handle.

That's all for this week! As always, this report comes from Debbik, your faithful chronicling kobold of the Ghetto. Until next time! All hail King Quetelmak! Until someone else replaces him, anyway.

DIPLOMATIC CONNECTIONS

The city rulers maintain distant but cordial connections to the Ghoul Empire and even more distant (but more cordial) connections to the Mharoti Empire. More often, they speak and trade with the Kobold Kings of Zobeck and sometimes with the goblins of Fandeval in the Shadow Realm. They send occasional emissaries to Baba Yaga or to the Red Queen of Courlandia, and that seems like more than enough attention to the Upper World for their liking.

The Lillefor kobolds maintain no formal connection to the Ironcrag Cantons, to the Blood Kingdom of Morgau, or to the Magdar Kingdom. They are sworn enemies to the gnomes of Niemheim, always happy to betray them to Baba Yaga.

While the cave dragons and kobolds rarely speak of it, they are enemies not just of gnomes and purple worms but also of the expansionist Ghoul Empire. From time to time, a ghoul patrol vanishes near Lillefor, perhaps devoured by cave dragons or slipped into a fiery magma trap. It is nothing so bold as a war, but when ghouls come too close to kobold territory, they are not welcomed.

Trade and Inhabitants

While much of the city focuses on creating a place for the smaller races to trade and thrive far from humans and darakhul, it still maintains a surprising amount of trade with neighbors in the underworld and on the surface. Lillefor's merchants and explorers carry raw materials and worked goods into Morgau and Krakovar, the Ironcrag Cantons, the Magdar Kingdom, and (most of all) to the Free City of Zobeck. The trade with Zobeck, while substantial, is largely invisible to the humans and dwarves of Zobeck. Rather than taking their subterranean goods to the marketplaces directly, the kobolds sell them to the Zobeck kobolds—who then pass them off as their own. Thus, the Zobeck ghetto seems to be an almost miraculous source of metal, jasper, and other goods.

MINERS AND MUSHROOMS

At the head of the Mercantile Brotherhood are Jiro the Explorer and Elder Miner and Chief Alchemist Jango Rikanrekko, who provides much of the metal and gemstones to merchants for trade. The merchants are skilled at loading up enormous pack lizards and mules to carry their silver, gems, coarse salt, and fine, worked devices to Zobeck and elsewhere and to bring back wine, silks, fine paper, and other goods.

In addition, the city has a small group of crucial mushroomfolk partners, the Wide Hat Clan. These include barbarians, druids, and rangers, who care for the city's bats, cave goats, and mushroom foodstocks, such as by caring for **boomer fungi** in entrance tunnels and producing **pixie's umbrella fungi** and **strobing fungi** for festivals (see *Tome of Beasts 2* for all three fungi). In return, the mushroomfolk are protected from the more dangerous creatures of the underworld.

ODD ITEMS OF KOBOLD TRADERS

d6	ITEM
1	**Ice Statue**. An iron statue of an owl in flight, the surface drops to freezing when touched by a warm-blooded creature, dealing 1d3 cold damage. It can expend this cold energy once per day and recharges at dawn. (3,000 gp, 85 lb.)
2	**Measuring Cups**. This set of nested measuring cups appears normal enough, but they are incapable of providing correct measurements as they constantly expand and contract when used. Not designed to do much other than ruin someone's day, the measuring cups are a treasured gag gift among the kobolds. (50 gp, 1 lb.)
3	**Moss Finger**. The small green tube snugly fits on the finger of a kobold or other Small humanoid. It can shoot a sticky silken strand up to 60 ft., up to 3 times per day. The thread attaches to any stone or metal surface and can bear up to 50 lb. (1,000 gp, 1/4 lb.)
4	**Spikeball**. Two spiked, perfectly balanced metal balls are connected with a woven cord that slips around a finger. When a wearer makes a melee attack against a foe within 5 ft., they can use a bonus action to deal an additional 1d3 slashing damage. (500 gp, 1/4 lb.)
5	**Toy Box**. Designed for a child, this wooden box can easily hold an assortment of toys. However, the curved lid also has a false panel (DC 12 to discover), revealing a drawer for weapons sized for kobolds. (200 gp, 25 lb. when empty)
6	**Wet Candles**. Candles of dark-blue wax, these are designed to glow even when submerged in water or other translucent, nonflammable liquids. They burn for 10 minutes when submerged and cannot be reused. (50 gp, 1 lb.)

Of as much note as the Merchant Guild, the Miner's Guild, and the Alchemists Guild is the Lantern Guild. They raise **lantern beetles** (see *Tome of Beasts 2*) and **lantern dragonettes** (see *Tome of Beasts*), which they sell to derro, dwarves, shadow fey, and shadow goblins along with lamp oils, magical mirrors, and many other items of kobold enchantment.

The living lights are at the heart of the guild— as much from tradition as anything practical (for many casters can conjure some form of light). Lantern dragonettes are considered lucky animals, and if one allows a person to feed or touch it, that person is considered a "dragon-friend" and gains respect among the kobolds of Lillefor.

The guild's leader, True Lantern Keeper Peepo Toddek, oversees lantern making, beetle breeding and hatching, and dragonette training. Most of his time, is lately devoted to strobing fungi and luminescent paints. The other guildmasters and journeymen think perhaps it is time for a change.

KOBOLD DELICACIES

d8	MENU ITEM
1	**Cave Fish Sushi**. A thin cut of raw cave fish, wrapped in fried snakeskin with a wild yam mash and served with a spicy mushroom aioli, this is a rare treat brought out on special occasions. (1 sp per piece, or 5 sp per 6-piece platter)
2	**Charred Fun Shrooms**. A warm treat that reminds even the most hardened kobold of their childhood, this fungus, when properly cooked, is no longer lethal while still retaining a mild hallucinogenic effect. Kobolds frequently adjust cooking times for too-talls to desired result. (4 cp per serving)
3	**Gristle Chips**. Fried to sizzling crisps and salted, these chips are made from shavings of whatever meat scraps are available, especially from tougher and older portions. (1 cp per serving)
4	**Kobold Milk Tea**. Whatever milk is on hand, usually ant, roach, or worm, is simmered and used to steep assorted spiced tea blends. (1 cp per mug, or free with additional purchase)
5	**Pudding Cups**. A kobold favorite, these are miniature pudding trifles of varying flavors. They are common at festivals. (4 cp per mug)
6	**Spiced Dirt Beans**. Fermented for years while buried in the dirt, these spiced beans provide a filling and flavorful meal. Earthy notes and the sweetness of the mold are well complemented by whatever fatty meat scraps are available. (1 sp per serving)
7	**Trash Juice**. This concentrated bone stock includes any number of whatever spices and vegetable castoffs become available. Great for sauces and marinades, many kobold kitchens keep a giant, perpetual pot, simmering constantly in a quiet corner, simply adding to it as needed. Also warming on a cold night! (3 cp per mug, or 5 cp with shot of spirits)
8	On second thought . . .

d20	ITEM TYPE	FEATURE	FIRST PART OF NAME	SECOND PART OF NAME
1	Axe	Attached fangs	[Choose a color]	[Same as **Item Type**]
2	Chisel	Bows and ribbons attached	[Kobold name]	Bleeder
3	Cooking utensil	Cheap gem inlays	[Same as **Item Type**]	Breaker
4	Crossbow/bow	Covered in Draconic runes	Brilliant	Bringer
5	Crowbar	Decorative feathers and bones	Claw	Carver
6	Hammer	Decorative rust	Clever	Destroyer
7	Instrument	Dragon carving/etching	Clutch	Device
8	Knife/dagger	Extra, unnecessary handle	Dark	Eater
9	Lockpicks	Faintly glows in the dark	Dragon	Finder
10	Mace/warhammer	Glued-on insect wings	Ever/Eternal	Fixer
11	Magnifying glass/spyglass	Gnawed-on handle	Excellent	Fury
12	Needles	Name written on it	Fang	Greed
13	Pen/brush	Painted, garish colors	Glorious	Helper
14	Pickaxe	Partially burned	Hollow	Mover
15	Polearm	Pitted with acid scars	Imperial	Seeker
16	Shears	Pointless chains/strings attached	Magnificent	Stabber
17	Shovel	Reeks of sulfur	Quick	Thing
18	Staff/club	Sparkly with gem dust	Rock	Trap
19	Sword	Wrapped in dead vines/flowers	Scale	Wrath
20	Roll twice*	Roll twice*	Roll twice*	Roll twice*

(*) keep both options and consider how they are put together, such as a staff with a spyglass attached to one end like a portable telescope or an item named Red Eternal Thing-Bleeder.

Kobold Tools

Kobolds have a unique relationship with their tools. Their favorites are designated as unmistakably theirs with a mix of decorative touches, unique (and mostly useless) modifications, and even partial damage. Throw in a predilection for giving their equipment proper names, and it's a rare kobold found without a signature item of some kind that they guard with jealousy. Roll a d20 four times and consult the **Kobold Unique Tool Generator** table, or choose from the entries to create an appropriate tool.

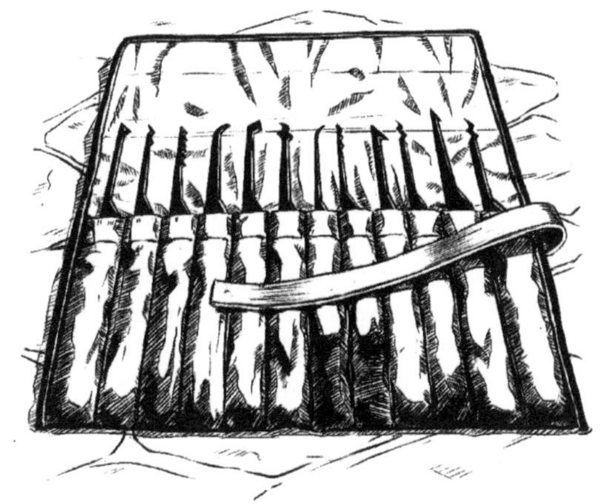

MISTO CHERNO: TREACHERY IN MOTION

By Richard Green, Ben McFarland, and Brian Suskind

"Many call us brigands, but we know challenges will find us, and we decide how to respond. Destiny brings the opportunities and misfortunes, and the merit of our skill will determine if we feed the crows…"

Overview and History

The histories all claim that Misto Cherno is a direct reflection of the uncertainty and unrest among the many tribes of the Rothenian Plain. If true, then the Rothenian Plain is undoubtedly a very sad place, for Misto Cherno has never been bigger nor stronger.

A long way from a mere quartet of walled wagons, Misto Cherno now boasts a rumbling flotilla of easily 250 massive wagons and dozens of smaller ones. The greatest of these are bound together with massive chains and connected with rope walkways to permit residents to travel between them, even as giants, horses, and oxen haul their wheeled metropolis over rolling hills toward the next potential target or campground. Herds of goats, sheep, and horses trail and swirl in its orbit, serving the populace.

Warbands petition for membership and serve a probationary period where they must acquire a declared amount of plunder, lest they be exiled and possibly attacked themselves. This makes the population of Misto Cherno a dynamic, shifting thing—and makes alliances between warband leaders more than just lip service.

VISITING

One who wishes to visit Misto Cherno peacefully must find it after nightfall and approach it with a gift of wine. A single skin is never enough, for you must offer the sentry and the city enough to slake a human's thirst. Once a visitor is welcome, they remain free to stay so long as they can barter or buy their room, board, and any other needs. This can be harder than it seems when the very landscape occupied by the city changes day to day. Outsider wagons may only join if a warband leader vouches for the driver and their crew.

THINGS TO KNOW

Grassweavers and other druids remain mostly unwelcome, but Misto Cherno responds violently to any who demonstrate the symptoms of the black strangles or longtooth. The whole population will burn down a whole wagon and its occupants before taking the chance the disease might ravage their community.

Otherwise, the need to defer to the strongest or most clever only extends until a chieftain might need to be called in, and traditions closely mirror those of other communities among the Khazzaki and Rothenian centaur

tribes. The residents take pride in their ability
to self-regulate. Bullies and intimidation have
their places, but those places are more often the
targets of a raid and not the next barstool.

REGULAR CAMPSITES

The route of Misto Cherno meanders and
dallies, for bandits hate hard work, preferring
to raid, ride, and lay about. While good water
and pasture is rarely overlooked, these are
reliable destinations.

Ingot Lake. Broad, deep, and cool, the wheels
of Misto Cherno know the shores of Lake Ingot
well. This wetlands and massive pool offers a
source of bog iron used for repairs and magic
arrowheads. A community of retired, former
Misto Cherno residents, who no longer wish
to wander but still like the fruits of brigands'
labor, happily sell the metal.

Mount Qaen. The Black City often begins its
itinerary at the volcanic springs beneath the
shadow of Mount Qaen's steep, forested cinder
cone. There, they trade with azer metalsmiths
and barter with two efreeti merchants who
bring goods from the City of Brass before
riding toward Vidim and points east.

Red Mounds of Rhos Khurgan. After a
successful season of raiding, Misto Cherno's
leaders never fail to return to this ancestral site
for raucous celebration and grateful sacrifice.
They stump for political support and affirm
their Great Khan for the next year's itinerary—
rarely a dull event.

STORY SEEDS

The prompts below can be used to introduce
Misto Cherno to a campaign:

- *Sundered and Undone.* A sorcerer has
  arrived with the intention of shattering the
  chains and warping the giants against the
  Black City. Able to magically shift their
  appearance, this spellcaster surreptitiously
  works through Misto Cherno, leaving
  mystic symbols on many of the great iron
  links holding it together, clearly planning
  some ritual that will destroy the bonds
  and fulfill some scheme. Can they be
  stopped before being brought to ruinous
  completion?

- *Waiting Emissary.* The party is sent to
  one of Misto Cherno's watering sites to
  parlay and protect their hometown from

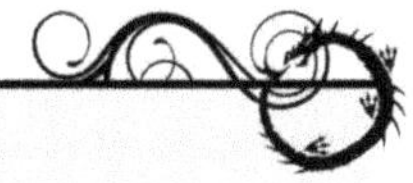

MISTO CHERNO, THE BLACK CITY

Symbol: A wheel of five white spears behind a
white horse head on a black field

Ruler: Her Most Fierce and Triumphant
Brass-Jawed Warhound of the Grasslands, the
Scourge of Vidim, Great Khan Yerude Dagasi
(CN **centaur chieftain**, see *Creature Codex*)
and the Thunderhooves

Bandit Warband Leaders: Osol Emberfist (CE
cacus giant, see *Creature Codex*) and Sakhen
Obzalov (LE human **thief lord**, see *Creature
Codex*) of the Baleful Brotherhood; Talgat
Freespoken of the Hellwains (NE tiefling **blood
mage**, see *Creature Codex*)

Important Personages: Garden Witch and
Grandmother's Daughter, Baba Vasilisa;
Master Karl Galway, Innkeeper (NE human
commoner); Thief of the East Wind, Kryvonis

(CN **windrunner elf**, see **Windrunner Elves**
later in this book)

Population: 9,000 (6,600 humans [primarily
Kariv, Khazzaki, Rhos, Vadim], 2,100 centaurs,
140 ogres & giants, 60 tieflings, 50 ravenfolk, 50
windrunner elves)

Regular Campsites: Lake Ingot, Mount Qaen,
Red Mounds of Rhos Khurgan

Prominent Structures: The Aerie, the Garden
Wagon, Giants' Yoke, Half-a-grog, Shepherds'
Conclave, Spear's Rest

Great Gods: Svarog (Volund, patron of the
Khazzaki), Loki, Perun, Veles, Yarila and Porevit

Trade Goods: Horses, oxen, foodstuffs, saddles,
plunder, tents (in order of importance).

a potential raid. However, a rival faction awaits them and steals what the group's patron planned to offer the bandits as a peaceful bribe. Can the PCs recover it before the Black City arrives, or worse, before the raiders' scouting parties capture the thieves themselves and take what was meant to be a gift?

Wagon Establishments of Misto Cherno

Hundreds of wagons make up the wandering bandit city, ranging from small carts to massive, multi-story vehicles connected to others by rope bridges. Other oddities include the Aerie Wagon where a group of windrunner elves has taken up residence alongside a rookery of ravenfolk, utilizing one of the taller wagons to launch their kites on the swift winds across the grasslands. Establishments of all manner can be found throughout the city, but a few of the most fantastic are detailed below.

GARDEN

Huge Wagon, Usually Near the Center of the City

Hanging greenery covers the exterior of this bi-level wagon in a tangle of vertical gardens, planting boxes, and trellises. The Garden is pulled by a pair of Huge awakened topiary hedges cut into the shapes of a pig and a cat.

A panoply of fruits, vegetables, herbs, rare medicinals, and flowers (including orchids) grows on the wagon. The plants thrive no matter the time of year, sustained by localized storm clouds and a greenhouse-like warmth exuded by the wagon when the weather is chill. Tiny fey tend the garden and delight in waving at gawkers.

Stepping into the wagon, visitors enter a small, comfortable sitting room decorated with mismatched chairs and a small table arrayed around an iron stove. Here, Baba Vasilisa offers tea and cookies to guests before dispensing her medicines, cures, and magics. A curtained doorway leads deeper into the wagon. The few who ventured within, and were foolish enough to tell the tale, whisper about an entire forest, strange fey creatures, and a hut standing on bird legs. Baba Vasilisa maintains a transitive pocket plane within the wagon, formed by a mixture of the Summer Lands layered with the Shadow Realm, where her fey companions can be comfortable. She also maintains an open portal to the current location of Baba Yaga's hut, wherever it may be.

Services. Potions, unguents, and all manner of medicine and healing. Baba Vasilisa can access every spell on the druid spell list and, given enough time, can certainly acquire any magical item (up to rare). For her services, she asks for rare plants, seedlings, important gossip, childhood memories, or days from a lifetime.

Story Seed: Comb the Skies. The PCs pass the Garden just in time to witness the notorious crooked nose thief Kryvonis (CN **windrunner** elf, see **Windrunner Elves** later in this book) escaping with Baba Vasilisa's jade scale comb! The item was a gift from the Emperor of Cathay and contains potent draconic magic. Chasing Kryvonis leads to the Aerie Wagon and an aerial battle on windrunner kites.

HALF-A-GROG

Huge Wagon, Northeastern Quarter

With tattered banners hanging from her tall mast, all stolen during their countless raids, the Half-a-Grog is literally the front half of a sailing ship mounted on a rolling frame. Reinforced bridges to the wagons on either side provide propulsion since no beasts pull the Grog. A wooden facade resembling the front of a three-story tavern seals off the rear of the ship and provides an entrance to the rolling inn and drinking den. Owned and operated by Karl Galway and his extended family, the Half-a-Grog is one of the most popular drinking establishments in Misto Cherno and is often frequented by adventurers and bandits alike. Galway maintains he is the younger brother of Ernst Goldtooth Galway, famed Pirate Lord of Graydock, and this is true to some extent.

Hidden Lore. Secretly, Galway is a denizen of Leng, magically transformed as part of a long-reaching infiltration campaign. Like Goldtooth Galway, Karl regularly funnels information and captives to Leng via a hidden portal in his chambers.

Services. Food, drink, and lodging. Rumors and information cost extra

Story Seed: Hunting the Spider. A **spider of Leng** (see *Tome of Beasts*) has been spotted near Misto Cherno. These enormous arachnoids are seldom seen so far from Leng, and Karl suspects his people's ancestral enemies seek to hinder his operations. He is arranging for a "spider hunt" and offers a hefty pouch of coin for bringing the creature back alive.

Tony DiTerlizzi

Gargantuan Wagon, Located at the Center of the City

Pulled by four elephant-sized **ankole** (see *Southlands Worldbook*), the great brass dome of the Ratusha forms the heart of Misto Cherno. Most of the wagon is a portion of an Ankeshelian flying vessel salvaged from a crash site deep in the Rothenian Plain and mounted on a massive wooden wagon frame. Though intended to be a city hall, the Ratusha typically functions as a social club, tavern, and den of debauchery for the bandit lords. Two ancient bearing golems (see *Tome of Beasts 2*) guard the entrance to the Ratusha and are keyed to protect the current lords of the city. The interior features a wide-open lounge beneath the brass dome, which is etched with odd stellar constellations. Here, the bandit lords drink, carouse, relish the plunder from their many raids, and plan new ones. Archways lead to many smaller chambers, perfect for clandestine meetings. Strangely, many of these doorways are high on the walls of the dome, accessible only by ladder.

Services. Quests (mostly assassinations, raids, and rescues). The bandit lords will occasionally purchase or sell items of rare or greater rarity.

Story Seed: Stealing City Hall. Arbela Artgnou (N dwarf veteran), the Cassadegan historian and archeologist, wants to "rescue" the Ankeshelian portion of the Ratusha and has a plan. All she needs is a tough and canny crew to pull off the job.

Misto Cherno's Most Wanted

Hundreds of bandits and ne'er-do-wells live in Misto Cherno, either on a permanent basis or for a season or so at a time. The Great Khan of Misto Cherno is chosen each season in a raiding contest held among the chieftains—the leader of the warband that brings the most valuable prize back to the city becomes its ruler.

Several of the most infamous bandit lords and their warbands are detailed below.

YERUDE DAGASI

This fearsome bandit leader is the current Great Khan of Misto Cherno. Yerude Dagasi (CN **centaur chieftain**, see *Creature Codex*) was

declared winner of the latest raiding contest when her warband, the Thunderhooves, stole a crate of magical gnomish mithral blades from the city of Janosgrod. Yerude is the elder sister of Anthal, leader of Clan Dargit, the Arrow Catchers, one of the most widely known of centaur clans. She was thrown out by her brother for stealing a length of precious heartwood the centaurs had taken from Domovogrod's Winter Tree in a raid and using it to make herself a mighty recurved *bow of accuracy* (see *Vault of Magic*).

Yerude has long dark hair, brown eyes, pale-gray hindquarters, and a black tail. She wears a brightly colored silk tunic on her upper body over her chainmail and a headdress made from gold and turquoise beads. The gold medallion shaped like a five-spoked wagon wheel that hangs around her neck is the badge of the Great Khan.

A fierce warrior and deadeye archer, Yerude can hit a series of targets while galloping across the steppes at full speed. Known as a daredevil with an irrepressible lust for life, she loves nothing more than taking on seemingly impossible challenges and winning. To join the Thunderhooves, a centaur must steal something in a daring solo raid and bring it back to Misto Cherno without getting caught. Typical items include a Niemheim gnome's red cap, a Kariv's horse, or a huginn's tail feather. Yerude enjoys carousing in the rowdy company of her comrades but insists anyone wishing to court her must first beat her in an archery contest. Many have tried, but none have succeeded.

Story Seed: King's Cut. Although all mithral blades stolen from the gnomes were valuable, one of them, a *mordant blade* (see *Vault of Magic*), was particularly prized. Intended as a gift for King Redbeard himself, its maker is desperate to get it back and is willing to pay the PCs a small fortune if they can steal it from Yerude Dagasi's wagon.

OSOL EMBERFIST

Driven out of his home in the mountains surrounding the Cloud-Soaked Cliff by the Kariv of the Lovari family, Osol Emberfist (CE **cacus giant**, see *Creature Codex*) wandered south onto the Rothenian Plain where he encountered the silver-tongued bandit chief Sakhen Obzalov (LE human **thief lord**, see *Creature Codex*). To avoid having his head bashed in with a rock, the quick-witted rogue persuaded the gullible giant that his warband, the Baleful Brotherhood, needed a new leader and that Osol was the giant for the job.

Osol has been convinced that he is the Brotherhood's chief ever since and has led the gang on many successful raids, nearly always planned and directed by his "little adviser" Sakhen. But Osol is hot-tempered and occasionally gets annoyed with Sakhen—usually when he thinks the human is being too cautious. When this happens, the giant insists the warband follows his own plan, typically a brutal, frontal assault on the target. Sometimes such direct tactics prove effective, but Sakhen is careful never to say "I told you so!" when they don't.

Osol stands 18 feet tall and has fiery-orange skin and a battle-scarred bald head. Foul-smelling smoke drifts out of his nostrils and mouth. He has Misto Cherno's five-spoked wheel symbol branded on his upper right arm, wears black iron armor, and wields a mighty greatclub with a head shaped like a fiery bull.

Story Seed: All In. The next raiding contest is due to take place soon, and the other bandit chiefs are desperate to ensure the Baleful Brotherhood do not win—as they only just prevented the complete collapse of Misto Cherno the last time Osol Emberfist was Great Khan. Either the PCs are enlisted by one of the warlords to sabotage the Brotherhood's raiding plans, or they are hired by Sakhen Obsalov to stop any attempts at interference by the other gangs and ensure victory in the contest.

TALGAT FREESPOKEN

Most of Misto Cherno's other bandit chiefs find Talgat Freespoken (NE tiefling **blood mage**, see *Creature Codex*) very unsettling. Talgat is the leader of the Hellwains, a warband of tieflings, centaurs, and **tusked crimson ogres** (see *Creature Codex*) with an unsavory reputation for leaving a trail of exsanguinated corpses behind whenever they raid a village or Kariv community.

The truth is even worse: as well as being a blood mage who practices dark magic, Talgat is one of the Master of Demon Mountain's bastard offspring. He remains loyal to his wicked father, spying on the other bandits of Misto Cherno and relaying information back to Demon Mountain through imps and other fiendish messengers. Yerude Dagasi suspects Talgat's true allegiance but has yet to gather sufficient proof to confront him.

Talgat has deep-crimson skin, silver eyes, long blue hair and a pair of tall, straight horns like a gazelle's. He dresses in black robes that hide the bloodstains from his vile activities and rides in an armor-plated wagon pulled by a pair of gorgons. A tusked crimson ogre named Moezig Spinebreaker acts as his bodyguard. Talgat used a tome of forbidden magic borrowed from his father to brew the bloody concoction that transformed Moezig from a regular ogre into what he is now.

Story Seed: What's in the Box. Rumors have reached Talgat's ears that a certain wooden puzzle box, holding a clue to freeing the Master of Demon Mountain, has surfaced in Misto Ellel (see *Warlock 34: Baba Yaga* or later in this book). Yakev Illyonevik, perhaps the Rothenian Plain's most enigmatic wizard, hires the PCs to obtain the box and bring it to him before it falls into the blood mage's hands.

BABA VASILISA

A denizen of Misto Cherno since its founding, Baba Vasilisa (use stats for **Baba Yaga**, see *Creature Codex*) occupies an odd position in the city. She does not, technically, have any standing among the bandit lords, yet all defer to her in magical matters or in the healing arts. The numerous stories about her suggest she is the younger sister of the infamous Baba Yaga, Grandmother in disguise, one of her daughters, a clone of the hag, or something entirely different, depending on the teller of the tale.

Unquestionably the most powerful creature in Misto Cherno, no one questions Baba Vasilisa's might. Her wagon, the Garden, produces fruits, vegetables, and herbs all year round and contains a forest inside. Fey creatures serve and protect her. Despite her powers, she seldom involves herself in the destiny of the city, only acting when directly threatened. Those foolish enough to confront her with violence meet their ends in grisly ways. Why she dwells in Misto Cherno is somewhat of a mystery. When asked, she only says she waits for something. In the meantime, she offers healing, potions, and magical items in exchange for trade, favors, and odd requests.

Baba Vasilisa appears to be a beautiful human woman in her early 20s with long golden hair, a kind smile, and solid black eyes with flecks of stars. Numerous fey creatures hide in the folds of her clothes or cling to her unseen. She has a patient and serene demeanor, though she seems constantly distracted as if listening to unseen voices. Her sense of humor is peculiar, often finding humor in otherwise gory and bloody events. The Motanka doll hanging from her belt can grow to Medium or Large size (use stats for **shield guardian**) and acts as her protector.

Story Seed: Black Days. A magical plague strikes Misto Cherno, and Baba Vasilisa needs a series of rare herbs to effect a cure in time to prevent the collapse of the city. Adventurers and bandits already scour the plains, but Baba Vasilisa needs the PCs to venture beneath the largest of the Red Mounds of Rhos Khurgan to recover a crucial ingredient.

MISTO ELLEL: THE THUNDERING TOWN

by Sarah Madsen

The gulyay-gorod, or "wandering towns," of the Rothenian Plain are a strange sight to behold. Whole settlements, safe behind sturdy walls, move across the landscape, drawn by horses or oxen or even stranger creatures. The arrival of such a wandering town can evoke wonder and fear in equal measure, as one never knows what the gulyay-gorod may bring. Misto Ellel is one of the most well-known of the wandering towns and is inhabited primarily by bandits, hunters, and mystics. The arrival of Misto Ellel brings the opportunity for trade and the risk of raids by the followers of the Horned Huntsman.

The Thundering Town. Nearly a mile wide, from a distance, Misto Ellel looks like a broad, squat hillside, floating across the horizon to an accompaniment of what some describe as the rumble of thunder, the roar of a massive waterfall, or the drumming of a rainstorm. At first, it is difficult to see what propels the town across the plains, for there are no horses or other beasts of burden harnessed to the moving structures. Up close, however, it becomes obvious: the city rides on the backs of hundreds of giant millipedes, their thousands of feet beating out a roar like a tempest on the hard earth. The marks of the city's passing are obvious in the mile-wide swath of trampled grasses, leaving a trail easy enough to follow for those bold enough to travel in the town's wake. When at rest, the millipedes settle into the earth beneath the city's foundation, allowing the town to settle nearly to ground level.

The town itself is made of the repurposed wagons favored by the Kariv, plus whatever additional materials the inhabitants have been able to scavenge, steal, or barter for along the way. Most of the homes and structures on the edge of the town are one story tall, all the better to hide behind the protective wall that rings the entire town, but the buildings gradually increase in height toward the center of the town. In the middle stands a four-story building comprised of several interlocking wagons, painted with bright colors and topped with a pointed cupola. This is the home of Tsura the Bold, the matriarch of Misto Ellel.

Wild and the Fallen

Misto Ellel is home to many, but the population is made up primarily of outcasts from the Rothenian Kariv and centaur communities. Centaurs that don't fit in well with their clans for whatever reason live on the outermost ring of Misto Ellel where they can easily throw open the wide gates in the city's walls and surge onto the plains to ride and pillage. Kariv who were exiled by their families or find themselves shunned by the greater Kariv community often find their way to Misto

Ellel, where Tsura the Bold welcomes all, regardless of reputation. Many members of the fallen families, such as the Heph, the Galati, and the Kalder, can be found within the walls of Misto Ellel, and any animosity between them is held in tight check, lest they find themselves facing Tsura's harsh judgement.

TSURA THE BOLD

Tsura the Bold, matriarch of Misto Ellel, is a Kariv, though which family she originally hailed from remains a mystery to most. Given her hold over Misto Ellel and her rumored ties with Baba Yaga, many believe her to be of the Kalder, though the Kalder in Misto Ellel deny any family ties with the wandering town's leader, and she steadfastly refutes any relation to any one family, insisting she's a leader for all.

A wide-shouldered but slender woman of some forty-odd years, Tsura wears layered skirts and is never seen without a saber on one hip and a curved, jeweled dagger on the other. She laughs easily but angers quickly, and she has little patience for those who would cause trouble in her town. Violence, theft, and raiding are acceptable outside the walls of Misto Ellel, but within, confrontations that escalate past a scuffle are quickly brought to heel. She does not expect everyone to get along all the time, but she treats Misto Ellel like the family she no longer has, and she despises infighting.

Tsura rose to power quickly after arriving in Misto Ellel about five years ago. Many attribute her accension to her claims to have outwitted Baba Yaga herself. Some say the fact that she still remains in power is the greatest support of her claim, for surely Grandmother would never let such a wild and baseless assertion stand, yet others assert that if Tsura had indeed outwitted the witch, talking loudly of such an accomplishment would be the quickest way to earn Grandmother's ire. But despite arguments over the origins of her power, the fact remains that Tsura the Bold rules Misto Ellel, and none have yet seen fit to challenge her.

Deals with Baba Yaga. Tsura the Bold's claim about Baba Yaga can be considered true, when viewed in a certain light. From other angles, the deal she brokered with Grandmother would be considered foolish and will prove to be her inevitable downfall. The truth is that Tsura's power does spring from Baba Yaga's magics. The Kariv bartered with the witch, promising to give whatever offerings were necessary in exchange for rulership over Misto Ellel. Baba Yaga demanded nothing in return except that

Tsura place a powerful relic, known as the *Eye of Baba Yaga*, at the highest point of the city where she could see in every direction at all times. The eye now resides in the cupola of Tsura's home, affixed with chains and overlooking the town and the plains beyond. Only Baba Yaga knows exactly how far—and how much—she can see from such a vantage and what exactly the eye is capable of.

THE EYE OF BABA YAGA

Suspended from the underside of the cupola in the center of Misto Ellel is an eye the size of a human fist. Pupils stare out from four sides, blending together like an hourglass where they meet, the irises around each a different color—brown, blue, green, and gold. Secured to the cupola by four hooks on chains, the eye allows Baba Yaga to see everything within Misto Ellel, even within homes and behind walls, and out into the surrounding area within a 1-mile radius. It is through the eye that Baba Yaga monitors Tsura, and the wandering nature of Misto Ellel allows her to observe the countryside of the Rothenian Plain and the peoples within it.

The *Eye of Baba Yaga* has darkvision with a radius of a mile. If it is destroyed (AC 10, 10 hp), Baba Yaga knows who destroyed it and can pinpoint the location of the creature on any plane of existence at any time. Baba Yaga may cast *bestow curse* (9th-level spell slot) through the eye once a day with the following modification: instead of a range of touch, the target must be within the walls of Misto Ellel.

KARIV

Many Kariv make their homes within the walls of Misto Ellel, making up the majority of the population, followed close behind by the centaurs. Kariv that live in the wandering town may have left their own family, or they may belong to one of the more unscrupulous Kariv families, such as the Kalder, that find suspicion even amongst their own. The Kariv of Misto Ellel are not required to give up their family ties, nor their loyalty to their blood or oaths, but must agree to hold Tsura's authority over all others.

Tsura welcomes all types to Misto Ellel, but the Kariv in the town are certain that, if things should come to it, Tsura would support them over the rest. Many of the non-Kariv share the same belief, and it is not unusual to find a Kariv taking advantage of a non-Kariv, both under the assumption that is how the arrangement should work. Whenever Tsura discovers such an arrangement, she is quick to disabuse all parties of the notion that the Kariv have higher standing than others within her town.

WOTAN'S UNKINDNESS

Though wielding no official power in Misto Ellel, a cloister of runemasters—composed of spellcasters from a variety of disciplines and backgrounds (including a few ravenfolk) but all with an expertise in runes—commands everyone's respect, and Tsura regularly seeks their counsel, especially regarding magical matters. The runemasters are responsible for the magical protection and maintenance of the town, including summoning the giant millipedes (or really whatever form of transport is most called for) that carry it across the plain.

The runemasters have perfected their own form of magical automatic writing in which they create single-use rune scripts that allow anyone to benefit from rune magic, similar to using a potion. Their services aren't cheap, yet their skills and wares are high in demand to those with means.

ZAGHARI AND THE WILD CENTAURS

The wild centaurs of Misto Ellel are, almost to a one, worshipers of the Hunter. They have been forced from the more civilized centaur clans or left due to irreconcilable differences. Some young centaurs stumbled upon Misto Ellel when they embarked on their bandit years and may leave to return to their home clans when their time is up. The centaurs primarily live along the edge of town, chafing at being within the walls, and many prefer to ride ahead or alongside the when it's in motion. Special ramps with wheels have been rigged to many of the gates and can be lowered when the city is on the move, allowing the centaurs easy access in and out of the city. They hunt and raid throughout the day and night, whenever the mood takes them, and often returned bathed in blood.

There is no official leader of the wild centaurs within Misto Ellel—Tsura claims leadership overall, regardless of race or ancestry—but if there was one, Zaghari would quickly claim that title. Zaghari is a roan-colored centaur with deep russet skin and black braids in his hair and tail. Zaghari is level-headed and patient, and he is renowned for his prowess in both battle and the hunt. When the centaurs have a dispute that they don't dare bring to Tsura's attention, they go to Zaghari for advice and mediation. Several of the younger or more rash centaurs have claimed Zaghari could and should unseat Tsura as ruler of Misto Ellel, but Zaghari is quick to hush any such talk. It is unknown whether he truly has no desire to rule the wandering town or if he's simply quietly biding his time, but Tsura seems confident in her position and has yet to oust the centaur.

Centaur Lodges. The Centaurs of Misto Ellel gather regularly in longhouses known as centaur lodges. These buildings are often used for rituals to the Horned Huntsman, for cleaning, skinning, and tanning, or just for social gatherings around barrels of mead or ale. A few serve a second, more ceremonial purpose, and these are known as Blood Lodges to the followers of the Horned Huntsman, and those in the know find it no surprise that Zaghari leads here as herl of the Misto Ellel Lodges.

Misto Ellel's Economy

Misto Ellel's economy subsists on three primary pillars: trade, hunting, and bandit raids. Within the city, coin of all sorts passes hands, and barter is a common occurrence.

TRADE

Those who are brave enough to venture into the wandering town will find goods from across the Rothenian Plain, and many merchants whisper of the wonderful items that can be found within. Trading in Misto Ellel carries its risks though as a merchant is just as likely to find themselves robbed of all of their goods and coin before they even make it through the city gates. Many merchants hire protection before venturing out to the town, or they offer bribes to the centaur scouts, or what passes as a city guard, to ensure safe passage. A handful of traders have arrangements with Tsura herself, and the raiders and bandits of Misto Ellel know better than to even look at them askance.

However, with great risk comes great reward. Misto Ellel's wandering nature allows the townsfolk to trade with—and steal from—people of all types. Often, rare items end up within the shops and homes here, and the owner has little idea of what they truly have hanging on their wall or in their display case.

HUNTING AND RAIDING

Misto Ellel is, at heart, a city of hunters, bandits, and raiders. The wild centaurs and other worshipers of the Horned Huntsman within Misto Ellel carry out routine raids in his name, rarely leaving behind survivors. Tsura does her best to balance the bloodlust of the followers of the Master of the Hunt and the needs of the rest of the town, and she restricts the bloodiest

CASLAV'S CABINET OF CURIOSITIES INVENTORY

d12	ITEM	PRICE
1	A set of three six-sided sandstone dice with the pips filed off.	4 cp
2	A dented silver fork missing two tines.	4 sp
3	A scarred purple leather pouch.	1 sp
4	A dusty arrangement of silk roses in a silver metal basin.	8 gp
5	A length of fishing twine dotted with semiprecious pebbles.	3 sp
6	A simple brass hooded lantern that, when lit, projects a racy image of two figures embracing.	20 gp
7	A black and red brocade jacket sized to fit an ogre.	5 gp
8	Three white alabaster chess pieces—the queen, a pawn, and a rook—and one black pawn.	8 sp
9	A pale-blue rhomboid crystal. It is an *Ioun stone of strength* mistaken for a mundane gemstone.	1 gp (or 5,000 gp if he's told of its magic)
10	A pair of pink silk shoes with holes worn in the soles.	5 sp
11	A wooden puzzle box shaped like a fox. Caslav has never been able to open it. It rattles as if there's something inside. If opened with a successful DC 18 Intelligence check, two human baby teeth (incisors) can be found within.	5 gp
12	A leather dog collar with a tag that reads "Jeannie-Bell."	1 gp

hunts to when the moon is full. She attempts to channel their need for carnage to the slaughter of beasts and monsters, providing meat and protection to Misto Ellel as well as sating the urges of her most ferocious citizens. So far, the strategy seems to be working, though some of the younger, more hot-headed and impulsive followers chafe at her restrictions.

Other, more circumspect hunters also serve Misto Ellel, orbiting the wandering town in small hunting parties of two to ten. Any outsider who stumbles upon such a party and proves their worth as a hunter may find themselves in the party's good graces and may even find a willing escort to the town.

Raids on merchant caravans and local settlements are common when Misto Ellel is nearby, and many villages will fortify their security and double or triple the number of

guards at the sound of rolling thunder on a clear day. Occasionally, these raiding parties can be bought off with bribes of gold or goods, but the spoils of a raid are always brought back and shared with the town—and Tsura.

Locations of Interest

The wandering town is filled with miscreants, criminals, and outcasts of all sorts and their families—grandparents, parents, spouses, siblings, children, grandchildren. Not everyone in town has a sordid past, but it's wise to tread lightly when inquiring into someone's history, for many are loathe to discuss their mistakes. Just as many, however, are proud of their actions and see themselves as an underdog, a freedom fighter, or a revolutionary, unwilling to bend their will to those that would oppress them.

AXIS

The Axis is the local name for the four-story structure at the heart of Misto Ellel that functions as both the town hall and the home of Tsura the Bold. The structure is made up of several repurposed wagons and brightly colored canvas awnings, and it's topped with an open cupola that helps keep the entire structure ventilated. It is the largest structure in town, and one could easily see miles in every direction from its roof—a favorite perch for the ravens that always follow the town.

CASLAV'S CABINET OF CURIOSITIES

Caslav's Cabinet of Curiosities is a tiny shop near the edge of town, wedged between a centaur lodge and a slaughterhouse. Caslav's Cabinet of Curiosities is no bigger than a wagon—and in fact its construction is simply a wagon with the wheels removed, the bottom flush against the ground. Inside, the walls have been covered with rough-cut shelving made from scavenged planks, and the shelves are cluttered with trinkets, junk, and sundry items.

The eponymous Caslav is a kobold of particularly diminutive size, and he stocks his shop with whatever items he can barter for when a trading caravan passes by or a raiding party returns to town—or the items he can scavenge from the remnants when the more influential merchants have had their pick. The items on Caslav's shelves are typically worthless garbage, but every now and then, the kobold gets lucky and scoops up a valuable (or magical) item that had been overlooked.

A selection of items for sale in Caslav's Cabinet of Curiosities can be found below.

WAGON WHEEL

The Wagon Wheel is a cramped tavern with food, drink, and one tiny room for rent above the kitchen (Misto Ellel doesn't get visitors often enough to warrant much in the way of lodgings). The exterior of the tavern is adorned with wagon wheels, and several hang from the low ceiling inside and serve as chandeliers, covered in candles and decades' worth of wax. The tables and benches are all bolted to the wood floor, and niches are carved into the tabletops to help steady plates, bowls, and cups in the event of rough terrain while the town is on the move. Upstairs are the living quarters for the Kariv owner, Adrina "Drina" Amel, and her wife, Volca. The roof of the tavern is covered in coops where Drina and Volca breed raille, a tiny flightless bird that serves as the centerpiece for much of the tavern's cuisine.

DOWN THE GULLET: ZOBECK'S DOCK DISTRICT

by Sarah Madsen

Zobeck is a bustling city of commerce, and nowhere is that more apparent than the Dock District. Bordered by the Derry River to the south and the River Argent to the north, this slice of the city is filled with taverns, shops, and markets that cater to all sorts, from wealthy merchants, escorting their wares, to the trod-upon dockhand, loading cargo onto boats bound for far shores. Criminals and beasts lurk in the shadows, weary travelers walk the streets, and newcomers to the city try their best to keep their bearings and their coin purses intact. Here are a few key locations throughout the district.

Altar of the Lorelei

Sailors have always been a superstitious lot, and those that work the River Argent are no different. For many locals, the lorelei—beautiful fey women who lure men into the river to drown them (see *Tome of Beasts* for more information on the lorelei)—are the river's handmaidens. The Altar of the Lorelei is a small wall fountain tucked in a quiet alleyway nearby, featuring a carving of a woman reclining on a rock and beckoning to passersby, the water pouring like a river around her and into a shell-shaped bowl beneath. Some say the lorelei are a mask of Yarila and that priestesses of the Green Gods tend the shrine. Sailors, travelers, and their loved ones toss coins or other small trinkets into its water as an offering to the fey before a journey.

Phylora Rhysen, an apparent priestess from the Temple of the Ocean Moon in Kammae, arrived some months ago. She has been preaching in the streets near the altar, calling out to the sailors and dockhands over the braying of donkeys and the lowing of cattle, exhorting passersby to put their faith where it's due—in Nethus. The sea god has never had any real footing in Zobeck however, and her impassioned harangues appear to have swayed few.

It is whispered that the shrine has a darker purpose for some. While most offerings are given to ensure a safe voyage, not all visitors to the fountain have such beneficent intentions. It is said that if a woman creates a poppet of a man who has wronged her and places it within the waters of the fountain on a night with no moon, the fey will find it and spirit it away. If the woman's anger is pure enough, her desire for vengeance strong enough, the man will meet a dark fate at the hands of a lorelei the next time he travels within earshot of a river.

Crafting a Poppet. Those who wish to call misfortune down upon their enemies can craft a poppet, a tiny doll made of rags and straw that serves as a proxy for focusing magic against a target. It is dressed and decorated to resemble the targeted individual, with hair, nail clippings,

teeth, or other sympathetic items from the target either stuffed inside or adorning its exterior. Poppets are neither good nor evil but simply a tool through which intentions are channeled, but those who craft them are likely to be viewed with suspicion and fear.

Bargeworker's Fellowship

Occupying a cluster of buildings on the west side of the district, the Bargeworker's Fellowship is a strange guild in that its members do all their best work up and down the river, at times far from Zobeck. They maintain close ties to the district's stevedores, working together in the loading and unloading of cargo. The bargeworkers are mostly sailors, rather than dockworkers, and often stay somewhat aloof.

Their guildmaster—the self-proclaimed Barge King (see *Zobeck Gazetteer*)—was recently removed and is currently serving 2 years in the Citadel for murder. Despite his many faults, rumor has it that he was framed for this, though why exactly or by whom is sheer speculation.

In the shakeup caused by the ouster of the Barge King, the city council made a surprising assertion of power and stepped in to ensure that the trade on the river wouldn't suffer, demanding a restructuring of the guild's leadership and a reevaluation of trade standards. The guild is now run by a council of three, to be elected yearly by the guild's active members, though the current trio was established by the city council itself: the human Jenna Gailey, the halfling Quinnie Wisewater, and the human Johan Greymark, distant cousin to Lord Volstaff Greymark (a fact he lets no one forget).

Any barge captain can attend the meetings and is invited to join the guild (and indeed is expected to) for a fee of 1 sp a year, and every barge captain who is a paying member gets a say in decisions concerning their trade. Meetings are held bi-monthly, or more often if a matter requires urgent attention, and a barge captain that will be absent can appoint a proxy to attend the meeting in their stead.

Recently, the kobold captains have appeared at meetings. At first, it was only a few, but their numbers are growing as their shipping enterprise expands. Their presence is making waves as no one quite knows how to deal with them. (Some members have suggested changing the meeting time from the evening to noon to avoid the problem entirely.)

Bengta's Radiance

With a prominent location near the center of the district, Bengta's Radiance, a recent addition to the district's offerings, does brisk business with those looking for a bit more than a tankard of ale and a bar fight to pass the time. Owned and operated by a bearfolk bard simply known as Madame Petra, the venue opens every evening at dusk and features performers of all stripes. Organized in the style of a cabaret, customers can sit at tables and enjoy mead, cocktails, conversation, and light food while taking in shows that range from refined to bawdy. Poets, musicians, clowns, comedians, thespians, and dancers all grace the stage, and the crowd loudly announces their pleasure (or displeasure) with the current act with their coins, cheers, jeers, and even a tomato or two. In fact, many of the local produce vendors find it worth their effort to take a cart of the day's cast-offs past Bengta's Radiance on their way home, selling rotten fruits and vegetables to passing patrons at a discount. To earn a spot on the stage, one must impress Madame Petra— though what exactly that means is up to some debate among the artistic circles in Zobeck.

The upstairs of Bengta's Radiance houses Madame Petra herself in a suite of rooms that could put some of the noble courts to shame. Richly appointed with plush rugs, thickly cushioned chairs and chaises, and a four-poster bed with heavy curtains, Madame Petra's slant-ceilinged chambers are suited to more intimate gatherings, and she often entertains private guests far past sunrise. Some of the staff claim there are nights that she admits no one, but they hear several voices in conversation within her chambers into the early hours of the morning nonetheless. Who exactly comes and goes without being seen is a question only Madame Petra can answer, and none are too keen to ask, for her tongue is sharp and her teeth sharper still.

It's rumored that Madame Petra chose this location, specifically so close to the Dancing Bear tavern that she holds in unhidden contempt, as a passive aggressive bid to take all the patronage away from that place.

Fey Haunts. Several locations throughout Midgard have a particular draw for the fey, and Bengta's Radiance is one of them. It is not unusual for fey to be hidden within the crowd, disguised as Zobeckers or anonymous travelers. Someone looking to strike a deal or carouse with the fey may wish to start their search here.

Blackened Fish Tavern

Unsurprisingly, given its locale, the Blackened Fish Tavern serves mostly sailors, stevedores, and other manual laborers that work the boats, docks, and nearby warehouses. The food here is questionable at best, but it's cheap, hot, and filling—and most importantly, goes perfectly with a large tankard of ale. The patrons are gruff and impatient, and the harried staff are brusque, but the place has an air of welcoming warmth nonetheless. One can easily find a raucous card game, a bar brawl, a boisterous tavern-sing, or a dark corner to skulk in here, and the other patrons respect all types—except anyone with a noble's attitude of entitlement.

A sizable establishment, the tavern sports a dining room lined with booths and filled with long tables where patrons sit elbow-to-elbow with strangers. Upstairs, ten spare rooms provide lodging. The kitchen sits at the side of the building, in a square offshoot with entrances from both the riverside to the north and Wharf Street to the south. Manned by three dwarves and a gearforged, the kitchen is cramped, busy, and hot. The dwarves are Drumdor, Belkorn, and Romir, three cousins who bicker constantly, while Bol, the gearforged, is calm and reserved.

In the kitchen, a set of stairs lead down into a low-ceilinged root cellar filled with barrels of salted fish and other foodstuffs. The space is laced with abjuration magic to keep out the waters of the River Argent. Expertly hidden on the back wall is also a secret door, and with the press of a stone, it swings inward, revealing a tunnel connecting to the Cartways. Drumdor, Belkorn, Romir, and Bol are all aware of the secret door and the tunnels beyond, though they will not speak of it, for they often host Morana's Smuggler's Market.

The three dwarves' aunt, Brunhilde, owns the tavern. She is old and doddering, and spends most of her time puttering around her room just above the kitchen. Though she seems ignorant of any illegal activities happening in or near her tavern, every now and then a keen glint flashes in her eyes, suggesting she may know far more than she lets on.

Blue Barbers of Wharf Street

A tiny-but-immaculate storefront sits poised on the south side of Wharf Street. It is here, inside the mirror-lined tonsorium, that the Blue Barbers of Wharf Street ply their trade. The dozen blue-haired gnomes wear elaborate hairstyles and carefully coiffed beards and mustachios, each distinctly different from one another. They provide cuts, trims, and shaves as well as restorative hair tonics, salves, shampoos, pomades, and oils, and they love nothing more than exchanging the latest news and gossip over a hot towel and straight razor.

The Blue Barbers claim they hail from the Court of Midnight Teeth, and rumors have followed on their heels like hungry dogs. While they have many loyal customers, some Zobeckers privately accuse them of being spies or assassins working for the shadow fey while others whisper behind their hands that the Blue Barbers are exiles on the run since angering their mistress, Countess Phylomara.

The truth is somewhere between the two. While the Blue Barbers of Wharf Street have in fact angered the countess (after passing on a particularly insulting rumor about the countess herself), instead of imprisoning or executing them, she ordered them sent to Zobeck with six of her enchanted mirrors. These mirrors now hang on the walls in their shop, each with a barber chair set before it, so the countess may eavesdrop on their conversations at her leisure or even pass through the glass and arrive in Zobeck at a moment's notice if it suits her. The Blue Barbers protect the mirrors and maintain wards over them, set against Duchess Shelessora, one of the countess's many foes (see *Warlock 16: Eleven Hells* for more information on Duchess Shelessora).

Kobold Shipping Consortium

On the north end of the Dock District, dockside to the River Argent, is the area referred to as the Gullet. Part of this is a narrow island, splitting the river, that was gutted years ago by fire: its warehouses were largely destroyed and the piers have offered only nominal usage until recently. The kobolds of Zobeck saw the potential in the unused land and launched into the new opportunities—the river trade business. Nearly overnight, ramshackle buildings and driftwood docks appeared, and the river began to fill with squat, flat-bottomed boats piloted by novice kobold oarsmen determined to move goods quickly from point *A* to point *B*. They have thrown many tiny wrenches into the well-oiled machine that is the Zobeck river trade industry, annoying the river halflings and others who have worked the waters for far longer.

Despite their rather chaotic business practices, the kobolds have made some headway and have picked up enough customers to encourage them to continue along their current path. The Gullet is now crawling with kobolds and is a maze of stacked crates, haphazard

construction, storage containers, and "warehouses" built from whatever material was on hand. There is no rhyme or reason to what kobold clans are involved or who is in charge, and those that go asking will get a different answer depending on who (or when) they ask. Currently, visitors to the island will likely get pointed to Trill Toothcut.

A kobold with a big voice and a bigger personality, Trill fancies himself a shipping magnate and dresses, to his mind, in a manner befitting his position. Wearing an oversized hat and carrying a sheaf of papers on a very important looking clipboard, Trill's ridiculous appearance hides a surprisingly keen mind. It's only under his guidance that the kobolds haven't devolved into complete chaos and infighting and have instead managed to complete several jobs successfully. Whether Trill can maintain his hold over the Kobold Shipping Consortium will have to be seen.

Ragman Alley

A narrow alley between clusters of ramshackle tenements in the poorest block in the district, Ragman Alley got its name from the junkmen, thieves, and the most destitute of Zobeckers that linger there. It is avoided by everyone except the most downtrodden and desperate, and those that accidentally stumble upon it pay for their folly in coin or blood—or both. Even the city guard refuses to enter Ragman Alley except in large numbers and absolutely never, ever after dark.

Ratfolk are most common here, living in the crumbling buildings that line the alley, followed by ravenfolk and then humans, dwarves, and elfmarked. Other creatures live here as well, skulking in abandoned apartments or hiding among the citizens huddled in doorways or beneath make-shift tents and preying on Zobeck's least fortunate, choosing their victims carefully as to avoid detection and quickly going to ground when suspicions are aroused.

Smuggler's Market

Though not a market in the traditional sense, goods and services are nonetheless exchanged for coin at the Smuggler's Market with startling frequency. The location changes weekly, commonly sharing space in the warehouses and backrooms of legitimate business concerns— whether with or without the permission of those merchants. The market runs afterhours and always wraps up by dawn, always trying to stay ahead of the authorities.

The market always has at least two employees present at any given time. It is currently operated by Morana Duskglow, a middle-aged ravenfolk woman with a striking pattern of white splashed across her deep-black feathers. Morana provides space for any and all organizations that are willing to pay her tithe, and she holds no loyalty to any one group. She brooks no violence within her walls, and indeed, the Smuggler's Market is one of the few places where members of opposing groups can be found in the same room together without blood being spilled. Those who break Morana's rules find themselves barred from the market— and may even be shunned by those criminals not willing to earn Morana's ire.

Morana has employed some of the most complex illusion magic in the city on this floating market, with magical camouflage layered upon the mundane as needed to remain hidden from the prying eyes of the city watch. The exact setup will differ, depending on the site, but a typical operation will provide a series of smaller rooms for private dealings and a larger space for storage and auctions. And multiple escape routes with easy access to the Cartways are always in place for Morana and her employees.

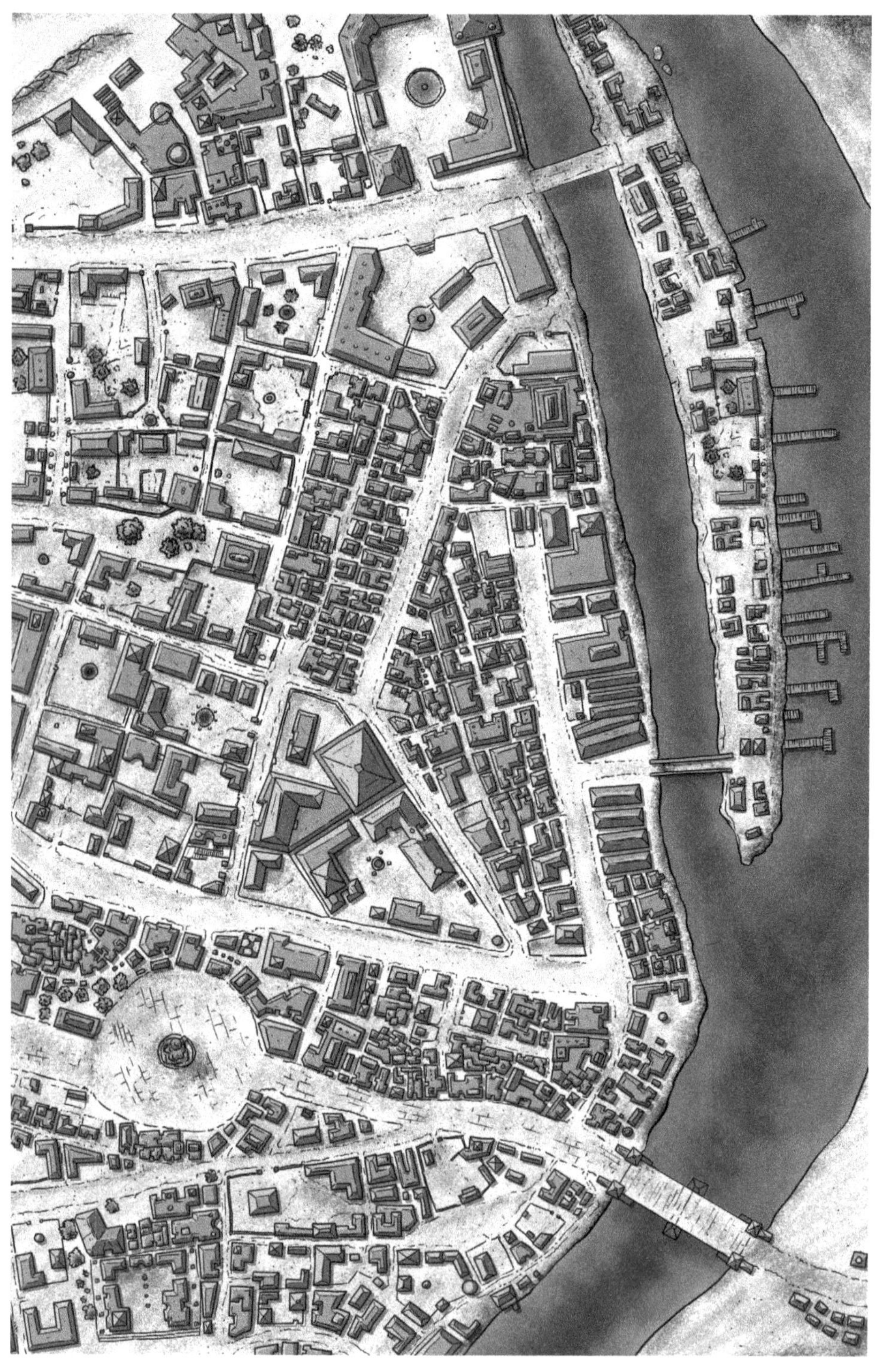

ENDLESS SKIES: ELEMENTAL PLANE OF AIR

by Brian Suskind

Imagine an endless expanse of azure skies. A pearlescent radiance of no discernable source perpetually shines upon drifting white clouds, dancing on determined currents of air. Those traveling to this plane often imagine an empty void of gas, but this is far from the truth. Though no ubiquitous and permanent stretch of "ground" exists, motes of terrain, ranging from miles across to merely pebbles, do float through the firmament. These islands host a variety of animal and plant life, and some boast settlements and even cities. Dangers and wonders exist in equal measure for those brave enough to explore the Elemental Plane of Air.

Subjective Gravity. Visitors to the Elemental Plane of Air must grapple with the plane's subjective gravity. For the most part, gravity functions as it does on Midgard, but—and it's a big *but*—creatures determine for themselves the direction from which gravity pulls. For unattended objects, the plane has no gravity at all. A creature simply imagines "downward" to be in a certain direction, and it will "fall" in that direction. Each round, a falling creature moves 500 feet in a straight line. (Falling damage from striking a stationary object is determined as normal.)

The nature of the plane does not allow a creature to control the strength of gravity, merely its direction. At the start of its turn, a creature can use a bonus action to make a DC 15 Wisdom check to set a new direction for gravity. On a success, the creature's movement in the previous direction slows to 150 feet. On the next turn, the creature will "fall" 500 feet in the new direction. On a failure, the creature continues to fall in the same direction and has disadvantage on its next check to determine a new direction for gravity.

In order to land on a solid surface, a creature must do the following. At the beginning of the round after the creature has successfully set a new direction for gravity, it can make a DC 15 Wisdom check to instead choose no direction. This causes the creature to stop falling. If the creature is within 50 feet of a Large or bigger solid object, it will float down toward it at a rate of 15 feet per round.

Cosmology

The Elemental Plane of Air has two distinct regions: Endalaus and Storoval.

Endalaus. The upper layer of the plane is commonly called Endalaus (meaning *forever*) and is the one most often visited by planar travelers. Endalaus features endless open skies dotted by clouds and floating islands. A complicated network of winds crisscrosses the layer, providing rapid travel for flying creatures. This layer is the home of powerful djinni lords, cloud giants, air elementals, and flying creatures of all kinds.

Storoval. Stretching out along the lower layer of the plane is Storoval, the Storm Wall. To a visitor standing on a mote of land in Endalaus, Storoval resembles a churning sea of black and gray storm clouds, stretching out forever. Lightning bolts flash upward from the surface of the storm, posing a hazard to nearby creatures in Endalaus. Within the layer, strong winds, driving rain, and obscuring clouds reduce visibility and present a dangerous environment for travelers. Storoval is the home of turbulent air elementals, storm giants, djinni, and any creatures who relish the storm.

NAVIGATING IN THE PLANE OF AIR

The complicated air currents of the wide-open skies can make navigation challenging. Luckily, motes of land larger than 200 feet across only drift at a rate of 1 foot per calendar year, making them useful as markers. Moreover, creatures in Endalaus can see twice as far as normal. For creatures without a flying speed, travel across the plane involves spotting a mote of land, falling toward it and successfully landing, and then sighting a new mote and repeating the process.

Despite Endalaus's reputation for endless blue skies, every weather condition exists here, including rain showers and thunderstorms. Amazed visitors often watch as the rain drifting "downward" from one cloud coalesces into another cloud. At times, the weather causes hazards for travelers. Natives instinctively avoid the strong winds, tornados, gales, and hurricanes when they occur. Due to the subjective gravity of the plane, tornados form into spinning toroids that pull nearby creatures into their whirling doom. In Storoval, storms or worse are the norm.

ELEMENTAL BREACHES

Planar storms in the open skies of the Elemental Plane of Air all feature driving winds, crashing thunder, and crackling lightning, but they take on additional traits depending on the other elemental planes involved. At a minimum, movement within any storm is considered difficult terrain and vision is lightly obscured:

- *Meteoric Tempest (Air/Earth)*. A chaotic, convulsing plume of crashing stones and poisonous vapors, any creature that begins its turn within the area of the storm must succeed on a DC 12 Dexterity saving throw or take 5 (1d10) bludgeoning damage and 5 (1d10) poison damage. Moreover, for every minute spent within the storm, a creature must succeed on a DC 12 Constitution saving throw (+1 DC per each additional minute) or be poisoned.

- *Twisting Vortex Pyrostorm (Air/Fire)*. This cyclonic firestorm features strong winds, weaving searing flames and clouds of superheated vapor into twisting vortices that revolve around a burning singularity. A creature that begins its turn within the area of the storm must succeed on a DC 12 Dexterity saving throw or take 5 (1d10) fire damage and 5 (1d10) bludgeoning damage. Failing the save by 5 or more results in the creature being flung 20 feet in a random direction. Moreover, for every minute spent within the storm, a creature must succeed on a DC 12 Constitution saving throw or gain a level of exhaustion from the intense heat.

- *Typhonic Maelstrom (Air/Water)*. At the heart of this storm of churning air and rain is a massive aerial whirlpool, dragging anything caught in its grasp into the void. A creature that begins its turn in the area of the storm is pulled 10 feet toward its center and must succeed on a DC 12 Strength saving throw or be pulled an additional 40 feet, taking 11 (2d10) bludgeoning damage, and restrained by wind and water. Failing the save by 5 or more results in the creature beginning to suffocate. At the end of each of its turns, a restrained creature can repeat the Strength saving throw, ending the effect on a success.

Reaching the Plane

Apart from forcible rifts in the fabric of the dimensions, the whims of Hune the Door Lord, and various spell-created portals, there are several other methods to travel to the Elemental Plane of Air.

Etherfalls (Ever River). Visible from across the plane, a massive cascade of water erupts from a perpetual cloud in the highest reaches of Endalaus to fall in a sparkling torrent into Storoval where it enters a lightning-wreathed tempest before exiting the plane. Ships sailing upon the Ever River can find a tributary leading to the Etherfalls, though the passage down the cascade, not to mention traversing the tempest, poses significant risks.

Pyramid Marked Door. In the Mharoti city of Harkesh, north of where the Sumarra River flows beneath the great aqueduct, is an establishment called Flights of Fancy. Specializing in flying creatures and flying magic, the shop's owner, Zingara, guards a door emblazoned with the alchemical symbol for air.

A creature stepping through this doorway emerges in the city of Qasfi Alasam in the Elemental Plane of Air.

Verdant Storm. Located in an equatorial region of Asaph, the Green Planet, is a swirling vortex of green-tinged clouds. Guarded by air elementals, this magical gateway offers a somewhat turbulent passage between the planet orbiting Midgard and the Elemental Plane of Air.

Wybren (World Tree). An 80-foot-wide tree branch stretches a mile between two floating clouds. Creatures can pass between Yggdrasil and the Elemental Plane of Air by climbing up or down this World Tree branch.

WHIRLWIND SPHERECRAFT

This fist-sized stone sphere is banded with iron strips decorated with twisting, coiling lines reminiscent of a vortex. The carvings move and flow across the surface of the sphere.

Professor and geologist, the gnome Ignacio Vartan was always envious of the great explorers, traveling to the farthest reaches of the world. He'd amassed a huge collection of travel tomes, works detailing those fated adventurers, and devoured every word.

Years passed and perhaps Ignacio would have languished in the forgotten stacks of academia if not for a strange scroll purchased from a traveling sage. It was old, complicated, and difficult to decipher, but with an uncharacteristic boldness, he fumbled through the casting only to be teleported to a ruin covered mote of stone suspended in the middle of a raging storm between the Elemental Planes of Air and Earth. Even more surprising, the storm spoke to him.

The two realized they were like minds and long to see the multiverse. So they devised a plan to place the storm in an artifact capable of making their dreams of adventure come true. It is not known precisely what became of Ignacio. Some legends have it that his plan succeeded, and he created the *Whirlwind Spherecraft*, escaping his mote of rock to travel the planes. Other accounts maintain that the plan went awry, binding both the gnome's soul and the spirit of the storm into the stone sphere. What is certainly true, the great work, *By Wind and Will: A Gnome's Travels Throughout the Planes*, is studied in many universities. It is also true that the strange stone sphere called the *Whirlwind Spherecraft* has appeared in many accounts over the centuries, to be used by one explorer or another before being lost again.

WHIRLWIND SPHERECRAFT

Wondrous Item, Fabled (5th-Level and Higher Abilities Require Attunement)

This fist-sized stone sphere has bands of iron inset into its surface and engraved with a storm-like image that seems to move slowly across its surface. While holding the sphere, you have advantage on Intelligence checks regarding elementals or the planes.

Ride the Storm (Requires Attunement). As your level increases, you gain the following benefits while holding the sphere.

5th Level. If you use an action to rotate one of the iron bands on the sphere, a powerful whirlwind lifts a circle of stone beneath you with a diameter of 5 feet into the air. The stone floats for a number of hours equal to your proficiency bonus, either all at once or in several shorter flights with each using a minimum of 1 minute from the duration.

The stone moves at your mental command. It has a flying speed of 15 feet and can carry you and any equipment you are wearing or carrying. Ranged attacks have disadvantage against you while you are traveling upon your stone. The effect ends if you step off the stone. When you do so, the stone vanishes and you descend 60 feet per round, taking no damage from falling.

As your level increases, the stone can move faster and carry more creatures and any equipment they are wearing or carrying:

- 30 feet and additional willing Medium or smaller creatures equal to half of your proficiency bonus (9th).
- 45 feet and additional willing Medium or smaller creature equal to your proficiency bonus (13th).
- 60 feet (17th).

9th Level. As an action, you can cast the *plane shift* spell, affecting the entire vessel and all onboard. The destination is restricted to the Elemental Plane of Air, the Elemental Plane of Earth, or the Material Plane. Once used, this ability can't be used in this way again until 24 hours have passed.

13th Level. While traveling upon the stone, you can use an action to rotate three iron bands on the sphere. The winds lifting the stone form a 30-foot-tall cylinder with a 10-foot radius, centered on the flying stone. Any creature in

the cylinder, other than you and those you chose to ride the stone with you, must make a Strength saving throw (DC equal to 8 + your proficiency bonus + your Charisma modifier), taking 6d8 bludgeoning damage and being flung up to 20 feet away from the whirlwind in a random direction and knocked prone on a failed save or taking half the damage and suffering no other effects on a successful one.

The whirlwind lasts for a minute. Once you use the sphere in this way, it can't be used in this way again until you finish a long rest.

17th Level. While piloting the vessel, you can cast the *reverse gravity* spell as an action. Once used, the vessel cannot be used again in this way for 1d4 + 1 days.

Inhabitants

As might be expected, flying creatures of all manner make their home in the Elemental Plane of Air. Air elementals make up the largest portion of its population, though various other creatures, entities, and beings call this plane home. Dragons especially seem to visit the plane frequently, lured by the freedom of unlimited space to fly.

The plane is also the domain of powerful djinni lords—elemental genie lords called "storm sheiks"—that construct beautiful palaces atop and around floating motes, forming strongholds of graceful towers and shining minarets that radiate outward in all directions. Most djinn live in independent holdings and are fiercely protective of their isolation, though all storm sheiks acknowledge the rule of the Grand Calipha to some extent. A typical sheik controls a palace community of 2–20 lower-ranked djinn and jinnborn as well as elemental servants and guardians. Fantastic cities encircle the palaces of some of the most powerful djinni lords and offer safe ports for voidships and other planar travelers.

The following are suggestions for various Plane of Air encounters:

- ***Low Level Encounters.*** **Couatls,** flying animals (such as **eagles** and **hawks**), **hippogriffs, radiant spark swarms** (see *Tome of Beasts 2*), **storm spirits** (see *Creature Codex*), **tusked skyfish** (see *Tome of Beasts*), and wyrmling **dragons**.

- ***Mid-Level Encounters.*** **Air elementals, al-Aeshma genies** (see *Tome of Beasts*), **fulminars** (see *Creature Codex*), **hongaeks** (see *Tome of Beasts 2*), **invisible stalkers, liosalfars** (see *Tome of Beasts*), **sparks** (see *Tome of Beasts*), **wyverns,** and young **dragons**.

- ***High Level Encounters.*** **Djinn, noth-norren** (see *Tome of Beasts 2*), older **dragons, planetars, rocs, stellar rorqual** (see *Tome of Beasts 2*), **theullai** (see *Tome of Beasts*), and various **sphinxes**.

Locations of Interest

Most motes of land in the Elemental Plane of Air feature ruins, a palace, or some interesting occupant.

Citadel of Bright Wind. This palace is the seat of power for the Storm Caliphate, ruler of the djinn. It is a vast, floating oval-shaped diamond carved by wind and magic into towers, domes, gardens, plazas, and labyrinths. The city of Qasfi Alasam encircles the citadel. The complex features no stairways, forcing visitors without the ability to fly to rely upon air elemental guides. Smaller spheres of ice and stone orbit it, housing guest chambers, barracks, and impressive defensive armaments. The latest name of the citadel was chosen by the current ruler of the djinn, Calipha Astallah al-Zahra bint Husam al-Balil.

Great Maelstrom. Deep within Storoval, howling winds draw the unwary toward a titanic whirlpool of storms and misfortune. The eternal whirlwind is large enough to swallow whole cities, if any were near enough to fall into its clutches. Each round, creatures caught in the maelstrom take 10 (3d6) bludgeoning damage and 10 (3d6) necrotic damage, and they have disadvantage on any ability check or saving throw they make to

escape. If a creature is pulled into the center of the maelstrom, it appears in the air above Evermaw, Plane of Undeath.

Qasfi Alasam, Steel City of Shining Ice. This large city is the capital of the djinn and rests on a massive white cloud that encircles the Citadel of Bright Wind, the palace of the Grand Calipha. The cloud beneath the city is infused with enough magic to render it solid. The spires and domes of Qasfi Alasam are fashioned from magically stable ice and polished steel, giving the city a cold, stark feel. However, the population—djinn, jinnborn, humans, and a scattering of other planar races—is welcoming and joyful for the most part. Some notable locations in Qasfi Alasam are the Jade Mosque of Endless Contemplations, the Flowing Gardens of Delight, and the Endless Souk, an enclosed marketplace that's larger on the inside.

Rorqual Brumes. Floating through the worst storms of Storoval are a few relatively calm

ELEMENTAL BREACH

The elemental planes of Midgard embody the core aspects of air, earth, fire, and water, representing the building blocks of creation.

These planes hang from the branches of the World Tree, each filled with strange creatures, fantastic locations, and thrilling adventures. Though they do not generally have extensive physical overlap, the planes intermittently interact with one another and can form elemental breaches. These come in two varieties. The more violent and transitory instances, called coterminous storms, are the more common, though why or even when they occur is not fully understood—a churning tempest of two clashing elemental energies, erupting without warning. The more permanent instances, or coterminous zones, can lie dormant for ages, existing in some complex, arcane dance between the planes as each plane's influence on the locale ebbs and flows over time.

Creating a Breach. The exact nature of these elemental breaches is left for GMs to fashion, according to the needs of the adventure. As a guideline, GMs wishing to create a breach should choose an element (air, earth, fire, or water), which is different from the plane the PCs currently occupy, and then envision an appropriate phenomenon made up of the two elements. For example, if the adventure is currently in the Elemental Plane of Fire, a coterminous storm with the Elemental Plane of Air could feature swirling tornados of wind that pull flames into a fire vortex. If they are in the Elemental Plane of Water, a storm with the Elemental Plane of Earth might be composed of massive rocks clashing together in raging waves.

Formation. A coterminous storm erupts into existence over the course of 3 rounds, beginning with a 30-foot radius and growing by 60 feet per round. Some storms remain small while others continue to grow until they dissipate. They can last between 5 rounds and 10 minutes, though some have been reported to last for hours or even days. Coterminous zones are generally permanent or cyclical to some degree, and they can be treated as storms made permanent although their effects are generally less tempestuous.

Hazards. Creatures attempting to move through such an elemental breach risk various hazards, depending on the elements involved. The descriptions of each plane provide some example phenomena.

Planar Travel. Using an elemental breach, travelers can attempt to cross from their current plane into the coterminous elemental plane. To make the crossing, a creature must reach a point within 15 feet of the center of the breach and use an action to make a DC 15 Wisdom saving throw to will themselves across the planar barrier. On a failed save, the creature is forcibly pushed 120 feet away from the center. On a successful save, the creature emerges at the edge of a similar elemental breach in the destination plane.

fogbanks of swirling clouds and eddying, nutrient-rich mist. **Stellar rorqual** (see *Tome of Beasts 2*) come to breed and give birth. The gigantic cetaceans generally ignore other creatures in the brumes, unless they pose a threat to the mothers or young. Rorqual brumes offer a rare safe zone in the otherwise perilous Storoval. Creatures that finish a long rest in a brume gain 10 temporary hit points that last for 8 hours.

Shattered Spire. Resting on a mote of land is a broken tower of cracked basalt, this towering spire was created by the four mighty Wind Lords soon after they manifested from the last breath of the giant Aurgelmir. It still features engravings honoring its creators: Chergui (East Wind), Shemral (West Wind), Khamsin (South Wind), and Boreas (North Wind). When Boreas turned against his siblings 2,000 years ago, he froze the spire in his anger, fracturing the upper floors. Recently, an archeological expedition of aeromancers from Aerdvall has begun to explore the spire, but mysterious injuries plague the team.

Personages of Note

Some of the plane's interesting inhabitants are described below.

Calipha Astallah of Bright Wind. A beautiful monarch with a bright outlook, Astallah al-Zahra bint Husam al-Balil (**djinni**) is one of the youngest rulers to take the Monsoon Throne. Though she still mourns the loss of her father, Caliph Husam, Astallah balances the often-squabbling ranks of her people with deft diplomacy and grace. Since taking the throne, Astallah has sought to avoid conflicts that might put her people at risk. Her other titles include Calipha of the Djinn, Mistress of Bright Wind, Daughter of Breezes, Commander of the Winds, and Storm of the Righteous.

Gray Sulka, Pirate Queen of the Hungry Tempest. Feared across the plane, even by the powerful djinn, Gray Sulka is a **doppelganger** buccaneer that shares a telepathic bond with her **carnivorous ship** (see *Tome of Beasts 2*), the *Hungry Tempest*. Sulka and her pirate crew operate out of a concealed redoubt deep within the storms of Storoval. Provoked by her raids on djinni holdings and other merchant vessels, she boasts a hefty bounty for her capture or elimination.

Lord Fuaran of Aqueous Imports. This gnome wizard and craftsman operates a small fleet of airships that "mine" clouds for water with a technique of his own invention. Once collected, he sells the water to the cities and communities of the plane. Currently, Fuaran alone knows the trick of cloud scooping, and he zealously guards his invention, often attacking other airships and creatures who seem too nosey for their own good.

Shabaan bin-Aqeel al-Basatar, General of the Azure Thunderbolts. The fierce and temperamental leader of the Citadel of Bright Wind's famed defenders, Shabaan (**djinni**) commands the djinni and elemental soldiers of the Thunder Legion. Though from all appearances loyal to the Calipha, Shabaan chafes under Astallah's peaceful reforms and longs for the days of the old Caliph's territorial expansions.

Adventure Hooks

Those brave enough to adventure in the Elemental Plane of Air contend with its variable gravity as well as its often-dangerous inhabitants. Despite the risk, great beauty and rewards await the courageous. A few possible adventures in the plane are described below:

- The Mharoti Empire's Collegium Elemental recently sent a group of professors and advanced students to the Elemental Plane of Air seeking a floating mineral rumored to lighten anything made from it. Using this mineral in the construction of new warships would make the Mharoti fleet the fastest in Midgard. However, the team is long overdue, and High Lector Jaaduu-gar Behistun seeks brave adventurers to find the lost expedition and return with the precious mineral.

- Calipha Astallah summons the PCs to her palace in secret, having heard of their prowess even in the skies of the Elemental Plane of Air. In order to solidify her grip on the throne, she needs the *Azure Scepter*, a djinni artifact of ancient power. The scepter is located deep within Storoval, in a trapped and guarded dungeon fashioned from solidified storm clouds. Great treasures will be theirs if the PCs return with the scepter. Unbeknownst to the heroes though, General Shabaan of the Azure Thunderbolts wishes to claim the scepter—and the throne—for himself and has dispatched an elite squad of jinnborn to the Stormwrought Delve.

- While in the Elemental Plane of Air, Malvie, a **sprite**, approaches the PCs with a plea for aid. A group of air elementals have captured a raiding party of Skybind aeromancers from Aerdvall and their powerful skyship. The aeromancers were seeking to capture the **air elementals** for their floating city. Malvie offers the PCs the location of an abandoned—and unlooted—djinni's palace as a reward for rescuing her friends.

FATHOMLESS SHOALS: ELEMENTAL PLANE OF WATER

by Kelly Pawlik

The Elemental Plane of Water is an endless expanse of liquid broken up by the occasional submerged land mass, reef, or eternally sinking hulk. The unending waters are in constant motion as temperamental, ever-shifting currents create wide, sweeping travel lanes only to narrow, veer suddenly, or change direction entirely.

Despite the vast, seemingly empty expanses of water, life abounds in the plane. The waters are rife with plankton and other microscopic organisms. Mollusks and crustaceans stud the land masses while fish of all sorts swim the expanse, feeding on their favored prey. Merfolk cities to rival any metropolis have been erected upon continent-sized reefs. Some inhabitants have grown to unimaginable size, and rumors speak of monsters the size of Midgard's moons in the far reaches.

Cold blue light filters through the central regions of the plane, penetrating through water and solid alike by some weird property it possesses. The farthest reaches however are as pitch black and frigid as deepest space. Where metaphysically close to the other elemental planes, the light changes, becoming a hellish orange-red near the Elemental Plane of Fire, a harsh white where it touches the Elemental Plane of Air, and a muddy brown where it meets the Elemental Plane of Earth.

Cosmology

Its ever-shifting currents combined with its seemingly limitless size make the task of mapping the Elemental Plane of Water a virtual impossibility. The difficulty is compounded by the distortion of relative distances experienced even by creatures adapted to aquatic environments. Planar scholars posit that the perceptual phenomenon is a result of the fluctuating viscosity of the waters combined with the unique gravitic force exerted by each solid object native to the plane.

The core of the plane, Bittereye, is a roughly spherical mass of rotating ice that is more than twice the size of Midgard's sun. This central mass holds the Arp of Gloaig, which serves as its primary source of natural light. Defying the physical laws that govern the rest of the plane, Bittereye has no gravitational field, despite its mass. Instead, chunks of ice that break away, some the size of terrestrial worlds, are slowly flung away from it, with each ice mass driving other objects away from it.

Surrounding Bittereye is the Aquan Totality, which is the turbulent, endless expanse of fresh water most Material Plane residents think of when they think of the plane. The Aquan Totality is punctuated with numerous salinized oceans, each of which has formed around a sizable solid mass. Most of the civilizations that

have developed in the plane have done so in these discrete bodies of water.

The outer reaches of the plane, called the Stygian Veil, are a lightless expanse of thick vapor. Where it is closer to the Totality, the Veil has a spongy, almost solid texture, but it thins the farther one gets from the center of the plane.

Subjective Directional Gravity. Like the Elemental Plane of Air, visitors to the Elemental Plane of Water experience subjective gravity. Unlike the other plane though, each solid object native to the Elemental Plane of Water has its own gravitational field with a strength determined by the size of the object in question. In simple terms, smaller objects "sink" toward the largest solid mass in their vicinity at a rate of 10 + 2d100 feet per round. For every 100 feet an object sinks, the currents it is subjected to cause it to drift 1d20 feet laterally in a direction of the GM's choice. A creature that succeeds on a DC 15 Strength (Athletics) check ceases to "sink" and can move in the direction it desires. A "sinking" creature that strikes a stationary object can use its reaction to make a DC 15 Strength (Athletics) check, taking 3 (1d6) damage for every 50 feet it sank on the turn in which it struck the object on a failed save or no damage on a successful save. Creatures with a swim speed do not need to make checks to move normally or avoid damage from striking solid objects.

Pressure. The waters of the plane exert the same amount of pressure on solid objects immersed in them, regardless of the differing factors between the various bodies of water. In practical terms, this allows creatures to travel safely from region to region within the plane without worrying about decompression sickness, otherwise known as the bends.

Likewise, most magic that allows travel between planes, such as *plane shift*, protects its subjects from the negative effects of moving from the relatively high-pressure environment of the Elemental Plane of Water to a lower pressure one, such as that of the Material Plane.

ELEMENTAL BREACHES

Despite how vicious they can be, planar storms in the boundless depths of the Elemental Plane of Water are surprisingly silent, often taking inexperienced marine explorers by surprise. These storms always have multiple competing currents, resulting in toroidal rings or other nightmares of swirling water. Some examples of coterminous effects in the plane follow:

- ***Drownspout (Water/Air).*** Where the howling winds of the Elemental Plane of Air meet the currents of the Aquan Totality, immense vortices form. At initiative count 20, all Huge or smaller creatures located within 1,000 feet of a drownspout are pulled 100 feet toward its eye. A creature can use its reaction to make a DC 20 Strength (Athletics) check to remain unmoved from its position. Creatures within 500 feet of the drownspout's eye have disadvantage on Strength (Athletics) checks they make to move away or maintain their position. Creatures that start their turn within 150 feet of the eye of the drownspout take 3 (1d6) bludgeoning damage. The damage increases to 14 (4d6), once a creature moves within 100 feet of the eye, and to 21 (6d6) once they are within 50 feet. Creatures that have 0 hp while they are within 100 feet of the eye have disadvantage on death saving throws. A creature that is sucked through the eye of a drownspout takes 52 (15d6) bludgeoning damage and is deposited in a random location on the Elemental Plane of Air. The eye of a drownspout usually has a radius of 30 feet.

- ***Seething Froth (Water/Fire).*** Where the heat of the Elemental Plane of Fire boils the oceans of the Elemental Plane of Water, it creates superheated steam bubbles that cook living flesh. A creature that starts its turn inside of, or moves through, an area of seething froth must make a DC 16 Dexterity saving throw, taking 17 (5d6) fire

damage and losing a Hit Die (as though it was expended to no effect) on a failed save or half as much damage on a successful one. If the seething froth forms around a land mass or other solid object, the object is affected as though subjected to *heat metal*.

- *Silt Churn (Water/Earth)*. Where the soil of the Elemental Plane of Earth finds its way into the Aquan Totality, it creates conflicting currents of thick mud filled with razor shards of stone. A creature that starts its turn in silt churn must make a DC 16 Strength saving throw, becoming restrained and taking 9 (2d8) bludgeoning and 5 (1d10) slashing damage on a failed save or half as much damage on a successful one. Creatures in the churn are heavily obscured. Areas of silt churn are usually 75 feet wide by 75 feet high by 150 feet long but can be much larger. The length of an area of silt churn is always double that of its other dimensions.

Reaching the Plane

Traveling to the Elemental Plane of Water from Midgard can be accomplished in many ways. The most commonly used method is via the *plane shift* spell. Several of Midgard's shadow roads can deposit a traveler in the plane. The Lotus Road, for instance, can lead those upon it directly to the Pearl Fane while those on the Pontoretto can exit to the frigid Glittering Hollow, and the Grey Way leads to the merfolk city of Kinvlemere. And there's a portal to the plane in the ruined marid city of Ammalsine at the bottom of Lake Debari (see *Southlands Worldbook*).

Mbardhi Pti. Creatures that enter the submerged tunnels located among the roots of the world tree Mbardhi Pti, a 400-foot-tall mangrove towering over the coast near the Gardens of Carnessa, might find themselves transported to a wide array of locations scattered across the plane. The serpentine roots of the tree seem to have a malevolent life of their own, and those who seek to use the tunnels are at risk of being pulled beneath the waves or crushed in their constricting coils.

Pearl Fane (Ever River). The Pasha of the Pearl Fane intimates that the origins of the Ever River are located near his seat in the Elemental Plane of Water. Whether or not this is true, a strong current of the waterway passes underneath the main entrance of his gem-encrusted palace. Other branches of the Ever River can deposit travelers on the Vaparean Shore, where the Aquan Totality meets the Stygian Veil, or on the banks of Lapplfite Beach in Kinvlemere. Creatures that swim to the Elemental Plane of Water via the Ever River are able to breathe air as well as water until they leave the plane.

Rivers Styx and Lethe. Though they are dangerous waters to travel, the Rivers Styx and Lethe both cut sluggish black ribbons through the plane. The wraith haunted River Lethe winds all the way through the plane, boring a tunnel directly through Bittereye and increasing the danger in that already hazardous location.

AQUA DESCENDER

This milky, translucent orb appears to be crafted from the eye of a creature of unimaginable size and coated in mother-of-pearl. Squirming cilia and flexing optic nerves guide the craft through the currents. Creatures that have observed the vehicle in motion report an uncomfortable sensation of being watched, even hours after it is no longer in sight.

After its death, the three eyes of the dead aboleth titan Pzu Gxa Ik were plucked from its drifting corpse and crafted into a trio of *Aqua Descenders*, vehicles that can be used to traverse the elemental planes. Each of the orb-like vehicles is large enough to hold a dozen standing Medium creatures and their gear. The interior of each descender is filled with the aboleth's vitreous slime. A pair of straps on the orb's floor are used to secure the pilot to the craft while a studded-steel skullcap is suspended from the ceiling by a brain stem-like stalk. Despite the fluid filling the craft, passengers can breathe freely.

AQUA DESCENDER

Wondrous Item, Fabled (5th-Level and Higher Abilities Require Attunement)

While strapped to the floor of this vessel and with the skullcap situated on your head, you can mentally direct it to move in any direction. It has a fly and swim speed of 150 feet per round (approximately 2 miles per hour).

If you aren't attuned to the aqua descender when you place the skullcap upon your head, you must succeed on a DC 25 Wisdom saving throw or have disadvantage on Wisdom checks and Wisdom saving throws for the duration of your voyage and for 24 hours after exiting the vehicle.

Eye of Command (Requires Attunement). As your level increases, you gain the following benefits while piloting the vessel.

5th Level. While within the vessel, you and all creatures with you are immune to cold and fire damage.

9th Level. As an action, you can cast the *plane shift* spell, affecting the entire vessel and all onboard. The destination is restricted to the Elemental Plane of Fire, the Elemental Plane of Water, or the Material Plane. Once used, this ability can't be used in this way again until 24 hours have passed.

13th Level. As an action on your turn, you can make three tentacle attacks with the vessel. You are considered to have proficiency with the tentacles, and when you make an attack with

them, you use your Wisdom modifier in place of your Strength or Dexterity modifier. Each tentacle deals 2d10 bludgeoning damage.

17th Level. While piloting the vessel, you can cast the *dominate monster* spell as an action. Once used, the vessel cannot be used again in this way for 1d4 + 1 days.

Inhabitants

Numerous intelligent species make their homes in the Elemental Plane of Water. Marids are native to the plane, and the Pasha of the Pearl Fane, a marid of immense power and status, rules the plane from his throne.

Merfolk. Merfolk settlements have been erected across the plane, ranging from isolated hamlets of only a few dozen individuals to the teeming metropolis of Kinvlemere, which boasts more than 250,000 residents. Where merfolk thrive, so too can merrow be found in great numbers. While they are hunted ruthlessly by their age-old enemies, the merrow city of Brine offers a haven to the maligned creatures.

Nomadic bands of sahuagin rove the endless waves, and it is said that they have discovered a secret that allows them to swiftly travel the vast distances between the oceans.

Elementals. Water elementals, as turbulent and temperamental as any body of water, can be found in untold numbers across the plane as can lesser elemental-kin, such as ice mephits. Though they aren't native, small communities of aboleth have migrated to the plane to hatch their eons-spanning plots.

Others. All types of fish, from tiny freshwater carp to giant sunfish to megalodons swim the waters of the plane as do marine dinosaurs, such as mosasaurs and plesiosaurs.

Ocean-going leviathans, such as sea serpents, dragon turtles, and the dread kraken can be found in the plane, though even there they are thankfully rare. Giant cephalopods, such as octopus and squid, are more common. Notably absent among the plane's denizens are whales and marine mammals, though a few addled-seeming travelers have made wild claims about encounters with vapor-surfing, carnivorous whales in the Stygian Veil.

Coral reefs make up most of the land masses in the plane—hundreds of thousands of square miles of area. A wide variety of seaweeds are scattered throughout the reefs (and elsewhere) and the combination of vegetation and coral substructure provide for rich ecosystems. Like the plant life found in most Material Plane oceans, it generally grows no taller than 30 feet, though within the Coriola Forest the seaweed can reach heights of 500 feet and provide ample hiding spots for ambush predators and prey fish alike.

Locations of Interest

A few of the many notable locations are detailed below.

Arp of Gloaig. This triptych of crystalline vortices is encased at the center of Bittereye at the ever-moving heart of the plane. The speed and direction in which the Arp rotates changes occasionally for reasons no scholar has yet been able to fathom, though it undeniably generates more light the faster it spins. The blue light it produces radiates outward through Bittereye and extends through most of the Aquan Totality, dimming the farther it travels before fading entirely near the Stygian Veil.

It is generally thought that the Arp of Gloaig is encased in solid ice since the rotation of Bittereye matches its movement. This belief is not true though, for the Arp actually spins in a nutrient-rich, high-viscosity, supercooled liquid. Living organisms that survive exposure to the liquid undergo rapid, beneficial mutation.

Glittering Hollow. The outer portion of Bittereye, and the ice that breaks free from it, are riddled with tunnels formed of faceted ice. The light that radiates outward from the Arp of Gloaig is at its brightest as it passes through the ice, creating the blinding effect the tunnels are named for. Expeditions, mostly mounted from the Material Plane, are occasionally made

to map the Glittering Hollow in order to find a path to the Arp at Bittereye's heart. The only complete map that has been produced is kept secured in the Pasha of the Pearl Fane's treasury.

Travelers without magical protection take 14 (4d6) cold damage at the start of each turn they spend in the Glittering Hollow or elsewhere in Bittereye.

Kinvlemere. The largest city in the plane also holds its greatest single concentration of merfolk and is by far the location most visited by creatures of the Material Plane. The metropolis is a work of art that integrates stone and crystal construction with bridges and walkways of living coral. Portions of the city, including its largest marketplaces, sit beneath great domes that allow any creature contained within them to breathe freely underwater. The city is located in the Sea of Pelenos and is completely surrounded by the 340,000 square miles of the Ullicor Ring Reef.

Pearl Fane. The marid Pasha Saliandla is the acknowledged ruler of the Elemental Plane of Water. His Pearl Fane is carved from a single perfect pink pearl he stole from Estreid, the Queen of Oysters. The aggrieved mollusk god sought to reacquire her treasure for centuries until Saliandla placated her by securing his fane to her shell. From time-to-time, Estreid forgets she has made peace with the pasha and seeks agents to assassinate him and return the Pearl Fane to her.

The fane itself is a confusing warren of small courtyards connected by wide corridors. Creatures that enter the fane with the intent of harming its primary resident find themselves caught in a loop of corridors, rooms, and plazas until the pasha tires of their presence and releases a battery of giant barracuda to devour them.

Spire of Qar. This spindle of solid onyx relocated itself from the Elemental Plane of Earth to the Elemental Plane of Water an eon ago during a particularly violent coterminous storm. Delighting in its uniqueness, the genie-kind of the plane built Nacre—their mother-of-pearl city—around it.

The marid Empress Quarrimaj built her palace, a replica of the Pearl Fane, carved from a giant, magically created golden pearl, in the in the genie city. Her decision, along with her harsh criticisms of Saliandla, has rewarded her with the increasing support of her peers as well as a steady stream of mortal petitioners attracted to her unique ability to grant wishes.

Personages of Note

Some of the plane's interesting inhabitants are described below.

Believers of the Blue Tide. This society of scholars and philosophers, mostly of merfolk descent, worships the Arp of Gloaig as a god and believes it is the origin of all life. While the organization began as a collective of like-minded ascetics, it has become increasingly militant as its popularity grows. A compelling young believer and her growing number of adherents have begun to rove the oceans, destroying temples to other divinities and assaulting their faithful. News of the groups actions has reached the ears of the Pasha of the Pearl Fane who seeks agents to intervene.

Pzu Gxa Ik. The blind aboleth titan's torpid body has been sinking for eons. Though it slumbers in a death-like state, the mind of the alien creature plots still, drawing creatures to it in order to carry out its plans. The sahuagin Slime-Slick Band has built an encampment on the titan's body, and its leader, Nykkekiy, is in constant communion with it. Through their telepathic link, Pzu Gxa Ik shares its desires with its disciple, and the warlock-priest accedes to its master's requests without hesitation. The sahuagin's current command is to reconnect its god with its missing eyes.

Adventure Hooks

Adventures in the Elemental Plane of Water can take many forms. Consider the following ideas to introduce the location to your campaign:

- The merfolk sage Sallashalla has heard that the Juno-Fin Band of sahuagin has discovered how to cross from one planar ocean to another in a matter of hours, regardless of the actual distance between them. She makes a request of the characters to find out if her information is true, and if so, she wants them to steal the secret from the sahuagin.

- One of the *Aqua Descenders* crosses paths with the characters. When the characters enter the craft, it connects itself to one of them and begins to travel toward Bittereye, despite the commands of its pilot. What reason does the vehicle have to travel to the least hospitable region of the plane?

- A tsunami striking the coast of the Wasted West has swept the town of Maravahr into the Stygian Veil. The characters, who were resting in the village when it shifted planes, must discover the secret of the settlements translocation and reverse it before the village is stuck in the cold black shoals forever.

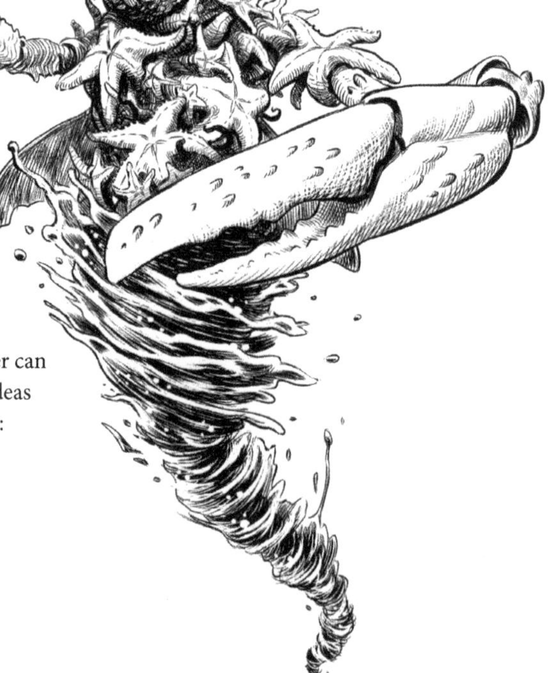

ONYX DEPTHS: ELEMENTAL PLANE OF EARTH

by Jonathan Miley

The Elemental Plane of Earth is a place of darkness and primordial earth. The majority of the plane is devoid of light, save for the odd luminescent fungal patch or roaming creature. This is a realm of subterranean mountains and canyons, of endless caverns that journey through stone in twisting tunnels. Artificial structures are all made of precious stone or carved directly into the rockfaces that reach deep into the darkness above. Those that have ventured up past the tallest mountain peaks are only greeted with the discovery of another ceiling of stone, dripping stalactites—just caverns within caverns.

Cosmology

The plane is a massive subterranean labyrinth of tunnels, interspersed with mountain ranges and ravines. The often-claustrophobic environs are earth and rock. The atmosphere is breathable, though a bit dusty and stale. The plane's denizens primarily communicate in Terran, if they know any language at all. Gravity functions as those from the Material Plane would call "normal."

ELEMENTAL BREACHES

Though most of the plane exists in varying degrees of never-ending darkness and stone, there are a few points where the other elemental planes intrude, creating places where the two elements come together in potentially dangerous circumstances. It might be worth

pointing out that, unlike the breaches in other elemental planes, those of the Elemental Plane of Earth are more static, less volatile, perhaps owing to the more unhurried nature of realm.

Obsidian Marsh (Earth/Water). A region of mud and running streams, this is where a connection to the Elemental Plane of Water lies as the Ever River bursts into the plane. Where the waters enter is a violent cataract, and the river then proceeds to snake throughout the realm. But the area immediately around the falls is dotted with stretches of deep, sucking mud (treat as quicksand), where many creatures have sunken to their demise. Steep slopes of stone gird much of the marsh.

Weird creatures are known to live here, such as **earth elementals** that resemble crayfish and that locals call crawlers. Stone formations jutting from the mud glow blue-green from the algae that coats them, giving the appearance of glowing stone trees.

A clan of **cave giants** (see *Creature Codex*) became stranded in the plane long ago and have made their home in the area.

Sea Noir (Earth/Fire). In a grey and black desert of limestone dust, a glowing portal of roaring flames hangs in the air above and serves as a sun to scorch the stretches below—and connecting to the Elemental Plane of Fire. This is also where the dao's Soul Forge is located, where pech master blacksmiths craft armor and weapons for their masters. The region presents a perilous journey for those who do not appreciate its dangers. **Purple worms** are known to nest in the area.

Zephyr Peaks (Earth/Air). One of the largest groupings of mountain ranges within the plane is the Zephyr Peaks, reaching far above and almost touching plane's ceiling. It is at this point that it connects to the Elemental Plane of Air. Temples carved into the peaks are kept by an ancient line of **gargoyles**. The incoming wind creates a constant howl.

Reaching the Plane

Traveling to the Elemental Plane of Earth from Midgard can follow many paths. Certain subterranean rapids might connect via the Ever River to this plane, such as in the Slate Ravine of Obsidian Marsh. Some of the highest peaks upon Midgard, for those brave enough to leap from their summits, might find themselves transported to the darkness of the Zephyr Peaks. Travelers exploring an active volcano or wandering the blistering deserts of the Southlands might find themselves in the Sea Noir.

ETERNAL RANCOR

The sailing ship's frame seems to be of oak, and the bow sports a silver-horned bull figurehead. The sails are white with a green sea serpent biting its tail. Two small ballistae of silver and oak sit amidships, along with a small cabin at the stern.

Another way of traveling to the Elemental Plane of Earth is a mystical sailing ship, the *Eternal Rancor*, whose story starts with the minotaur mage-turned-corsair named Meja the Neverlost. The corsair had been sailing the coast of Kyprion when an unnatural storm came out of nowhere. The treacherous waters pulled her down. Desperately using her magic to save her ship, she inadvertently connected to the Pontoretto ley line, and the ship was imbued with the elemental energies of earth and water.

Meja went on to find her second life, traveling the Ever River through the multiverse. Before she passed away, she gave her ship to another like her, who was in need and of a fearless curiosity. Its captains have since maintained this tradition—and the ship seems to indicate to its captain the proper time and the proper entity for such a transference.

ETERNAL RANCOR

Wondrous Item, Fabled (5th-Level and Higher Abilities Require Attunement)

The *Eternal Rancor* can sail over sea or land, magically parting the dirt and stone and trees, and sailing just as if it were water, leaving no trace of its passing—and you are its captain.

Seas of Fate (Requires Attunement). As your level increases, you gain the following benefits as captain of the vessel.

5th Level. As captain, the ship's lanterns respond to you and can only be extinguished at your command, you have advantage on ability checks made using navigator's tools while aboard, and any part of the ship that has been damaged or destroyed will magically repair itself daily at dawn.

In addition, the ship can now dive, whether on sea or land and with a swim and burrow speed equal to its sailing speed, creating a protective bubble of breathable air for its crew. There is no limit on the amount of time this ability can be used.

9th Level. As an action, you can cast the *plane shift* spell, affecting the entire vessel and all onboard. The destination is restricted to the Elemental Plane of Earth, the Elemental Plane of Water, or the Material Plane. Once used, this ability can't be used in this way again until 24 hours have passed.

13th Level. The ship's connection to the planes grants it various abilities: it is immune to fire damage, it can't be capsized, the sails are always filled to provide the speed desired, and its maximum traveling speed is doubled.

17th Level. As an action, the ship's ballistae can fire 1d4 + 1 bolts that trigger the *fireball* spell (6th level) when they hit (DC equal to 8 + your proficiency bonus + your Charisma modifier). The vessel regains these uses daily at dawn.

Inhabitants

The realm is ruled by the dao. Their slaves—that is everyone else, according to them—spend their lives digging endless mines in the search of gems and riches for their tyrant masters. The dao overlord, Khagan Ghorek, rules over the plane as the head of the Council of Khans. Currently, the other members of the council are the khans of the two largest and most important regions within the plane: Golnaz, Keeper of Shadows, and Delatam, the Emerald Mage. (Delatam has been absent of late, but the council has kept it secret. The prevailing theory is that the mage was tricked into partial servitude by a mortal on Midgard.) Other dao serve under the council, each having successively more power and authority than other creatures in the plane.

Other than the dao, some of the plane's most notable inhabitants are earth elementals, gargoyles, pech, and xorn.

Elementals. **Earth elementals** of various shapes and sizes fill the plane, either bound, following the orders of their dao masters, or wild and roaming the land. The region of the plane can have a marked impact on the elementals' nature, such as the form taken on by the crawlers of the Obsidian Marsh, the fast-flying **gargoyles** of the Zephyr Peaks, or the sand and lava elementals of the Sea Noir.

Pech. **Pech** (see *Creature Codex*) make up the majority of the realm's slaves. Their ability to craft and mine is invaluable to the dao. Though a pech's natural inclination is to please their masters, there are some that meet in secret and work toward freeing their people. They sneak other pech out when they can, such as through newly discovered portals to Midgard, where they live out their lives in freedom. To stamp out the resistance, the council has elevated one of the pech's own to the role of mining boss: a greedy and ruthless pech, Overseer Abdiesus is loyal to the dao and leads the efforts in crushing the spirits of the slaves.

Xorn. **Xorn** have also been preferentially enslaved to help fill their dao masters' appetite for more gems and precious metals. Few xorn tribes have avoided capture, but those on the loose have banded together under the leadership of the massive Scarlet Maw, trying to attack and deteriorate dao rulership where they can.

Others. Plant life consists of various types of fungi and algae, with the greatest concentration being around Obsidian Marsh. (The local crawlers cover their bodies with the glowing algae.) Within the Sea Noir, the increased light gives rise to varieties of plant life seen nowhere else in the plane, but the scarcity of water keeps this to a minimum.

Locations of Interest

A few of the many notable locations are detailed below.

Jagged Tooth Ravine. Spikes of stone jut from the ravine ridgelines, looking like a massive maw filled with sharp teeth. Wild earth

elementals roam the area, but the dominant group are the xorn, led by the massive Crimson Claw, that currently use the ravine to gather. Many are the hunting parties that have come to bring the xorn in as tribute for the council only to never be heard from again.

Soul Forge. Located deep in the Sea Noir is a cluster of rocks surrounded by a sea of limestone dust. Nested at the formation's center, under the scouring light of the Buried Sun (a portal to the Elemental Plane of Fire), there is a temple made of limestone that houses the Soul Forge, where enslaved pechs forge whatever their dao masters demand. The temple is guarded by power earth elementals controlled by the Council of Khans.

Sunken Citadel. Deep in Obsidian Marsh, there are a cluster of stone structures, slowly sinking into the mud. The structures were built by the earliest earth elementals in the region, those that evolved into the crawlers, which currently maintain and rebuild any that submit to the elements. The crawlers do not follow the dao, and the dao—oddly—do not pursue the crawlers. But no one knows why.

Throne of Earth. The seat of power for the Council of Khans, the Throne of Earth, is a multi-level fortress carved from emerald. It is lavishly appointed, an unsubtle reminder of their great wealth and power. This is where the council meets to discuss things of great matters, sitting around their onyx table.

Personages of Note

Some of the plane's interesting inhabitants are described below.

Delatam, Khan of the Emerald Expanse. Also known as the Emerald Mage of the Onyx Depths, the dao is a standing member of the Council of Khans but is currently missing. Unknown by the others on the council, Delatam is currently imprisoned in a magical flask in the hands of a wizard in Midgard's Magdar Kingdom.

Ghorek, Khagan of the Onyx Depths. Also known as the Iron Sword of the Onyx Depths, the dao is the overlord of the plane, ruling as head of the Council of Khans—and is known for his rage. He is feared by all as a warrior of great renown. His body is covered in dark stone, and glowing veins of fire courses through just under the surface. Though a master of many weapons, he greatly favors his massive great sword. Ghorek is greatly angered over Delatam's disappearance and how it makes him look weak.

Golnaz, Khan of the Sapphire Threshold. Also known as the Keeper of Shadows, the dao is a member of the Council of Khans and is a mage of great power. Her skin is as dark as onyx. There are stories told by slaves that she uses her magic to give her sight through all the mineral veins throughout the planes, allowing her always to know one's secrets. Golnaz has a penchant for entering pacts with mortals, who gain power in her name while she furthers her own agenda.

Overseer Abdiesus. The pech slave's loyalty to his masters has earned him the role of mine boss, overseeing the other pech slaves. Abdiesus stands out among his kin by not appearing filthy. He also collects trinkets and gadgets and keeps that handy on his person, displaying or brandishing them prominently, basking in the importance he feels they provide him, such as a golden spyglass and a magical steel collar that acts as a communication device with his masters. He is known to be cruel to his own people and follows without reservation the wishes of his dao masters.

Scarlet Maw. A **xorn** of massive size, the Scarlet Maw moves quickly through solid earth and stone, appearing out of nowhere to bring chaos and destruction to the dao. The creature's followers are thought to be all the displaced wild xorn from all the tribes the dao have rooted out and enslaved. They regularly attempt to free their kin and raid the dao's supply chains.

Adventure Hooks

Wanderers venturing through the Onyx Depths are seen as outsiders, if they're lucky, or potential slaves. Though with all the many plots in motion in the plane, there is often need for hardy and experienced adventurers. Here are some recent events for adventurers to tackle:

- The Council of Khans is doing everything in their power to keep the news of the missing khan a secret. Any veteran adventuring party that has proven their skill and discretion could be offered vast riches by the remaining council to return their missing brother.

- There is a sizeable bounty on the xorn known as the Scarlet Maw. The council are literally opening their vaults and granting their favor to whomever succeeds.

- Sensing something is amiss with the Council of Khans, the pech are organizing a massive rebellion, encompassing more slaves by far than any other in memory. They are seeking anyone with a good heart (since they don't have much else to offer) and willing to assist in their continual efforts to free their people.

CONSUMING FLAME: ELEMENTAL PLANE OF FIRE

by Tim Hitchcock

Fire—the element of passion, life, chaos, creation, and destruction—ties all life to the time before existence. In the Elemental Plane of Fire, the flames rise and fall, igniting and smoldering in the eternal, churning dance of primordial powers. Violent and inhospitable, the wild, burning landscapes of the plane remain in a state of constant change. Jagged stretches of basalt and mirror-black obsidian gleam beneath the burning sky. Ripping torrents of scalding wind whip drifts of black sand, ash, and cinders. Smoke clots the air. Gouts of steam and fire spew from cracks in the rock while molten streams rip through the lands. Sulfurous clouds race across the burning sky, raining ash, flaming cinder, and brimstone.

The Elemental Plane of Fire is probably the least hospitable plane of the multiverse to mortals, yet this has done little to dissuade travelers and lore seekers over the passing eons, those who remain ever drawn to the majesty and mystery of the plane and its infamous City of Brass.

Cosmology

The Elemental Plane of Fire is flat, expanding outward from its center, a roiling orb of flames utterly destructive to all life. Planar natives call the core the Everflame, and many believe that it's sentient, perhaps even an ancient god, and that fire elementals entering the core become one with their creator—or at least commune with it. Around the edges of the Everflame, gateways mark the paths of flame and incineration. Powerful constructs dedicated to fire gods, such as **altar flame golems** (see *Creature Codex*) and **tophets** (see *Tome of Beasts*), stand guard. A current of heat moves from the center outward to where the edges become coterminous with other worlds, creating a series of rings with varying environmental conditions.

Surrounding the core lies the Sea of Ash—a vast, desert-like wasteland of scalding sand encrusted with ribbons of thick ash. The sky is bright red with clouds of flame and cinder, and delicate bits of ash fill the sky, drifting upon the winds like falling snow or forming terrifying burning blizzards when the scalding winds race across the sea. The Sea of Ash extends for miles, eventually washing against the edge of a long, twisted mountain range cut with glistening obsidian spires. A "no man's land" known as the Ebon Spires marks the third ring's border. The smooth surface is chipped into sharp, bladed edges, making climbing the spires impossible. Over the eons, travelers have carved precariously narrow footpaths through the rock. Thousands of passages wind and twist throughout the range, creating a vast and unnavigable maze. Within

its chasms and deep ravines lurk outcasts—escaped slaves from the City of Brass and other renegades that survive as scavengers and raiders. On the opposite side of the Ebon Spires, the peaks taper off into a broad expanse of flat black stone known as the Basalt Barrens. Intense heat rises from the stone, blurring vision and transforming everything beyond 60 feet into wavering images and unrecognizable shades. Past the Basalt Barrens, the plane loses its form and transforms into the Molten Rim, where Yggdrasil's roots attempt to thread into the edges. The Rim also lies coterminous with the Ever River, connecting it to the Evermaw and the Shadow Realm.

By its violent and inhospitable nature, the Elemental Plane of Fire burns everything that isn't immune to fire. All planar natives possess immunity to fire, and fire makes up some form of their physiology. Conversely, visitors need to protect themselves when traveling its harsh environments. In various locations of the ring, travelers may encounter a variety of hazards.

Spontaneous Combustion. Creatures not immune to fire damage occasionally burst into flame with little reason or explanation other than they don't belong in the Elemental Plane of Fire. Once per day, non-natives roll 1d20. If they roll under their character level, they begin to combust. The victim begins smoldering and must make a DC 15 Constitution saving throw, taking 13 (3d8) fire damage on a failed save or half as much damage on a successful one. At this point, PCs should work to cool the victim by any means available, such as cold or water-based spells. If the victim isn't cooled, then they catch on fire on the next round. After that, the victim continues to burn until someone extinguishes the flames or until they combust. Each round, the victim remains on fire, roll 1d6. On a roll of 6, the victim combusts. Creatures within 10 feet of the explosion must make a DC 15 Dexterity saving throw, taking 55 (10d10) fire damage on a failed save or half as much damage on a successful one. The combusting individual makes this save with disadvantage.

ELEMENTAL BREACHES

Fire has such a domineering presence in the plane, it can be challenging to notice the influence of the other planes. Yet their presence is never missing for long.

Burning Sirocco (Fire/Air). Searing winds, burning cinders, and hot blinding ash frequently rip across the plane. Near Everflame and across the Sea of Ash, travelers have a 50 percent chance of encountering them per hour. The chance decreases to 30 percent in the Basalt Barrens and 15 percent at the Molten Rim. PCs caught in a sirocco have obscured vision and take 1d6 fire damage per minute. Each minute they remain in the area, they must succeed on a DC 12 Constitution saving throw (+1 DC per each additional minute) or gain a level of exhaustion from the intense heat. A character reaching three levels of exhaustion within the area of effect is also blinded. If the character reaches five levels of exhaustion, ash fills their lungs, and they begin suffocating.

Flame Spouts (Fire/Water). A tangled warren of flame-hot tunnels weaves through the plane, starting at the center and snaking outward toward the rim, and these fill with the waters of the Ever River. Fluctuations in the Everflame occasionally send the temperatures in the tunnels into a critical range, superheating the waters and forcing a cascade of surface eruptions, showering everything in a 15-foot radius of each with steam and scalding water. Creatures in the area must make a DC 15 Dexterity saving throw, taking 21 (6d6) fire damage on a failed save or half as much damage on a successful one. Fortunately, before a flame spout bursts, it makes weird popping noises in the soil. PCs that associate the popping noises with flame spouts can attempt a successful DC 13 Wisdom (Perception) check to gain advantage on Dexterity saves to avoid the flame spouts.

Lava Floods (Fire/Earth). Those traveling
the Basalt Barrens, near the edges of the Ever
River or its fiery tributaries, may occasionally
witness lava floods. These occur when a
sudden influx of water or other matter
causes lava to spill over and sweep across the
plains. Once the disturbance ends, the lava
retreats into the river. Lava floods are sudden,
spreading outward from the shore at a rate of
20 feet per round. They typically expand for
1d6 + 2 rounds before receding at the same
rate. As a result, PCs caught in a flood zone
come in direct contact with lava.

Reaching the Plane

The Elemental Plane of Fire explodes into
coterminous rifts capable of reaching into
every plane. These rifts exist in the eye of every
flame and the sparks of every strike of the
blade. Creatures of pure fire have little trouble
reaching the plane—but most creatures cannot
travel through fire, so other means are required.

Cinderwood. Where Yggdrasil's roots coil
against the Molten Rim stands an endless
forest of dead, leafless trees whose charred
branches never cease smoldering. A pale,
ashen crust forms upon the root surfaces
and the tips of the dead branches. Known as
Cinderwood, a powerful **thorned sulfurlord**
(see Planar Flora in *Creature Codex*) guards
its thoroughfare and demands payments of
mortal flesh for those attempting passage.

Ever River. A tributary of the Styx-Lethe
flows from the Eleven Hells through the Lock
of Erebus, passing into the Elemental Plane of
Fire. The water around the lock roils, churns
wildly, and drops into dark, unfathomable
depths. Giant serpentine **alnarr demons** (see
Creature Codex) coil about the lock, seeking
easy prey. While many have tried to bargain
with them, their demonic hunger typically
wins over. Beyond the lock, the Ever River's
surface catches fire, and the water boils,
scalding all life. Its main channel runs straight
through the Basalt Barrens and then splits into
dozens of smaller tributaries that wind across
the land.

Rifts of Light and Shadow. Chasms between
the Ebon Spires cut through the plane and
rip into the Shadow Realm. Soot-feathered
raptors known as **eala** (see *Tome of Beasts*)
manifest in coterminous bleeds between the
two planes. They swarm around the haunted
Road of Black Embers that leads to Smoke in
the Shadow Realm. (Of note, similarly, the tips
of the tallest spires rip into the heavens.)

Transcendental Incineration. This plane is
the true source of all flames. Whenever and
wherever a flame manifests, it's drawn directly
from the Elemental Plane of fire—essentially,
passing through a coterminous rift to whatever
plane on which the flame manifests. Creatures
born of pure flame can pass through these rifts
as can the spiritual essence of those whose
material form becomes entirely consumed
by flame. Those who worship fire call the
phenomenon transcendental incineration.

Withered Walk. This root path passes
through Evermaw. After passing through the
realm of undeath, the root's color fades to a
yellow-gray and becomes nearly lifeless. A
winding path of dust and dried bone follows
a series of iron lanterns, hanging from metal
gallows. Upon the gallows hang desiccated
corpses. Violent undead, such as **wraiths**
and **firegeists** (see *Tome of Beasts*), possess
the corpses and rise to steal life from mortal
travelers.

Yggdrasil. The Elemental Plane of Fire
connects with Yggdrasil through the great
tree's roots. The roots burrow through the
Void, creating a tangled path that passes
through neighboring planes of existence. The
two most common routes are Withered Walk
and Cinderwood.

PHOENIX CARPET

The thing looks like the burning corpse of a giant phoenix, drawing eight kilim carpets suspended in the air like kites. Upon landing, the flaming vehicle extinguishes, revealing a raptor-shaped mechanical framework.

During the primordial age of rifts, the Elemental Lords of Air and Fire formed a pact to arm their mortal champions with an eldritch flying vessel to travel between their worlds. The vehicle became known as the *Phoenix Carpet*, and the elemental lords shared it, taking century-long terms of possession. At present, the Lords of Fire possess the airship. In the past, they have lent it to mortal petitioners. Unfortunately, this act has also drawn the jealous ire of the Lords of Air, who have made several attempts to get the vessel back.

PHOENIX CARPET

Wondrous Item, Fabled (5th-Level and Higher Properties Require Attunement)

In order to access the *Phoenix Carpet*, a mortal must petition and make a pact with whomever currently possess of the vehicle. This requires a caster capable of summoning the lord and making a substantial offering. If the lord accepts, the individual along with allies and gear can board the vehicle and be transported to an arranged destination on the summoner's plane.

The *Phoenix Carpet* can carry up to 16 passengers (two per carpet), or eight passengers and a ton of additional cargo. It can travel at a speed of 30 mph, has AC 15, 300 hp, and a damage threshold of 15. Control can be temporarily relinquished by the lord to the creature to be attuned to it, per their pact. The carpet is controlled by the will of whomever is attuned to it.

Creatures traveling on the *Phoenix Carpet* gain immunity to the energy type associated with the elemental lord they have entered their pact with. If the vessel is attacked, it automatically defends itself with a breath weapon based on the same lord:

- ***Breath Weapon (Recharge 5–6).*** The *Phoenix Carpet* exhales either a cyclone in a 15-foot radius centered on it (if pact made with air lord) or a gout of flame in a 60-foot line (if pact made with fire lord). Each creature in the area must make a Dexterity saving throw (DC equal to 8 + your proficiency bonus + your Dexterity modifier), taking 63 (18d6) thunder damage (if a cyclone) or fire damage (if a gout of flame) on a failed save or half as much damage on a successful one.

Pact of Wind and Flame (Requires Attunement).

The elemental lord that the pact is made with grants you temporary stewardship over the vessel. While attuned to the *Phoenix Carpet*, it remains in your service until you dismiss it, the lord that granted you stewardship over the vehicle ends the stewardship, or some magical force breaks your attunement.

As your level increases, you gain the following benefits

after gaining access to the *Phoenix Carpet*. Using some of the more powerful abilities can terminate the elemental pact, breaking the individual's connection to the vessel along with their attunement. If the pact breaks in this manner, the *Phoenix Carpet* completes its flight, taking its passengers to the last agreed upon destination before returning to the possession of its elemental lord.

Jealous Lords. Whenever you attempt to command or control the *Phoenix Carpet*, you risk evoking the ire of a rival elemental lord. Roll d100, and if you roll your character level or lower, you attract the attention of a rival elemental lord who comes seeking to reclaim the vessel. If you refuse to surrender the vessel to the rival lord, it sends a legion of elementals to seize the vessel by force.

5th Level. At any time, you can direct the vessel to change course and travel to additional locations in the same plane or to stop and wait at a location until you command it to travel again.

As an attack action, you can also command the vessel to make a Breath Weapon attack.

9th Level. As an action, you can cast the *plane shift* spell, affecting the entire vessel and all onboard. The destination is restricted to the Elemental Plane of Air, the Elemental Plane of Fire, or the Material Plane. Once used, this ability can't be used in this way again until 24 hours have passed.

13th Level. You can command the vessel to unleash waves of elemental energy in a 60-foot radius. Creatures caught in the burst must make a Dexterity saving throw (DC equal to 8 + your proficiency bonus + your Charisma modifier), taking 22 (5d8) fire damage and 22 (5d8) thunder damage on a failed save or half as much damage on a successful one.

Using this ability more than once per week breaks the pact and your attunement to the vessel.

17th Level. You can command the vessel to utter a plane ripping cry that slashes a rift between your location and either the Elemental Plane of Air or the Elemental Plane of Fire. The rift forms a coterminous storm (see **Elemental Breach** sidebar) that draws all creatures within 60 feet of it toward its eye and pulls them into the coterminous plane.

Using this ability breaks the pact and your attunement to the vessel.

Inhabitants

By nature, fire is somewhat anarchic. The motivations of the fire elementals—and perhaps even the plane itself—make it impossible for mortals to determine any overarching rule. Pockets of authority form in the various city-states, such as the City of Brass, forming unique microcosms within the largely inhospitable plane. The efreet of the City of Brass command its social and political structure. Because they frequently extend their influence beyond the Elemental Plane of Fire, most outsiders base their conceptions about the plane on the efreet and their magnificent city. However, other power groups operate throughout the plane, each holding court and sway over the various rings and the surrounding Void.

Nevertheless, the true sovereign of the plane is the Everflame, which the elementals and several other races worship as a deity. They claim the core possesses sentience, that they can commune with it and that its will dictates the ebb and flow of all entities in the plane. Due to the City of Brass's proximity to the core, many of its efreeti lords view themselves as avatars of the fire god. Other races vehemently dispute this claim.

Azers. The dwarf-like **azers** build their largest settlements along the edge of the Basalt Barrens. Though they dominate the region, they lack a centralized authority and organize themselves as a loose federation of independent clans. Azers live in colonies and jump-mine the metallic asteroids orbiting in the Void drift. Still, independents see themselves as part of a larger federation. They settle disputes and conflicts internally, with most matters arising over mining rights, trade, and resource access. A small percentage of azers live outside of azer society, working as merchants, manufacturers, advisors, and guides in the City of Brass. Others operate interplanar caravans, smuggling operations, or courier services.

Efreet. The undisputed rulers of the fifth ring and the most potent and organized creatures of the plane, **efreet** run the City of Brass, the most trafficked location in the entire plane. The Smoldering Citadel's influence even extends outside of the plane and most non-natives picture the City of Brass as their conceptualization of the entire Elemental Plane of Fire.

Fire Elementals. **Fire elementals** are the most frequently encountered creatures in the plane. Born from the Everflame, they manifest anywhere along the rings without

suffering limitations. As a result, fire elementals maintain a powerful connection to the plane and converse with it as one might commune with a god. Some believe fire elementals are extensions of the plane in a material form. Others think the elementals are its children. In either case, fire elementals continually blossom, and like the element that birthed them, their primary goal remains to seek, burn, spread, grow, and devour.

Salamanders. A hegemony of **salamander** clans claims the wastes within the Sea of Ash. A clan leader's ability to establish a bloodline to the first god-emperor determines their value in the societal hierarchy. Over the centuries, warlords and mystics have contested individual claims. As a result, territorial clan borders frequently shift during power struggles. Clans center territories on temple-cities dedicated to their god. Clan rulers and mystics claim they receive direct instruction from the Everflame, which they believe to be their fire god and progenitor. Salamander ideology places them as superior to all other races. Still, some suggest salamanders act under the exploitative manipulations of Baal or efreeti pashas. Regardless, infighting over bloodline rights prevents the salamanders from increasing their dominance in the plane.

Others. Nearly all life native to the Elemental Plane of Fire is at least partially composed of flame and immune to fire damage. Elemental fire assumes plant-like forms that blossom quickly and soon after burn out. Flora first emerges along the edges of the Sea of Ash, where flaming tumbleweeds race wildly until they incinerate into dust. Where the tributaries of the Ever River and other coterminous rifts enter the Basalt Barrens and the Molten Rim, small groves of fire blossoms and burning trees emerge.

Similarly, nearly all sentient creatures birth from elemental fire. **Fire dancer swarms** (see *Tome of Beasts*) drift across the rings of fire while **firebirds** (see *Tome of Beasts*) soar across the sulfuric skies. Wild herds of sarsaok (see *Tome of Beasts 2*) roam the Ash Wastes and Basalt Barrens. **Magma mephits** lurk throughout the plane, especially in the churning rivers of in the Molten Rim, acting as emissaries and servants to **lava keepers** (see *Tome of Beasts 2*) and **magmin. Steam mephits** are more common along the banks of the Ever River and near gates and coterminous rifts that border with the Shadow Realm and the Elemental Planes of Air and Water. Travelers should be wary of mephits outside their spheres of influence as efreet frequently summon them to serve as messengers and toadies. **Giant sootwing moths** (see *Creature Codex*) are more common along the edges of the plane, often swarming around areas of coterminous flux. One may even encounter the occasional **red dragon** or **brass dragon**. Non-native fire-born dragons infrequently hold council with powerful beings in the City of Brass or attend business with dragons in the coterminous Void.

Locations of Interest

A few of the many notable locations are detailed below.

Blazing Chasms. At various locations throughout the Basalt Barrens, the earth splits into gaping chasms that descend deep into the plane. From the chasms protrude massive basalt columns with stepped tops, rising within a vortex of flame. Azer clans seek out these chasms and build mining encampments in the largest ones. They navigate the chasms upon sagging bridges of charred black chain precariously stretched between the columns.

City of Brass. The best-known and most accessible location of the Elemental Plane of Fire is the City of Brass, a neutral ground for trade and diplomacy and a haven to all diabolic exiles and curiosity seekers held under the absolute authority of the efreet and their Grand Sultan Ixingaltrix. Passing centuries unveiled numerous accounts of the wondrous city and its outlandish denizens (see also *Warlock 6: City of Brass*).

Ebon Spires. This anarchic wasteland lies broken into smaller territories ruled by refugees, exiles, cacus giants, or whatever outcast can claim them. In this ring, individuals seize positions of authority by guile, charisma, and force.

Helspyre. Against the blazing edge of Everflame lies a rift gate that connects to the fire giant kingdoms in Valhalla. The fire giants constructed a fortress of bladed towers known as Helspyre around the gate to protect the passage. Currently, a clan of fire giant berserkers under the command of the merciless warpriest Ragiir Blisterbrand occupies the fortress.

Molten Rim. Along the plane's edge, fire and lava spill into the Void. The ground becomes a shifting swamp of molten and semi-solid rock and metals. Most denizens wandering the rim form from the molten morass. Nearly all these creatures offer their fealty to an ancient lava keeper known as the Amorphous Consciousness of Irathris-Ko.

Azers also build mining outposts along the rim and repel off the edge into the Void to mine asteroids. Smeltport, the largest azer outpost, developed into a major hub for trade, crafting, and shipping, and voidships from numerous planes line its docks. In recent years, Smeltport has attracted the attention of the ahu-nixta and now suffers from their increasing raids.

Temple City of the Blistering God. Atop one of the highest peaks in the Ebon Spires, cacus giants chiseled a series of cliff walks and caves that precariously coil around a gigantic effigy of their fiery lord, sculpted into the massive spire's apex. During raids, these giants capture prisoners to sacrifice to their god by lighting them on fire and flinging them from the top of the temple spire.

Personages of Note

Some of the plane's interesting inhabitants are described below.

Cacus Giants. Clans of foul-tempered, violent **cacus giants** (see *Creature Codex*) keep court

in the Ebon Spires. They chisel out crude caves high in the taller spires and crags, allowing them to keep watch over everything below. Most of their resources come from raids and open warfare. Cacus giants worship the Elemental Plane of Fire as a god and believe themselves its progeny. Over the centuries, both the efreet and the salamanders have attempted to conscript or enslave them. As a result, they are fiercely xenophobic and attack all outsiders on sight.

Glauvistus. Glauvistus (adult **flame dragon**, see *Tome of Beasts*), the primordial fire dragon, keeps a hidden lair somewhere in the Elemental Plane of Fire, beneath the Molten Rim in the underbelly of the plane. It is likely near a gate or time ripple through which she can travel freely. Beyond the rim, her dragon disciples and children live in nesting lairs within the drifting rock floating in the Void.

Igris-Syr the Immolator. An enormously bloated salamander empress of the city-state of Irathhriiyer seeks to unite all the cities of the Sea of Ash under her banner. Rumors circulate that she holds pacts with several arch-devils, and her ultimate goal is to lead a united nation against the City of Brass, to seize control of the entire plane as an offering to the lords of the Eleven Hells. Half the city-states support the Immolator's claim while the rest remain resistant. The escalating struggles create a constant demand for mercenaries, spies, and assassins.

Recused. Within an isolated chasm in the Basalt Barrens, a fortified encampment of exiles sits at the mouth of one of the larger and more stable flame spout tunnels. Operated by escaped slaves from the City of Brass and the salamander empires, they call themselves the Recused. Under the guidance of a small council of elders, the Recused actively work to help other victims and exiles escape servitude from the efreet, salamanders, and other would-be lords. Over the centuries, they successfully navigated several reliable routes through the volatile warrens of the flame sprouts.

Adventure Hooks

The Elemental Plane of Fire isn't a place for the unmotivated. Luckily, there is limitless potential. Here are a few possibilities for adventuring parties:

- An azer mining colony recently uncovered a new mineral on a giant asteroid drifting off the Molten Rim. They've been using the mineral to produce an alloy capable of absorbing massive amounts of heat. Several interested parties now target the colony, each desperate to acquire and weaponize the discovery. One of the interested parties hires the players to pay a visit to the colony, establish a relationship with the miners, and defend them against those who seek to take the alloy by force.

- A demon escapes from a celestial prison, slaying several of the angelic host with a sacred blade. His escape led him into conflict with the **Herald of Fire** (see *Creature Codex*). The herald now holds the demon captive and wishes to trade his prisoner. The temperamental herald has called for a summit to discuss his terms and demands. However, he refuses to meet anywhere but the Elemental Plane of Fire. PCs are sent to negotiate his terms and, if possible, return with the prisoner.

- The PCs extinguish three magical, flaming seals to enter an ancient, treasure-laden tomb. Doing so grants them access but unwittingly awakens and releases the tomb's primary occupant, a **mummy lord**. Desperately outmatched, the adventurers must find a safe route of escape. Through exploration and investigation, the adventurers discover they can only rebind the mummy lord by traveling to the Elemental Plane of Fire to reignite the flaming seals.

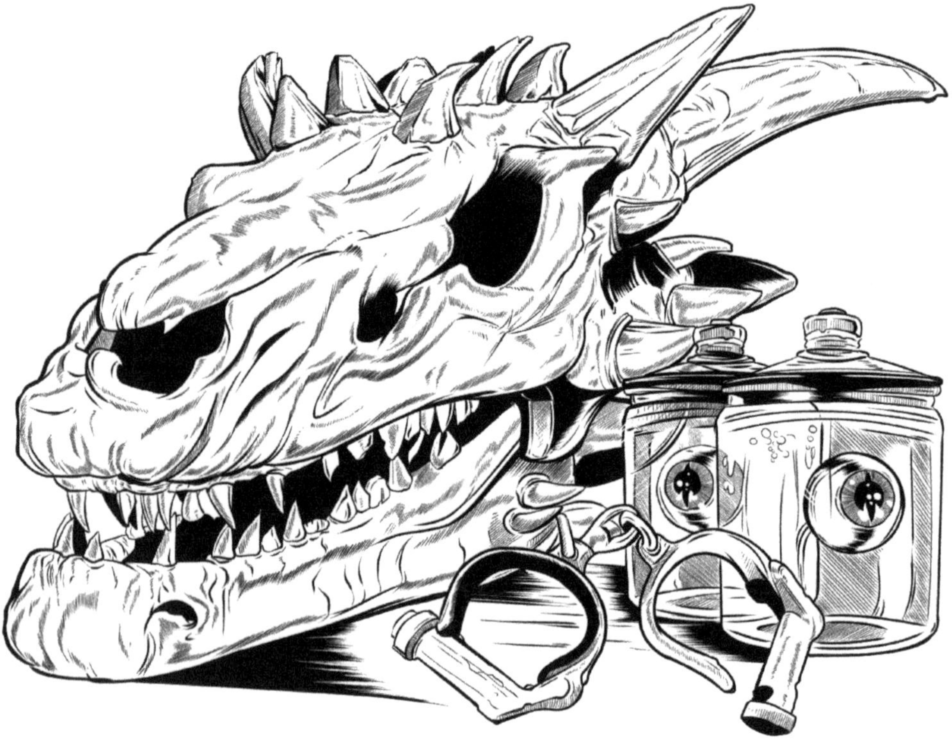

MONSTERS

AHU-NIXTA: HIVEMIND OF THE CONCORDANT CHRONOSPHERE

by Tim Hitchcock

In the time before Midgard, there was only the Void—and within that twilight dwelled the ahu-nixta. While mortals use the name to define an ancient race of aberrant, Void-spawned tyrants, it may just as easily represent an ideal or the wellspring of the ahu-nixta's very existence. It is a primordial name, given to these same aberrations by the dragons who coined it from a repeated syllabic phrase pulled from their incessant maddening chatter.

At one time, the ahu-nixta held dominion over many races. Cruel masters, they fed upon the younger entities and stole from them those elements they needed to transcend the Void. They broke the creatures they enslaved—salvaging flesh and bone, dominating thoughts, harvesting fears—and they warped them into vessels for their own designs. But just like those creatures, the encasements built from them proved weak and inefficient, prone to physical aging and damage. No matter how the ahu-nixta manipulated the raw materials, the result was always insufficient. To overcome these flaws, they sought out other raw materials, metals and crystals and other elements, the same the mortal races forged into tools and machinery. Using these new resources, they copied and cobbled, implanted and spliced, creating new forms, each stronger and more lasting.

In the fabled *Codex of the Endless Void*, one of the authors theorizes the ahu-nixta as both belonging to the Void and being the physical embodiment of the Void itself. She further claims that the ahu-nixta exist to expand the Void into other realms by building themselves—or rather, *itself*—into pieces of the realm. (The text is unclear whether the ahu-nixta are multiple entities or but a single entity spread through multiple forms.) The hive mind then warps the pieces, devouring the realm from the inside out. The theory also attempts to define the Concordant Chronosphere, the prime hive mind intelligence of the ahu-nixta.

Hive Nodes. Ahu-nixta reproduce from clusters of organic matter encased in a resinous, amorphous mass—a hive node. Occasionally these clumps take the form of long, weblike strands and sometimes as blankets of unnaturally sticky or caustic slime. Some believe a hive node's appearance depends on the manner of its creation, but no substantial evidence supports this theory. Nodes range in size from a foot in diameter to the size of an elephant, and when ready to burst, they can disgorge from one to over a dozen various ahu-nixta: a large node may be filled with a swarm of drudges (see *Tome of Beasts 2*) while a smaller node may hold a single large, heavily armored ahu-nixta. It's unknown how long a node can exist in stasis before bursting, but they have been found in ancient and long-abandoned vessels, adrift in the Void, buried in the ruins of sunken cities, and attached to debris, hurling through the planes.

The largest of these nodes is known as Node Prime, a titanic mass of pulsing biomechanical clockwork the size of a small planet. Node Prime serves as something of a homeworld to the ahu-nixta. From Node Prime, the Concordant Chronosphere communicates with the rest of the hive nodes scattered through the Void and beyond. Some consider the Concordant Chronosphere to consist of just Node Prime while others argue that it exists within all hive nodes simultaneously and that it manifests on Node Prime merely due to its magnitude—and some see it as all of the ahu-nixta combined.

Manifestations. Of the myriad forms that the ahu-nixta and their armor takes, three types are most frequently encountered by mortals. The first appears as a spheroid clockwork horror, which is what most creatures imagine when they think of the ahu-nixta (see *Creature Codex*), and the others are called drudges and cataphracts (see *Tome of Beasts 2*) with drudges assuming the role of servitor and cataphracts acting as violent and domineering juggernauts. Still, owing to their constantly evolving forms and the violent creativity brought to bear in their clockwork encasements, there exist countless lesser-known manifestations of the ahu-nixta, roaming the Void and occasionally slipping beyond.

Cephaloid Form

Whatever is floating before you has an appearance like a brain, floating free of its mortal shackles—or maybe a putrid cuttlefish. But it also has several little appendages and eyes popping up all over its form.

While terrifying within their near invulnerable clockwork encasements, once plucked from their shells, they appear far less imposing. The creature's mature form bears an uncanny resemblance to a putrefied cuttlefish. In the larval stage, bodies possess a similar texture to the adult, though lacking any consistent shape. In cephaloid form, an ahu-nixta can alter its body dramatically, allowing it to stretch its soft and pliable tissues within other structures. This allows them to occupy existing matter and manipulate it. They can also fuse together to manipulate larger objects, working in pairs or even entire colonies, depending on the nature and size of the encasements. Other times, they use their own larva as building material, for mature cephaloids are able to control larva at will. It is unknown if the creatures can also fuse their consciousnesses, though such an ability would account for their advanced intellects and mastery of arcane secrets, void magic, and clockwork constructions.

An ahu-nixta larva has the following quick statistics: Tiny or Small, AC 9, hp 2, speed 10 ft., Int 3. Additionally, any ahu-nixta larva will automatically do the bidding of any mature cephaloid (whether encased or not) within 120 feet. Provided a larva is capable of performing

A RANGE OF CEPHALOIDS

The cephaloid listed is the base size and power for a mature ahu-nixta cephaloid. Because of their rapidly evolving forms though, the details may vary from one specimen to another. See each ahu-nixta's Clockwork Encasement trait for details on how to use each cephaloid when free of its encasement.

the commands, it obeys them to the best of its ability—including even those commands that would result in the larva's destruction.

AHU-NIXTA CEPHALOID

Medium Aberration, Neutral Evil

Armor Class 12 (natural armor)
Hit Points 32 (5d8 + 10)
Speed 20 ft., fly 20 ft. (hover), swim 20 ft.

STR	DEX	CON	INT	WIS	CHA
9 (−1)	15 (+2)	14 (+2)	19 (+4)	13 (+1)	10 (+0)

Skills Perception +3
Damage Immunities psychic
Condition Immunities prone
Senses darkvision 60 ft., passive Perception 13
Languages Deep Speech, Void Speech
Challenge 1/2 (100 XP)

Spellcasting. The ahu-nixta's innate spellcasting ability is Intelligence (spell save DC 14, +6 to hit with spell attacks). The ahu-nixta can cast the following spells, requiring no material components:

 At will: fear, firebolt (2d10), telekinesis

Ahu-Nixta Tapper

The creature's clockwork armor resembles the slender, segmented form of a metallic spinal column, ending in an ovoid metal centerpiece, and an articulated arm mounted with a boring drill bit swings freely on top. Metallic appendages dangle from the creature's ventral region, each tipped with a tiny, barbed claw.

Tappers collect psychic energy from intelligent creatures. They often come in swarms and attack by affixing themselves to a host with their barbed claws and tapping into the base of the skull with their boring bits. Why the ahu-nixta need this energy remains unknown, though most speculate they use psychic energy to create the bond to their clockwork armor.

The creature inside the clockwork encasement, once a larval ahu-nixta, now lacks a cohesive form and fills the encasement as a viscous, jelly-like substance with only enough

sentience to fulfill the commands of the hive mind directing it.

AHU-NIXTA TAPPER

Tiny Aberration, Unaligned
Armor Class 17 (clockwork armor)
Hit Points 10 (4d4)
Speed 30 ft., fly 30 ft., swim 30 ft.

STR	DEX	CON	INT	WIS	CHA
10 (+0)	16 (+3)	10 (+0)	3 (−4)	12 (+1)	10 (+0)

Damage Immunities lightning, poison, psychic
Condition Immunities charmed, exhaustion, frightened, paralyzed, petrified, poisoned, prone
Senses darkvision 60 ft., passive Perception 11
Languages does not speak but understands Void Speech
Challenge 1 (200 XP)

Clockwork Encasement. The creature within the machine is a shapeless mass, both protected and given concrete manipulators by its armor. The clockwork armor has a few manipulators that the ahu-nixta can use to attack or to interact with objects outside of the armor. Unlike other ahu-nixta, the tapper can't live outside its armor and dies when its armor is reduced to 0 hp.

Electrostatic Field. Once a tapper attaches to a target, it generates an electrostatic field to protect itself while draining its victim. Once per round, the first time something makes physical contact with the tapper, it triggers a 10-foot-radius burst of electrostatic energy. All creatures caught in the burst must succeed a DC 13 Dexterity saving throw or take 3 (1d6) lightning damage. The burst doesn't affect the tapper.

Immutable Form. The tapper's clockwork armor is immune to any spell or effect that would alter its form, as is the creature that controls it as long as the ahu-nixta remains within the armor.

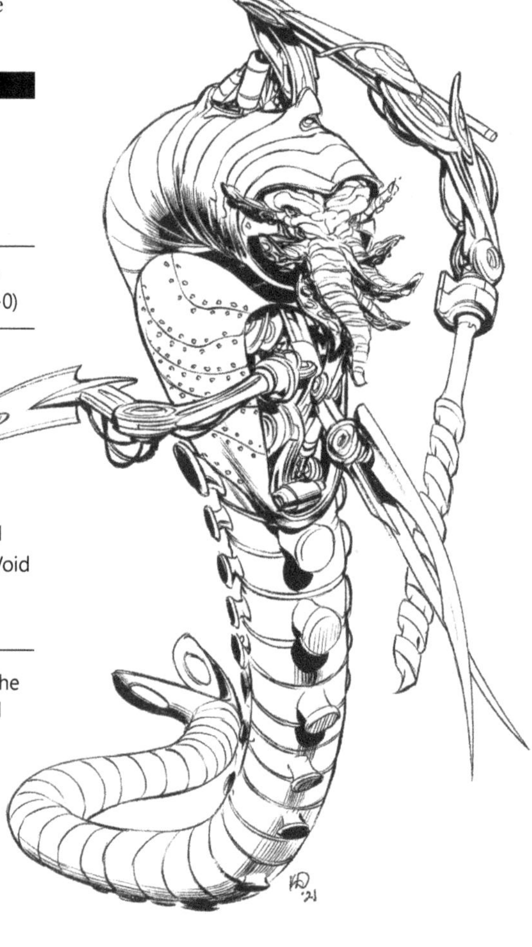

ACTIONS

Psychic Tap. *Melee Weapon Attack*: +5 to hit, reach 5 ft., one creature. *Hit*: 6 (1d6+ 3) piercing damage, and the tapper attaches to the target. While attached, the tapper doesn't attack. Instead, at the start of each of the tapper's turns, the target takes 6 (1d6 + 3) psychic damage as its brain is tapped. The tapper can detach itself from its target by spending 5 feet of its movement and will detach after dealing 12 psychic damage or after the target dies. The tapper can be ripped free with a successful DC 13 Strength (Athletics) check, though doing so also injures its target, dealing 7 (2d6) slashing damage.

Alpha Node

The massive sphere just floats in the distance. Its mass, with a roughly 30-foot diameter, appears to be a conglomeration of debris—a floating junkyard of clockwork components all mashed together. Sluglike creatures can occasionally be seen moving on its surface before disappearing again within its mysteries, and bits of free-floating material slowly drift toward it, swirling in strange eddies.

Alpha nodes are massive conglomerations of ahu-nixta, comprising dozens of strange clockwork devices and slowly drifting through the Void. Those who have encountered them claim that strange currents engulf these colossal structures, drawing objects to it, and that as one draws closer the sound of maddening gibberish grows louder and louder.

The alpha node is a collective, a sort of hive mind that gathers to spawn individual ahu-nixta. Despite the node's appearance, it is a living creature and possesses a fierce though utterly alien intelligence.

ALPHA NODE

Gargantuan Aberration, Neutral Evil

Armor Class 20 (clockwork armor)
Hit Points 310 (20d20 + 100)
Speed 0, fly 10 ft. (hover)

STR	DEX	CON	INT	WIS	CHA
10 (+0)	16 (+3)	20 (+5)	21 (+5)	13 (+1)	15 (+2)

Saving Throws Con +12, Int +12, Cha +9
Damage Immunities cold, necrotic, poison, psychic
Condition Immunities blinded, charmed, exhaustion, frightened, incapacitated, paralyzed, petrified, poisoned, prone, restrained, stunned
Senses true sight 120 ft., passive Perception 11
Languages Deep Speech, Void Speech, telepathy 120 ft.
Challenge 21 (33,000 XP)

Clockwork Encasement. The clockwork encasement of the alpha node is the collective encasement of dozens of ahu-nixta in various stages of development and stasis. When the alpha node is reduced to 0 hit points, its clockwork encasement breaks apart, flinging dozens of somewhat shapeless masses, both half-developed larval ahu-nixta and mature cephaloids, into the surrounding Void. The node's Void Current trait inverts, and the surrounding space fills with hundreds of chunks of broken clockwork and 1d10 + 20 ahu-nixta larva and cephaloids (see **ahu-nixta cephaloid** above). Once outside of their armor, the creatures' pulpy mass no longer receives the benefits of the listed Damage or Condition Immunities, except for psychic and prone. An ahu-nixta can exit or enter the clockwork collective as a bonus action.

Collective Assimilation. Any ahu-nixta can merge with the alpha node. Whenever an ahu-nixta chooses to assimilate, it merely needs to come into contact with the alpha node, and as a reaction, the alpha node absorbs the creature into its body. The alpha node gains a number of hit points equal to half of the absorbed creature's maximum hit points.

Immutable Form. The clockwork armor of the alpha node is immune to any spell or effect that would alter its form, as are the creatures that control it as long as the ahu-nixta remain within their respective encasements.

Innate Spellcasting. The alpha node's innate spellcasting ability is Intelligence (spell save DC 20, +12 to hit with spell attacks). The alpha node can innately cast the following spells, requiring no material components:

At will: *fear, firebolt* (4d10), *telekinesis*
3/day: *chain lightning* (12d6), *programmed illusion, power word stun*
1/ day: *time stop*

Magic Resistance. The alpha node has advantage on saving throws against spells and other magical effects.

Void Current. The alpha node channels the Void. As dark energies siphon through the node to other dimensions, it creates a current that draws creatures toward itself. Creatures within 240 feet of the alpha node are slowly pulled toward its center at a speed of 5 feet per round. As the individual moves nearer, the force increases: +5 feet for every 40 feet of distance closer to the node, to a maximum

of 30 feet per round within 40 feet of the alpha node. Within 40 feet, the current travels counterclockwise around the alpha node, causing objects trapped in the current to orbit the alpha node. Creatures entering into the Void Current can attempt a Strength (Athletics) check to resist the pull (DC 8 + current's speed). If they succeed, they can move half their movement speed away from the node.

ACTIONS

Multiattack. The alpha node makes three Clockwork Gear Launcher attacks. It can instead use Forced Assimilation or cast one spell in place of two of those attacks.

Clockwork Gear Launcher. *Ranged Weapon Attack*: +10 to hit, range 120/300 ft., one target. *Hit*: 22 (4d10) bludgeoning damage and 11

(2d10) necrotic damage. A creature must succeed on a DC 20 Constitution saving throw, or the launched gear begins bonding to its flesh and hardening, encasing it like an ahu-nixta's encasement and mentally connecting the individual to the node. If the creature fails its save, its AC increases by +1, and the alien interface fills its thoughts with the chattering voices of thousands of ahu-nixta. The target can't take reactions until the start of its next turn and must roll a d8 to determine what it does during that turn: on a 1–4, the creature does nothing; on a 5–6, the creature takes no action but uses all its movement to move in a random direction; on a 7–8, the creature makes one melee attack against a random creature or does nothing if no creature is within reach. The target can make a new save each round to attempt to suppress the voices for that round, but they return each round thereafter until the link is broken by a *remove curse* spell or similarly powerful magic. On a successful save, there is no effect.

Forced Assimilation (Recharge 5–6). The alpha node can attempt to forcefully assimilate any creature with whom it maintains a mental connection. All affected creatures must succeed a DC 20 Charisma saving throw or be compelled to move toward the alpha node at full speed on their next turn and on subsequent rounds, continuing to move toward the node until they either touch it or the mental connection is broken.

If the target touches the alpha node, they become grappled by the clockwork encasement, which attempts to engulf them. Each round, allies (or the target itself if it breaks the mental connection) can break the grapple by making a Strength (Athletics) check contested by the Strength check of the alpha node; on the second and third rounds, the alpha node has advantage on this Strength check. After 3 rounds of contact, the target is fully engulfed (grappled and restrained) and will remain inside the node's mass until the node is destroyed.

LEGENDARY ACTIONS

The alpha node can take three legendary actions, choosing from the options below. It can take only one legendary action at a time and only at the end of another creature's turn. The alpha node regains spent legendary actions at the start of its next turn.

- ***Cast a spell (Costs 3 Actions).*** The alpha node casts a spell using its Innate Spellcasting.

- ***Chatter of the Cogs (Costs 3 Actions).*** The alpha node can command one individual, with whom it has a mental connection, as if it were under the effect of a *dominate monster* spell. The domination only lasts until the end of the creature's next turn.

- ***Reverse the Void Current (Costs 1 Action).*** The node can cause the void current to flow in reverse until the start of its next turn.

- ***Spawn Ahu-Nixta (Costs 2 Actions).*** Ahu-nixta emerge from the clockwork conglomeration (alpha node's choice): 2d4 **ahu-nixta** (see *Creature Codex*), 1d4 **ahu-nixta cataphracts** (see *Tome of Beasts 2*), or an **ahu-nixta harpooner** (see below). Any spawned ahu-nixta appears in an unoccupied space on the node's surface and acts as its ally. It is reabsorbed into the node after 1 minute unless either it or the node dies or the node reabsorbs it as an action before that.

Ahu-Nixta Harpooner

A giant armored, clockwork spider with harpoon cannons for legs stands before you. From a small glass dome atop the carapace, a sloshing mass of jelly appears to look out at you with myriad eyes. Another glass window rests on the contraption's head, revealing a second gelatinous form within. The creature rears on its hind four legs and brings the points of the front harpoons to bear on you.

Ahu-nixta unceasingly innovate on their clockwork encasement designs, incorporating from the various components and materials taken from their foes and recrafting them into something new—and always lethal. Harpooners are one example, crafted from the chitinous carapaces of one of the greatest nemeses of the ahu-nixta: a spider of Leng.

AHU-NIXTA HARPOONER

Large Aberration, Neutral Evil

Armor Class 20 (clockwork armor)
Hit Points 165 (22d10 + 44)
Speed 40 ft. climb 30 ft.

STR	DEX	CON	INT	WIS	CHA
18 (+4)	19 (+4)	15 (+2)	19 (+4)	11 (+0)	10 (+0)

Saving Throws Con +6, Int +8
Damage Immunities poison, psychic
Condition Immunities charmed, exhaustion,
  frightened, paralyzed, petrified, poisoned, prone
Senses darkvision 60 ft., passive Perception 10
Languages Deep Speech, Void Speech
Challenge 12 (8,400 XP)

Armored Ball. As part of its move action, the
harpooner instantly collapses in upon itself,
folding its entire body into a giant metallic
ball. As a bonus action, it unravels. While in
its Armored Ball form, the harpooner gains
resistance to all types of damage but is blinded
and unable to climb. (The harpooner's Death
Roll attack is unaffected by it being blinded
unless it was blinded from the start of its turn.)

Clockwork Encasement. The machine is occupied
by two ahu nixta (see **ahu-nixta cephaloid**
above), and each is a somewhat shapeless mass,
protected and given concrete manipulators by
their armor. The clockwork armor has

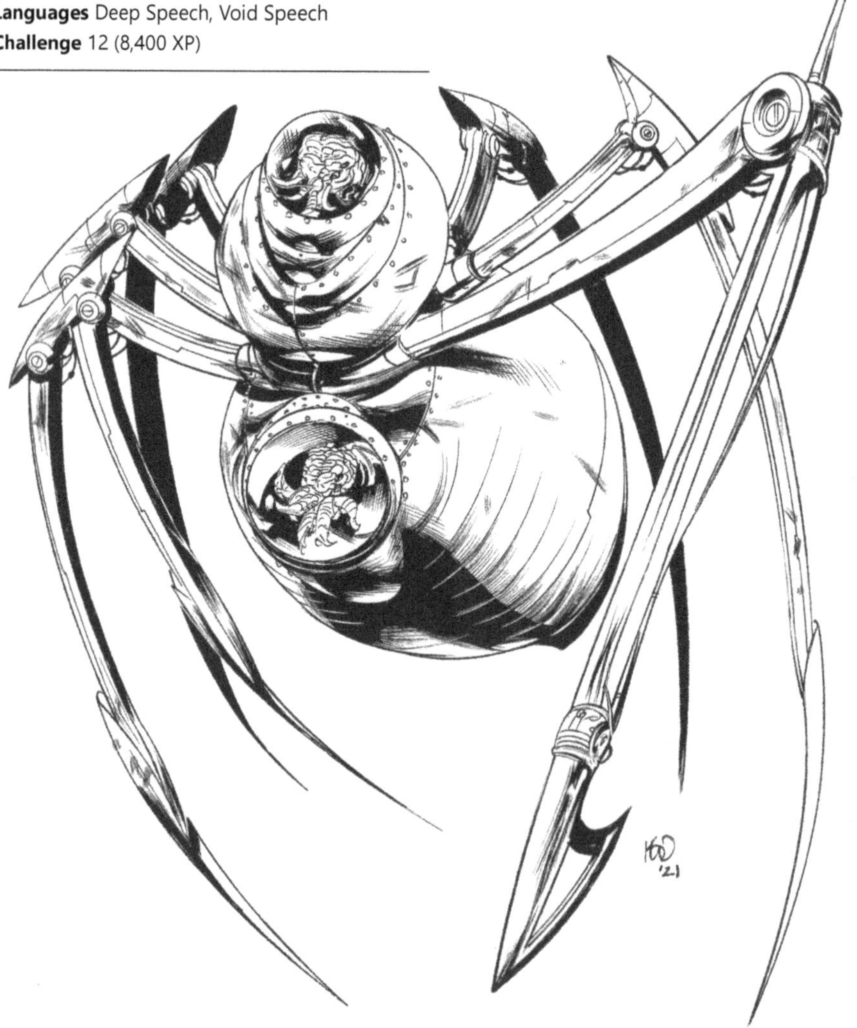

a variety of manipulators that the ahu-nixta can use to attack or to interact with objects outside of the armor. When the ahu-nixta is reduced to 0 hit points, the clockwork armor breaks, and the two ahu-nixta exit it. Once out of their armor, the creatures' pulpy mass no longer receives the benefits of the listed Damage or Condition Immunities, except for psychic and prone. Without their clockwork armor, the ahu-nixta have the following statistics: AC 12, hp 37 (5d10 + 10), Strength 9 (−1), and their speed is adjusted as follows: 20 ft., fly 20 ft. (hover), swim 20 ft. In addition, they have no attack actions, though they can still cast their spells. The bodies of the ahu-nixta can form eyes, mouths, and grabbing appendages. Their grabbing appendages can pick up objects and manipulate them, but the appendages can't be used for combat. The extra appendages can open and close glass-covered viewing ports in the clockwork armor, requiring no action, so they can see and interact with objects outside the armor. An ahu-nixta can exit or enter the clockwork armor as a bonus action.

Immutable Form. The ahu-nixta's clockwork armor is immune to any spell or effect that would alter its form, as are the creatures that control it as long as they remain within the armor.

Innate Spellcasting. The ahu-nixta's innate spellcasting ability is Intelligence (spell save DC 16, +8 to hit with spell attacks). The ahu-nixta can innately cast the following spells, requiring no material components:

At will: *fear, firebolt* (2d10), *telekinesis*

ACTIONS

Multiattack. The harpooner makes three Harpoon Cannon attacks. It can instead use Death Roll in place of two of those attacks.

Harpoon Cannon. *Melee or Ranged Weapon Attack*: +8 to hit, reach 10 ft. or range 90/180 ft., one target. *Hit*: 17 (3d8 + 4) piercing damage, and the target must succeed on a DC 18 Constitution saving throw or be restrained. If the harpoon is embedded in a target on the start of the ahu-nixta's turn, the target takes 17 (3d8 + 4) piercing damage, and if the target is a Huge or smaller creature, it must succeed on a Strength contest against the ahu-nixta or be pulled up to 20 feet toward the ahu-nixta. If the target, or an allied creature, succeeds on a Strength contest with the ahu-nixta, the harpoon is removed from the target.

Each of the ahu-nixta's eight legs is equipped with a Harpoon Cannon. However, it can only attack with up to three each round.

Death Roll (Recharge 5–6). If the harpooner has already moved at least 20 feet on its turn and has at least 20 feet of unobstructed space between itself and its intended target, it can launch itself up to 40 feet in a straight path as an attack. The target must make a DC 18 Dexterity saving throw. On a failure, the creature takes 36 (8d8) bludgeoning damage and falls prone. On a success, the target takes half the damage and suffer no additional effects.

REACTIONS

Fast Ball (Recharge 5–6). If targeted with a ranged attack, the harpooner can quickly collapse itself into a giant metallic ball, as its Armored Ball trait. It remains in this form until it takes the requisite bonus action on its turn to unravel.

IZRAVENES: ANGELS OF UNDEATH

by Kelly Pawlik

Izravenes are the personification of avarice and gluttony, and they represent the largest contingent of non-undead beings on Evermaw, the Plane of Undeath. They hold the amassing of personal power as the highest of achievements—even when compared to other fiends. They are self-centered with virtually no capacity to imagine taking an action that wouldn't advance them in some way toward their goal of metamorphosis.

Heralds of Corruption. Izravenes erupt, writhing and maggot-like, from a titanic figure that hangs crucified upon a series of dusty, mountainous spires deep within Evermaw. The titan's name is lost to time, but some of the ancient and undying residents of the plane dimly remember it was once a celestial power that represented goodness and glorious fecundity. Izravenes are as debased as their progenitor was virtuous, and they gain their purest pleasure in reducing innocent people into undead horrors. Each type of izravene represents a specific type of spiritual or physical corruption that can manifest itself in a form of undead.

Gluttonous Traitors. With every mortal life an izravene takes, it absorbs a portion of the mortal's soul. The consumed soulstuff compounds until the izravene undergoes metamorphosis into a more advanced form.

The method of their evolution spurs izravenes to kill as many mortals as they can in the most efficient manner possible. The fiends are drawn to places where the dying can be dispatched with little effort, such as battlefields, plague villages, and surgeries. Izravenes are also apt to prey upon other izravenes of their type as the killer will gain the soulstuff their victim has already consumed. Due to their backstabbing natures, izravenes rarely work together, doing so only when threatened and berated by a much more powerful izravene.

Disagreeable Schemers. Izravenes are rapacious, but they do not act hastily or carelessly. Even the least of them knows that a sword wielded by a single valorous fool can spell the end of their ambitions. Though they find it frustrating, they carefully plot out their activities. They spend time investigating the areas they would like to hunt and make sure they won't have to contend with an overabundance of heroic mortals. After each kill, they cautiously gauge any response before striking out again.

An izravene may accept a position as the lesser partner to another more powerful creature, but it will immediately start plotting to take control of the venture. Devils in particular sometimes see the value in conspiring in a limited fashion with an izravene.

Hidden in Plain Sight. The older an izravene and the more it has metamorphosed, the more likely it is to act with caution and patience. More highly evolved izravenes spend centuries spying upon humanoid communities in order to perfect their ability to hide among them. Sometimes they take on a persona and simply live a seemingly normal life for as many years as they can without drawing undue suspicion from their neighbors. In this manner, some settlements have harbored a greedy fiend for decades, none the wiser for its presence. The patience of older izravenes is matched only by their cowardice. The more they have experienced, the more greedily they hold onto their immortality. Truly ancient and powerful izravenes, such as masavenes and azraevenes are rarely seen or discovered, hidden as they are behind armies of guardians, servitors, and possibly other izravenes.

Three of the most commonly encountered types of izravenes are detailed below.

Alamravene

This disgusting creature looks like a decaying maggot with six rotting humanoid arms erupting from the upper portion of its body. One end of its body terminates in a yellowing, bloodshot eyeball, and it holds itself aloft upon four tattered, membranous wings.

Zombies gather around alamravenes as flies gather around dung. They are among the least of izravenes, in keeping with their dominion over the lowest and most common form of undead. Hordes of zombies tend to arise wherever alamravenes go about their activities, but the sly creatures are clever enough to leave an area before a response to their horde can be organized.

Alamravenes are venal and treacherous, even when compared to other izravenes. They spend much of their time hunting and killing other alamravenes in the hopes of paving a quick path to their metamorphosis. For this reason, alamravenes encountered on the Material Plane are usually newly born, trying to amass

souls and status, or they are very near their time of transformation and need only a few more souls to be reborn into an even more powerful and terrifying form.

Small Fiend (Izravene), Neutral Evil
Armor Class 13 (natural armor)
Hit Points 65 (10d6 + 30)
Speed 30 ft., fly 30 ft.

STR	DEX	CON	INT	WIS	CHA
13 (+1)	14 (+2)	17 (+3)	10 (+0)	15 (+2)	14 (+2)

Damage Resistances necrotic
Damage Immunities poison
Condition Immunities poisoned, unconscious
Senses darkvision 60 ft., passive Perception 12
Languages Abyssal, Celestial, Common, Infernal
Challenge 3 (700 XP)

Corpse Sense. The alamravene can sense the presence of a corpse within 150 feet of itself. The alamravene knows in which direction the corpse lies and its approximate distance in relation to itself.

Mortal Form (1/Day). As a bonus action, an alamravene can transform into an unremarkable-looking mortal of any race. The alamravene returns to its true form if it takes any amount of damage or if it uses its bonus action to do so.

ACTIONS

Death Touch. *Ranged Weapon Attack:* +4 to hit, range 120 ft., one creature. *Hit:* 21 (6d6) necrotic damage. The target must succeed on a DC 13 Constitution saving throw, or its hit point maximum is reduced by an amount equal to the damage taken. This reduction lasts until the target finishes a long rest. The target dies if this effect reduces its hit point maximum to 0.

A humanoid slain by this attack rises 24 hours later as a **zombie** under the alamravene's control unless the humanoid is restored to life or its body is destroyed. The alamravene can have no more than six zombies under its control at one time.

Animate Corpse (3/Day). As an action, the alamravene can animate a corpse within 60 feet

of itself as a **zombie**. As a bonus action on its turn, the alamravene can mentally command a zombie it has animated to move and take an action. If the alamravene has more than one zombie under its control, they all move in the same direction and take the same action.

REACTIONS

Life from Death. If the alamravene is reduced to fewer than half its maximum hit points, it can use its reaction to deal 14 (4d6) necrotic damage to a **zombie** that is within 60 feet of it, and the alamravene regains hit points equal to the amount of necrotic damage dealt. A zombie that is reduced to 0 hit points by this feature is destroyed and gains no benefit from its undead fortitude.

Gurravene

The creature appears as a gaunt, hairless feline that flies with a pair of bat-like wings. Its torso writhes with dozens of gnashing, slobbering mouths filled with sharp teeth. Instead of a head, its long neck ends in a slavering maw, inside which a single large eye is situated directly above its gaping gullet. A second, smaller eyeball is situated at the end of its sinuous tail.

Like the ghouls they represent, gurravenes hunger ceaselessly. The places they lair, whether on Evermaw or another plane of existence, are reeking charnel pits filled with decaying flesh and carrion creatures to feed upon it. Despite not requiring food for subsistence, gurravenes devour every scrap of the creatures they kill while also trying to keep their larder stocked with ripening flesh. Gurravenes are fascinated by mechanical devices, particularly traps, and tend to place them throughout their lairs, more to examine the suffering they cause firsthand rather than to keep their demesnes safe.

Each gurravene styles itself the master of its domain and grooms ghoul and ghast servitors to see to its desires. When they use their ability to take on a humanoid aspect, they gravitate to poor areas with large settlements where they feel a few missing people won't be noticed. Gurravenes find darakhul too strong-willed and difficult to keep control of. Alliances between the two types of creatures are almost always short-lived and often end with the gurravene attempting to destroy its darakhul ally.

GURRAVENE

Medium Fiend (Izravene), Neutral Evil

Armor Class 15 (natural armor)
Hit Points 76 (17d8)
Speed 30 ft., fly 60 ft.

STR	DEX	CON	INT	WIS	CHA
13 (+1)	17 (+3)	10 (+0)	13 (+1)	12 (+1)	14 (+2)

Damage Resistances necrotic; bludgeoning, piercing, and slashing from nonmagical attacks
Damage Immunities poison
Condition Immunities charmed, poisoned, unconscious
Senses darkvision 60 ft., passive Perception 11
Languages Abyssal, Celestial, Common, Infernal
Challenge 5 (1,800 XP)

Mortal Form (1/Day). As a bonus action, a gurravene can transform into an unremarkable-looking mortal of any race. The gurravene returns to its true form if it takes any amount of damage or if it uses its bonus action to do so.

Unholy Aura. Undead within 30 feet of the gurravene have advantage on saving throws against any effect that turns undead.

ACTIONS

Bite. *Melee Weapon Attack:* +6 to hit, reach 5 ft., one target. *Hit:* 12 (2d8 + 3) piercing damage plus 21 (6d6) necrotic damage.

A humanoid slain by this attack rises 24 hours later as a **ghoul** under the gurravene's control unless the humanoid is restored to life or its body is destroyed. The gurravene can have no more than five ghouls under its control at one time.

Summon Ghouls (1/Day). The gurravene summons 3 (1d4 + 1) **ghouls** from Evermaw. The ghouls appear in spaces within 30 feet of the gurravene that it can see, and they can attack creatures of the gurravene's choice when they arrive. The ghouls remain on the plane to which they were summoned until they are destroyed. As a bonus action on each of its turns, the gurravene can mentally command all of the ghouls it has summoned to move to a specific location and take an action of its choice.

The gurravene can summon 1 (1d2) **ghasts** instead of ghouls if it wishes.

REACTIONS

Devour. If the gurravene kills a living creature with its bite, it can use its reaction to completely consume the creature. A creature devoured by the gurravene cannot be resurrected by anything short of a *wish* spell.

Sharavene

Hundreds of eyes dot the insubstantial, moth-like body of this creature. The unsettling orbs blink open and closed at irregular intervals. The sharavene's wings become even less substantial at the outer edges where they appear to fade away into the gray pall that shrouds the creature.

Sharavenes feel more of an animosity toward ghosts and other insubstantial undead than an affinity for them. The mere presence of a sharavene causes incorporeal undead to attack any living creature near them in a near-mindless frenzy. Sharavenes prefer to remain hidden in areas where ghosts can't interact with them but where they are close enough that any humanoid slain by the ghost rises as a new ghost itself.

Despite their disdain for ghosts and their ilk, sharavenes enjoy using their ability to take on a ghostly aspect to manipulate mortals. A favorite tactic of theirs is to take up residence in the home of a mortal and convince them they are a deceased relative or former resident. They then ask their roommate to undertake a series of tasks, often of bizarre or unsettling nature, in order to put their spirit to rest. When the unfortunate victim of their prank realizes they are being toyed with, the sharavene kills them and raises them as a ghost that they quickly abandon.

SHARAVENE

Medium Fiend (Izravene), Neutral Evil

Armor Class 13
Hit Points 90 (20d8)
Speed 0 ft., fly 90 ft. (hover)

STR	DEX	CON	INT	WIS	CHA
7 (−2)	17 (+3)	10 (+0)	13 (+1)	12 (+1)	18 (+4)

Damage Resistances acid, fire, lightning, necrotic, thunder; bludgeoning, piercing, and slashing from nonmagical attacks
Damage Immunities cold, necrotic, poison
Condition Immunities charmed, grappled, paralyzed, petrified, poisoned, prone, restrained, unconscious
Senses truesight 30 ft., passive Perception 11
Languages Abyssal, Celestial, Common, Infernal
Challenge 7 (2,900 XP)

Ghost Form (1/Day). As a bonus action, a sharavene can transform into an insubstantial yet unremarkable-looking mortal of any race. The sharavene returns to its true form if it takes any amount of damage or if it uses its bonus action to do so.

Heart of Evermaw. Living creatures within 15 feet of the sharavene are vulnerable to necrotic damage. A creature killed by necrotic damage while within 15 feet of the sharavene rises as **ghost** at the beginning of its next turn. Ghosts that rise because of this feature will not attack the sharavene.

Incorporeal Movement. The sharavene can move through other creatures and objects as if they were difficult terrain. It takes 5 (1d10) force damage if it ends its turn inside an object.

Spirit's Wrath. The sharavene's presence enrages undead that are capable of incorporeal movement. Such an undead that is within 20 feet of the sharavene cannot be reasoned with or interacted with diplomatically. Additionally, the undead deals an extra 7 (2d6) necrotic damage with any attack it makes that deals necrotic damage.

ACTIONS

Corrupting Touch. *Melee Weapon Attack*: +6 to hit, reach 10 ft., one creature. *Hit*: 31 (8d6 + 3) necrotic damage. The target must also succeed on a DC 15 Constitution saving throw or be unable to benefit from magical healing for 1 hour. A creature that makes this saving throw is immune to the nondamaging aspects of this feature for 24 hours.

Frightful Moan (Recharge 5–6). Each non-undead creature within 30 feet of the sharavene that can hear it must make a DC 15 Wisdom saving throw, taking 28 (8d6) psychic damage on a failed save or half as much damage on a successful one. A creature that fails its saving throw is also frightened for 1 minute. A creature frightened by this feature can make a new Wisdom saving throw at the end of each of its turns, overcoming the condition on a successful save.

REACTIONS

Escape the Light. If the sharavene takes radiant damage, it can use its reaction to teleport to an unoccupied space it can see within 150 feet of it.

Izravene Arbiters

Some few izravenes have existed long enough and consumed such unimaginable amounts of mortal soulstuff that they have undergone apotheosis into an izravene arbiter. Arbiters are the ancient and cunning master schemers who rule over all lesser izravenes, though their independent-minded subjects dispute that the arbiters exert any true control over them. There are currently three izravene arbiters active on Evermaw, though there have been as many as five in millennia past.

Meticulously Paranoid. Izravenes do not become arbiters by being careless or by making ostentatious displays of power. They calculate each maneuver, only taking action once the benefits are guaranteed and any foreseeable consequences are mitigated to the extent possible. Each plan an arbiter makes includes several different routes to achieve success as well as several exit points should the scheme turn sour.

Arbiters insulate themselves against their enemies in a number of ways. Each of them adopts several false personas, using them to draw out and snuff opposition before they become aware of the truth. They also groom minions whose job is to act as the arbiter in public and social situations. Almost every encounter with an izravene arbiter is actually with an underling posing as its master. Arbiters place spies with every potential threat or rival they can gain access to as well as placing loyal agents within their own organizations in order to root out traitors and betrayers.

Lust for Power. Like every other izravene, arbiters crave power and dominance over their kind and their rivals. Despite the precautions they take against betrayal, the reaches of Evermaw are dotted with the husks of fallen izravene arbiters. While some of the dead are the victims of celestial crusades, demonic incursions, or elemental stampedes, most destroyed izravene arbiters fell to the machinations of another arbiter. As lesser

izravenes prey upon each other for soulstuff, so too do the apex izravenes. The difference between the two is simply in scale as an arbiter has no qualms about devastating a continent or an entire world in its quest for absolute power.

MARIZZET

In their true form, Marizzet appears to be a beautiful, androgynous celestial with alabaster skin and gray-feathered wings dotted with hundreds of blinking yellow eyes. This form is rarely seen however as the fiend most often appears to be an immense, decrepit-looking owl whose face is a decaying, maggot-filled hollow. The form has sickly yellow and red scales that create eye-like patterns across their torso and wings.

Marizzet, the first izravene, was the first creature to erupt from the nameless titan and is among the most powerful creatures on Evermaw that have not attained true divinity. They are incalculably ancient and plot to assume control of reality by simultaneously slaying all life on the Material Plane and immediately animating it all as undead. A few millennia past, Marizzet almost achieved their goal but were derailed by the betrayal of their former stand-in, ally, and lover Lizzil. The sting of treachery burns in Marizzet's breast still, and they have made several frustrated attempts to destroy the deceiver.

ULLIVIRE

Ullivire usually appears in the form of a tiny, decaying winged snake whose eyes have been pecked out. In truth, their appearance is of a desiccated, eight-eyed raven from which bone dust constantly puffs. The number of wings and legs Ullivire sports ranges from two to eight.

Ullivire ascended to the ranks of the arbiters merely a few millennia ago. Since their apotheosis, there have been no actual sightings of the creature as they have hidden themself as the familiar of Uch-Tal Hirbaruss, a lich of middling power and import. Under the lich's protection, Ullivire has used their so-called master's resources to build a vast information network to keep abreast of happenings on the Plane of Undeath.

LIZZIL

Lizzil spent thousands of years as a stand-in for Marizzet, and their true form is the same as their former lover's false one, but the pattern of the scales is the reverse of Marizzet's. Lizzil never adopts a different form.

While alternately treated as a plaything and a servant by Marizzet, Lizzil hoarded their secrets like a miser stockpiles copper coins. Before gaining freedom from the first izravene, Lizzil disassembled key components of Marizzet's entropy engine and stole the schematics, casting them into Ginnungagap, the Yawning Void, beyond their former companion's reach. Since then, Lizzil seems to be lurking just out of Marizzet's sights, waiting for just the right moment to spring.

YUGOLOTHS: VINTNERS OF SUFFERING

by Amber Stewart

Vintners of Suffering. Lie Weavers. Feasters of Misery. The Unwelcome Strangers Bearing Gifts. They have many names, and answer to them all, though the name they call *themselves* is simple and with no translation: yugoloth.

And so too, they have myriad self-spread origins. That they emerged from the Void itself as concepts taken flesh is the principal story spoken by sages and by the 'loths themselves. A secondary legend though tells that they derive from a fallen celestial race who turned on the gods upon discovering some dark secret hidden from the rest of creation. Time and again, they delight in seeding the minds of mortal scribes with ever more spurious tales of their own genesis, and in this vacuum of truth, they have yet another name: the Lost.

Unrestrained by *order* and devoid of its antithesis, *chaos*, yugoloths are beholden to naught but *evil* itself, pure and unsullied beings of abstract malevolence taken physical form. Yet the 'loths themselves have long been something of an enigma in so far as what their true nature, origins, and goals might be beyond the facile surface they present as self-absorbed paragons of malice.

Native to the Void but frequently found scattered about other planes—in particular the Eleven Hells—they travel far and wide, selling their services to the highest bidder.

This behavior characterizes the activity of the most common and least powerful yugoloths, but their greatest desire lies in spreading an abstract form of suffering and misery in their passage. They are paid in agony just as much as any other form of currency. They prefer to act against mortals, savoring that taste as the sweetest, and in a way, they obsess over this favorite quarry. Fascinated by the mortal experience, they seem to envy mortals for reasons unexplained. And the more powerful of yugoloths seek their worship and the chance to possess and manipulate them, which ultimately leads to ruin for the mortal.

No singular pattern categorizes yugoloth forms, though indeed there seems a hidden rationale underlying each type. The forms of each yugoloth caste are the finished product of raw evil and spiritual suffering poured into metaphorical molds and crafted about the lost wax of half-remembered, dark reflections of those most populous species they consumed into extinction.

The dark and buried truth of it all is they're ever emigrants through the branches of the World Tree, burning out one doomed sun after another, feasting upon them and abandoning them, like maggots blooming into flies and leaving the long-putrefied remains from which they were nourished. Their highest remember this truth and others, and they

seed it all selectively to those below them, for a yugoloth ascends to higher castes only by achieving some threshold of personal power and achievement—a concurrent initiatory revelation and understanding. Yugoloth society operates as a mystery cult with the higher-ranking yugoloths seeding pieces of their truth down through the ranks, pulling the puppet strings of their lessers while blind to the strings pulled by those from above.

The specific manner in which yugoloths ascend into higher forms is unknown, but some manner of ritualized suicide or equally ritualized and torturous sacrifice is presumed. As tightly guarded as their layers of initiatory knowledge are, it is likely that a given yugoloth has no idea of what awaits it when their rulers decide to promote them, right up until it occurs, and attempts by non-yugoloths to divine these secrets by magic or torture invariably lead to only resounding silence, to a refusal by the 'loth to divulge their knowledge even when faced with obliteration by the hands of those attempting to gain what is not meant for them.

Regardless of how it occurs, form by higher form, yugoloths ascend the ranks of caste until they reach the penultimate position of Ibshalek, those unique yugoloth lords of the Void, a title which very roughly translates as "We Who Will Feast, We Who Remember the Feast."

The Ibshalek. There are said to be twelve Ibshalek, though only six of their names are commonly known—the others collectively called "The Waiting Ones," who may or may not actually exist. The best known of the core six, and most powerful, include Shirveka the Weaver of Corrosive Promises, Alogeth the Blind Oracle-Prince, Voromek the Lord of Bitter Chains, and Y'voloka the Regent of Silent Songs. The yugoloth lords command legions of their kind like a blending of secular emperors and religious prophets, organizing the sale of those forces to other planar powers and on behalf of their own mysterious goals across the planes.

Lower tiers of yugoloths whisper to themselves that the Ibshalek serve as prophets and oracles of a singular bleak divinity, a malevolent, transcendent hunger with no name and no title, so profoundly unholy as to be unknowable but to those chosen few.

This however is nothing but a lie.

This yugoloth god the Ibshalek serve as bleak apostles is a lie that they whisper to themselves, propagated from highest to lowest caste to unify their kind and leash their own self-serving desires to a greater power. Only the Ibshalek know this, and it is only they who have any understanding as to what actual truth underlies their own mythology, both self-created and exogenous. It is possible they have wholly forgotten their true origins, only to travel the World Tree and spread misery to sate the hollow void of meaning within themselves, abandoned by their creators. Lost in every meaning of the word.

Despite the semblance of unity the Ibshalek present to others, there is perpetual rivalry and jockeying for power and influence, and a gulf of distrust hangs wide between these so-called equals. Consumed by their own lies, they doubt their knowledge, fearing that each closely held secret truth, stolen from a long-obliterated forbearer, is nothing but a lie, the same as those they whisper to their servitors.

Emwabbik Em. Yugoloths have long migrated from the Void to other planes, and they found a second home in the Eleven Hells. Perhaps it's the lessened impact of the Void or the nature of the hells or something else entirely, but whatever the cause, new types of yugoloths have distinctly increased. And while the highest caste of the yugoloths of the Void traditionally culminates in the Ibshalek, recent aeons have seen the rise of at least one new caste—witnessed in Xecha Zecha Amblamar, the Lady of Pure Distillate, lord of Emwabbik Em, the Alien Hell of the Acid Abyss—that could rival the old hierarchy. Only time will tell what happens with this potential rift.

The connections between the Ibshalek of the Void and the lord of Emwabbik Em are simply not clear—even to yugoloths. To some, the Lady of Pure Distillate is nothing more than a brilliant, heretical opportunist who departed the Void and struck out without the constraints of bending a knee to others of her kind. For a paragon of self-centered malice, it would make sense. But is it true? Or is she the first hyphae rising from virgin soil, seeding a new line to drink deep and corrupt, a rot concealed beneath an earth soon to be populated with fruiting bodies. She has certainly found ample sustenance in the Alien Hell of the Acid Abyss.

The abyssal layer also has a number of little-known connections of importance to yugoloths and others, including to the ahu-nixta, devoted servants of Xecha Zecha Amblamar. Flickering in and out of being, like dark mirages on the shimmering horizon of some alien desert, transient portals to the Void can be found, hinting at the ruler's connection to her original home. It is possible that these portals might be stabilized by the presence of yugoloths or other Void natives, allowing them easy entrance and egress from the plane. This seems likely given that yugoloths are found here more commonly than any other layer of the hells. Many of them are present on myriad contracted jobs, serving as guardians, escorts, and mercenary armies purchased on behalf of one or another fiendish power. Beyond these however, clusters of them have been observed there without any patron, far from their native plane and often far from population centers, in transit to and from unknown locations, travelers on some unknown pilgrimage. Dovetailing on this suggestion are isolated shrines to various of the Ibshalek, located in the realm's hinterlands, many of which show signs of active, recent use and even magical wards to prevent non-yugoloths from approaching.

Some of the more commonly encountered types of yugoloths are detailed below.

Ezkiloth

Perched upon its master's shoulder, this creature's vaguely humanoid body is wasted and unnaturally thin, covered in glossy, translucent flesh like smoky quartz, fading to ruddy purples at its wickedly clawed extremities and the end of its prehensile, barbed tail. Within its pupils, floating above crimson sclera, a glowing rune of its Ibshalek lord marks it for what it truly is.

Ezkiloths are diminutive yugoloths, bequeathed to a mortal master by an Ibshalek's blessing, to serve while secretly corrupting.

Hidden Forms. Their bodies vaguely modeled after their mortal master's species, ezkiloths are loathe to show their true forms, obscuring their faces or taking on the guise of familiars such as cats, ravens, or even imps and quasits. They prefer to hide their natures—and that of their master's—from suspicion while urging them to ever greater evils.

THE SATARRE

As fellow residents of the Void, it would seem natural perhaps that the satarre would be convenient allies of the yugoloths, but that assumption would be far from a more nuanced truth. Despite (seemingly) hailing from the same native plane, yugoloths view the satarre as inconvenient fellow travelers at best and more often as ideological rivals whose desire for death and destruction runs counter to the yugoloth desire for suffering and to their subsequent near obsession with mortal life as the source of such. The satarre on the other hand see the yugoloths as cowards and backstabbing schemers whose actions delay their own wished-for end of existence. It is not uncommon for the two fiendish races to clash, though in the face of outside opposition, especially by celestials, the two grudgingly cooperate.

Selfish Paradox. Ezkiloths seek to increase the sum total of cosmic suffering while remaining fiercely protective of their masters, at least so far as keeping them alive. Through their master, they can inflict wickedness upon the Material Plane and experience the range of mortal emotions, reveling in a taste of existence their own native plane inures them to.

The Smallest of Puppeteers. Ezkiloths will, over time, emotionally isolate their masters, working behind their backs to drive away family, lovers, and confidants either directly or by sowing seeds of doubt and mistrust, leaving only them in control.

EZKILOTH

Tiny Fiend (Yugoloth), Neutral Evil

Armor Class 13 (natural armor)
Hit Points 14 (4d4 + 4)
Speed 20 ft., fly 30 ft.

STR	DEX	CON	INT	WIS	CHA
6 (−2)	14 (+2)	12 (+1)	14 (+2)	10 (+0)	14 (+2)

Skills Deception +4, Persuasion +4, Religion +4, Stealth +4
Damage Vulnerabilities radiant
Damage Resistances acid, cold
Damage Immunities necrotic, poison
Condition Immunities poisoned
Senses darkvision 60 ft., passive Perception 10
Languages Common, Void Speech, telepathy 30 ft. (with master only)
Challenge 1/2 (100 XP)

Hidden Form. The ezkiloth can use its action to polymorph into a beast form that resembles a cat (speed 40 ft., climb 30 ft.), a rat (speed 20 ft.), or a raven (speed 10 ft., fly 50 ft.), or back into its true form, which is fiend. Its statistics, other than speed (as noted), are the same in each form. Any equipment it is wearing or carrying isn't transformed. It reverts to its true form if it dies.

Magic Resistance. The ezkiloth has advantage on saving throws against spells and other magical effects.

Protect the Feast. The ezkiloth grants its mortal master advantage on death saving throws.

ACTIONS

Multiattack. The ezkiloth makes two melee attacks: one with its bite and one with its barbed tail.

Bite. *Melee Weapon Attack*: +4 to hit, reach 5 ft., one target. *Hit*: 4 (1d4 + 2) piercing damage.

Barbed Tail. *Melee Weapon Attack*: +4 to
hit, reach 10 ft., one target. *Hit*: 5 (1d6 + 2)
slashing damage.

Magical Intuition. The ezkiloth can utilize a
wand or similar device known to and usable by
its master, activating a single use of the item.

EZKILOTH FAMILIARS

Ezkiloth are often granted to mortal devotees
of a particular Ibshalek or otherwise obtained
through willing rituals, gaining a living
conduit to the erstwhile lords of the Void.
Should the mortal already possess a familiar,
the ezkiloth devours and replaces it:

Familiar. The ezkiloth can serve another
creature as a familiar, forming a magic,
telepathic bond with that companion. While
the two are bonded, the companion and
ezkiloth can sense what the other senses
as long as they are within 1 mile of each
other. While the ezkiloth is within 10 feet of
its companion, the companion shares the
ezkiloth's Magic Resistance trait. At any time
and for any reason, the ezkiloth can end its
service as a familiar, ending the telepathic
bond.

Reciraloth

*Not only slick, reptilian scales cover this fiend,
but plates of armor are fused to its flesh. It
ambulates somewhere between upright and
quadrupedal on limbs with unnatural joints.
With eye sockets covered over by bare flesh,
it would seem blind, yet eyes still twitch in
their sockets beneath the flesh. In the dark, the
creature glows, light seeping from its form.*

Reciraloths are yugoloth shock troops, eternal
soldiers in a never-ending struggle to control
the suffering.

Blind Malice. Reciraloths display no
outwardly visible eyes, showing only an eerie
glow below their fleshed-over sockets when
in darkness, but they see as well as any other
creature. In fact, their strange ocular organs
allow them a preternatural sense, regardless of
visibility conditions.

Undying Evil. Among the lowest ranking
yugoloths, reciraloths are considered a
disposable, renewable resource by their
masters—and with good reason. Each
reciraloth that dies finds their essence funneled
back to the Void, where their soulstuff is
pooled, and they are crafted anew. This
resurrected fiend is not precisely the same, but
every reciraloth has faint memories of every
untold time they have died. With no true
death, they have no fear in battle.

Unknown Origins. Reciraloths display slavish
obedience to higher-caste yugoloths and a
pack-like devotion to others of their kind in
battle. Yet outside of combat, they can and will
betray one another for personal gain as the
base essence of yugoloth-kind shows through,
and this betrayal is the first step toward their
transfiguration to a higher caste.

RECIRALOTH

Medium Fiend (Yugoloth), Neutral Evil
Armor Class 15 (natural armor)
Hit Points 60 (8d8 + 24)
Speed 30 ft., climb 40 ft.

STR	DEX	CON	INT	WIS	CHA
18 (+4)	16 (+3)	16 (+3)	10 (+0)	12 (+1)	12 (+1)

Saving Throws Str +7, Dex +6, Con +6
Skills Athletics +7, Perception +4,
Stealth +6
Damage Vulnerabilities radiant
Damage Resistances acid, cold; piercing and
slashing from nonmagical attacks
Damage Immunities necrotic, poison
Condition Immunities blinded, poisoned,
frightened
Senses blindsight 20 ft., darkvision 60 ft., passive
Perception 14
Languages Abyssal, Infernal, Void Speech
Challenge 5 (1,800 XP)

Pack Tactics. The reciraloth has advantage on an
attack roll against a creature if at least one of
their allies is within 5 feet of the creature and
the ally isn't incapacitated.

Slaves of Evil. The reciraloth has advantage on initiative checks when ordered to act by a yugoloth with a greater challenge rating.

Spider Climb. The reciraloth can climb difficult surfaces, including upside down on ceilings, without needing to make an ability check.

Undying Soldiers. The reciraloth has no fear of death, knowing it will be reborn anew within the Void. When reduced to 0 hit points, rather than fall unconscious, the reciraloth continues to fight for a number of rounds equal to its Constitution modifier, and then if still at 0 hit points, it instantly dies.

ACTIONS

Multiattack. The reciraloth makes two claw attacks. If both claws hit a target, the reciraloth mauls the creature, dealing an additional 2d8 slashing damage and forcing the creature to make a DC 15 Strength saving throw or be dragged 5 feet closer. If the creature is already within 5 feet and both claws hit, the reciraloth gains a free bite attack (in addition to the additional slashing damage).

Bite. *Melee Weapon Attack:* +7 to hit, reach 5 ft., one target. *Hit:* 13 (2d8 + 4) piercing damage.

Claw. *Melee Weapon Attack:* +7 to hit, reach 10 ft., one target. *Hit:* 11 (2d6 + 4) slashing damage.

Viridriloth

Difficult to distinguish from the surrounding gloom, this sinuous creature seems little more than a shadow, though one moving independently of anything casting it. Only in moments of movement can its true form be visualized, outlining its draconic wings, piercing emerald eyes, and elongated claws.

Viridriloths are yugoloth spies and taskmasters, lording their knowledge over all beneath them.

Lurking Terror. Viridriloths prefer to hide in darkness or within the cloaking presence of underlings' shadows. Especially crafty beings,

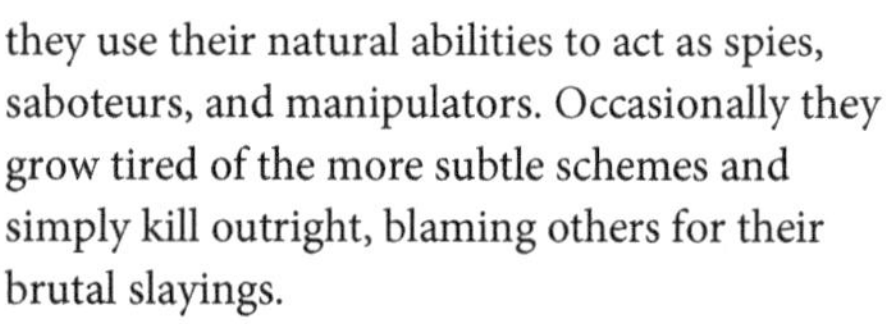

they use their natural abilities to act as spies, saboteurs, and manipulators. Occasionally they grow tired of the more subtle schemes and simply kill outright, blaming others for their brutal slayings.

Corporeal Envy. Viridriloths envy their corporeal brethren and as such are prone to be brutal taskmasters of lesser yugoloths. That envy is multiplied tenfold toward non-yugoloths—and particularly mortals. Viridriloths delight in possessing mortals and indulging their cruelty while masked in mortal flesh.

The Edge of Gnosis. Near the middle of the yugoloth religious hierarchy, though not yet initiated into the higher mysteries reserved for more powerful yugoloths, viridriloths lord their presumed secret knowledge over

lesser yugoloths. This belies a profound insecurity and hunger for understanding, both qualities intentionally stoked by higher castes to increase their usefulness and urge them toward promotion.

VIRIDRILOTH

Medium Fiend (Yugoloth), Neutral Evil
Armor Class 17 (natural armor)
Hit Points 105 (14d8 + 42)
Speed 30 ft., fly 30 ft.

STR	DEX	CON	INT	WIS	CHA
12 (+1)	22 (+6)	16 (+3)	16 (+3)	16 (+3)	16 (+3)

Saving Throws Dex +10, Int +7, Cha +7
Skills Deception +7, Intimidation +7, Perception +7, Stealth +14, Persuasion +7
Damage Vulnerabilities radiant
Damage Resistances acid; bludgeoning, piercing, and slashing from nonmagical attacks
Damage Immunities cold, necrotic, poison
Condition Immunities charmed, exhaustion, frightened, grappled, paralyzed, petrified, poisoned, prone, restrained
Senses darkvision 60 ft., passive Perception 17
Languages Abyssal, Common, Infernal, Void Speech
Challenge 10 (5,900 XP)

Incorporeal Movement. The viridriloth can move through other creatures and objects as if they were difficult terrain. It takes 5 (1d10) force damage if it ends its turn inside an object.

Stand in the Shadow. A viridriloth standing within 5 feet of another creature gains advantage on Stealth checks as it hides within the other creature's shadow.

ACTIONS

Multiattack. The viridriloth makes two attacks, but it can use its Drain Will only once.

Claw. *Melee Weapon Attack:* +10 to hit, reach 5 ft., one target. *Hit:* 13 (2d6 + 6) slashing damage plus 4 (1d8) necrotic damage.

Drain Will. The viridriloth saps the willpower of a creature within 30 feet of it. The target must make a DC 16 Wisdom saving throw. On a failure, the target takes 28 (8d6) psychic damage, and the target's Wisdom score is reduced by 1d4. The target dies if this reduces its Wisdom to 0. Otherwise, the reduction lasts until the target finishes a short or long rest.

Possession (Recharge 6). One humanoid that the viridriloth can see within 10 ft. of it must succeed on a DC 16 Charisma saving throw or be possessed by the viridriloth; the viridriloth then disappears, and the target is incapacitated and loses control of its body. The viridriloth now controls the body but doesn't deprive the target of awareness. The viridriloth can't be targeted by any attack, spell, or other effect, except the *banishment* spell and similar effects, and it retains its alignment, Intelligence, Wisdom, Charisma, and immunity to being charmed and frightened. It otherwise uses the possessed target's statistics but doesn't gain access to the target's knowledge, class features, or proficiencies. The possession lasts until the body drops to 0 hit points, the viridriloth ends it as a bonus action, or the viridriloth is banished or forced out by an effect like the *dispel evil and good* spell. When the possession ends, the viridriloth reappears in an unoccupied space within 5 ft. of the body. The target is immune to this viridriloth's Possession for 24 hours after succeeding on the saving throw or after the possession ends.

Xethiloth

This tall figure's form is hidden beneath elaborate layers of vestments, silken veils, and a shroud of darkness and shifting distortion. It gestures with two hands while a pair of grasping tentacles hold wands or symbols of station. Their face masked from sight, the symbol of their chosen Ibshalek hovers over their veiled head.

Xethiloths are yugoloth priests who insure that the transformative arc of these fiends stays true.

Priests of the Unholy. Xethiloths serve as the yugoloth priestly caste, agents of the Ibshalek, though there are yet other and more highly exalted religious stations. They oversee yugoloth religious rites, determine a lower-caste yugoloth's fitness to ascend to a higher form, and enact the actual transformative rituals that allow such.

Veiled Majesty. Perpetually cloaked by obfuscating robes, veils, and illusions, xethiloths' true appearance is unknown. Observed differences in their cloaked forms suggest a myriad of true forms, varying by Ibshalek served, or otherwise suggest a shapeshifting ability.

Reclusive Masters. Xethiloths are rarely seen by non-yugoloths, usually only when they are present to speak on behalf of one of the Ibshalek or as a threat and display of yugoloth power. Cloistered in their masters' realms, they seem to be nowhere yet simultaneously omnipresent among their flock, aware of any miniscule transgression or failure.

XETHILOTH

Large Fiend (Yugoloth), Neutral Evil

Armor Class 18 (natural armor)
Hit Points 189 (18d10 + 90)
Speed 30 ft., fly 30 ft.

STR	DEX	CON	INT	WIS	CHA
18 (+4)	16 (+3)	21 (+5)	19 (+4)	23 (+6)	20 (+5)

Saving Throws Int +9, Wis +11, Cha +10
Skills Deception +15, Insight +11, Perception +11, Religion +14
Damage Vulnerabilities radiant
Damage Resistances cold, fire, lightning, psychic; bludgeoning, piercing, and slashing from nonmagical attacks
Damage Immunities acid, necrotic, poison
Condition Immunities exhaustion, frightened, poisoned
Senses darkvision 60 ft., truesight 30 ft., passive Perception 21
Languages Abyssal, Infernal, Void Speech, telepathy 120 ft.
Challenge 14 (10,000 XP)

Innate Spellcasting. The xethiloth's innate spellcasting ability is Charisma (spell save DC 18, +10 to hit with spell attacks). It can innately cast the following spells, requiring no material components:

> At will: *detect magic, dimension door, dispel magic, divine favor, invisibility* (self only)
> 3/day each: *black tentacles, hold monster, mirror image*
> 1/day each: *finger of death, harm, plane shift, teleport* (self only)

Magic Resistance. The xethiloth has advantage on saving throws against spells and other magical effects.

Masters of Form. The xethiloth can change form, as per the *shapechange* spell, into any yugoloth of lower CR or any neutral evil creature lower than CR 10. This otherwise acts as the spell.

Shepherds of Evil. As a bonus action, the xethiloth blesses any yugoloths within 30 feet of it in the name of its patron Ibshalek, granting them advantage on any attack rolls or ability checks that they make before the start of the xethiloth's next turn.

ACTIONS

Multiattack. The xethiloth makes two attacks, one of which can be Invocation of the Ibshalek.

Claw. *Melee Weapon Attack:* +9 to hit, reach 10 ft., one target. *Hit:* 17 (3d8 + 4) slashing damage plus 10 (3d6) necrotic damage, and the target must make a DC 18 Constitution saving throw or gain a level of exhaustion.

Necrotic Lash. *Ranged Spell Attack:* +9 to hit, range 60 ft., one target. *Hit:* 31 (6d8 + 4) necrotic damage.

Invocation of the Ibshalek (Recharge 5–6). The xethiloth calls forth the power of their unholy patron. Non-yugoloth creatures within 30 feet must make a DC 18 Wisdom saving throw, taking 35 (10d6) necrotic damage and becoming frightened on a failed save or taking half as much damage and suffering no additional effects on a successful one.

SHIRVEKA, IBSHALEK OF CORROSIVE PROMISES

Held aloft on skeletal wings, draped in black and purple silks, the creature wears a crown of swirling soul gems from which it periodically feeds—a grand connoisseur of agony. Six arms, two humanoid and four skeletal, hold arcane accouterments. Her jackal head is partially stripped of putrefying flesh while her reptilian tail ends in a swirling globe of sickly yellow light, like a dangling lure of some deep-sea predator.

Shirveka, the Weaver of Corrosive Promises, is a being of titanic intellect and magical prowess—and one of the Ibshalek. Few see beyond the highest reaches of her realm, a place of dark elegance where she holds court. Below this, like hungry shadows swimming below the ice of a dark and foreboding lake, lies a storehouse of secrets, foul experiments, and bound souls tortured in activities somewhere between ever-evolving art and religious suffering.

Face of the Ibshalek. Shirveka acts as a public face and speaker for her kind toward other fiendish divinities, yet she prefers to audibly speak through servitors infused with a spark of her essence. She speaks using telepathy when she personally holds court, her keen, loquacious tongue hiding the abject malice behind her every action.

Keeper of Secrets. Shirveka hoards knowledge and secrets, trading them like some base commodity. Unwary buyers are liable to purchase immaculately crafted lies, tailored to their desires, there to set in motion a ruinous chain of events in Shirveka's favor.

Cults of Shirveka. Shirveka's mortal cults are a mixture of secretive, initiatory groups whose rank and file may not be aware they worship an Ibshalek. Her followers seek to bring discord and ruin, especially through magic or political manipulation, though without an overt body count as a goal since the dead cannot continue to suffer.

SHIRVEKA

Large Fiend (Yugoloth), Neutral Evil
Armor Class 22 (natural armor)
Hit Points 322 (28d10 + 168)
Speed 30 ft., fly 60 ft. (hover)

STR	DEX	CON	INT	WIS	CHA
18 (+4)	18 (+4)	22 (+6)	24 (+7)	24 (+7)	23 (+6)

Saving Throws Dex +12, Int +15, Cha +14
Skills Arcana +23, Deception +22, Insight +15, Perception +15, Persuasion +14, Religion +23
Damage Vulnerabilities radiant
Damage Resistances fire, lightning; bludgeoning, piercing, and slashing from nonmagical attacks

Damage Immunities acid, cold, necrotic, poison

Condition Immunities charmed, deafened, exhaustion, frightened, poisoned

Senses truesight 120 ft., passive Perception 25

Languages all, telepathy 120 ft.

Challenge 25 (75,000 XP)

Innate Spellcasting. Shirveka's spellcasting ability is Intelligence (spell save DC 23, +15 to hit with spell attacks). Shirveka can innately cast the following spells, requiring no material components:

At will: *confusion, detect magic, dispel magic, mirror image, modify memory*

3/day each: *dominate person, reverse gravity, telekinesis, teleport*

1/day each: *disintegrate, gate, time stop*

Legendary Resistance (3/Day). If Shirveka fails a saving throw, she can choose to succeed instead.

Magic Resistance. Shirveka has advantage on saving throws against spells and other magical effects.

Magic Weapons. Shirveka's weapon attacks are magical.

ACTIONS

Multiattack. Shirveka makes three attacks: one bite and two claws. She can use Corrosive Promise in place of her bite.

Bite. *Melee Weapon Attack*: +12 to hit, reach 10 ft., one creature. *Hit*: 17 (3d8 + 4) piercing damage, and the target must make a DC 23 Constitution saving throw, taking 42 (12d6) necrotic damage on a failed save or taking no damage on a successful one. If Shirveka scores a critical hit and the target fails the saving throw, the target is disintegrated (as the *disintegrate* spell).

Claw. *Melee Weapon Attack*: +12 to hit, reach 10 ft., one target. *Hit*: 17 (3d8 + 4) slashing damage plus 7 (2d6) necrotic damage. If the target is a creature, it must succeed on a DC 23 Wisdom saving throw or be poisoned until the end of its next turn.

Corrosive Promise (Recharge 5–6). Shirveka telepathically whispers to a single target she can see within 120 feet of her. The creature must make a DC 23 Wisdom saving throw or be compelled to attack their nearest ally. They

may refuse but, in doing so, are then subject to a duplication of any damage or negative effect suffered by that ally within the next round. The target repeats the saving throw at the end of its next turn, ending the effect on a success. The effect lasts until the creature receives a *greater restoration* spell or comparable magic.

LEGENDARY ACTIONS

Shirveka can take three legendary actions, choosing from the options below. Only one legendary action can be used at a time and only at the end of another creature's turn. She regains spent legendary actions at the start of her turn:

- ***At-Will Spell***. Shirveka casts one of her at-will spells.
- ***Phase Shift***. Shirveka magically teleports, along with any equipment she is wearing or carrying, up to 120 feet to an unoccupied space she can see.
- ***Promise of Agony (Costs 3 Actions)***. Shirveka screams a curse in Void Speech at a single target within 120 feet. The creature must make a DC 23 Wisdom saving throw, taking 42 (12d6) necrotic damage and becoming incapacitated for 1 minute on a failed save or taking half as much damage and suffering no additional effects on a successful save. An incapacitated creature can repeat the saving throw at the end of each of its turns, with disadvantage if the yugoloth is within sight, ending the effect on itself on a success. Each non-yugoloth creature within 30 feet of the target creature that can hear Shirveka must also succeed on a DC 23 Wisdom saving throw or take 21 (6d6) necrotic damage.
- ***Promise of Opposition (Costs 2 Actions)***. Shirveka's telepathic whispers corrupt the spellcasting of a single creature that she can see within 120 feet. The creature must succeed on a DC 23 Wisdom saving throw, or the next spell they cast will be directed to another target of Shirveka's choosing.

SHIRVEKA'S LAIR

The Inverse Tower of Weeping Words is located deep within the Void. A vast and labyrinthine structure, it rests between two extinct volcanoes, entrapped by an ancient obsidian flood. Only the tower's highest floors rise above the frozen glass, and the remainder

extends below ground in the original structure and in excavated tunnels into the surrounding matrix, the walls carved with the glowing names and contracts of every being to have bargained with her.

LAIR ACTIONS

On initiative count 20 (losing initiative ties), Shirveka takes a lair action to cause one of the following effects; Shirveka can't use the same effect 2 rounds in a row:

- Shirveka magically calls one or more yugoloths of cumulative challenge rating 15 or lower to aid her. The called creatures act as allies of Shirveka and remain until Shirveka uses this lair action again.
- The contracts bound into the walls of Shirveka's lair glow with a beguiling magic, and any creature within 20 feet of a wall is fascinated and called to examine their words unless they succeed on a DC 20 Wisdom saving throw. Creatures failing this save are considered restrained. Creatures may attempt a new saving throw each round.
- The misery of spirits bound within the walls of her lair erupts in a 20-foot-radius burst of manifested agony, directed at one or more creatures within 120 feet of her that Shirveka can see. A target must succeed on a DC 20 Wisdom saving throw, taking 28 (8d6) necrotic damage and being stunned on a failure and taking only half the damage and suffering no other effects on a success.

REGIONAL EFFECTS

The region containing Shirveka's lair is warped by her magic, creating one or more of the following effects:

- While within 3 miles of Shirveka's lair, creatures that are not neutral evil in alignment hear a susurrus of beguiling whispers, playing upon their fears and desires. When taking a short or long rest, a creature must succeed on a DC 15 Wisdom saving throw or fail to regain expended class features during that rest.
- The area within 1 mile of Shirveka's lair disrupts the use of magic by any good-aligned creatures. For these creatures, casting a spell requires a DC 15 Wisdom saving throw or else the spell is lost. On a roll of 1, the creature is exhausted for the next hour.
- Shirveka can choose to see or hear through the senses of any yugoloth or member of her cult within 10 miles of her lair and can speak through them while doing so.

If Shirveka dies, these effects fade over the course of 3d10 days.

The Broken Path

The demiplane known as the Broken Path has long served as a manifest enigma, promising to some sages a glance inside the quasi-religious secrets of yugoloth society itself. To others however, it seems a poisoned lure to draw those very same who would seek to expose that knowledge to the light, devouring them instead, either by slaughter or by corruption. Regardless, the Broken Path promises knowledge to initiates who dedicate themselves to exploring and understanding the patterns in its bizarre, alien architecture. But while it offers rewards and power, like yugoloth promises to mortals, every step of progress toward gnosis that they make drags them deeper into its grasp and unknowingly binds them to it, more and more deeply until they are physically unable to leave without succumbing, one way or another.

Only 6 miles wide in its entirety, roughly half of that space is beholden to the ruins of an utterly ancient fortress of alien design and its surrounding debris field of bones, seemingly comprised of the remains of every known creature, save those of any yugoloth. As befitting its extreme age, much of the structure has fallen to rubble, though the central ruins are in better condition due to a deep swath of protective wards that keep portions intact and standing, even with the absence of proper load-bearing support. Of the keep itself, its plan

is a series of labyrinthine, spiraling corridors, both aboveground and passages burrowing deep below, with a central chamber, several acres wide, open to the looming, roiling sky above. Surrounding the keep are a pentad of slender ancillary towers, of which one is toppled. And another is sheared off halfway up, as if some angry titan had swung at it with a fist millennia earlier, with the upper portion of the tower still suspended in the sky and a roughly 40-foot gap of missing stairwell and walls between it and the extant lower portion.

Runes in the yugoloth dialect of Void Speech spiral across every inch of stone, carved by thousands of different hands, crowding against one another for position and bizarrely appearing on the undersides of fallen stones as well, not just what would have been exposed surfaces in the original structure. The nature of the carvings varies. Most of them are elaborate prayers for various of the Ibshalek, including some either no longer extant or potentially counted among the Waiting Ones, some are tantalizing promises, some are magical formulae of deeply obscure purpose, and still others are warnings directed toward the reader. One motif is repeated, especially upon the ruined entrances, "Travel the path supplicant, seeking and finding. Know and transcend. Know and find freedom." The direct translation of *freedom* in the yugoloth tongue is dubious and can mean a number of related concepts from "release from slavery" to "knowledge" to "oblivion," and the specific wording is reported to change when observed by different readers.

The Broken Path has no apparent native life. Whatever purpose it held for its original builders, it is seemingly abandoned, and only the occasional planar traveler is found within. There is, however, evidence of past occupation, both by mortal explorers and by yugoloth pilgrims. The former litter the ruins' periphery with abandoned and still half-stocked campsites, suggesting that they hurriedly fled or never actually left while the latter leave behind numerous impromptu shrines to the Ibshalek,

including sacrifices of all manner of sentient creatures and a panoply of scattered ritual materials, the aftermath of religious rites of a distinctly yugoloth flavor.

There are two caveats to this absence of native life. Visitors over the past century report one permanent resident, a disheveled human wizard by the name of Verig Renelik. Obsessed with the Broken Path, the wizard is prone to long, meandering diatribes to himself, his familiar, and non-existent persons who may have been former—though now missing— companions. Left to his own devices, he is non-violent, but if interfered with, he is merciless. Visitors describe him rambling on and on about some great reward promised to him, some unknown truth that he has learned that is otherwise reserved for the Ibshalek themselves. Powerful and paranoid, Verig is convinced that he is close to discovering some final hidden and powerful truth. Often dismissed as mad, others are convinced by one curious realization: the wizard has apparently not aged over the course of the past 200 years, despite the normal flow of time within the Broken Path.

The other caveat resides in the wizard's familiar, Xera, an ezkiloth. This tiny yugoloth urges on its master's obsession and claims to be the fruit of his advanced understanding of the Broken Path's obfuscated truths. If the demiplane generates yugoloth familiars for those visitors who follow the path, so to speak, it would lend credence to there actually being a dark and hidden truth waiting for the worthy to understand.

So what is that truth? Is it a honey trap to lure powerful and ambitious mortals and, there, bind their souls and thus them into fiendish service? Is a powerful yugoloth, perhaps even one of the so-called Waiting Ones, lurking secluded deep within its core, luring powerful victims to an unknown end? As with everything involving the 'loths, every deeper exploration, like the Broken Path itself, brings no answers but only an ever-deeper and more dangerous level of questions.

GRANDMOTHER'S DAUGHTERS: SECRETS OF THE VILA

by Kelly Pawlik

The brave and foolhardy souls who attempt to catalog the life and deeds of Baba Yaga have often wondered at the relationship between her and her so-called daughters, the beguiling vila. As with many of the confusing and conflicting stories about Grandmother, there are numerous tales explaining the origin of her relationship with the vila, but the following tale is one of the more common ones.

The Fiend, the Fairy, and the Beldam

When she was younger, Baba Yaga had many dealings with that diabolical glutton Mammon. His coffers swelled with the treasures she paid him to gain access to the knowledge of the Eleven Hells and the hierarchies of arch-devils and demon lords. Mammon knew what the crone was gaining could be dangerous to other mortals, but what damage could a simple witch, even a powerful and long-lived one such as her, do to one as mighty as him? Satisfied with the growing pile of coins, gemstones, and trinkets in his treasury, he allowed the deal to stand as centuries drifted by.

Grandmother knew Mammon would eventually discover his folly in allowing her such access to his vast body of knowledge. She anticipated his reaction and the trickery he would use to strip her of what she had gained, and she prepared herself for his wrath. The wily witch gathered favors, performing deeds for whomever might agree to her terms, be they a desperate pauper, a petty tyrant, or an exalted demigod.

Some unfathomable span of time later, while he performed an accounting of his holdings, Mammon realized just how much he had profited from Baba Yaga—and conversely, how much she had gained from him. He realized she had lived well beyond what he considered acceptable for a mere mortal. The fiend knew in his empty black chamber of a heart that the crone had used knowledge forbidden to mortals, knowledge learned from his own scriptoriums and libraries, to achieve her unbelievable age. She knew that his desire for wealth would blind him to the truth of her treachery. Worse still, she had built a loyal following of devotees, making her not unlike a deity in her own right, and she passed some of the knowledge she had stolen from him to her adherents to cement their loyalty to her. The hells shook as Mammon raged in his realization. But after a while, the fiend's temper cooled. He could repair this and show the overblown magician what the cost was for attempting to deceive the lord of the Hells.

Mammon disguised himself as a simple peddler laden with goods both mundane and magical. He set up a blanket at a marketplace located at a crossroads on the plains at the foot of Demon Mountain, a mortal location close to the devil's husk of a heart. He cried out about his incredible wares to all who passed, and he cajoled them to spread the word.

Baba Yaga heard the tale of the peddler on the plains, about his stock of bottled worlds, genie-filled lamps, and elixirs of eternal youth, and she knew the time had come to put her preparations to action. She went to the market, taking a brief detour to call in a favor in the shadowed city of Corremel, where the fairy courts held sway. When she saw the peddler, she knew at once that she had been right. Mammon himself stood before her, nearly quaking with bitter mirth at the lesson he was going to teach her.

Grandmother perused the peddler's stock, asking questions about this bottle of iridescent pink liquid or that jar holding the eye of a dead god. The devil's patience thinned as she slowly looked over every single item he had brought with him. She made a sour face and turned to go.

"Where are you going?" the peddler asked.

"I don't see anything here I don't already have," she explained. "I am looking for something no one has ever seen before."

The peddler frowned. "I assure you that I have what you need. Describe what you want, and I will find it," he said, indicating to his bulging pack.

Baba Yaga pursed her lips, doubtful of his proclamation. She thought for a moment. "If you can do as you claim, I will give you everything I have in exchange."

Mammon's eyes shone with greed. He licked his lips and then repeated, "Describe what you want."

"I want a creature like a horse but a bit smaller. It must have four legs and brown fur dappled with white," Grandmother said.

The peddler opened his bag and dug around while murmuring. A moment later he pulled out a fawn and presented it.

"Here you are. Exactly as you wished," he said. His eyes burned like embers.

"That is just a deer," Baba Yaga dismissed and turned to go. "Obviously you were just telling me a story."

"No, no!" The peddler exclaimed. "I have what you want. Describe something else."

"How about a creature slightly larger than a mastiff but with shaggy gray fur," she inquired.

"Easily done." He dug in his pack and pulled out a wolf cub and presented it to her.

"That is a wolf. They are common in the forests not so far from here.

"Of course, they are. I
see you are too canny for
these simple creatures.
Try something more
interesting," the fiend
commanded.

With a nonplussed look she
tried again. "How about a
feline as big as a mountain
lion but with a feminine
intelligence?"

The peddler's brows
waggled as he drew forth a
wampus cat, cursing from its
human head. "I think it's time for
you to pay up now," he stated.

"That is a wampus cat. I have seen
them detailed on a scroll I saw on
Totivillus's table," she stated, waving her
hand in boredom.

The peddler clenched his fists.
"How about something even
more fascinating ?" he asked,
drawing a deerlike creature
with the trunk, arms, and
head of a human from the
sack.

Baba Yaga shook her head as
a little girl shouted, "That's an
alseid. My mama says they roam
the Margreve Forest."

"Fine," shouted Mammon. "Is there no
one that create something new for this
impossible-to-please woman?"

"It is not so difficult," said Sarastra, the Queen
of Night and Magic, stepping from the growing
crowd. "Though possibly that is not true for one
with only the creativity granted to them by the
hells," she finished.

Mammon ground his teeth but smiled as he
said, "Milady, please demonstrate your skill."

"Can you make me a creature with antlers like
a deer, hair as green as the grass in spring, skin
like the wood of the beech tree, and eyes as grey
as the ocean in autumn?" Baba Yaga asked the
fey lady.

Sarastra threw three seeds on the ground, and
each swiftly grew into a beautiful woman with
features as Grandmother described.

"They are new and never seen before by the
eyes of mortal or immortal," Sarastra said,
gesturing at them. "And they are yours if you
wish them." She then faded away to her home
in the Shadow Realm.

Mammon's eyes crinkled as he grinned. "Have
you seen these before?" he asked.

"No. I think I will call them vila." Baba Yaga
replied.

"Call them what you will," the peddler spat
back. "It is time for you to pay me now."

"Pay for what, peddler?" Grandmother asked
him. "You claimed to have what I needed, but

you did not. The Queen of Night and Magic made these vila."

Mammon gaped. The crone had tricked him again. "There will be a reckoning for this, witch." He disappeared in a burst of flame and the stench of brimstone.

"Perhaps," replied Baba Yaga, "but now I have granddaughters. Let us see what they can learn." And she took those first three vila and taught them all she knew.

VILA REQUESTS

d20	FAVOR REQUESTED
1	Make a promise to nurse an injured animal back to health.
2	Forswear the eating of venison for one year.
3	Lead a small herd of sheep to a nearby wolf pack.
4	Spend a month planting trees.
5	Agree to be a vila's protector for one month.
6	Plant a vegetable garden.
7	Drive all the loggers out of the vila's forest.
8	Promise to plant a pine tree on four different mountaintops.
9	Only wear clothing made of woven grasses.
10	Do not wield or wear iron for a fortnight.
11	Carry a message from the vila to one of the lords of the shadow fey.
12	Spend one hour dancing around a fire each night for one month.
13	Do not curse or swear for one year.
14	Wear only sandals on your feet for one month.
15	Free all the livestock owned by a grumpy old farmer.
16	Do not use fire for any purpose, mundane or magical, for one week.
17	Deliver the honey from a sacred beehive to an ill-tempered bear.
18	Sit unmoving on an uncomfortable stump for one day.
19	Agree to carry a horse's burden for one day.
20	Remain silent for a week.

Vila Boons

Whether they gained the ability from their association with Baba Yaga or from some other divine being or phenomenon, vila can grant favors to mortals. Most often, these are given as payment for a service a mortal has performed for a vila, but a few magnanimous individuals occasionally grant a boon freely or on a whim. Some others use their boons in a more punitive fashion, where they act more as a curse to the recipient than as a benefit.

Vila boons always have a drawback. It isn't known whether they are able to grant favors that are open and free of complication or fey trickery, but the fact is that they never do. There is always a cost, and that cost must always be borne by the recipient of the boon.

Typical of all fey, the service required from a mortal to obtain a vila's boon often seems nonsensical or pointless to the petitioner, and the wording of the request itself can obfuscate the creature's true desire. Nonetheless, a vila adheres to the letter of any verbal agreement she makes with a mortal, and she always delivers the favor agreed upon if such an agreement was reached before the boon is granted. The **Vila Requests** table lists a number of potential favors a vila might ask for in exchange for a boon.

The vila boons listed herein consist of the boon's name, a description of the benefit gained by the recipient, and the drawback of the boon to be borne by the recipient. The drawback associated with each boon is a suggestion. If the drawback isn't fitting for your campaign or the character that received the boon, you should feel free to assess a different, more fitting one.

DANCING HUT

A vila allows you to borrow her dancing, chicken-legged hut. The hut can comfortably hold six Medium or smaller creatures and has a movement rate of 50 feet. As an action, the occupants of the hut can speak the name of the vila who loaned them the hut to instantly transport themselves up to 500 miles to a

location one of them has visited before while the hut remains in the place. Speaking the vila's name again returns all the occupants to the interior of the hut. Once the hut has been used in this fashion, it can't be used again until dawn the next day.

Duration. One week or until you break your promise.

Drawback. Creatures that finish a long rest in the hut have disadvantage on the first attack roll, saving throw, or ability check they make on the following day.

GRANDMOTHER'S HONEY

You are given a small pot filled with fragrant honey. As an action, you can rub a handful of the honey on yourself to gain resistance to fire and lightning damage for 1 minute. Once you have used the honey, you can't do so again until dawn the next day. At the end of the duration, the pot crumbles, and any honey remaining crystalizes.

Duration. One month or until you break your promise.

Drawback. Bees, stinging insects, and **stirges** are attracted to you. **Giant wasps** and similar creatures have advantage on attack rolls on you.

HUMMINGBIRD HEART

For the duration, when you use your action to Dash, your movement is equal to three times your speed, after applying any modifiers, and you have advantage on Dexterity saving throws until the start of your next turn.

Duration. One day or until you break your promise.

Drawback. If you don't move on one of your turns, your movement is reduced to 20 feet until the turn after you move again.

NATURE GUT

For the duration, you can subsist on grass, leaves, bark, and moss and are immune to the dangerous or debilitating effects of plant-based foodstuffs, such as alcohol. As a bonus action, you can recover hit points as though you had expended a Hit Die. Once you have recovered hit points, you must finish a long rest before you can do so again.

Duration. One week or until you break your promise.

Drawback. Herbivores and omnivores, such as bears, focus their attention and attacks on you over other targets.

THUNDER TONGUE

For the duration, your voice is amplified to a volume that can be heard clearly for 1,000 feet, regardless of other noise in the area, such as hurricane winds, a collapsing tower, or a roaring dragon. If you cast a spell with verbal components, your allies are heartened by your voice and have advantage on saving throws until the beginning of your next turn.

Duration. One week or until you break your promise.

Drawback. Every creature within 500 feet of you that can hear, hears every word you speak, regardless of how quiet you think you are.

Wayward Daughters of Baba Yaga

Not all vila venerate, or even respect Baba Yaga. Some of them have gone so far as to band together with mortals to counter her machinations and wrest some of the old witch's power away from her. These groups focus their activities on divining where objects Grandmother will be drawn to are located and taking possession of them. Often, this means moving the item in question to the Shadow Realm or the Summer Lands, where the vila feel the native populations of fey can keep them safer than mortals can.

These groups don't officially have a name, though some of the members ironically refer to themselves as wayward daughters, for they don't feel like they are anyone's daughters. Each cell of wayward daughters is self-contained, rarely numbering more than a dozen members, though groups of them do occasionally

intermingle with other groups, especially to pull off more dangerous undertakings. Groups seek outside assistance from time to time as well, hiring specialists as the need arises. As often as not, these specialists are paid in vila boons and magical items rather than coin.

The largest numbers of wayward daughters can be found in places Baba Yaga is known to frequent, such as the Rothenian Plain or the Margreve Forest. The Blood Kingdoms can also boast many cells as can the Grand Duchy of Dornig. Most other regions host one or two small cells that often require assistance in pulling off their operations.

JOINING THE WAYWARD DAUGHTERS

Wayward daughters are very selective about whom they allow into their tight-knit cells. A prospective mortal member might assist a cell with a dozen or more missions over a handful of years before they are offered full-time membership by the vila in charge. An ideal candidate for membership has few familial bonds or intimate friendships when they join, though they will likely build strong bonds with those of their cell.

Prospective members can expect to have their loyalty and wits tested at random intervals by the existing members of the group. As Baba Yaga is known to be a powerful witch, tests are aimed at ensuring a potential recruit can see through illusions, overcome enchantments, resist being transformed against their will, and endure any physical tortures they are subjected

to. Wayward daughters that come from the mortal world need to be well rounded with strong physical skills, a reasonable body of knowledge, and the ability to interact with others without drawing attention to themselves. Despite their name, there is no bias with regard to gender amongst the wayward daughters, and any mortal that meets their exacting requirements can find admittance eventually.

WHAT IS EXPECTED OF A MEMBER

Wayward daughters must be subtle, swift, and sometimes ruthless. Operations requiring theft, destruction of personal property, and assassination are carried out with enough frequency that individuals who are overly concerned with matters of right and wrong or who have a very black and white view of morality have a hard time coping. The general methodology of a wayward daughter cell is to discover something, be it an object, person, or situation, that Grandmother Baba Yaga might take an interest in and remove it from her sphere of influence, no matter how that needs to be done.

After an operation, the cell leader expects that members will remain silent about it. The details are to remain secret and unspoken, except possibly to one another. Wayward daughters that can't maintain discretion are dealt with harshly. It isn't unheard of for a member who has run afoul of their own cell to have their memory permanently erased or to simply to be executed.

ALLIES AND ENEMIES

Not surprisingly, the biggest enemy of the wayward daughters is Baba Yaga herself. The canny old witch has more power and influence at her disposal than any cell of daughters can muster. Baba Yaga's agents are also a danger to the groups. Her adherents will stop at nothing to gain Grandmother's favor, and delivering a single member, let alone an entire cell, to her is a sure way to win ancient and forbidden knowledge.

Despite the fear that the wayward daughters have about Baba Yaga's attention, no known cells of them have ever been the subject of her aggression. It isn't known if the crone is aware of these so-called daughters of hers that work against her interests, but some of the vila leaders wonder if they aren't just working toward Baba Yaga's inscrutable goals somehow.

BENEFITS OF BEING A WAYWARD DAUGHTER

Given the difficulty of gaining membership, the benefits of joining a cell of wayward daughters are significant for mortals:

- If they are within 60 feet of another wayward daughter, a member can add their proficiency bonus to initiative checks.
- Members have advantage on Dexterity (Stealth) checks while on a mission for their cell.
- Members are immune to the Dance of the Luckless and Fascinate abilities of all vila.
- Members have advantage on saving throws to avoid being put to sleep or magically knocked unconscious.

WAYWARD DAUGHTER ADVENTURE HOOKS

Baba Yaga has agents and interests all over Midgard, so the wayward daughters can be found anywhere, working to curtail her power and influence. Consider the following hooks to involve them in your campaign:

- A beautiful, antlered woman approaches the party's leader and inquires if their services are available. She needs to recover the staff a cagey wizard stole from her—and if the wizard ends up dead in the process, so much the better.
- The party, while seeking a relic in a tomb, encounters a group of wayward daughters seeking the same artifact. The daughters are willing to use whatever means are necessary to fulfill their objective.
- One of Grandmother's agents hires the party to investigate a series of thefts in town. A cell of wayward daughters has been stealing magical trinkets to keep Baba Yaga from gaining control of them. Both groups are actually seeking an artifact they suspect to be in the town and the agent that hires the party is hoping they'll stumble into it first.

AZURE BAND: ORGANIZED CRIME IN THE DRAGON EMPIRE

by Basheer Ghouse

The grand dragons of the Mharoti Empire have never cared much for the jambuka: dragons rule, dragonkin are the true citizens, and everyone else are subjects, beholden to the law, beholden to their masters, and rarely benefiting from the relationship. Judges and guards care little for the affairs of any but the richest humans, leaving vast gaps in the empire's social fabric.

Of course, where the law leaves a void, crime is happy to fill it.

Across the empire, poor humanoids turn to a dark network of smugglers, brutes, loan sharks, and fixers to meet their needs. They enforce contracts, mediate disputes, and maintain something resembling peace. In the process, they link in great networks of organized crime, immiserating the millions under their heel, spreading criminal enterprises across the empire and beyond, and growing rich in the process.

Greatest and most violent of these criminal networks is the Azure Band.

History of the Azure Band

The Azure Band was founded 92 years ago by Zahid Saab. It began its life as a minor smuggling ring, a way for the towering djinn to rebuild his wealth on the Material Plane. They smuggled alchemical reagents, weapons, and other illicit goods across the empire's borders with the aid of djinn magics and elemental servitors.

As the Azure Band expanded, it found itself broadening its operations by necessity. Enforcers were needed to ensure they weren't cheated or that employees didn't flee to the authorities, trusted parties to mediate disputes, fences to sell excess goods. This expansion, in turn, found them enemies.

Other criminals opposed the expansion. The Azure Band had pressed into their turf across the empire, disrupting existing smuggling networks and destabilizing local power structures. Feuds, territorial disputes, a spreading brushfire of quiet wars erupted in the empire's vast criminal underworld. An initiation by fire into the Mharoti Empire.

The constant fighting slowed—though didn't stop—the Azure Band's expansion. Negotiations found rivals turned into allies, brutal feuds fixed territorial lines, and when things were truly desperate, Zahid Saab flexed the might of a genie lord, ripping souls from bodies, freezing hideouts, and wiping bitter enemies from the face of Midgard. Within two decades, the group morphed from an up-and-coming smuggling ring to a brutal, omnipresent fixture of the Mharoti underworld.

From there, it sought special considerations from the ruling class. They bribed local officials, became useful to governors and morzas, and found niches where they could remain profitable without drawing draconic ire. The group became a part of the empire, a layer between the powerful and the truly miserable, letting satraps and emirs enrich themselves without managing the desperate themselves.

In doing so, it became the most widespread criminal organization in the Mharoti Empire.

Such has been the status quo for half a century. Entire generations of impoverished jambuka have grown up, their local enforcer more present than their local lord, their local smuggler a more trusted arbiter than a judge.

Ozmir Al-Stragul's coup has thrown things into chaos though. The Dread Sultan is less lenient to upstart jambuka and perceived threats to his rule. His declaration of a new Age of Scales has seen corrupt officials thrown out and replaced with fanatics while many jambuka agents are seen as inherently untrustworthy. Several Azure Band operations have been curtailed by arrests or shut down entirely— and suffering most cataclysmically, its grand smuggling ring in Harkesh.

In response, the group has begun to expand its operations beyond the empire. Smuggling cells pop up across Nuria Natal, thugs ply their trade as mercenaries and spies in the Seven Cities, and unmarked boats deliver weapons to minotaur pirates.

The Azure Band has found itself on the back foot. While this is an opportunity for its enemies, it's also a profoundly dangerous state of affairs, for they will quite happily do anything and kill anyone to resecure their position.

Operations and Organization

The Azure Band were smugglers first, and even at the height of their power, smugglers they remain. Their criminal empire is arranged like a tree's branches. The central trunk is a vast, hidden smuggling network. Most of its component operators don't know that they're part of the Azure Band, merely that they're paid to ignore customs on certain merchants or take extra cargo on their caravans or some similarly innocuous tasks.

However, Azure Band smugglers carry far more valuable cargo than most merchants: magic items, crates full of weapons, drugs capable of intoxicating dragons, alchemical reagents. They consider no cargo taboo, no risk too great, so long as there's a proportional profit in store. Even adventurers might find use of their services. After all, they're unlikely to ask why you need 200 flasks of alchemist's fire. Or why you need to be smuggled out of the city the next morning.

The network of handlers, managers, and enforcers who organize the network stay in the background, doing their best to ensure their smuggling is indistinguishable from far more

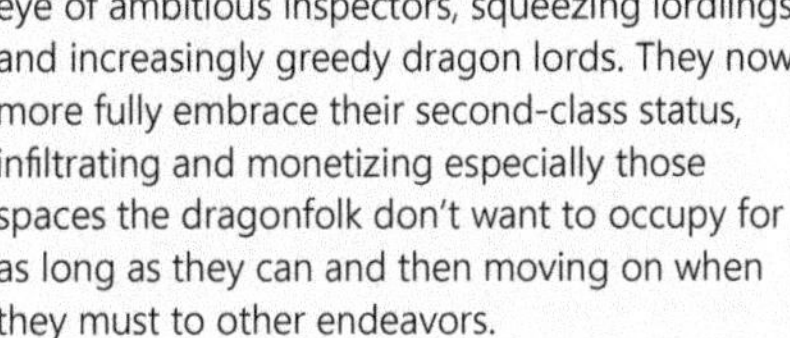

RECENT YEARS AT A GLANCE

The Dragon Empire of recent years, under the Dread Sultan's rule, has been marked by ambition and conquest. This renewed focus brings with it a greater presence of both governmental agents, such as active tax collectors, and military movements throughout the empire—a general effort to concentrate wealth and power. This in turn has made operations more challenging for the Azure Band, and they've had to adapt, becoming nimbler in order to avoid the constant eye of ambitious inspectors, squeezing lordlings, and increasingly greedy dragon lords. They now more fully embrace their second-class status, infiltrating and monetizing especially those spaces the dragonfolk don't want to occupy for as long as they can and then moving on when they must to other endeavors.

minor sorts of graft. Azure Band smuggling operations are often surrounded by a network of subsidiary operations—drug pushers, fences, collectors, farms, mines, and storefronts that supply contraband on one end and convert it to cash on the other. Many of these operations aren't directly controlled by the Azure Band, and plenty of pirates, street gangs, and bandits rely on its smugglers without realizing it.

The Azure Band's visible arm is its enforcers, loan sharks, and informers. A network of thugs, mercenaries, fixers, and thieves that patrol every slum in the empire. They enforce contracts, protect turf, racketeer relentlessly, and ensure that the Azure Band is known, feared, and obeyed.

Azure Band loan sharks are almost stamped out of a mold: thin, genial folk possessed of warm eyes, good reputations, and comprehensive ruthlessness. They are simultaneously community figureheads, funding minor public works projects or offering opportunities to the needy, and brutal criminals trapping folks in debt. Most set themselves up as mediators, helping their unwilling constituents handle crime (at least that of their competitors) and property disputes while managing friction arising with their clients.

Debtors to the Azure Band find themselves pressed into service. The unskilled are sent to various subsidiary ventures: gemstone mines, drug farms, or warehouses can always use the laborers, and the charges for food and board keep the indebted locked in place for months or years. Merchants might be made to smuggle dangerous routes while adventurers might perform tasks. Some, especially veteran soldiers, are instead offered jobs as enforcers.

Enforcers and informers are the twin hands of the Azure Band. Identified by brilliant blue bracers and belts, they serve to enforce the band's will throughout the empire's criminal underworld. They're allowed wide latitude and functional independence but are careful not to be openly associated with the Azure Band's smuggling fronts. Instead, they run racketeering rings, back-alley pit fights, freelance spy rings, and debt collections. Their superiors ensure the group's other operations are protected "coincidentally" and designate targets to be beaten, brutalized, or killed. The enforcers are a prestigious position for many poor jambuka, who see some measure of money, status, and respect, but they're rarely promoted to higher ranks. Zahid Saab prefers his thugs expendable.

The Azure Band conspicuously avoids thievery. Most within the group view it as beneath them and counterproductive. Robbing the rich brings too much attention to their operations, robbing the poor takes money they could get more easily in other fashions, and cultivating a thief's skills risks those talents being turned on their employers. When thieves are needed, the local shawish is expected to hire some adventurers to handle it.

Key Figures

The Azure Band spans countless individuals but a few of the more important, more interesting ones are detailed here.

Khorug Oglu. Khorug (CN gnoll **warlock of the genie lord**, see *Tome of Beasts 3*) is a lean, one-eyed gnoll with misshapen limbs. Victim of a mining accident as a youth, Khorug's life would likely have ended there but for a friendship with the son of an Azure Band shawish. Khorug's friend convinced his parents that he was a smart youth and would be an asset to the company, so the injured gnoll was given a single chance to prove his worth, managing the books for a racketeering operation.

To everyone's surprise, including his own, Khorug excelled. A lifetime of stolen lessons, harsh rationing, and no small amount of intelligence helped him organize a clean, efficient, and quiet operation while catching a Shawish skimming money off the top. A last chance turned into a permanent position, which turned into a promotion to a smuggling operation in Cogelu, to an escalating series of administrative positions.

Now, Khorug is one of the most highly ranked people in the Azure Band. He's respected, rich, and well-liked by his subordinates, who see a rags-to-riches story who treats them fairly because he *was* them not so long ago. He may be amoral and in service to a sprawling criminal empire, but he's dispassionate and pleasant in person.

Alas, Khorug Oglu is now regularly exposed to Zahid Saab. The gnoll's patron and boss torments him regularly, scheduling meetings in rooms difficult for him to reach, making jibes about his appearance in public, and undermining him to his peers. The simple wealth of his position, the material comforts compared to his life as a miner, has cushioned the experience so far, but Khorug has begun to take his frustrations out on those around him, and it is only likely to get worse.

Mara Fahan. Mara (LE human **field commander**, see *Tome of Beasts 3*) is a tall woman with light skin, broad shoulders, curly hair, and a penchant for heavy, imported armor. She dresses in Illyrian fashion, Seven Cities and Nurian suits cut for men, or ceremonial armor won in various duels. She's charismatic and bold, quick to reward underlings who impress her and not afraid of joining raids on rivals on the front lines.

Mara is the daughter of a satrap whose career in the military was stonewalled due to her status as jambuka. With no other way to advance her career, she left the army and joined the Azure Band. Military training, good instincts, and noble resources saw her progress rapidly through the ranks. She crushed rival gangs, protected and expanded smuggling operations, and slowly took over half a dozen gem mines on the Empire's western coast. Her successes saw her promoted again and again until she was put in charge of the Azure Band's Rumelan operations.

Rumela is still a growing command. The Azure Band fights resistance groups, occupation officers, criminals, and even the mysterious ghost folk. They're a new force in a set market, rather than the overwhelming

juggernaut they are at home. Fortunately for her, Mara's military experience and hands-on leadership has served her well, letting the Azure Band fend off competitors, avoid suspicion from the Muhta, and establish a solid foothold in the new province.

However, Mara Fahan has an inconvenient streak of patriotism. She may be a ruthless criminal, but she's a ruthless *Mharoti* criminal, and she's taken the existence of opposition to Glauvistus strangely personally. Enforcer squads ignore local gangs to hunt down or expose rebel cells, weapons meant to go to the highest bidder find their ways to occupation garrisons at reasonable prices, and the Muhta receives a steady stream of tips from Azure Band enforcers. While this has given them a degree of favor with Glauvistus's court, it's also an uncomfortable degree of exposure and is beginning to cut into their profits.

Zahid Saab. Zahid (LE **djinni**, 224 hp) is a 14-foot-tall djinni with vibrant blue-green skin and a lean, muscle-bound frame. He is handsome, clever, and wise and possesses a keen understanding of other people and a knack for planning that has served him well in founding a criminal empire. He has a particular skill for finding what people want out of the world and making himself the path of least resistance to getting it. He lives in a grand palace on the outskirts of Qiresh, filled with servants and sapphire-studded decor, living as an advisor and confidant to the powerful.

Ninety-four years ago, Zahid Saab was a prince in the Elemental Plane of Air, a widely considered contestant to its throne. He attempted a coup, to wrest control from his aunt, but it failed, and he fled in disgrace. Humiliated, impoverished, and with no supporters, he arrived in Harkesh with a handful of still-loyal servants and a dozen contacts willing to speak with him. Over the following nine decades, he built the Azure Band from the ground up, rebuilding his wealth and reputation and styling himself as the Azure Emir.

However, there is a fatal weakness that ended his political career on the Elemental Plane of Air and now plagues the Azure Band: Zahid Saab is an awful jerk.

He is reflexively cruel to those around him. He makes jibes about their insecurities, pokes at the worst moments of their lives, and refuses to respect their boundaries. For all his cleverness, for all his wealth, for all his ability to ensure cooperation is the smartest option for others, he manages to relentlessly alienate his allies.

On the Elemental Plane of Air, this destroyed his coup attempt. Courtiers were unwilling to risk their reputations for him, noble families who had everything to gain refused to give their habitual tormenter the throne, guards valued their dignity over bribes, and even his personal guard refused to stick with him when betrayal proved momentarily profitable.

Much of the Azure Band's decentralized, secretive nature is a reaction to this failure. Few ever meet Zahid in person or stay with him for any length of time. To most, his jabs are a minor annoyance during rare meetings rather than an unending stream of slights.

However, such measures have their limits. The purge at Arkesh was prompted by Hamad bin Soori, a high-ranking lieutenant who Zahid had tormented over the death of his father at every meeting for years. Pushed past the brink, Hamad sold out Azure Band operations in the capital to the sultan's office and is now one of their most committed opponents.

NPCS

The NPCs below provide an easy way to introduce the Azure Band in an encounter.

AZURE BAND ENFORCER

The most visible limb of the Azure Band is its enforcers—a presence in every slum of the Mharoti Empire. They're criminal foot soldiers who protect operations, extort locals, and kill foes. Enforcers are chosen for loyalty. They are more lightly armed than even many

bandits since full blades and armor draw too much attention in cities. They make up for this vulnerability in improvisational brutality, knocking foes to the floor and then pummeling them into submission before they can recover.

Medium Humanoid (Any Race), Lawful Evil
Armor Class 13 (leather armor)
Hit Points 33 (6d8 + 6)
Speed 30 ft.

STR	DEX	CON	INT	WIS	CHA
14 (+2)	14 (+2)	13 (+1)	9 (−1)	14 (+1)	7 (−2)

Saving Throws Str +4, Dex +4, Wis +3

Skills Insight +3, Perception +3

Senses passive Perception 13

Languages Common

Challenge 1 (200 XP)　　**Proficiency Bonus** +2

ACTIONS

Multiattack. The enforcer makes two Dagger attacks. If the enforcer hits a creature with two Dagger attacks in the same round, that creature must succeed on a DC 12 Strength saving throw or be knocked prone.

Dagger. *Melee or Ranged Weapon Attack:* +4 to hit, reach 5 ft. or range 20/60 ft., one target. *Hit:* 4 (1d4 + 2) piercing damage.

REACTIONS

Cheap Shot. When a creature within 5 feet of the enforcer stands from prone, they take 4 (1d4 + 2) bludgeoning damage. That creature has disadvantage on the next attack roll or saving throw it makes.

AZURE BAND SHAWISH

Shawish are mid-ranking officers in the Azure Band. They're entrusted with the secrets of its smuggling operations and genie magics with which they oversee various operations and intervene personally when things go wrong.

Shawish deal with most issues through deception, leveraging their personal charisma, criminal resources, and illusion magics to solve problems and divert investigations. When violence erupts, they command from the back, enchanting the weapons of their underlings and battering enemies into submission with powerful magic.

Medium Humanoid (Any Race), Lawful Evil

Armor Class 15 (*mage armor*)

Hit Points 54 (12d8)

Speed 30 ft.

STR	DEX	CON	INT	WIS	CHA
8 (−1)	14 (+2)	11 (+0)	12 (+1)	14 (+2)	19 (+4)

Saving Throws Int +3, Wis +4, Cha +6

Skills Deception +6

Senses passive Perception 12

Languages Common

Challenge 4 (1,100 XP)　　**Proficiency Bonus** +2

ACTIONS

Multiattack. The shawish makes two Eldritch Blast attacks.

Dagger. *Melee or Ranged Weapon Attack:* +4 to hit, reach 5 ft. or range 20/60 ft., one target. *Hit:* 4 (1d4 + 2) piercing damage.

Eldritch Blast. Ranged Spell Attack: +6 to hit, range 120 ft. *Hit:* 9 (1d10 + 4) force damage.

Overpressure (1/Day). The shawish claps their hands, emitting a destructive shockwave in a 60-foot cone. All creatures in the area must make a DC 14 Constitution saving throw, taking 18 (4d8) thunder damage and being knocked prone on a failed save and half as much damage and no additional effects on a successful one.

Weave Lie (3/Day). The shawish casts *arcanist's magic aura, hypnotic pattern,* or *major image.*

BONUS ACTIONS

Air Ward (1/Short Rest). The shawish cloaks themself in a gust of wind. For 10 minutes, they gain half cover against all ranged attacks and do not provoke opportunity attacks with movement.

Thunderclap Boon (1/Short Rest). The shawish blesses a creature it can see within 30 feet of itself. Whenever that creature is hit with a weapon attack, the attack deals an additional 4 (1d8) thunder damage. This effect requires concentration and lasts for 1 minute.

WARREN GUILD: ALL HAIL VINZLO (NOW PASS THE PUDDING)

by HH Carlan (with Sarah Madsen, Trapmaking Competition flyer)

Beneath the streets of Melana, there lies a second Melana: the sprawling Undercity, a complex system of tunnels and caves, buzzing with opportunity and, for the unsuspecting stranger, looming regret.

The dwarves of the city initially brought the kobolds in as cheap labor to work the mines and similar jobs, treating them like animals, but with the election of Censor Vinzlo, there came a new dawn for the kobolds, and they discovered hope. The Warren Guild is there to ensure their continued relevance and prosperity, to elevate the lives of the kobolds of Melana—by whatever means necessary, leaning in on their propensity for subterfuge and mischief.

TIME IS PUDDING

The Warren Guild have come to be known for their motto: "Time is pudding." Vinzlo coined the original phrase, "Time is short, and victory is pudding," on the eve of the great Raid of Garments, but now the kobolds recite their abbreviated motto as a call to arms. At the time, the canton heavily taxed pudding, so after the raid, after the kobolds stole the surface humans' clothes, they feasted on tubs of prohibition pudding.

Guild Members

The Warren Guild's roster boasts members from all kobold clutches within Melana, living and dead, as their ghosts are etched into the walls of the caverns and considered to be active members of society. Members range from seamstresses to assassins, and all the young kobolds complete an initiation on the eve of their tenth birthday. The newly admitted kobolds claim their assignments after tests which include rafting, sword-fighting, completing a labyrinth, and a pudding-eating contest.

The guild has need of kobolds of all stripes. At the helm of their crew reigns the beloved Archking Vinzlo, who sits in the largest tunnel on an intricate wooden throne. Now showing the signs of age, Vinzlo continues to oversee the activities of the guild through his daughters. Unlike his sons, who all took on combat roles, his daughters excelled early in leadership. Now, Vinelope oversees all trade, Vinchelle directs all social matters, and Vinarriet is the chief of strategy. Regardless of their direct command, all kobolds revere Vinzlo, and his word is final.

Two of the more infamous members of the Warren Guild maintain a credible and deadly reputation both in the Undercity and on Melana's surface. The first is a mapmaker whose knowledge of the surface rivals that of the most: Fingers is a smaller-than-average kobold with beautiful handwriting. He has drawn some of the most exquisite maps found in Melana—and will also write invitations for weddings when paid enough. His twin brother,

Toes, is a pastry chef and thief who benefits from his brother's maps and informs him of the changes within the city. Both are slight, even for kobolds, and in their hands, their chosen utensils are also deadly weapons.

BY THE FINE FINGERTIPS OF VINTINA

ASSASSIN'S LAMP

Wondrous Item, Very Rare (Requires Attunement)

A gold, gilded lamp with three transparent orbs that glow without flame. However, once attuned, the lights can be extinguished with their command word, casting *darkness* for all within range except for the attuned.

MURDER SPOON

Weapon (Shortsword), Very Rare

A standard wooden spoon with slots cut into its bowl to strain solids from soup, this spoon has a detachable handle that reveals an extending shortsword. You gain +1 bonus to attack and damage rolls made with this weapon.

Life in the Warrens

Descending into the tunnels and eventually the warrens of the Undercity, travelers discover a confusing odor of sweet earthiness. The hollowed paths continue deep within the earth, and the seemingly ever-present smells of dessert permeate the galleries. Optimally carved for the physical dimensions of kobolds, taller creatures, including humans, must crouch or crawl through the tunnels, allowing the kobolds time to outrun enemies and quickly access the safety of their living quarters. The kobolds snicker and giggle at the too-talls navigating their homelands.

The grandest space within the warrens is the Doom Room. A sizeable cavern, tall enough for even a human to stand, the Doom Room is the strategy room where Vinzlo oversees the guild. Tables and bookshelves line the walls, trinkets and weapons fill the shelves—not a book is in sight. Hand-drawn maps cover most surfaces, and though most have been drawn on by bored kobolds over the years, from longstanding games to mocking cartoons, they also contain useful notations and plans, such as for heists or trap design.

ADVENTURE SEED: WHISPERS OF CHAOS

The Warren Guild have come to be known for their motto: "Time is pudding." Vinzlo coined the original phrase, "Time is short, and victory is pudding," on the eve of the great Raid of Garments, but now the kobolds recite their abbreviated motto as a call to arms. At the time, the canton heavily taxed pudding, so after the raid, after the kobolds stole the surface humans' clothes, they feasted on tubs of prohibition pudding.

Since the ascension of Vinzlo, now archking and guildmaster, the kobolds are no longer banished to the shadows. Kobold society, supported within the Warren Guild, creates a robust subculture beneath the busy streets of Melana, composed of popular tradesmen, craftsmen, assassins, and proprietors of goods and services common, uncommon, and for enough coin, illegal.

Kobold Scheming

Pressured to create alliances with the surface dwellers, Vinelope tasked the older kobolds with creating intricate boxes and weapons, laced with traps and secret compartments. Through decades of refining their crafts, their works are now highly valued and sought after by those with the taste and means. Their works are attributed to the fictitious artist Zlokin and sold through surface connections. Travelers frequently ask

ADVENTURE SEED: VESPER'S SHADOW

Creaking floorboards ache beneath the heavy footsteps of a troubled man. "Nikswen's gone missing," Spire Dwell announces from the tavern stage. Rumors of the singer's disappearance had been building for days, and the only good lead is a mysterious woman seen about town. What the troubled proprietor is not mentioning is that his black book of secrets is also missing, which is problematic for the Warren Guild and the Freeholders if it fell into the wrong hands. Luckily, the last kobold to see her alive is sitting at the next table, and he has a story to tell.

ADVENTURE SEED: COMMUNITY DOOMED

It's a warm night, and businesses in Melana have closed early due to rumors of an impending conflict. Threats of violence against Censor Seppo Voller and Merzlo Regon have the entire city on high alert. The entrance to the Undercity is flanked with heavy wooden crates, and as darkness settles, the crates explode, leaving the entrance in shambles and shaking the area. Merzlo was seen hiding among the buildings right before the explosion, and her guards are nearby. The entrance is destroyed, and thousands are now stranded belowground. Cries for help echo through the streets. How many will die tonight? Who will save them?

The 3rd Tri-Annual Zobeck Kobold Trapmaking Competition

KOBOLDS ONLY

AMAZING CONTRAPTIONS! EXCITING EXPLOSIONS! FANTASTASTIC PRIZES!

Sponsored by the Kobold Shipping Consortium!

1st Place: 200 gp and first dibs on the losers' scrap
2nd Place: 100 gp and second dibs on the losers' scrap
3rd Place: 50 gp (That's all, so do better next time!)

THE CONSORTIUM ARENA (GULLET)
Ceresday @ Sundown

Entrants must apply by DAWN on Ceresday and present their tools for inspection!
NO EXCEPTIONS!!!

ENTRY FEE
Competitors: 10 gp per team
Spectators: 5 sp for safe seats, 1 cp for blast zone seats*

NO ANIMALS ALLOWED, ESPECIALLY DOGS

*Spectators sitting in the blast zone assume all risk and responsibility associated with sitting in the blast zone. Such risks include, but are not limited to, first-degree burns, second-degree burns, third-degree burns, acid burns, shrapnel injury, loss of sense of smell, loss of hair, loss of limb, loss of life. Ponchos (1 cp) and shields (2 cp) can be purchased on site or bring your own. Risk also includes loss of poncho.

RULES AND REGULATIONS
Kobolds ONLY!

Clarification: Assistants can be non-kobolds, but the primary engineer must be kobold!
More Clarification: ASSISTANTS ONLY ASSIST, THEY DON'T BUILD!
You must bring your materials and tools with you. If it's not in your workspace when the starting gun goes off, you can't use it! There will be a pile of scrap for competitors to raid for extra materials. NO FIGHTING ALLOWED AT THE SCRAP PILE!

All items must be built from SCRATCH. No pre-building allowed!
THAT MEANS YOU, GERDA!

NO ATTACKING THE OTHER COMPETITORS OR THEIR ASSISTANTS!
No magic tools allowed!

Magic can be used ONLY to create materials, heat metal, or enhance triggers. Magic cannot be used to fabricate traps! MAGIC CANNOT BE USED TO ATTACK OR INFLUENCE THE OTHER COMPETITORS OR THEIR ASSISTANTS!! Judges are the final ruling on this!

NO ATTACKING THE JUDGES! MAGIC ALSO CANNOT BE USED TO ATTACK OR INFLUENCE THE JUDGES! LEAVE THE JUDGES ALONE!!!

Melana shopkeepers if they have anything new from the mysterious crafter. Believed by the locals of Melana to be the creator of their fine goods, this Zlokin has never made an appearance on the surface and is contacted only though the Warren Guild.

On occasion, a traveler might request a weapon made "by the fine fingertips of Vintina." This is a code for assassins who wish to buy weapons crafted by Zlokin. If a shopkeeper has one in stock, they typically sell the mysterious weapon no matter the buyer. These weapons sometimes appear as harmless items, such as lamps and utensils, but they quickly reveal deadly capabilities when in the right hands (see **By the Fine Fingertips of Vintina** sidebar).

The guild maintains alliances with other subterranean groups, relying on gossip and trade to further their goals. Common phrases heard in the Warren Guild are "friar's poke," which means something is good (such as it being a valuable deal or a positive outcome), and "looks like pudding," which is code for impending conflict or combat. However, if a stranger passes through and talks about Zlokin, they are likely to be ambushed. It is rare for the Warren Guild to openly reference their secrets, so such a public misstep would be considered an attack and handled appropriately.

Vinzlo and Freigyrdawn (a rising leader among the dwarves and member of the Freeholders, whose interests are not currently clear) are old friends and meet weekly at the Silver Crown to discuss their goals and how they can aid one another. Freigyrdawn uses his connections to both ensure the kobolds stay supplied from the surface and to assist in the trade of the kobolds' unique crafted items.

SILVER CROWN TAVERN

The Silver Crown Tavern boasts a notorious reputation in the Undercity as the source of shady deals and even shadier patrons. The alliance between the Warren Guild and the dwarven Freeholders is not the only political intrigue in the Undercity, but if the barkeeps at the Silver Crown Tavern are approached by someone who means the Warren Guild or the Freeholders harm, they will more likely be served poison instead of ale.

The close relationship between the kobolds and Spire Dwell, the proprietor of the Silver Crown, means the tavern's kitchens have crafted a specialty pudding recipe after years of experimenting. Beloved by the Warren Guild, the recipe is proudly displayed in a gilded frame behind the bar at the tavern.

Enemies of the Guild

While the kobolds built a great friendship with the dwarves, they also created plenty of enemies to keep them busy. The foes of the Warren Guild come from all areas: surface and subterranean, flesh and fey.

- The greatest threats to the kobolds are the humans on the surface of Melana. Specifically, the humans of the vocal Temperance League—a political organization led by Merzlo Regon and her sycophants who espouse "peace" and "community"—secretly plot the demise of the Undercity and its inhabitants. Merzlo Regon is an ally to the leadership of Melana, but her personal agenda is to cause chaos and unrest between the surface and the Undercity. Her greatest ambition is to seal off the opening to the Undercity and forget it ever existed.

- The shadow fey linger throughout Melana and frequent the Undercity to incite conflict. Motivated by their desire to sow chaos, for Zobeck in particular, and to see the mysterious prophecies come to fruition, the shadow fey typically do not attack, nor even show themselves undisguised, but instead orchestrate disaster from a distance and try to secretly insert themselves into society.

- A variety of subterranean creatures threaten the kobolds and their homes.

Pechs (see *Creature Codex*) occasionally dispute territory boundaries and mineral veins with the kobolds and the dwarves. A **corpse worm** (see *Tome of Beasts 2*) lives at the edge of a frontier cavern where the kobolds throw their trash—and where many Undercity criminals throw their victims—and when it has not fed for a while, it attacks kobolds. A nest of **crypt spiders** (see *Creature Codex*) keep the corpse worm company and frequently hunt recently dead bodies or those close to death to bring back to their cavern.

The King's Prophecy

The often seemingly prophetic insights of Relvina seem to be more and more relevant over time. Many dwarves continue to look to them for guidance. A mining crew recently uncovered a bundle of previously unknown fragments, and dwarven scholars vigorously debate the countless interpretations:

- *"Friendship is sweet, but Valor is divine."* Some consider this to support a divine right to Seppo Voller's leadership, and it stokes the monarchists' zeal. His detractors, however, still contend he is merely self-interested and exploiting his family lineage for personal gain.

- *"Trust the daughters for they carry the wisdom of mothers."* Many kobolds and dwarves believe this passage speaks to capabilities and responsibilities of their daughters and they are prepared to make it reality.

- *"The gifts from the lizard people will bring peace to our land."* The use of the word *gifts* causes some turmoil between the kobolds and the dwarves. The dwarves interpret it as a metaphor for skill and labor, but the kobolds interpret it as literal presents. So many kobolds focus on creating gifts, from folded paper dragons to bundles of reeds painted with the blood of enemies.

BLUE HOUSE, RED TIDES

by Adam W. Roy

The Blue House is a largely unassuming compound—though with cold-iron-barred windows and walls of striking robin's-egg blue—found just down the hill from Zobeck's mighty Citadel (in the Citadel District). Surrounded by a high wall, gated, and guarded by "plainclothes" guards, it is perhaps the most important building in Zobeck, after only the Citadel and the Arcane Collegium, for it is here that Lady Fenyll Marack, scion to one of the oldest and wealthiest families in Zobeck, holds sway as Zobeck's spymaster and head of the city's "secret service," whose operatives are respected and feared within the Free City and without.

The striking "bluewash" of the buildings is said to be part of a complicated Collegium matrix of permanent spells that protect it and its occupants from all forms of scrying and clairvoyance and prevents ingress or egress by any magical means (such as by *dimension door* or *teleport* spells or otherwise from the Astral or Ethereal Planes) without Lady Fenyll's express permission . . . and the use of her *key scepter.*

The few that have been inside the Blue House (and are able and willing to talk about it) claim that it is a luxurious manse above, as befits Lady Fenyll's status and nearly uncountable wealth, but below there is a vast catacomb of reclaimed kobold tunnels that run underneath Citadel Hill and connect to no other kobold warrens underneath the Free City. The dungeons are said to contain numerous cells, "interrogation" rooms, and the magically warded vaults that contain vast magical and monetary treasures. It is said when troublesome adventurers are arrested in the city, they are often brought here, where the lady or one of her agents makes said party an "offer they can't refuse," such as spying on Morgau, as an alternative to torture and execution. Some rumors also tell of secret, magically trapped tunnels that run to secret entrances and exits in the Citadel, the Arcane Collegium, and even outside the walls of the city to the edge of the Margreve Forest—all of which are keyed to her magic scepter.

Within Zobeck

Though she does not officially sit on the Free City Council, she does have tremendous influence as a "shadow consul," especially through her sister, Consul Lady Wintesla Marack, and Consul-General Jorun Haclav, Captain of the Hussars. She respects and admires the wisdom and patience of the First Consul Ondli Firedrake, the worldly dwarven sage and priest. She often consults him for advice on dealing with the Ironcrag Cantons or for access to oracles of his goddess, Rava, Mistress of Fates.

It is said she was pivotal in the election of the current mayor, the dwarven merchant Constantia Olleck. Working behind the scenes, Lady Fenyll is a known proponent of the mayor, for they are both wise, widowed, and wealthy merchant women. They both fear and plan for the rise of banditry outside of the city walls, the expanding borders of the Greater Duchy of Morgau in the northwest, and the incursions of the Dragon Empire into the Seven Cities to the south.

The rest of the consuls, it is said, she has leaned on or bribed with gold and magical gifts to help her with her diplomacy and spying with the allies and enemies of the Free City. Guildmaster Selena Harbeck feeds her information about the productivity and mood of the city and its citizens via her guildhalls and guildmasters, so Lady Fenyll always has her finger on the pulse of the city and its citizens.

Myzi the First, the Mouse King and Lord of the Undercity, she has simply bought outright with bribes of gold and gems (and the occasional magic scroll or weapon from her vaults), so she can keep tabs on the Underbelly of the Free City and its unwholesome elements, many of whom she recruits or extorts into joining some of her more distasteful and dangerous missions abroad. She is also free with "gratuities" of gems and gold to the two kobold consuls, Kekolina and Quetelmak, to stay informed on doings in the Free City's kobold warrens and smithies. Lady Fenyll has also been known to do favors for the Bard-Consul Melancha Vendemic to make sure honeyed words are dripped into the right ears. The consul has proven effective in stressing the threat posed by the Dragon Empire to the Free City.

She distrusts Consuls Streck and Orlando from the Collegium but finds uses for some of their students in creating magic items she needs to stay informed and to keep the Free City safe. She is actively working to find a recruit among the students to elect as a replacement for the love-blinded and retiring Orlando and openly mistrusts his lover Aldona, suspecting her to be an agent of Morgau or Demon Mountain.

Her most public anger, however, is reserved for a recently retired member of the Free City Council: Lord Volstaff Greymark. Greymark's

family wealth is one of the few to rival that of the Marack sisters and grows daily with his new trade with Prince Lucan of Morgau. The Marack sisters have denounced the House of Greymark's trade with Morgau, saying he is aiding and abetting a threat to the Free City. It is also possible she is playing a deeper game, that he is her double agent, using his trade with Morgau to spy on the prince and Morgau's plans for further conquest, enslaving the Free City and its strategic crossroads. Or is he a triple agent, playing both sides for his own benefit. As the reaver dwarves say, "Only time and blood will tell."

Outside the City Walls

With undead and dragon armies encroaching ever closer to the Free City's stout walls, Lady Fenyll seeks to shore up and create strong alliances of mutual aid and military might with other neighbors that are equally threatened by the agents and armies of the Vampire Prince and the Dragon Sultan.

The strongest military allies to the Free City so far are Perunalia and the Kingdom of Magdar. The three realms recently formally renewed their century-old alliance of mutual aid and military assistance in the event that any of the three realms is threatened by invasion. At a grand ceremony held in the Royal Konytari of Perunalia, the Three Free Realms signed new and broadened treaties of aid: Lady Wintesla, Lady Vendemic, and Mayor Constantia signing of behalf of Zobeck; Duchess Baretta, daughter of the Widowed Magdar Queen, signing on behalf of the Magdar Kingdom; and Her Divine Transcendence, the Demigoddess Duchess Vasilka Soulay, signing on behalf of the duchy. Some watchers reported that Lady Fenyll met quietly and privately with the duchess after the ceremonies, reportedly to seek further assurances of aid from her divine siblings in time of need, even perhaps the favor of her father, the storm god Perun. Since that covert meeting, Lady Fenyll has sent Zobeck agents to reclaim Thunder's Seat, to see if arcane agents could do what the Order of White Lions could not: clear the undead and deadly hauntings from the strategic Perunalian fortress.

After these two primary allies, Lady Fenyll and her agents probably spend the most time treating with the fractious Free Cantons of the Ironcrags to varying degrees of success. The dwarven clans are not particularly known for taking on risky military ventures, but Lady Fenyll and her numerous envoys (with the help of Mayor Constantia and First Consul Ondli) have made a number of bilateral strategic trade deals with several of the cantons. Guaranteeing to keep the Free City well supplied with coal, wood, black powder, cannons, and ammunition in exchange for gold, trade, and clockwork artifacts, these treaties have emergency clauses to increase the level of military supplies significantly in times of war. Lady Fenyll has negotiated such treaties with Bundhausen and Lower Nordmansch (timber and coal), Kubourg (black powder weapons), Hammerfell (metal armor, cannons, and siege weapons), and St. Mishau (adamantine, black powder, and alchemical supplies). Bareicks and Juralt have agreed to send war wagons and mercenaries to join the effort, being the only two cantons bloodthirsty and greedy enough to commit actual troops to the defense of Zobeck. She has also negotiated the first order of armored airships and lift gas for Zobeck from the Templeforge of Favgia Baselgia for a display of military airpower, intended to reinforce the famed Griffon Riders of Zobeck—and perhaps eventually replace them—as the number of riders and mounts seem to dwindle every year.

Lady Fenyll and her allies do not rest their hopes of survival on their nearest neighbors alone however. She has sent envoys (and spies) to any number of powers and potentates near and far: the Kariv, the centaur tribes, the Khazzaki and Vidim, even the Magocracy of Allain. She has sent representatives as far west as Dornig and Barsella, north to the Wolfmark,

Huldramose, Björnrike, and Nordheim, and as far south as Nuria Natal and the Dominion of the Wind Lords. She has sent ambassadors and agents to the hut of Baba Yaga, to the fey courts, to the Shadow Realms, and even to Niemheim and the Master of Demon Mountain with notably fewer (and deadlier) results. Few of these representatives return, at least not in one piece. Hence her recruiting from "disposable" ne'er-do-wells in her dungeons under the Blue House.

She taps the same dark "wells" for spies and agent provocateurs to send into the Dragon Empire and the dark realms of Morgau. Recruiting agents for these missions is particularly difficult, given the non-human (and non-living) inhabitants of those kingdoms. She has had some success however: kobold "traders" moving about Rumela and deeper into the Empire, reporting on war preparedness (or the lack thereof); werefolk "mercenaries" that embed themselves in Morgau's dark armies and hierarchies; even a Nurian mummy theurge that has ingratiated herself into Prince Lucan's inner circle. This immortal spy keeps the Blue House well informed on Morgau troop movements and military preparations, though Lucan has recently begun to mistrust her interest in military matters over the arcane. As far as active military and sabotage missions go, she has managed to insert a tiny cadre of suicidal saboteurs into the province of Mezar in the Dragon Empire where they have had some small but surprisingly effective successes: collapsing minor keeps and dragon lairs, ambushing military convoys, and even closing a major military road through a small mountain pass by crashing a large avalanche into it. Made up of zealous minotaur saboteurs and crazed Zobecker kobold sappers, they call themselves the Dusty Dozen.

Magic of the Blue House Vaults

The Blue House has raised the magic of spycraft to an artform.

AMULET OF INSIGHT

Wonderous Item, Rare (Requires Attunement)

These large, round amulets bear the solar-disk symbol of Khors, the sun god. Most of the known amulets are platinum, hung on silver neck chains, and set with nine lapis lazuli and epidote gemstones around the edges. You gain advantage on all Wisdom (Insight) checks. Additionally, all Wisdom (Insight) checks made against you are made with disadvantage.

If nine successful Wisdom (Insight) checks are made against you between two long rests, the stones turn grey, and the amulet becomes inert and nonmagical.

GIFT OF THE GOLDEN TONGUE

2nd-Level Enchantment
(Bard, Sorcerer, Warlock, Wizard)

Casting Time: 1 action
Range: Touch
Components: V, S
Duration: 1 hour

You touch a willing humanoid, and for the duration, the target has advantage on all Charisma checks. Additionally, any Charisma checks made against the target have disadvantage.

At Higher Levels. If you cast this spell using a spell slot of 3rd level or higher, you can either target one additional creature or increase the duration of the spell by 1 hour for each slot level above 2nd.

NOTHING TO SEE HERE

1st-Level Enchantment
  (Bard, Sorcerer, Warlock, Wizard)

Casting Time: 1 action
Range: Touch
Components: S
Duration: 1 hour

Creatures relying on eyesight and with a Wisdom score of 11 or less ignore the target as if they were not there—unless directly attacked or addressed by the target. Creatures relying on eyesight and with a Wisdom score of 12 or higher can make a Wisdom saving throw to pierce the illusion and see the target of the spell. Blindsight and tremorsense work normally.

At Higher Levels. If you cast this spell using a spell slot of 2nd level or higher, you can either target one additional creature or increase the duration of the spell by 1 hour for each slot level above 1st.

PERCIPIENT PEARL EARRINGS

Wonderous Item, Rare (Requires Attunement)

While wearing these pearl-drop earrings, you have advantage on all Wisdom (Perception) checks involving sound. Additionally, when within the area of effect of a *silence* spell, you can still cast spells with a verbal component and can choose to ignore the deafening effect of the spell.

Once per long rest, you can also perform each of the following magical effects:

- Listen to any conversation within 500 feet with perfect clarity and fidelity by pressing both pearls with two fingers.

- Record 1 minute of a nearby conversation by pressing the left earring with two fingers as a bonus action. The conversation can be played back for up to 24 hours by pressing the right earring with two fingers. You decide if only you can hear the recording or if it can be heard by anyone within 10 feet.

Both effects can be activated at the same time, if desired.

RAGGED SHROUD

Wonderous Item, Uncommon (Requires Attunement)

These ragged grey cloaks are death shrouds taken from actual tombs and enchanted to hide a living humanoid creature from the notice of the undead. All undead with a Wisdom score of 11 or lower consider you as undead and ignore you unless directly attacked or addressed by you. Any undead with a Wisdom score of 12 or higher can make a DC 15 Wisdom (Perception) check to see through the illusion. (If you are in sunlight, the undead rolls with advantage.)

The shroud becomes non-magical and quickly crumbles to dust 24 hours after it is first worn or if it is exposed to sunlight for more than an hour.

RINGS OF EMBASSY

Wonderous Item, Rare (Requires Attunement)

These rings are always found in pairs. They are pewter bands, smooth on the outer surface, and on the inside surface, the runes for *voice* and *distance* are engraved. You can use an action to cast a *sending* spell. The target is the attuned wearer of the other ring. The message can be up to fifty words and does not need to be said aloud. You can sense if there is no attuned wearer for the matching ring. There is no chance of message failure, even if the other ring wearer is on another plane. The *sending* spell can only be used once per short rest. If one of the rings is destroyed, the other becomes inert and nonmagical.

SLIPPERS OF SUBTLETY

Wonderous Item, Rare (Requires Attunement)

While wearing these spider-silk slippers, you make no sound, regardless of the surface trod upon. You make Dexterity (Stealth) checks with advantage. Additionally, three uses of the following abilities, in any combination, can be made per long rest:

- Ignore difficult terrain for up to a minute.
- Cast one of the following spells: *jump, pass without trace, spider climb.*

STEAL MEMORIES

4th-level Enchantment (Bard, Sorcerer, Warlock, Wizard)

Casting Time: 1 action
Range: 60 feet
Components: V, S
Duration: Instantaneous

You attempt to steal another creature's memories. One creature that you can see must make a Wisdom saving throw. If you are fighting the creature, it has advantage on the saving throw. On a failed save, you steal their memories. (If the target succeeds their save by 5 or more, they realize that someone tried to access their memories. If they succeed by 10 or more, they have a mental picture of the caster and are immune to further attempts for 24 hours.)

You state the type of memory you are looking to steal, such as "the assassination of the arch-duke" or "the password of the day for entrance to the thieves' guild hideout." If the memory does not exist in the mind of the target, the spell fails. If the memory is there, the GM describes exactly what memory is transferred. Any memories include sensations for all senses. The memory returns to the target in 24 hours without them being any wiser.

At Higher Levels. If you cast this spell using a spell slot of 5th level or higher, you can target one additional creature or one additional memory for each slot level above 4th.

CHITTERINGS OF THE RAT CULT

by Wolfgang Baur

For long centuries, the least of all the demon cults has been in the cities, where a morsel of food laid at a half-neglected shrine of the rat cult of Chittr'k'k (pronounced CHIT-er-ek-ek) often brings some boon. Indeed, the small glint of greenish fire that indicates a sacrifice has been accepted is one of the ways that the cult itself recognizes the presence of its demonic patron, and such light is often mimicked by its adherents in their rituals and secret countersigns.

In Zobeck, the cult occasionally appears on the docks but far more often in the cartways and crypts of the undercity. The cult is often pursued and extinguished in one or another city along the River Argent, from Zobeck all the way to its mouth at the Ruby Sea, but as soon as it is wiped out, another brother or sister of the rat is sent to reestablish contact.

Chittr'k'k Cult Goals

The cult of Chittr'k'k has rather simple goals: eat, breed more rats, summon avatars of their lord. At the same time, its demonic master revels in fouling and destroying the goods and foodstuff of others. Indeed, the scouting of food and despoiling of grain, beans, and other nourishment is a common practice of both rats and Chittr'k'k's followers.

However, the goal of summoning more rats is an even more compelling urge, either through feeding and breeding normal rats, through magical summoning (see below), or through the use of magical idols.

IDOLS OF THE RAT LORD

The cult carves and maintains small statues of Chittr'k'k, which it places in small niches or under eaves or in culverts, as impromptu shrines to the Rat Lord. Some are even found on ships, hidden in bilgewater or a ballast hold. They are usually of carved wood, showing the bright teeth and sometimes the fiery green tail of the demon lord, and its small, clawed hands are typically open enough to hold a small object. The cult values the oldest of these statues highly, treating them as divine or saintly relics, often with particular names, like Old Buck, Nabby Tooth, or Whisker Prince. They will strive to recover any of these believed lost or taken by their foes.

As objects of veneration, believers and others seeking some small blessing leave bits of hair, meat, candles, and even bread or blood offerings at the statue, either smeared on its mouth or placed into its claws. Cat fur and cat paws are popular sacrifices. In return, Chittr'k'k sometimes dispenses a minor boon.

These boons never involve true healing or the mending of broken objects or broken hearts, as with more benevolent godlings. Indeed, Chittr'k'k's power is very weak and diffuse in all the cities and ships where he has followers,

but it is strong enough to provide at least the illusion of warmth, comfort, wakefulness, and the like. In most such cases, the boon provides no actual warmth, sleep, or nourishment, but the illusion of comfort is very distinct and pleasing in the moment.

A priest or paladin of Chittr'k'k need not roll for the effect but gains the one desired.

When an idol has granted sufficient boons, it has also acquired divine power, which the cult's priests and preachers use to summon hordes of rats, to contact Chittr'k'k himself, to summon a **rattok** (see *Creature Codex*) servant of Chittr'k'k, or (in the case of truly ancient idols, brimming with divine power) even an avatar of the demon lord (see also **Chittr'k'k** in *Creature Codex*). The details of this level of summoning are best left to the GM but typically involve a ritual sacrifice or the destruction of a trove of food or magic.

d12	RESULT
1	No effect.
2	*Rat's Eye*. A sense of wakeful alertness, as after a short rest.
3	*Stolen Meal*. A sense of fullness, as after a good meal.
4	*Demonic Word*. Adds 1d4 to one ability check within the next hour.
5	*Scathing Insult*. An enemy of Chittr'k'k suffers disadvantage on their next roll within the next hour.
6	*Rat Gossip*. You can pass a message to a friend of the cult within 120 feet within 1 minute.
7	*Hand of the Rat Lord*. Adds 1d4 to the believer's next saving throw roll within 1 hour.
8	*Darkness Creeps In*. One normal candle or lantern is extinguished.
9	*Soul Fire Touch*. The believer loses 1 hp and adds 1d4 necrotic damage to their next damage roll within 1 hour. (The believer must still attack normally, though magical attacks are also strengthened.) This appears as a flash of green fire.
10	*Rat's Path*. You slip beneath a door or through bars normally too small for you.
11	*Rat's Paw*. An object you desire (less than 1 pound in weight), floats from a high place to the floor.
12	*Glory to the Chittering Horde*. A *bless* spell graces all the followers of Chittr'k'k within 200 feet.

DESTRUCTION AND LOSS

While the cult often pretends to help people, its goals as a group are starvation for humanoids and the rise of ratfolk everywhere (see also *Midgard Heroes Handbook* for more on ratfolk). They are most active in cities, abandoned villages, wastelands, and other regions where rats can thrive in the absence of humanoid extermination. They are sometimes aligned with other forces of destruction, such as goblin tribes, gnolls, or dragons of the Mharoti Empire who use them as spies and saboteurs to weaken a place before they send in valuable dragonborn troops.

The **Rat Sabotage** table shows a number of different targets for the rat cult to attack and typical strategies.

Cult Leaders & Followers

Priests of the rat cult are few, though devotees and followers (even relatively indifferent followers) are common enough. Farmers leave an offering to keep rats off the threshing room floor, millers sprinkle flour at a shrine to avoid rats in the meal-bins and grain sacks, and even sailors often leave bits of bread or cheese out to avoid having their mooring lines and sails gnawed and spoiled.

Those priests who do follow Chittr'k'k are often pantheist priests (see *Midgard Heroes Handbook* for more on pantheist priests). They have access to the Vermin domain (see *Southlands Player's Guide*) or the Darkness domain (see *Deep Magic*).

In addition, the rat cult is widespread among beggars, ratfolk, sewer dwellers, kobold rogues, smugglers, and others. Dock workers, stevedores, bargefolk, and sailors are all at least familiar with it, though most are wise enough to distrust its claims.

THE RABBLE OF RATS

The best-known leader of the rat cult in recent years is a human rogue named Marienga "Mischief" Slodna (LE human **bandit lord**, see *Tome of Beasts*), a very young and extremely clever leader of ratfolk, humans, and a few rattok demons. Raven-haired Marienga often presents herself as a fortuneteller, bard, or

RAT SABOTAGE

d12	RESULT
1	Puncturing barrels or wineskins to spill the contents.
2	Eating the choicest stored food and defecating on the rest.
3	Gnawing through mooring lines or ship's rigging.
4	Removing caulk and sealant from a barge or ship's hull.
5	Devouring all the fruit in an orchard overnight.
6	Digging tunnels to undermine a statue, standing stone, or waymark.
7	Stripping an aristocrat's kitchen bare overnight.
8	Opening pens full of small animals, such as chickens or rabbits.
9	Fouling an altar or holy stone circle with blood and feces.
10	Destroying a hut by chewing through one of its load-bearing beams.
11	Chewing through fine clothes, making them rags.
12	Tipping over lanterns or candles to start fires.

druid, but her green eyes shine brightest when she is up to thievery and mischief. Some believe she is a devil or imp in human form, and she certainly delights in tormenting the weak and the powerful alike.

The Rabble of Rats is her nomadic and devoted crew, spreading the word of Chittr'k'k up and down rivers, along navigable coasts, and in graveyards and undercities. They spend their days thieving small valuables, spoiling harvests, cutting mooring ropes at midnight, and stealing livestock—just enough to bring to a farmer's market early in the morning, selling them to some unwitting buyer as if they were Marienga's own flock or herd.

Working with Marienga to spread the word of Chittr'k'k is Brother Peal Tkonnar (NE ratfolk **druid**) who often calls groups of rats to some place as a distraction (such as in a market) while the rest of the gang makes off with valuables elsewhere. He is usually able to scrabble down into sewers or through narrow windows to escape pursuit, and on the rare occasions when he is imprisoned, he always seems to find his way out by dawn.

THE CHITTER SISTERS

Lesser followers of the cult are twin sisters, Yelash and Yelanna, both **vampire spawn** with an innate ability to cast *conjure rats* (see below) once per day. The sisters call home crypts and catacombs, prone to moving their resting chambers twice per year. They often travel with zombies, necromancers, or other hangers-on and seem especially fond of traveling by boat.

RAT PROPHETS

The cult of the rat lord believes that some living rats and some statues of Chittr'k'k are endowed with the gift of prophecy, foretelling storms, harvests, deaths, and the arrival of ratcatchers and trappers. These "true-speaking rats" are beloved and coddled members of any such cult, fed the choicest treats and generally pampered in exchange for their insight. While some non-believers claim these are frauds perpetrated through ventriloquism and cantrips, the cult itself does often seem to enjoy early warning of shipwrecks, poisoned bait, enormous storms, and failed harvests.

The sisters claim to be seeking a holy relic, the *Teeth of Old Naga-Nar*, which once belonged to a **wererat** saint. On his death, the saint's teeth transmuted into divinely blessed (or demonically tainted) objects of worship, but they were given to each of his many disciples, weakening their power. Some believe that Yelash and Yelanna themselves are the grandchildren or great grandchildren of Naga-Nar.

Cult Magic Items

The cult of the rat lord tends to be destructive rather than creative, but occasionally it fashions statues of its god or makes weapons and objects of veneration. The cultists are particularly fond of vile potions, a magical whip called the *rat's tail*, and the *Teeth of Old Naga-Nar*.

LOTION OF PURE FILTH

Potion, Common

Frequently used by toshers (sewer-dwellers who seek discarded valuables in the undercity), the *lotion of pure filth* covers the user in a sticky coat that resembles mud or grease. This layer prevents contact with any of the filth or debris in a sewer, swamp, or dungeon, rendering the user immune to contact poisons, disease spread by touch, and even sticky spiderwebs—all such things slide off the layer of protective filth for 4 hours or until scrubbed away with clean water.

POTION OF PERSISTENCE

Potion, Rare

When you drink this potion, you gain immunity to one type of damage for 1 minute. The GM chooses the type or determines it randomly from the options below.

d10	DAMAGE TYPE	d10	DAMAGE TYPE
1	Acid	6	Piercing
2	Bludgeoning	7	Poison
3	Cold	8	Psychic
4	Lightning	9	Slashing
5	Necrotic	10	Thunder

POTION OF REGURGITATION

Potion, Uncommon

When you drink this potion, you can use your action to devour any object you hold, weighing up to 2 pounds. This object remains within an extradimensional space until any time up to 1 hour later, when you can use a bonus action to vomit it back up. If you vomit an item back up before 1 hour has elapsed, you can use the effect again on the same object or any other item you hold of up to 2 pounds. You automatically regurgitate any swallowed item once the hour is up.

RAT'S TAIL

Weapon (Whip), Very Rare
 (Requires Attunement)

This magical whip resembles the fleshy tail of a full-grown rat. You gain a +2 bonus to attack and damage rolls made with this magic weapon. On a hit, the whip wraps itself neatly around a creature's throat. For living, breathing creatures, this immediately engages suffocation. The creature is also restrained and takes 1d8 psychic damage per round while suffocating. (Constructs, undead, plants, and creatures of size Large or greater are unaffected). On its turn, the target can make a DC 15 Strength check to cut or remove the whip, ending all effects.

TEETH OF OLD NAGA-NAR

Wondrous Item, Artifact
 (Requires Attunement)

A normal rat has four incisors, the teeth used for gnawing. A normal wererat has eight incisors. Saint Naga-Nar was a completely obsessed zealot of Chittr'k'k, and the stories claim he had twelve incisors, all of which became holy items on his death. Each such tooth grants its bearer the ability to cast *gnaw* (see below) once per day. Anyone carrying two or more teeth can also cast *conjure rats* (see below) once per day. Anyone with a necklace of four or more of his teeth can also cast *Chittr'k'k's soul fire* or *spoil food and water* (see below for both) once per day.

Cult Magic

The cult of Chittr'k'k has a number of low-level spells known to its followers, which are not widely found outside those circles. These are described below.

CHITTRK'K'S SOUL FIRE

2nd-Level Illusion (Bard, Sorcerer, Warlock, Wizard)
Range: 60 feet
Casting Time: 1 action
Duration: Up to 1 minute (concentration)
Components: S, M (a stick of charcoal or a chip of moonstone worth 5 gp)

You summon a bit of greenish fire to the top of your head, into one hand, or at the tip of your tail. It flares brightly, and all creatures that see your soul fire must make a Wisdom saving throw. On a failed save, the creature becomes charmed for the duration. While charmed by this spell, the creature seeks to follow the light, even into areas of bright light or darkness or into shallow water. The spell ends for an affected creature if it takes any damage or if someone else uses an action to shake the creature out of its stupor.

CONJURE RATS

1st-Level Conjuration (cleric, druid)
Range: 60 feet
Casting Time: 1 action
Duration: Up to 1 hour (concentration)
Components: V, S

You summon rats or ratfolk that appear in unoccupied spaces that you can see within range. Choose one of the following options for what appears:

- One mildly hostile **wererat** (CR 2), which does not obey your verbal commands but might defend itself.
- One **ratfolk rogue** (see *Tome of Beasts*) (CR 1).
- Four **swarms of rats** or four **ratfolk** (see *Tome of Beasts*) (CR 1/4).

- Eight **giant rats** (CR 1/8).
- Sixteen normal **rats** (CR 0).

Each rat disappears when it drops to 0 hit points or when the spell ends. The summoned rats are friendly to you and your companions. Roll initiative for the summoned rats as a group, which has its own turns. They obey any verbal commands that you issue to them (no action required by you), except the wererat. If you don't issue any commands, they defend themselves from hostile creatures but otherwise take no actions. The GM has the creatures' statistics.

At Higher Levels. When you cast this spell using higher-level spell slots, you can choose one of the summoning options above, and more creatures appear: one additional creature with a 2nd-level slot or three additional creatures with a 4th-level slot and any summoned wererats obey verbal commands.

GNAW

Cantrip (Cleric, Druid)
Range: Touch
Casting Time: 1 action
Components: V, S, M (a rat's tooth)

You touch a piece of wood, rope, cloth, thatch, or other organic material, and a hole appears through it up to 3 inches long and 1 inch in diameter, circumscribed with tooth marks as if chewed by rodents or other vermin. You can see through this hole and use line-of-sight spell effects to the other side.

This spell can be used to cut any rope or snap any branch up to 2 inches thick. It has no effect on metal or stone objects.

RAT PLAGUE

3rd-Level Necromancy (Cleric, Druid)
Range: Touch
Casting Time: 1 action
Duration: 3 days
Components: V, S

Your touch inflicts disease. Make a melee spell attack against a creature within reach. On a hit, you afflict the creature with one of two possible rat plagues, described below. At the end of each of the target's turns, it must make a Constitution saving throw. After failing three of these saving throws, the disease's effects last for the duration, and the creature stops making these saves. After succeeding on three of these saving throws, the creature recovers from the disease, and the spell ends. Since this spell induces a natural disease in its target, any effect that removes a disease or otherwise ameliorates a disease's effects apply to it.

Rat Fever. A creeping horror of rats, ratfolk, wererats, and all other rat-like creatures enters the creature's mind, and it fears contact with rats and is terrified of crowds. The creature is frightened for the duration.

Rat Shakes. Violent shivers convulse the creature's limbs, its speed is halved, and it cannot use the Dash action. After making any melee or spell attack, the creature falls prone.

SPOIL FOOD AND WATER

3rd-Level Conjuration (Cleric, Druid)
Range: 30 feet
Casting Time: 1 action
Duration: Instantaneous
Components: V, S

You spoil 45 pounds of food, grain, or seeds and 30 gallons of water, ale, or other potable drinks on the ground or in containers within range, normally enough to sustain up to fifteen humanoids or five steeds for 24 hours. The food becomes moldy, rotten, vermin-infested, or liquified. The water is filthy and foul-smelling, and any creature consuming either the food or the beverage is ill for the next 24 hours, moving at half speed and with disadvantage on all ability checks and saving throws.

At Higher Levels. If cast at 4th level, you spoil up to 150 pounds of food and 100 gallons of beverage. If cast at 5th level, you spoil up to 500 pounds of food and 300 gallons of beverage.

CAVEAT EMPTOR: ODD VENDORS OF THE CITY'S UNDERBELLY

by Kelly Pawlik

It has been said many times that anything can be found in the Cartways. This warren of tunnels runs the length and breadth beneath Zobeck, serving as a dark mirror to the tangled streets of the city above. While use of the Cartways is officially prohibited by the city watch, the tunnels remain active, particularly below the Dock District, where criminals, charlatans, thrill-seekers, and desperate people of all types rub shoulders as they search for goods and services that are impossible to find in the sunlit streets above.

The Black Market

The Black Market runs on both sides of a wide tunnel with the most prominent merchants, including the Imperial Slave Block, situated between the thick stone pillars running at regular intervals down the center of the tunnel. Merchants come and go. Some appear for only one night and are never seen afterward while others appear for a day or two before disappearing, only to return weeks or months later for another day or two.

In the Black Market, the susurrus of voices is occasionally broken by an argument or a scream. Newcomers flinch at each outburst while regular visitors to the market are wise to its ways and keep to themselves. Opportunistic eyes peer out from every shadow, and it is a rare week indeed when some unfortunate newcomer to the Black Market doesn't end up on the slave block or in someone's belly. Cartways vendors expect to dicker over the price of their goods with every potential buyer, and they always open by asking for the highest price they feel they could feasibly receive.

Black Market Vendors

Listed here are some of the stranger merchants of the Black Market, including suggestions for how often they appear and how difficult they are to negotiate prices with.

ANTON'S MENAGERIE

Frequency of Appearance: 1 week every 4 months.

To look at Anton Ladescu (LE **dhampir**, see *Creature Codex*, **mage** who can cast *animal friendship* and *charm person* at will), with his noble air and the manner of dress of a minor aristocrat, you would never think he spends the bulk of his time training animals. Like clockwork, however, Anton and a small coterie of dazed-looking assistants wheel his caged carts into the Black Market every 4 months. Primarily Anton has trained **ravens**, **rats**, **giant rats**, and **wolves** to offer for general sale, though he usually has one or two other trained beasts such as an **owl** or a **brown bear**.

Anton trains his animals hard with a mix of brutal conditioning and magical enchantment, which results in creatures that are completely loyal to their owner. Once they are purchased, Anton teaches their new master the verbal commands and visual cues that they have learned to quickly obey. Beasts are trained to a specific purpose. Those trained to attack on command are not also trained to defend their master or to retrieve items. Trained beasts only respond to the commands of Anton and a single other master, usually the being who purchased it.

In addition to trained beasts, Anton sells his services as an animal trainer for an exorbitant fee. Despite the cost, it is rare for him to leave the Black Market without having contracted to train one or two beasts. Those who spend the gold for such a service often have him train more exotic creatures than mere animals, such as **owlbears**, **griffons**, and **death dogs**. Anton cannot train creatures that lack the raw intellect to learn beyond responding to their natural instincts. Creatures with an Intelligence of 1 cannot be trained.

Pricing: Price depends both on the type of beast and the type of training it has received. Common training and examples of animals that have received it are listed here:

- *Attack*. As an action, the creature's master can issue a verbal command to attack a creature within range of its movement. Once the trained animal has attacked a creature on command, its master can use a bonus action to command it to continue attacking the same creature on subsequent rounds. If the trained beast has been ordered to attack, it does not defend itself even if attacked by another creature. Example attack beasts and their costs:
brown bear 4,000 gp, **giant badger** 1,200 gp, **giant rat** 700 gp, **mastiff** 900 gp, **wolf** 1,500 gp.

- *Defend*. This creature's master can use their reaction to order the beast to make a melee attack against a creature that is standing within 5 feet of it and that has attacked its master. This creature defends itself when necessary but doesn't willingly move more than 5 feet from its master. Example defense beasts and their costs: **brown bear** 3,000 gp, **mastiff** 700 gp, **wolf** 1,100 gp.

- *Deliver Message*. This beast has been trained to deliver messages or goods to specific locations. Once the message

has been delivered, it returns to its master's home. A beast so trained can know a number of delivery locations equal to double its Intelligence. It takes 1 week to train the beast to recognize a location. Rats and giant rats are popular choices for messenger beasts since they can get messages and contraband to difficult-to-reach locations. Example messenger beasts and their costs: **cat** 300 gp, **giant rat** 700 gp, **hawk** 1,000 gp, **rat** 300 gp.

- *Steal Item*. This beast has been trained to enter a location, identify the most valuable item it can carry, and take that item to its master. The creatures are trained to take jewelry and gemstones before other items. This creature has proficiency with Dexterity (Sleight of Hand and Stealth) checks. Its proficiency bonus is +2. Example **robber beasts** and their costs: cat 1,000 gp, **giant rat** 1,500 gp, **rat** 800 gp, **raven** 2,200 gp, **weasel** 1,000 gp.

Beast Training: Anton will train a creature for a cost of 100 gp per day. A creature with an Intelligence of 2 requires 3 weeks of training for each task Anton trains it to do. A creature with an Intelligence of 3 requires 2 weeks of training for each task. A creature with an Intelligence of 4 or higher requires 1 week of training per task.

Haggling DC: If a character succeeds on a DC 20 Charisma (Persuasion) check, Anton will reduce the price of his trained animals by 10 percent. If he is requested to train a creature for more than one task, he reduces his rate to 80 gp per day.

MERRY SISTERS' MEAT MARKET

Frequency of Appearance: Permanent location.

Hester Umbrecht (NE human **noble**) and Glynnphidea Gerhardt (CE gnome **cult fanatic**) operate this tidy, colorful tent from which they sell neatly butchered and artfully arranged cuts of humanoid meat. Their wares are arrayed on ice Glynnphidea magically creates inside a trio of small carts that have been brightly painted in primary colors. A fourth cart holds uniced cuts of meat for buyers who prefer their meat aged naturally. Tidy signs display the type of meat being offered, and the date it was butchered. Residents of Zobeck above would be disturbed at how brisk business tends to be at the sisters' macabre stall.

A tent, also bright blue, yellow, and red, has been erected behind the carts. Inside, Hester expertly butchers corpses on a long stone table. Blood and other fluids flow in runnels along the edge of the table and then drain into a wooden pail. Hester takes pride in the quality of her work and in being able to skin, gut, joint, and filet a Medium humanoid in under 10 minutes. She enjoys her job and has no qualms about slaughtering those that end up on her slab while still alive, regardless of their age, race, gender, or social status. There is little waste produced by the enterprise as organs and blood are ground, spiced, and made into sausages or pate, and bones are ground into meal.

Glynnphidea hawks her cart's wares like a sideshow huckster, extolling their quality and freshness, or lack thereof if some cuts have been lingering on display for a time. She takes care of procuring bodies to butcher and maintains cordial business relationships with surgeons, morticians, gravediggers, and the leaders of criminal gangs in the city above. She also has an arrangement with Dobricar, the captain of the Imperial Slave Blocks. When he has slaves that aren't selling, he passes them to the sisters who slaughter and butcher them, keeping 30 percent of each and passing the remainder back to the darakhul to do with as he will.

Pricing: The sisters charge more for desirable, tender cuts of meat and less for tougher, gristlier ones. Additionally, the price per pound drops by about 2 cp each day it remains on display, though never below 1 cp.

Haggling DC: If a character succeeds on a DC 15 Charisma (Intimidation or Persuasion) check, Glynnphidea will reduce the price by 15 percent per pound.

A rough price range for commonly available meats is as follows: **dwarf** 1 cp to 2 sp per lb., **elf** 1 sp to 5 sp per lb., **dragonborn** 2 sp per lb., **gnome** 3 sp to 1 gp per lb., **goblin** 1 cp per lb., **halfling** 5 sp to 2 gp per lb., **human** 3 cp to 1 sp per lb., **kobold** 1 cp to 8 cp per lb., **shadow fey** 3 sp to 2 gp per lb., **troll** 1 cp per lb. (A startling number of trolls donate portions of their flesh for coin, secure in the knowledge it will regenerate.)

PETRA THE MASK-MAKER

Frequency of Appearance: On the fifteenth day of each month.

For one day each month, an extravagant sign proclaims the presence of Petra the Mask-Maker. The sign further advises patrons to place 100 gp in the dish to gain entry. Other than the sign and a wooden bowl sitting in the air at a height of 3 feet above the ground, there is no sign of a stall, shop, or any other occupation. When a creature places 100 gp in the dish, the money disappears, and an unsupported wooden door gilded in silver and gold appears and swings open in the space before them.

A patron entering the doorway appears in a richly appointed sitting room with two comfortable chairs sitting on a thick woolen rug. A table holding a full glass of wine stands next to one of the chairs, and a card on the table exhorts the patron to sit, drink, and relax. In the winter, the wine on the table is mulled, filling the space with the scent of spices, and a fire roars in the hearth. The space can hold multiple patrons at once, but each customer arrives in their own sitting room.

After a short time, Petra, the shop's owner, appears in the sitting room, sits in the opposite chair, and explains that they can remake the customer's appearance to reflect their wishes, within reason. They will also provide documents to match the new identity for an additional fee, if so wished.

Pricing: After the 100 gp to enter the establishment is paid, Petra charges an additional 1,000 gp to transform a patron's appearance. If forged documents are required, they charge an additional 300 gp, and the documents are delivered to the customer at a place of their choosing within 7 days. The forged documents are easily sufficient to pass a casual viewing. A creature that spends 1 minute examining the documents can make a DC 16 Intelligence (Investigation) check to detect their false nature.

Haggle DC: None. Petra does not negotiate with patrons over the price of their services.

PETRA THE MASK-MAKER

Petra is a **doppelganger**, changing the challenge rating to 4 (1,100 XP) and adding the following Spellcasting trait and Transform Humanoid action:

Spellcasting. Petra's spellcasting ability is Charisma. They can cast the following spells, requiring no material components:

At will: *floating disc*

1/day: *magnificent mansion*

Transform Humanoid. As an action, Petra can transform the appearance of a humanoid. They can change the creature's height, weight, facial features, the sound of their voice, hair length and color, and any other distinguishing characteristics. These changes do not alter the target's statistics. The transformation cannot change the target's size or basic shape. Despite any racial traits the target may appear to have after the transformation, it retains its original race. The transformation is permanent once complete. An unwilling creature can make a DC 12 Constitution saving throw to prevent the transformation from occurring.

Customers that refuse to cease haggling after politely being asked to stop are immediately ejected from the sitting room, back to the Black Market.

TEARS TO FORGET

Frequency of Appearance:
The day of the new moon as well as the day preceding and following it.

For years, Xanarla Gloomyn (CE **derro witch queen**, see *Creature Codex*) has unrolled her tattered quilt in the Black Market for 3 days each month. On the frayed patchwork, she piles an array of waxed and stoppered phials, jars, and amphoras in a dizzying array of colors and materials. Each of the containers holds water from the River Lethe that the derro has enchanted to erase specific memories the imbiber wishes to forget. In addition, she sometimes sells other trinkets she's picked up in her travels, which run the gamut from mundane curiosity to minor bits of magic.

A less known service Xanarla offers is the procurement of specific goods from other planes. She makes a tidy sum from magic users and alchemists that desire fiendish organs and ichors, blood of celestials, jars of living shadowstuff, bark from a World Tree, or ratatosk brains.

As a result of imbibing her own draughts, Xanarla has forgotten her clan in favor of satisfying her own whims. For their part, the members of her clan have been seeking their wayward queen for years. When they find her, they will put her to death, so her soul can pass to the next witch queen, and they will no longer be without a leader-servant.

Pricing: Xanarla is happy to accept trade, service, or favors in exchange for her goods. While she seems as scattered and random as other derro, she has a fine memory for faces

and names, and she never lets a favor go unasked for long.

Haggling DC: If a character succeeds on a DC 17 Charisma (Deception or Persuasion) check, Xanarla will reduce her prices by 30 percent. She finds intimidation rather humorous and doesn't respond to it as a form of negotiation.

Example items and their costs: *draught of forgetfulness* (see sidebar), phial 100 gp, *draught of forgetfulness*, jar 500 gp, *draught of forgetfulness*, bottle 1,250 gp, *draught of forgetfulness*, amphora 7,500 gp, nonmagical trinkets 5 gp, magical items of uncommon rarity 250 gp.

Smuggler's Market Vendors

The following stall appears as a regular at the Smuggler's Market, which randomly changes location weekly throughout the Dock District.

JAN'S MOST EXPEDIENT CARRIAGES

Frequency of Appearance: Permanent location.

Jan Wonderdelver (N dwarf **mage** with *teleportation circle* prepared) only recently opened his stall, consisting of a single ornate carriage made of glossy, black-stained mahogany and gilded in silver, in the Smuggler's Market. The interior of the carriage acts as a *teleportation circle* that transports the contents of the carriage, be they goods or people, to an agreed upon destination.

Jan has memorized the sigil sequences for teleportation circles in the following locations: Trombei in the Seven Cities, Savoyne in Verrayne, Bemmea in the Magocracy of Allain, Bad Solitz in the Grand Duchy of Dornig, the Free City of Siwal in the Southlands, and Stannasgard in the Northlands.

Pricing: Jan charges 150 gp for each person that is transported and 20 gp per pound for cargo.

Haggling DC: Jan doesn't haggle over the price, but the lecherous dwarf reduces the fee per person to 100 gp if they are an attractive dwarf or gnome of any gender, though the beneficiary of his largesse has to endure his likely unwanted advances.

DRAUGHT OF FORGETFULNESS

Potion, rare

This liquid is a pure, inky black. When exposed to air, it seems to absorb light, causing the area around it to become slightly dimmed.

At the time you willingly drink this potion, you set the memory of a time firmly in your mind. Within 10 minutes, the memory you had in mind is completely wiped away and forgotten. The amount of time you forget, in consecutive days, depends on how much of the draught you imbibed, as indicated on the table below.

An unwilling or unaware imbiber of this potion is poisoned for 1 minute and must make a DC 16 Constitution saving throw, taking 7 (2d6) poison damage on a failed save or half as much on a successful one. The damage increases to 14 (4d6) if a jar is so imbibed, 21 (6d6) if a bottle is so imbibed, and 35 (10d6) if an amphora is so imbibed. An unwilling or unaware imbiber doesn't suffer any loss of memory as a result of drinking this potion.

CONTAINER SIZE	NUMBER OF DOSES	DAYS FORGOTTEN (PER DOSE/IF FULL CONTAINER IS CONSUMED)
Phial	1	1/1
Jar	5	1/7
Bottle	25	1/30
Amphora	250	1/750

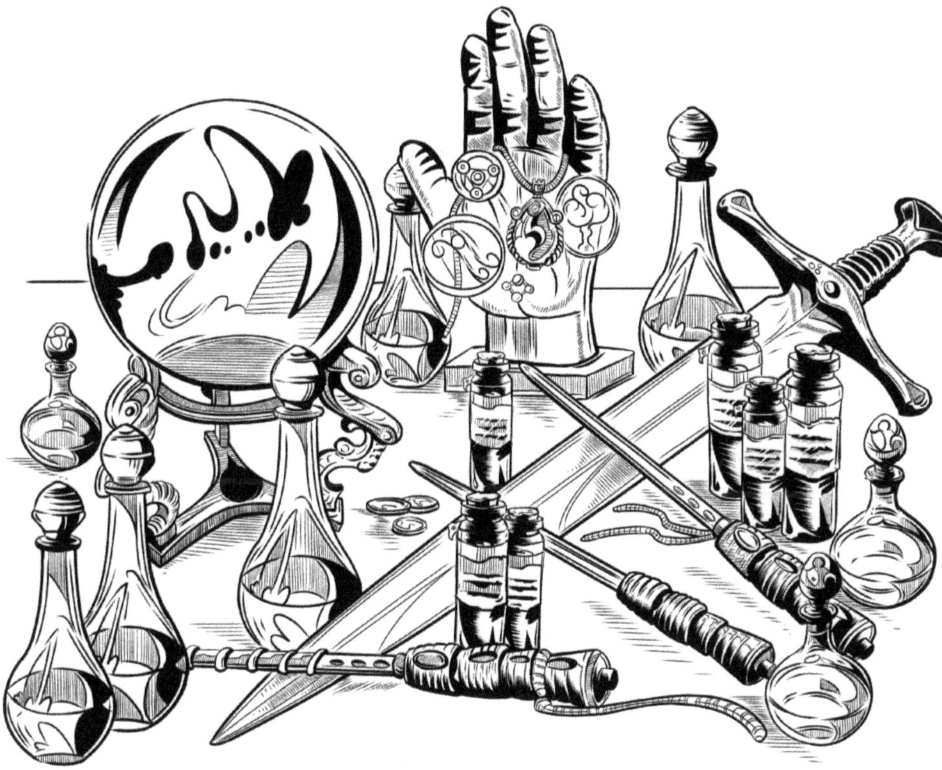

MAGIC

DEEP KNOWLEDGE: THE SHORES OF ANKESHEL

by Paul Scofield

We've spent decades unlocking the secrets of vril technology. It was time well spent, for the very enemies against which it was initially developed seem to be returning for long-sought revenge.
—*The Power of Vril and the Founding of Cassadega,* by Elder Arch Kallimachus

Founded and built on the ruins of a sunken empire, the city of Cassadega is a boomtown of technological wonders. On seemingly every corner stands a workshop, some built on the rubble of previous failed experiments, analyzing and tinkering with discoveries extracted from the ruins beneath the streets. Arcane scholars, artificers, craftspeople, entrepreneurs, and a healthy dose of seedy criminals come to the "city-on-the-city" to find the next big breakthrough.

Some seekers of lore want to understand the Ankeshel people themselves and others to steal the technologies for their own schemes. All the while, something massive awaits in the deep, grumbling in barely contained agitation. It sank a city once, and after millennia, it itches to do so again.

Places of Note

Walking the streets of Cassadega, it's hard not to find something fascinating. The place is filled with wonder.

ADIE EXCAVATION

Once Adie Muldoon broke through into the tomb of Thalassos IV and brought the first working vril battery out into the public eye, Cassadega was born. Now backed by the Kallimachus estate, Muldoon's heirs continue to be the most prolific and popular excavation and research company in Cassadega. Rumors persist of them being on the threshold of discovering the tomb of Thalassos III. There are just as many rumors that they are being fed artifacts by an unseen benefactor who steals from other companies. The implication is that they haven't legitimately discovered something new in several years. Orthan Kallimachus dismisses this, of course, as the rantings of jealous rivals.

BARRIOT'S AQUATIC ESCORTS

Home and establishment of the merfolk Barriot Thinfin, this establishment, asking only a "reasonable fee," will provide escorts for those who wish to explore the underwater ruins of Ankeshel. With a slew of magical diving methods for those that breathe air available to rent and guides of every persuasion, they offer tours throughout some of the most dramatic (though picked over) areas of the ruins. Most of their income comes from the uninitiated and tourists. Still, occasionally they are contracted by larger outfits to lead more dangerous excursions into unexplored regions or those known to be stalked by undersea predators. Sometimes Barriot himself will lead these trips as he's developed a possibly unhealthy taste for ever greater risk.

BRESLEY TUNNELS

Vril researchers and historians would pay a handsome price for access to the body of an Ankeshelian preserved enough to allow a *speak with dead* spell to be used. Besides vril, glyphs and other written secrets abound within the ruins, but no linguist has yet been able to fully decipher the language of Ankeshel. The sunken tombs have yielded no results, so Thoriva Bresley, with the backing of the Braner Estate, started the Bresley Tunnels Expedition. Their goal is to find commoners' catacombs instead of exploring the conspicuous noble tombs. They've had luck uncovering ancient skeletons here and there, but unfortunately, the remains have proven uncommunicative, and some have attacked their discoverers outright. Bresley is always looking to hire extra security to accompany her expeditions.

DEEP DIVE

Perched on the edge of the Brink—the tremendous continental shelf that descends into the abyssal depths—stand two submerged, crane-like elevators operated by merfolk. For 10 gp, they will lower the cages into the depths. For 20 gp, they will bring you back up. Safety along the descent is loosely guaranteed, and linkages at various depths allow expeditions to abscond into sunken ruins to search for treasures. The closer to the surface, the less there is to find, so deeper descents are becoming more common. The merfolk have noted that more and more customers pay to go down but never signal to come back up.

MIDTOWN MARKET

If ever there was an epicenter to the chaos of the city of unearthed secrets, it would be the innocuously named Midtown Market. While most gear for exploration and adventuring is found here, the real treat is the newly discovered and displayed technologies that inventors and other artisans bring out. New demonstrations happen often, and crowds turn out to watch and wager on whether it will be a delight, dud, or disaster. Security is tight, but that brings out the best thieves, and the greater attention could lead to an even more entertaining heist.

SPIRE

The lighthouse demarking the edge of Lower Cassadega is the home of Elder Arch Kallimachus. It is a neutral ground for meetings between the surface leaders of the city and the merfolk that dwell below. Kallimachus himself is rarely seen aside from his early morning excursions to watch the depths and cast a few spells, though it's not obvious what his castings are for. When asked by those able to get close enough to talk to him what he is waiting for, he often frowns and says cryptically, "You already know."

Working with Vril

The key to vril technology is, at its core, a reaction between vril fluid and an arcane-infused alloy of gold and copper called orichalcum. This reaction produces volatile energy that can be channeled through various materials to produce electricity, raw force, or even vitalizing rays of energy. Without proper precautions, the technology can be hazardous,

and being that both materials are scarce, only the most intelligent, powerful, and resourceful can work with it.

RECHARGING VRIL BATTERIES

One of the most closely guarded secrets among the vril engineers of Cassadega is how they can repair and recharge vril batteries. Without direct arcane assistance, the process is lengthy and expensive, often costing 1,000 gp to replace the metal plates and solution, called vril fluid, in a standard 50-charge battery. A vril battery requires 1 ounce of vril fluid for every 10 charges it holds, and each ounce is 100 gp on the open market of Cassadega. Outside of the city, prices can double or triple, assuming you can find a seller. It also requires pure orichalcum and other supplies worth 200 gp.

An engineer proficient in vril engineer's tools (see below) can spend an hour per ounce of vril fluid required, using a complete set of vril engineer's tools, to recharge a vril battery. The engineer cannot gain the benefits of a rest during this time.

REPAIRING VRIL TECHNOLOGY

If an engineer wishes to repair a damaged or incomplete piece of vril weaponry or armor, they must first gather the necessary parts. Assuming a market is available to purchase such things, they tend to mimic the cost of creating a magic item of similar rarity. (The GM may modify the cost of parts needed based on how extensive the damage to the piece.) Repairing the item itself is a long, laborious, and sometimes dangerous task, taking an hour for every 500 gp in value to repair the piece. The engineer must have access to a vril laboratory complete with vril engineer's tools, smith's tools, and alchemist's supplies. The engineer can work no more than 8 hours a day and 40 hours a week without gaining a level of exhaustion. At the end of this time, the vril item, armor, or weapon is fully functioning again. Vril artifacts cannot be repaired in this way without using a *wish* spell.

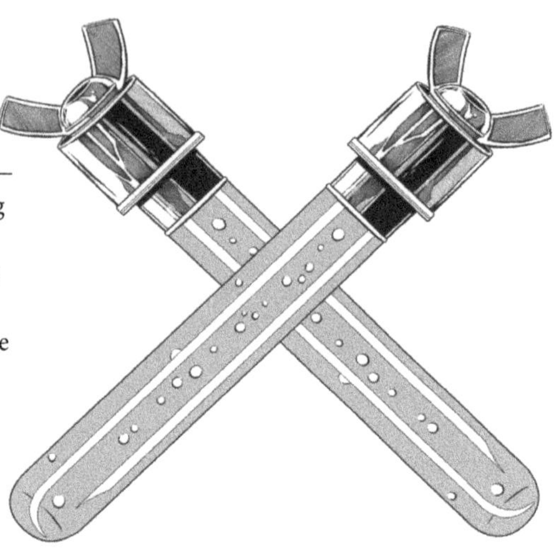

New Technology

New discoveries are made every day, but the devastating effect of millennia of exposure to seawater has left most of these as barely worth recording. Still, as more and more technologies are unearthed and those who study them learn to replicate them, the market streets have grown wild with merchants selling new and exciting wares. Some of them even work while others maybe should never have seen the light of day.

For more on vril technology, see also *Midgard Worldbook* and *Warlock 10: The Magocracies*, which is reprinted in *Warlock Grimoire 2*.

ANKESHELIAN DISINTEGRATION RAY

This sleek, pistol-like weapon of polished orichalcum was found sealed in a vault deep beneath what was believed to have once been a military general's estate in ancient Ankeshel. It was tested once, by those who discovered it, to devastating results. That night, the entire archaeology team disappeared along with the weapon. Its current whereabouts are unknown.

You can connect a vril battery to this weapon, and each use drains 50 charges from the attached battery. If the battery has less than 50 charges, the weapon does not activate, and the battery is irrevocably destroyed, all valuable parts being converted to lead. If the battery is drained to 0 charges, it is similarly destroyed. Successfully activating the weapon causes a white-hot blast of electrified plasma to spring from the barrel to a range of 60 feet. A creature targeted by this must make a Dexterity saving throw against a DC equal to 10 + your dexterity modifier + your proficiency bonus if you are proficient in vril weapons. On a failed save, the target takes 6d12 + 30 force damage. The target is disintegrated if this damage leaves it with 0 hit points.

A disintegrated creature, including everything nonmagical it is wearing or holding, is reduced to a softly glowing pile of blue ash. Only a *true resurrection* or *wish* spell can restore the creature to life. Magic items are unaffected by this ray, but any Large or smaller nonmagical object is automatically disintegrated. Huge or larger objects lose a 10-foot-radius sphere of mass originating from the point struck. This ray does not affect magical forces, such as the wall created by a *wall of force* spell.

BOOMFIST

This heavy, articulated gauntlet of orichalcum and lead is laced with wires that terminate in copper knuckle plates. Just behind the hand of the gauntlet is a housing for a vril battery. A boomfist does not operate if you are wearing a magical ring on the hand the boomfist. You cannot wield a weapon in the same hand, and you automatically fail any Dexterity checks that require the use of your hand. Making a successful unarmed attack with a boomfist allows you to spend 1 charge from the installed vril battery to add 1d12 lightning damage to your normal unarmed

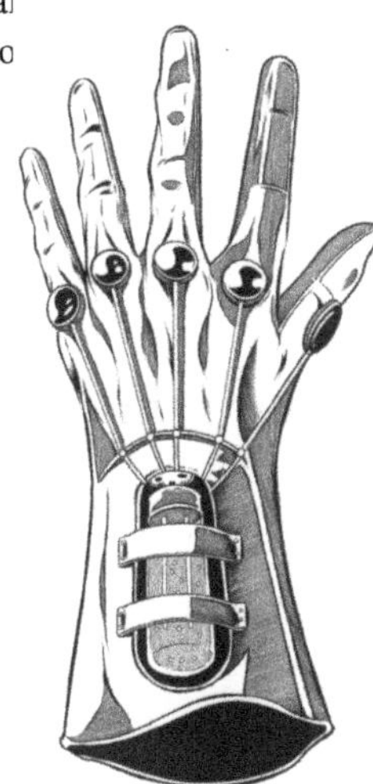

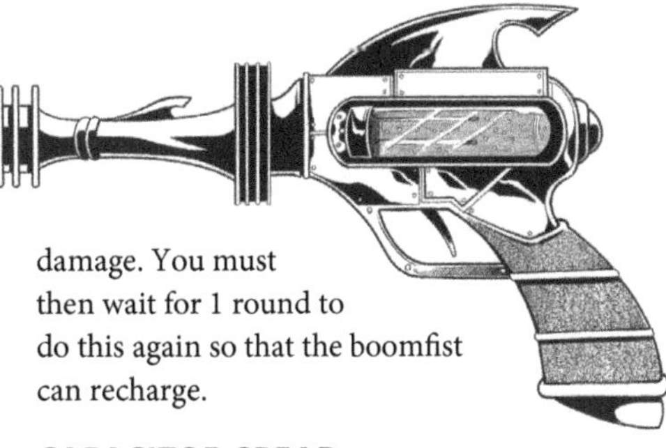

damage. You must then wait for 1 round to do this again so that the boomfist can recharge.

CAPACITOR SPEAR

This heavy spear is made of orichalcum-laced steel and features a housing at the base of its head to accept a vril battery. This weapon functions as a normal spear.

In addition, as a reaction when you are subjected to lightning damage, you may divert half the damage suffered into the spear. For every 5 damage so diverted, rounded down, you recharge one charge of the attached vril battery. If overcharged, make a Dexterity saving throw with a DC equal to 10 + the number of charges overcharged. (You can add your proficiency bonus to your saving throw if you are proficient with vril weapons.) If you fail, the battery explodes, and everyone within 5 feet of the spear takes 2d6 lightning damage. The spear cannot be used until it has been repaired. Overcharged charges are lost.

CASSADEGAN ARC THROWER

This heavy device is slung around your shoulders, hanging near your waist. It features a massive array of orichalcum-filigreed glass tubes, filled with a softly glowing blue liquid, that converge on a copper tube extending a meter out the front, and the tip holds a jagged piece of crystal. One hand must operate a rear triggering mechanism, and the other supports and aims from a handle sticking out of the top while calibrating the arc emissions. The arc thrower requires two vril batteries to operate, and each use drains 2 charges from each battery. As an action, you may activate the Cassadega arc thrower, which then creates a blast of arcing electrical energy, originating

from the crystal. Each creature within a 30-foot cone must make a Dexterity saving throw with a DC equal to 8 + your dexterity modifier + your proficiency bonus if you are proficient in vril weaponry. On a failed save, a target takes 3d6 lightning damage and is stunned. On a successful save, a target takes half as much damage and suffers no additional effects.

CASSADEGAN REJUVENATION TABLE

Some scholars in Cassadega have discovered that vril is useful for more than triggering blasts of lightning or plasma, that it has links to the energy inside every living thing. One of the results of this discovery, for which the wealthy local patrons pay richly to develop, is the rejuvenation table. This Large casket-like device is linked via tubes and wires to a series of pumps, dials, and other strange electrical devices, including four spots to attach the vril batteries required to operate the table. One Medium or smaller creature may lie in the casket at a time. The rejuvenation table has three functions:

- You may spend 10 charges from each attached battery (40 total) to allow the user inside the casket to experience the effects of a short rest in 1 minute.
- You may spend 25 charges from each attached battery (100 total) to allow the user inside the casket to experience the effects of a long rest in 1 hour. Spellcasters that use this function retain the same spells they prepared at their last long rest.

- You may spend 50 charges from each attached battery (200 total) and irreversibly destroy the attached batteries to regrow a lost limb on a still-living creature.

CASSADEGAN THUNDERBUSS

When refining the coil rifle to a working condition, some enterprising engineers took the initial design and sought to improve upon it. Instead of using the coils to launch a ferromagnetic projectile directly, they created a crossbow-like device that used the energy of an attached vril battery to launch whatever happened to be at hand.

You must plug the thunderbuss into a vril battery to fire it. Each shot fired uses 1 charge from the battery and destroys its ammunition. For ammunition, you may use a bonus action to jam a handful of any rigid, non-combustible, nonmagical material, such as pebbles, nails, or the like, into the receiver compartment.

FULMINATOR ROD

This short bar of carved orichalcum houses a vril battery and is tipped with two reinforced copper tines. On a successful melee attack, which consumes 1 charge from the attached vril battery, the target takes 1d6 lightning and 1d6 thunder damage. The explosion of electrical energy can be heard up to 300 feet away.

ORICHALCUM PROSTHETIC

Complex clockworks have been available for a long time that could mimic the movements and responsiveness of natural appendages, when driven by magic, but these rare items are only available to those with great money and resources. However, developers in Cassadega have found a way to link vril directly to a conscious mind to power often beautifully crafted prosthetics. Fine woods infused with vril liquid, encased in a framework of orichalcum filigree, and crafted to match the size and shape of the lost limb—a vril craftsperson can spend 8 hours fitting and tuning one of these devices to a single creature missing a limb. Once fitted for such a device, this nonmagical prosthetic moves and behaves as the lost limb once did. It can be attached or removed as an action, and damage to it heals while it is worn as living tissue normally would.

VRIL DUAL-CHARGE RIFLE

A derivative of the Cassadega coil rifle (see *Midgard Worldbook*), this vril device instead fires wooden darts infused with vril liquid. The rifle requires two vril batteries. Each shot costs a charge from each battery and a wooden dart, fed by an internal magazine of eight darts. One of the batteries powers the firing mechanism and the other infuses the ammunition. The vril dual-charge rifle can infer your intent when fired, requiring a certain amount of focus, and thus the vril dual-charge rifle can only ever be fired once per round. On a successful ranged attack, the dart explodes in a spray of sparks and the target takes 2d6 lightning damage.

NEW VRIL WEAPONS

NAME	COST	DAMAGE	WEIGHT	PROPERTIES
Melee Weapons				
Boomfist	1,000 gp	Unarmed + 1d12 lightning	5 lb.	Light
Capacitor spear	1,000 gp	1d6 piercing	5 lb.	Thrown (range 20/60), versatile (1d8)
Fulminator rod	1,000 gp	1d6 lightning, 1d6 thunder	2 lb.	Light
Vril saber	2,000 gp	1d12 Force	2 lb.	Finesse, light
Ranged Weapons				
Ankeshelian disintegration ray	10,000 gp	See description	3 lb.	Loading (see description)
Cassadegan arc thrower	8,000 gp	3d6 lightning	25 lb.	Special, two-handed
Cassadegan thunderbuss	5,000 gp	2d6 piercing	12 lb.	Ammunition (range 20/60), loading, two-handed
Vril dual-charge rifle	6,000 gp	2d6 lightning or 1d6 healing	10 lb.	Ammunition (range 30/90), loading, two-handed

NEW VRIL EQUIPMENT

ITEM	COST	WEIGHT
Ammunition		
Cassadegan rejuvenation table	10,000 gp	500 lb.
Orichalcum prosthetic	1,000 gp	As limb
Vril engineer's tools (artisan's tools)	50 gp	10 lb.

You may also instead shoot an ally. On a successful ranged attack, the dart infuses its vril energy into the ally, and they regain a number of hit points equal to 1d6. An ally who understands the nature of the rifle—and is aware of their ally attempting to shoot them with it—may use their reaction to grant advantage to the ally's attack.

VRIL ENGINEER'S TOOLS

These artisan's tools include ratchets, lubricants, wire tools, and other implements needed to work with vril-powered clockworks and machinery. Proficiency with these tools lets you add your proficiency bonus to any ability checks you make to understand or repair vril technology. Also, proficiency with these tools is required to recharge vril batteries.

VRIL SABER

This intricate, hilt-like device is made of orichalcum and has a compartment that allows the housing of a vril battery. Assuming the attached battery has at least 1 charge, you may activate or deactivate the saber as a bonus action, causing a 3-foot electric-blue beam of arcing plasma to emerge from the hilt. The energy blade deals 1d12 force damage on a hit, draining 1 charge from the attached battery each time. The blade is hot enough to burn or melt nonmagical materials on contact (the details of which are left to the GM's discretion). Rolling a natural 1 on an attack with the vril saber means you've overestimated the weightless nature of the blade and struck yourself, suffering the damage.

Wizards of Cassadega

Many great mages are drawn to the crumbling ruins of the sunken city of Ankeshel in order to unlock its great mysteries, but few are able to grasp the true nature of vril and wield its power with the same ease the Ankeshelian people once did.

NEW ARCANE TRADITION: VRIL ADEPT

The connection between vril and magic is tenuous at best. However, some have learned to bridge these divergent sources of power and harness the power of the Ankeshelian battery. Vril adepts master a tradition of wizardry that incorporates lost technology, tapping into the powers of vril and utilizing orichalcum to bend the contained power to their wills.

Devoted for decades to researching these lost technologies, those who intend to become vril adepts often start with an unfinished vril spell harness (see below). The first steps of their

journeys often involve fine tuning this device
to suit their style, unlocked completely as they
reach 2nd level.

Secrets of the Deep

At 2nd level, you gain proficiency with vril
weapons, vril armor, and vril engineer's tools.

Vril Spell Harness

Starting at 2nd level, you created a harness of
leather, fine woods, and orichalcum. It weighs
15 pounds, counts as both vril armor and a
set of vril engineer's tools, and grants you an
armor class of 12 + your Dexterity modifier.
Additionally, this harness of vril-infused
machinery and tools counts both as an arcane
focus and as your spellbook: orichalcum
plates are sewn into the seams as the "pages,"
where diagrams and incantations are carefully
stamped with a hammer and fine chisels.

A vril battery can be attached to the harness,
and through careful meditation and tinkering,
you may spend 1 minute and one unused spell
slot to recharge the battery, restoring 1 charge
per level of the spell slot spent in this way. This
vril battery is now intrinsically linked to you
and can only be utilized with vril equipment
that you are operating.

Additionally, you gain resistance to lightning
damage while wearing your vril spell harness.
At 6th level, you gain resistance to thunder
damage, at 10th level, you gain immunity to
lightning damage, and at 14th level, you gain
resistance to force damage.

Lightning Rod

At 6th level, you may now permanently mount
a vril battery into your vril spell harness. As
a reaction, when you cast a spell that causes
lightning damage, you may spend a charge from
the attached battery to reroll any damage die
rolling 1 for the spell and take the new result.

Vril Arsenal

At 10th level, while wearing your vril spell
harness, you may add your Intelligence
modifier (minimum of +1) to the damage you
deal with any vril-powered weaponry.

In addition, repairing or recharging vril
equipment takes either half the time or half the
cost in materials, your choice.

Discharge

At 14th level, you've learned to extract vril
from the life force of the environment. You
may spend 24 hours using vril engineer's tools
to convert 20 pounds of living matter (plants,
animals, and so on) into 1 ounce of vril fluid.

In addition, once per long rest you can create
a feedback loop within the structure of vril
equipment. You may target vril weapons,
armor, or items with the *overcharge* or *greater
overcharge* spells (see below).

The Spells of Ankeshel

Research into vril technology and the
occasional discovery of ancient texts have
yielded new arcane spells that have gained
traction among the spellcasters of Cassadega.

AWARENESS

*1st-Level Divination | Sorcerer, Warlock,
Wizard*

Casting Time: 1 action
Range: Touch
Components: S, M (a glass bead)
Duration: Concentration, up to 1 minute

You touch a creature and grant it a heightened
awareness of its surroundings. For the spell's
duration, the target creature can make Wisdom
(Perception) checks as a bonus action.

BALL LIGHTNING

*5th-Level Evocation | Sorcerer, Warlock,
Wizard*

Casting Time: 1 action
Range: 120 feet
Components: V, S, M (a bit of fur; a piece of
amber, glass, or crystal rod; and a silver bead)
Duration: Concentration, up to 1 minute

You create a ball of arcing lightning in an
unoccupied space you can see within range.
The ball sheds bright light in a 20-foot radius

and dim light for an additional 20 feet. The ball buzzes and crackles with electricity and occupies a 5-foot space.

When a creature gets within 5 feet of the ball for the first time on its turn or starts its turn there, it is targeted by arcs of electricity, and it must succeed on a Constitution saving throw or take 8d4 lightning damage.

On each of your turns after you cast this spell, you can use an action to move the ball up to 60 feet in any direction.

At Higher Levels. When you cast this spell using a spell slot of 6th level or higher, the damage increases by 2d4 for each slot level above 5th.

GREATER OVERCHARGE

7th-Level Transmutation | Sorcerer, Warlock, Wizard

Casting Time: 1 action
Range: Touch
Components: V, S, M (a bit of string and a rare or very rare magic item, which the spell consumes, see description)
Duration: Concentration, up to 1 minute

You touch a rare or very rare magic item that has charges and isn't cursed. This funnels loose magical energy into it beyond its normal capacity, causing it to thrum and vibrate with barely contained arcane power. It is clear there is something wrong with the magic item. When the spell ends, the magic item detonates with a blast of deadly arcane energy. All creatures within 30 feet of the magic item must make a Dexterity saving throw. On a failed save, the creature takes 8d12 force damage and is knocked prone. On a successful save, the creature takes half as much damage and suffers no additional effects.

INSIGHT

2nd-Level Divination | Sorcerer, Warlock, Wizard

Casting Time: 1 minute
Range: Self
Components: V, S, M (a small gear or mirror)
Duration: Concentration, up to 10 minutes

You choose one mechanical, nonmagical trap or puzzle that you can see and gain an insight into how to defeat or bypass it. You may choose to receive a clue from the GM, which ends the spell immediately. The GM should provide a helpful clue to help solve a puzzle or determine the best way to disable or avoid a trap. Otherwise, you may gain advantage on any ability checks to disable the trap or solve the puzzle for the spell's duration.

MUCUS

2nd-Level Conjuration | Sorcerer, Warlock, Wizard

Casting Time: 1 action
Range: 60 feet
Components: V, S, M (a snail shell)
Duration: 1 minute

A thick layer of coagulated slime covers the ground in a 10-foot-square centered on a point within range and turns it into difficult terrain for the duration.

When the mucus appears, each creature within its area must succeed on a Constitution saving throw or be poisoned until the end of its next turn. A creature that enters the area for the first time on a turn, or starts its turn there, must also succeed on a Constitution saving throw or be poisoned until the end of its next turn.

OVERCHARGE

4th-Level Transmutation | Sorcerer, Warlock, Wizard

Casting Time: 1 action
Range: Touch
Components: V, S, M (a bit of string and a common or uncommon magic item, which the spell consumes, see description)
Duration: Concentration, up to 1 minute

You touch a common or uncommon magic item that has charges and isn't cursed. This funnels loose magical energy into it beyond its normal capacity, causing it to thrum and vibrate with barely contained arcane power. It is clear there is something wrong with the magic item. When the spell ends, the magic item detonates with a blast of deadly arcane energy. All creatures within 20 feet of the magic item must make a Dexterity saving throw. On a failed save, the creature takes 4d12 force damage and is knocked prone. On a successful save, the creature takes half as much damage and suffers no additional effects.

THUNDERCRACK

3rd-Level Evocation | Sorcerer, Warlock, Wizard

Casting Time: 1 action
Range: Self (30-foot cone)
Components: V, S, M (a tuning fork)
Duration: Instantaneous

A wave of pressure explodes from your extended hand in a 30-foot cone with a thunderous sound, audible out to 300 feet. Each creature within the cone must make a Constitution saving throw. On a failed save, a creature takes 6d6 thunder damage and is deafened for 2d4 rounds. On a successful save, the creature takes half as much damage and suffers no additional effects.

At Higher Levels. When you cast this spell using a spell slot of 4th level or higher, the damage increases by 1d6 and the duration of the deafened condition increases by 1d4 for each slot level above 3rd.

Foes of the Deep

The shores near Cassadega and its ruins are not free from dangers. Creatures twisted by the strange vril energies, ancient defenses of the once mighty nation, and the people who come to plunder them all pose threats to explorers.

GARGANTH

A crab-like machine—smooth panels of chromed orichalcum surmounted by a broad, armored carapace—wades toward you on eight articulated legs. A massive pincer covered in jagged ridges snaps at the air while another appendage spins up three articulated barrels to a high rate of speed. Arcs of blue-white electricity surround it as it moves.

Antediluvian Death Machine. In a last-ditch effort to combat the aboleth, Ankeshelian engineers constructed the garganth. Many believe only one was ever created, but rumors and scraps of ancient lore indicate others may be waiting dormant in the depths to fulfill some ancient order of defense or destruction.

Endless Obedience. The garganth was created with defense in mind. However, their instructions have worn down over millennia. Whether because of logical misinterpretations, newly developed vagaries, or ancient instruction, a garganth rises and proceeds on some unknown mission. Scholars hope that these misguided goals are limited to the depths of the fathomless seas, but some insist that it's only a matter of time before one's path is directed toward the shore.

Powered Construction. A garganth doesn't require air, food, drink, or sleep.

GARGANTH

Huge Construct, Unaligned
Armor Class 19 (natural)
Hit Points 229 (17d12 + 119)
Speed 15 ft.

STR	DEX	CON	INT	WIS	CHA
20 (+5)	12 (+1)	24 (+7)	2 (−4)	10 (+0)	1 (−5)

Saving Throws Con +13, Wis +6, Cha +1
Damage Resistances cold, thunder; bludgeoning, piercing, and slashing from nonmagical weapon attacks that aren't adamantine
Damage Immunities fire, lightning, poison, psychic

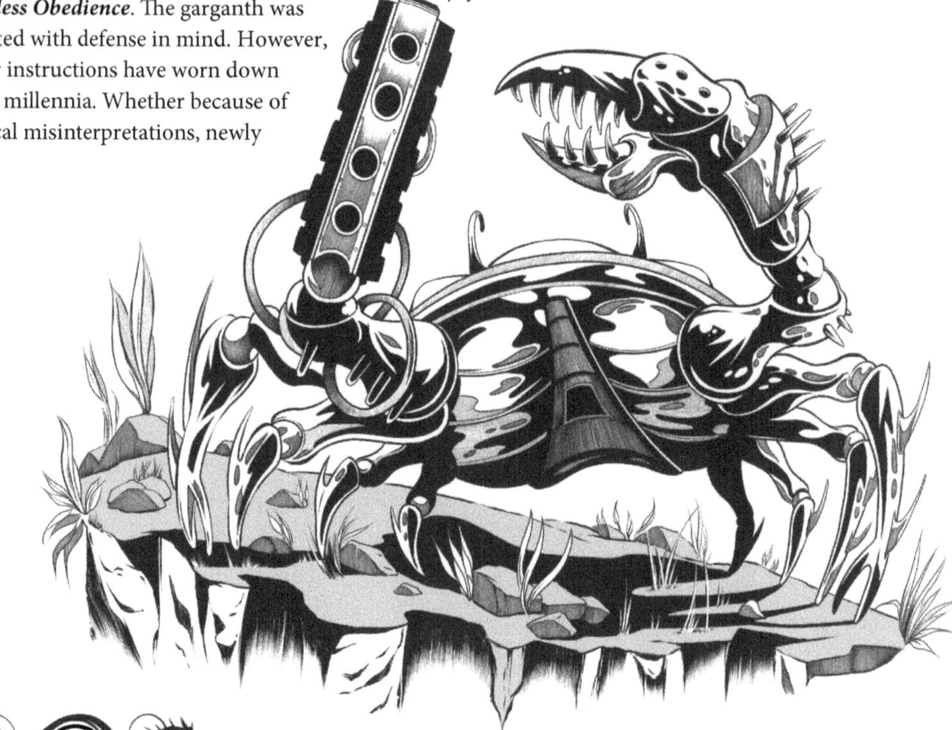

Condition Immunities charmed, deafened, exhaustion, frightened, paralyzed, petrified, poisoned, prone, unconscious

Senses darkvision 120 ft., passive Perception 10

Languages understands one language of its creator but can't speak

Challenge 18 (20,000 XP)　**Proficiency Bonus** +6

Ethereal Sight. The garganth can see into the Ethereal Plane up to 60 feet, though it cannot affect objects or creatures there.

Immutable Form. The garganth is immune to any spell or effect that would alter its form.

Legendary Resistance (3/Day). If the garganth fails a saving throw, it can choose to succeed instead.

Magic Resistance. The garganth has advantage on saving throws against spells and other magical effects.

Magic Weapons. The garganth's weapon attacks are magical.

Stable Platform. The garganth is unaffected by any force that would move it against its will.

ACTIONS

Multiattack. The garganth can use its Arc Field. It then makes either one Pincer attack or one Claw attack and two Foot Slam attacks.

Claw. *Melee Weapon Attack:* +11 to hit, reach 15 ft., one target. *Hit:* 18 (3d8 + 5) slashing damage plus 22 (5d8) lightning damage. If the target is Large or smaller, it is grappled (escape DC 19).

Foot Slam. *Melee Weapon Attack:* +11 to hit, reach 5 ft., one target. *Hit:* 14 (2d8 + 5) piercing damage.

Arc Field. Every creature within 10 feet of the garganth must succeed on a DC 19 Constitution saving throw or take 22 (5d8) lightning damage. If the creature is in contact with the same body of water as the garganth, they make their saving throw at disadvantage.

Coil Autocannon (Recharge 5–6). The garganth fires a fusillade of ferromagnetic bullets in a 60-foot cone. Each creature in the cone must make a DC 19 Dexterity saving throw, taking 66 (12d10) piercing damage on a failed save or half as much damage on a successful one.

Pincer. The garganth makes a Claw attack against a grappled target. On a hit, the target takes 32 (6d8 + 5) slashing damage plus 22 (5d8) lightning damage. If this attack reduces the target to 0 hit points, the garganth kills the creature by cutting it in half. Otherwise, it severs one of the creature's limbs, selected randomly, and the creature is no longer grappled.

LEGENDARY ACTIONS

The garganth can take three legendary actions, choosing from the options below. Only one legendary action option can be used at a time and only at the end of another creature's turn. The garganth regains spent legendary actions at the start of its turn:

- ***Claw.*** If the garganth is not currently grappling a target, it uses its Claw attack.
- ***Detect.*** The garganth makes a Wisdom (Perception) check.
- ***Move.*** The garganth moves up to its speed without provoking opportunity attacks.

CASSADEGA VRILWATCH

The guard appears to be wearing a strange suit of bronze armor. But you quickly realize it's charged orichalcum plate, and the quarterstaff they are leveling your direction is an articulated coil rifle.

Elite Troopers. As the valuable technology increases in prevalence on the streets of Cassadega and, for that matter, the rest of the Magocracy of Allain, some seek to ensure their treasures and newly uncovered secrets don't fall into hands of wrongdoers—or competitors. The best of their best guards are outfitted in the very technology they seek to protect.

Arms Race. In any technologically advanced society, a type of arms race often emerges. Both sides of the law deploy greater and greater power to try and outstrip their opponents. Wise commanders keep vrilwatch in check unless necessary to protect the peace, mainly because they don't want their enemies to get their hands on vrilwatch equipment should they fail.

If I Can't Have It... Many cunning patrons ensure their vrilwatch have dead switches installed to ensure their rivals don't get a hold of the valuable equipment.

CASSADEGAN VRILWATCH

Medium Humanoid (Any Race), Any Alignment
Armor Class 17 (vril half plate)
Hit Points 84 (13d8 + 26)
Speed 30 ft.

STR	DEX	CON	INT	WIS	CHA
13 (+1)	18 (+4)	14 (+2)	12 (+1)	13 (+1)	12 (+1)

Saving Throws Dex +6, Con +4, Wis +3
Skills Insight +3, Perception +3
Damage Resistance lightning
Senses passive Perception 13
Languages any one language (usually Common)
Challenge 4 (1,100 XP)   **Proficiency Bonus** +2

Dead Switch. If a vrilwatch is reduced to 0
hit points, their armor and weapons short
circuit, venting vril fluid and fusing electronics,
rendering them useless.

Vril Charged Half Plate. Any creature within
5 feet that strikes the vrilwatch takes 4 (1d6)
lightning damage. This may happen 10 times
before the vrilwatch must have their suit
recharged.

ACTIONS

Multiattack. The vrilwatch makes two Charged
Rapier attacks.

Charged Rapier. *Melee Weapon Attack:* +6 to hit,
reach 5 ft., one target. *Hit:* 8 (1d8 + 4) piercing
damage and 4 (1d8) lightning damage.

Coil Rifle. *Ranged Weapon Attack:* +6 to hit,
range 40/120 ft., one target. *Hit:* 10 (1d12 + 4)
piercing damage.

VRIL-YA

*A legless being with scintillating gold skin drifts
toward you. Whisps of bluish vapor seem to
indicate wing-like appendages emerging from its
back. It extends a tentacle toward you.*

Failed Experiments. Ancient Ankeshelian
practitioners once thought to use vril to
enhance elemental beings and inadvertently
created the vril-ya. A vril engineer can extract
3d8 ounces of vril fluid from a dead vril-ya.

Mindless Hunger. These ageless abominations
roam the deep oceans, psychically draining any
sentient life they find. Occasionally, in their
starvation, they roam inland.

Elemental Nature. A vril-ya doesn't require
air, food, drink, or sleep.

VRIL-YA

Medium Elemental, Neutral Evil
Armor Class 13 (natural)
Hit Points 45 (7d8 + 14)
Speed 0 ft., fly 30 ft. (hover), swim 30 ft.

STR	DEX	CON	INT	WIS	CHA
16 (+3)	16 (+3)	15 (+2)	3 (−4)	10 (+0)	7 (−2)

Damage Resistances cold, fire, psychic;
bludgeoning, piercing, and slashing damage
from nonmagical weapon attacks
Damage Immunities lightning, poison
Condition Immunities exhaustion, paralyzed,
petrified, poisoned, prone, unconscious
Senses darkvision 60 ft., passive Perception 10
Languages telepathy 60 ft.
Challenge 4 (1,100 XP)   **Proficiency Bonus** +2

Magic Resistance. The vril-ya has advantage on
saving throws against spells and other magical
effects.

Vril Cloud. Once per day, the vril-ya can emit
a cloud of vril vapor, filling a 10-foot-radius
sphere of air or water around it. The first time
on a turn that a vril-ya enters the cloud or if it
starts its turn within the cloud, the vril-ya heals
2d8 damage. A strong current or wind can
disperse the cloud.

ACTIONS

Tentacle. *Melee Weapon Attack:* +5 to hit, reach 5
ft., one target. *Hit:* 7 (1d8 + 3) psychic damage.
If the target is Medium or smaller, it is grappled
(escape DC 14).

Psychic Drain. The vril-ya makes one Tentacle
attack against a Medium or smaller creature it is
grappling. If the attack hits, the target takes 22
(5d8) psychic damage. The vril-ya will continue
draining once the target reaches 0 hit points,
forcing failures on death saving throws until the
target is dead

THE DEEP DIVINE: MASKS OF THE PRIESTHOOD

by Tim Hitchcock

Despite their best efforts, mortals will never understand the true nature of the universe, its state of perfect entropy. In wonder, fear, and desperation though, they petition the divine for such revelation, for the purposeful meaning of their existence. Nevertheless, even the gods do not divulge these secrets—and it is uncertain if they even could. They appear immortal only to the short-lived creatures of the mortal world, but to the vast infinity of the void, they too are only a blink in the eye of eternity.

One of the unique aspects of Midgard's pantheons is the inclusion of divine masks— different manifestations of the same deity. Within the game world, while priesthoods might accept that a deity could possess alternate manifestations, the idea of divine masks is little more than a fringe topic in theological discourse. But that doesn't mean a character can't explore the deep mysteries of their faith, bringing them, perhaps even unknowingly, to the doorstep of one of their deity's masks

Considering Masks. Within the game, these masks might represent a deity's manifestation during the transition from one stage of existence to another. And if time does work differently for the gods, the future and past quickly become irrelevant. A divine mask might represent how a god appears depending on its followers: Veles, the great serpent, for instance, may appear in the guise of any

god, and worshippers believe the serpent to be the only god and all other gods simply divine representations of Veles. Occasionally, a mask represents ideologies or practices contradicting or opposing the faith's primary tenets. For mortal worshippers, the dichotomy of structure and belief explains the occurrence of various events, such as cataclysms, war, disease, and death. It divorces deities from mortal conceptualizations of morality, implying the existence of a greater divine morality and creating a further distinction between deities and their mortal worshippers.

Assuming a Divine Mask

Within the priesthoods of every major religion, select clerics devote themselves to a deeper understanding of their deity. These clerics explore the intricacies and subtleties of the scriptures and attempt to decipher their meaning. Inevitably the search leads to lost or forbidden lore associated with the worship of their deity—and leading to the exploration of their deity's divine masks (see **Masks in Your Game** sidebar).

If a cleric character desires to explore the deep and often apocryphal mysteries of their deity (that is, their masks), choose a single god to designate as their primary god. Next, choose one domain associated with one of that deity's masks. This domain becomes the

character's secondary domain. By attuning to a specially crafted focus mask, you can use Channel Divinity to shift your primary domain to the domain represented by the divine mask. In effect, you become a cleric of a different domain, though you maintain devotion to the same deity. You can only access a single domain at any given time.

Each cleric holds a profoundly intimate and personal relationship with their deity. Therefore, before creating and attuning to a focus mask, establish the character's reasoning for assuming such a mask associated with the deity. Use the **Reason for Assuming a Mask** table for inspiration.

Backlash

Not all priesthoods or religions acknowledge these deeper mysteries (or masks) for their chosen gods, and many clergy formally denounce their belief as sacrilege. Backlash intensifies when individuals honor divine masks that espouse contradictory philosophies or openly challenge a priesthood's tenets. Conversely, the blasphemous concept that one's deity is mere divine mask or minor aspect of another deity demands confrontation. While the devout occasionally question their faith, they rarely tolerate when another priesthood claims their deity only exists as a mask. At best, they may accept or argue that another deity is a mask of their own deity. As a result, clerics that serve multiple aspects of the same deity often keep their practices covert. Depending on circumstances, a cleric assuming a divine mask may pretend to worship the mask's aspect as their primary deity or avoid assuming the mask altogether.

Basics

A cleric that attains 3rd level gains access to the *imbue divine mask* spell. This allows you to delve into exploring various divine masks associated with your deity. The spell allows you to bless a specially crafted focus mask that establishes a divine connection to one of your patron deity's masks.

IMBUE DIVINE MASK

2nd-Level Divination (Ritual) | Cleric

Casting Time: 1 hour
Range: Touch
Components: V, S, M (a focus mask worth at least 250 gp, see text)
Duration: 1 day or until completing a long rest (see text)

When you cast this spell, you temporarily bless a specially crafted relic in the form of a focus mask that grants you the ability to commune with one divine mask associated with your primary deity. The focus mask represents an alternate manifestation of your primary deity, whose divine mask you wish to assume. Creating a focus mask requires unique woods, metals, gems, paints, and other materials that cost no less than 250 gp, takes a month to create, and requires proficiency in an appropriate set of tools for the crafting.

After creating the focus mask, you imbue it with a divine enchantment, allowing you to attune to a divine mask associated with your patron deity. The focus mask is associated with a specific deity and establishes your bond to that deity. The focus mask is considered a holy item as long as the blessing remains. It serves as your personalized divine focus, and only the caster who created it may use it effectively. The enchantment lasts until you cast the spell upon another focus mask or your focus mask is destroyed. After that, you may attune to the focus mask and use it as a magic item.

Once attuned to the focus mask, you can spend one use of your Channel Divinity class ability to become an agent of your deity's divine mask. Then, you temporarily sever your connection to your primary domain (your chosen cleric domain) and bind yourself to a secondary domain associated with one of your patron deity's divine masks. While bonded to the secondary domain, you replace all the domain spells and domain powers associated with your primary domain with all the domain spells and domain powers associated with the appropriate divine mask. In effect, you temporarily switch domains while retaining your connection to your chosen deity.

Assuming a focus mask requires near-blind devotion and absolute surrender to the whims of your deity. You assume the role of the deity's mortal vessel and accept the manifestation of multiple masks. Whenever a cleric shifts focus masks, they invoke a struggle between fate and independence. Each divine mask carries distinct obligations. This can also introduce moral challenges when divine masks of the same deity do not share the same alignments or values and do not make the same moral distinctions.

Wearing a divine mask for too long may cause a cleric to lose their primary domain and permanently shift to the secondary domain associated with the divine mask. A divine mask can only be worn for a day or until you complete a long rest. To avoid the risk of losing your primary domain (chosen cleric domain), you must wait at least a week before assuming the divine mask again. If you assume the divine mask before a week passes, you must succeed on a DC 10 Charisma saving throw

MASKS IN YOUR GAME

The idea of masks is a gaming device for when dealing with the gods of the Midgard campaign setting (see *Midgard Worldbook* for more information on masks). This abstraction of the gods is not really a topic that characters in Midgard would likely talk about or even comprehend, aside from perhaps in the most rarified conclaves of divinity scholars—certainly not among the common folk. The reality in the game world is that the beliefs and practices of the various religions merge and evolve in various combinations over time (known as syncretism). So a cleric character exploring a "mask" of their primary god is really just exploring the deep mysteries of that god's teachings, likely apocryphal, and might never actually intone or even consider the name of the mask deity while still benefitting from the corresponding alternate domains. The character would likely still view any newly espoused beliefs as belonging to their primary god.

We are, however, using the term *mask* here freely in relation to characters for the ease of incorporating the related mechanics should you choose to experiment with them.

d6	REASON
1	You assume a different incarnation of the same character, a sort of split soul, perhaps even shifting through time and space.
2	You experience a wild personality shift. When you assume the mask, you have no memory of your previous personality.
3	You believe the divine mask to be the true form of your deity. The revelation occurred after you first assumed the focus mask.
4	You believe the divine mask connects your deity to ancient philosophies, which you must somehow sever. Unfortunately, you must assume the focus mask to help break those cosmic bindings.
5	You believe you must spend time serving each of your deity's opposing divine masks to help maintain cosmic balance.
6	You worship a deity shunned or despised by the dominant culture and assume their divine mask to covertly continue your services to the priesthood and other followers of your faith.

or permanently lose your primary domain's spells and powers. The domain associated with your deity's divine mask replaces your original domain. If the alignment associated with the divine mask is different from your alignment, it shifts to reflect the values of the divine mask. On a successful save, you can remove the focus mask. However, each additional day you assume the divine mask increases the DC to lose your primary domain by +1. In effect, clerics who continue to assume the belief systems associated with a specific mask incur a permanent shift in their beliefs.

A cleric incurring a permanent shift in their beliefs loses access to the domain power of their former primary domain. After that, they can never assume the divine mask associated with the domain they forsook. Any further attempts to assume the mask anger the deity. If the character wants to continue being a cleric, they must perform a series of ritual penances to regain the deity's favor or find a new patron deity altogether.

PENANCE

A cleric seeking to reestablish a connection with their deity's primary mask chooses to represent their former domain. To regain favor, they must perform one or more of the following acts in penance.

Convert. The cleric must prove the sincerity of their devotion by converting outsiders into the deity's service. The number of followers should be of an equal CR to the cleric's level plus their proficiency bonus.

Founding. To increase the deity's influence, the cleric must build a foundation dedicated to the deity that provides community service, typically the establishment of a church or temple. If the settlement already has a church or temple, the deity may request the establishment of a hostel, mission, or orphanage.

Quest. The cleric must undertake a quest to prove their sincerity. Quests may include recovering a relic, pilgrimage to a sacred site, leading followers to a more fruitful location, or irradicating the influence of a rival deity.

DIVINE INTERVENTION AND MASKS

Once you assume a divine mask, the connection to an alternate sphere of influence also influences the 10th-level Divine Intervention ability. Whenever you use the ability to call upon your patron deity, you cannot be sure which of your patron's divine masks will answer. Each divine mask you access increases the probability that any associated mask hears your petition. However, different mask aspects likely interpret petitions in ways that create unintended consequences. Consequences vary

according to the philosophy and alignment of the divine mask.

When you roll your Divine Intervention check, you roll a d20 for your primary domain and a d20 for each divine mask you have ever assumed. The lowest roll represents the mask that manifests to offer assistance.

If the lowest roll is your primary domain, the Intervention functions normally. If not, consult the **Unintended Consequences** table.

MASKED PRIESTHOODS

While an individual cleric might explore the facets of a deity's masks independently, entire priesthoods are devoted to worshipping their deity's every aspect. These masked priesthoods represent cults or sects that create a dichotomy within a religion's foundational tenets. The critical element to building a masked priesthood requires the struggle of the duality between two (or more) distinct philosophies and coming to terms with that balance as a servant of that deity.

The Midgard campaign setting has many deities, with each entry containing a section describing the deity's specific masks. A mask often represents regional and cultural differences between similar deities and reflects how the same entity might appear to different peoples. A good example is the northern deities Freyr and Freya who appear as Yarla and Porevit to elven counterparts. The tripartite deities Thor, Perun, and Mavros offer another example of this type of relationship. While this makes for colorful storytelling, neither of these examples make good candidates for building a masked priesthood because they lack conflict between their counterparts.

Similarly, the belief that all deities exist as aspects of one grand deity (as with Veles, the Great Serpent) makes a poor choice for building a masked priesthood. The core assumption of a monotheistic deity that appears in many forms to all beings overrides a need for covert duality. There is no conflict between sects and beliefs, and all philosophical conflict becomes inner conflict and explains the convoluted nature of reality, which can be all things and one thing.

SAMPLE MASKED PRIESTHOODS IN MIDGARD

Below are some examples of masked priesthoods. It is important to note that the following mask lists are examples only to illustrate how the relationships between masks might appear in your game. The Goat of the

UNINTENDED CONSEQUENCES

d8	CONSEQUENCES
1	The mask refuses to speak to you until you activate your focus mask and attune to their domain.
2	The divine mask demands some sort of tribute or sacrifice in exchange for granting the request. The tribute or sacrifice should be proportional to the request.
3	The mask is capricious or fickle and withholds a tiny element of the request without first bothering to inform you of the alteration.
4	The divine mask grants the request but then demands you never again call upon them for aid. As a result, your focus mask crumbles to dust, and you can never again communicate with that aspect of your deity.
5	The mask offers the aid but expects you to perform a favor or quest in return.
6	The divine mask requests you forsake your current primary domain and instead patronize the divine mask as your primary domain.
7	After granting the request, the deity temporarily cuts off all access to your Channel Divinity until you take a long rest.
8	The mask severs your access to all domain powers associated with their primary domain until you take a long rest.

Woods, Hecate, and Loki hold no greater importance—unless perhaps you number among their faithful—than those listed as their masks, for in truth they are masks themselves. These lists could have easily been that of Ninkash, Thoth-Hermes, and Baal or any number of other pairings.

GOAT OF THE WOODS

The masks of the Goat represent the ancient deity's progression from one eon to the next. However, the older beliefs still cling even through the transformation and occasionally surface when triggered by need or circumstance. Alternatively, priests most dedicated to the Goat and her primal and savage rites use the masks of her later incarnations to hide within society and infiltrate current cultures more effectively.

Bacchana. Clerics of this priesthood believe Bacchana represents the Goat of the Woods during another age before she became corrupted and alien. Clerics attune to the domains of Lust or Prophecy

Ninkash. Some claim that Ninkash, the deity of drunken mirth, is a mask of the Goat of the Woods. Many find the claim ironic, considering the rivalry between Ninkash and Baccho. Still, there remains an undeniable connection between drunken celebration, debauchery, and regret. Clerics of this priesthood attune to the domains of either Beer or Life.

Vardesain. This masked priesthood believes that the Goat of the Woods assumes the mask of Vardesain when she seeks to communicate with the void. They believe the mask of Vardesain is an incarnation of the Goat and one of her many spawns. Clerics of the Goat of the Woods who assume Vardesain's mask use it to attune to the Void domain.

HECATE

Magic is by nature wondrous and sinister, and its mysteries frequently lie hidden in dark and disturbing origins. Worshippers of Hecate hold their goddess as the sum of all these mysteries. Each mystery represents the embodiment of one of her many masks. The following examples present some of the masks to which a priesthood of Hecate might attune.

Azuran. The draconic god of the four winds connects the magical forces between sky and earth. Clerics of this masked priesthood often assume the mask of Azuran during the day and return to Hecate when her blessed moon rises. Human clerics attune to the domains of Speed and War while dragonkin worshippers attune to the Dragon domain. Alternatively, dragonkin believe Hecate is a mask of Azuran.

Marena. Marena, the red goddess, represents Hecate's attunement to magic derived from fear and death. Clerics dedicated to Marena's mask acknowledge Hecate's connection with depravity and unspeakable evils. The masked priesthood typically attunes to the Death domain, but those following a more primal expression of magic attune to the domain of Lust.

Seggotan. This priesthood views Seggotan's mask as Hecate's connection to the elemental magic of water. Clerics of this priesthood attune to the Tempest or Water domains.

Thoth-Hermes. Hecate typically manifests as a city god, though she can quickly spread her reach beyond city walls. Clerics of this masked priesthood assume the mask of Thoth-Hermes when wandering the world and frequently attune to the Travel domain.

LOKI

Loki is a great deity to use to build a masked priesthood. As the trickster god, he changes his appearance, never manifesting as expected. It lies in the nature of his priesthood for members to assume alternate guises and wear the masks of other beings manipulated by Loki. Conversely, sinister deities such as Chernobog assume the mask of the trickster to appear less monstrous or deviant in their intentions. They don Loki's mask and disguise their intentions' foulness by intertwining them with the trickster's playful pranks. The following examples focus on priesthoods that might choose Loki as a mask.

Baal. Loki represents a human aspect of Baal, a blasphemous belief within the Dragon

Empire. Of all deities that assume Loki's mask, Baal is the most philosophically dissonant. Clerics of this priesthood believe a link between Chaos and Law allows Baal to maintain cosmic balance. They typically choose Knowledge or Trickery as their secondary domains.

Chernobog. Death and darkness often hide secrets. Clerics of this priesthood believe that Chernobog's command of fear lies in his ability to disrupt reality. Clerics of Chernobog who assume Loki's mask use it to attune to the Trickery or Knowledge Domain. Priesthoods concerned with bringing death to all things use Loki's mask to assume his role as the bringer of Ragnarok and attune to the Apocalypse domain.

Surastra. The goddess of the shadow fey and realms of illusion needs to manifest in many forms, especially when she must confront mortals who might question or distrust her motives. The priesthood's clerics assume Loki's mask to attune the Travel domain.

Thoth-Hermes. Clerics of this priesthood focus their concerns on uncovering lore, knowledge, and power. The priesthood attunes to Knowledge as their secondary domain.

Veles. The Midgard serpent takes many forms. Clerics of this priesthood believe that Veles sometimes uses the mask of the trickster to appear before mortals to tempt, trick, or deceive. Clerics of Veles who assume Loki's mask use it to attune to the Trickery domain.

DIVINE INTERVENTIONS: REWARDS FOR THE FAITHFUL

by Rajan Khanna

For most of the clerics and priests of Midgard, the reward for their religious service is divine magic, the ability to shape and alter reality. But while a devoted cleric can gain access to great magic, this is merely a fraction of a given god's power. For the most faithful of priests, those who significantly further their god's goals or effectively spread their faith, additional rewards are possible. These rewards can take various forms, but they generally fall into three general categories: blessings, magic items, and spells:

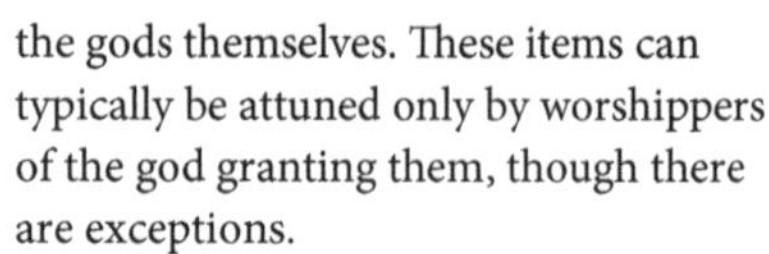

- **Blessings.** Blessings are generally limited-use powers or abilities that the gods grant to their top priests, and their power varies in relation to the how effective that priest has been. A low-level reward, for example, might be a one-time-use ability while a deity's most worthy champions might receive a permanent ability.

- **Magic Items.** Magic items are yet another reward that faithful divine servants can receive from the gods. In many cases, these magic items have been held by the priesthood, stashed away in churches and sepulchers, guarded until one is called to use them. Still, the most beloved champions may receive their items from emissaries of the gods or, in rare occasions,

the gods themselves. These items can typically be attuned only by worshippers of the god granting them, though there are exceptions.

- **Spells.** Clerics receive divine spells from the gods already, but on occasion a deity will grant a specific follower access to a spell that they normally couldn't cast. These can be new spells or spells from another class's spell list. Some of these new spells are detailed in the following pages.

Earning Rewards. The specifics of what earns one of these rewards depends on the god in question and can vary widely. Typically, however, a reward is given either after a great service or labor or in preparation for one. In the latter case, the blessing, item, or spell, is bestowed to aid the cleric in their efforts.

Note that while this article focuses primarily on clerics, these rewards can be bestowed on any dutiful follower, regardless of class. For these followers, the rewards usually take the form of blessings or magic items, unless the follower is already a spellcaster (in which case spells are a possibility). For wizards, these spells are often given in the form of spell pages, which can be copied into the wizard's spellbook.

Below are examples of these rewards for some of Midgard's gods.

Bastet

The goddess Bastet is known to reward her most faithful in sudden and surprising ways, as befits the goddess of cats. She tends to favor hunters and other bold followers who throw themselves into their actions. Gifted perfumers and alchemists might also receive her favor, as do those who destroy powerful serpents or servants of the god Set.

Bastet most often sends a special black cat messenger, fur glinting like starlight. These cat messengers speak, bearing Bastet's message to the chosen. Items are carried by these cats while blessings and other spells are often bestowed with a touch.

Bastet herself appears only to the worthiest of followers. First as a simple messenger cat—or in the wilds as a lion—before transforming into the cat-headed humanoid she is most often depicted as. In presenting her reward, she also marks the recipient with a scratch, a swipe of a single claw that always draws blood. Those so marked wear the resulting scar with honor for the rest of their days.

BLESSINGS

Instill Essence. Bastet's patronage of perfumers can sometimes take the form of a blessing the goddess rewards to her faithful. After a long rest, you can touch a vessel or container of perfume and instill it with a mote of Bastet's essence. Choose one of the options below. The next creature to wear the perfume before your next long rest gains the selected effect for 1 hour:

- *Imposing Presence.* The creature has advantage on Charisma (Intimidation) checks.
- *Seductive Presence.* The creature has advantage on Charisma (Persuasion) checks.

MAGIC ITEMS

The following item may be presented as a boon from Bastet. Other item rewards may include the *courtesan's allure*, figurine of wondrous power (golden lions), luring perfume*,* or *slippers of the cat*.*

(*) see *Vault of Magic.*

BASTET PENDANT

Wondrous Item, Rare (Requires Attunement by a Worshipper of Bastet)

This pendant holds a carved ebony cat with a crescent moon carved in its side. While wearing the pendant, you can use your action to cast

the *polymorph* spell on yourself, transforming into either a **cat** or a **lion**. While you are in one of these forms, you retain your Intelligence, Wisdom, and Charisma scores.

SPELLS

The following spell may be presented as a boon from Bastet. Bastet may also reward her faithful with catfolk spells (see *Southland Players Guide*).

CONJURE CATS

2nd-Level Conjuration | Cleric
Casting Time: 1 action
Range: 60 feet
Components: V, S
Duration: Concentration, up to 1 hour

You summon celestial spirits that take feline form and appear in unoccupied spaces that you can see within range. Choose one of the following options for what appears:

- One **lion**
- One **tiger**
- Four **panthers**
- Eight **cats**

Each beast is also considered a celestial, and it disappears when it drops to 0 hit points or when the spell ends.

The summoned felines are friendly to you and your companions. Roll initiative for the summoned creatures as a group, which has its own turns. They obey any verbal commands that you issue to them (no action required by you). If you don't issue any commands to them, they defend themselves from hostile creatures, but otherwise take no actions.

At Higher Levels. When you cast this spell using certain higher-level spell slots, more creatures appear with your chosen summoning option: twice as many with a 4th-level slot, three times as many with a 6th-level slot, and four times as many with an 8th-level slot.

Khors

Since the worship of Khors is in decline, he sometimes pays more attention to his most ardent followers in hopes that they can help inspire others to honor him. Those who bring others into the fold might earn a reward, as might followers who slay powerful demons and devils. Because of Khors's warrior nature, he often rewards paladin worshippers in addition to his clerics, as well as the occasional devout fighter. Khors's rewards often appear in a ray of sunlight or are bestowed by angels with radiant swords.

BLESSINGS

Radiant Weapon. This blessing is bestowed upon a single weapon of your choice. As a bonus action, you can cause the weapon to emit bright light in a 15-foot radius and dim light for an additional 15 feet. The light is sunlight. When you hit a creature with the weapon while it emits sunlight, the creature takes an extra 1d6 radiant damage (undead creatures instead take an extra 2d6 radiant damage).

MAGIC ITEMS

Magic item rewards from Khors include the *dawn shard*, sun blade*, and *vial of sunlight**. (*) see *Vault of Magic*.

SPELLS

For his most faithful clerics, Khors offers access to the following spells, though often on a limited basis: *branding smite, searing sun* (see *Deep Magic*), *sunbeam*, and *sunburst*.

Loki

Loki doesn't pay much attention to his priests or worshippers, instead urging them to act with skill and cleverness while flouting the rules and strictures of society. As such, he is not known to award his followers with much beyond their typical spells. There is, however, one exception—clerics of Loki who make him

laugh. What exactly will make Loki laugh is a matter of great debate. Some believe only the massive and unexpected absurdity of the fickle and chaotic world can elicit such a laugh while others believe it can only be accomplished by plans within plans, schemes within schemes, all laid to defy and belittle the authority of the powerful, be they rulers or gods. In any case, these rare few might receive the following blessing from the trickster god, and it is almost always a one-time use reward.

BLESSINGS

Loki's Ear Serpent. As a bonus action, you can sing a simple melody or speak a simple phrase that works its way into the ears of a nearby creature, enabling you to affect its mind. Choose one creature that you can see and that can hear you, within 60 feet of you. That creature must make a Wisdom saving throw against your spell save DC. On a failed save, the creature has disadvantage on ability checks, attack rolls, and saving throws for 1 minute as the melody or phrase continues to repeat in its mind. In addition, you can choose one of the following effects:

- ***Serpent's Bliss.*** The creature is charmed by you for 1 hour and is friendly to you and your allies. This charm lasts for the duration, until you or one of your allies attacks the creature, or until you use a bonus action to dismiss it.
- ***Serpent's Hiss.*** The creature is frightened of you for 10 minutes.
- ***Serpent's Kiss.*** The creature is poisoned for 1 minute.

On a successful save, the creature has disadvantage on attack rolls, ability checks, and saving throws for 1 minute but doesn't suffer any additional effects.

Nakresh

Nakresh is a dark god, though one who nevertheless likes to reward the best of his followers, who might be rogues or wizards as well as clerics. Nakresh intentionally foments an air of desperate competition among his most devout followers, including the members of the Five, the leaders of his cult. Nakresh often rewards those followers that commit great acts of theft or who discover or steal magical secrets or powerful magic items.

BLESSINGS

Monkey Familiar. Nakresh sometimes rewards his faithful clerics with access to a monkey familiar. You can cast the *find familiar* spell as a ritual without using any material components. When you cast the spell in this way, your familiar always takes the form of a monkey (use the statistics of a **baboon**, though its size is Tiny).

MAGIC ITEMS

The following item may be presented as a boon from Nakresh.

GLOVES OF NAKRESH

Wondrous Item, Rare (Requires Attunement by a Rogue or Wizard who Worships Nakresh)

These gloves appear to be made from thin, brown leather, or maybe even the skin of a humanoid. They are unadorned save for the images of stars painted on the palms.

While attuned to these gloves, you can use a bonus action to cause a pair of illusory arms to appear in place of your normal arms while your real arms and hands become invisible. Objects that you carry in your hands also become invisible as long as your arms and hands are. While these illusory arms are in place, you gain the following benefits:

- Dexterity (Sleight of Hand) checks are made with advantage.
- If you have the Sneak Attack ability, you don't need advantage on the attack roll to

use your Sneak Attack against a creature if you are within 5 feet of it and you don't have disadvantage on the attack roll.

- While casting a spell, you can conceal its' somatic and material components.

The illusory arms last for a minute or until you use a bonus action to dismiss them. You must complete a long rest before you can use the gloves again.

The following spell may be presented as a boon from Nakresh. In addition, Nakresh can share with his followers the *scattered images* spell (see *Demon Cults & Secret Societies*).

WALL OF HANDS

6th-Level Conjuration | Cleric
Casting Time: 1 action
Range: 120 feet
Components: V, S, M
Duration: Concentration, up to 1 minute

A wall of writhing, animated humanoid hands appears at a point you choose within range. The wall appears within range on a solid surface and lasts for the duration. You can choose to make the wall up to 60 feet long, 10 feet high, and 5 feet thick. The hands reach out from both sides of the wall. The wall blocks line of sight.

If the wall cuts through a creature's space when it appears, the creature is pushed to one side of the wall (your choice). Any creature that enters a space within 5 feet of the wall or starts its turn within 5 feet of the wall must make a Strength saving throw. On a failed save, the creature is grappled and has disadvantage on ability checks and attack rolls until the start of its next turn. If a creature succeeds on the saving throw, it is not grappled but still has disadvantage on attack rolls and ability check rolls.

Additionally, you can cast a spell with a range of touch and have the spell originate from a point on the wall instead of from you.

Ninkash

The Mother of Beer likes to reward those of her followers who excel both at the brewing of beer and the ability to bring people together (often over that beer). Some of her most favored worshippers start breweries and alehouses. Ninkash speaks to her followers through ale, often bestowing her rewards through drunken visions.

BLESSINGS

Because beer and ale are temporary, enjoyed in the consumption, Ninkash's blessings are almost always temporary, often single-use abilities, with the exception of the following blessing.

Ale-chemy. You can hold a container of beer or ale and use an action to infuse it with the blessings of Ninkash. Choose one of the following options. That effect takes place when a creature consumes the infused beverage within the next hour:

- *Aid.* The creature has advantage on the first attack roll or skill check that it makes in the next 24 hours.
- *Fortify.* The creature has a +1 bonus to all saving throws for 1 hour.
- *Heal.* The creature regains 1d8 hit points.

MAGIC ITEMS

The following item may be presented as a boon from Ninkash. In addition, Ninkash sometimes rewards followers with a *wand of fermentation* (see *Vault of Magic*).

BOTTOMLESS TANKARD

Wondrous Item, Very Rare (Requires Attunement by a Follower of Ninkash)

While beer is meant to be consumed and not kept for long periods of time, this tankard allows you to store multiple varieties of beer or other liquids in it. Five magical runes are

inscribed upon this tankard. If you pour a liquid into the tankard and press one of the runes, it is transported into an extradimensional space. Pressing that rune again will fill the tankard with that liquid. Once all five runes are used, no more liquid can be stored within the tankard until one of the runes is emptied.

SPELLS

The following spell may be presented as a boon from Ninkash.

TOAST THE GODDESS

3rd-Level Transmutation | Cleric
Casting Time: 1 action
Range: Touch
Components: V, S, M (a full tankard of beer or ale)
Duration: Instantaneous

When you cast this spell, you create six full tankards of beer or ale that resemble the tankard and beverage used in the casting. Creatures that consume one of the tankards within the next hour gain temporary hit points equal to your spellcasting ability modifier.

Ogun

Ogun most often rewards his followers in the guise of the Keeper of Keys and Dungeons. Explorers, those who open closed doors, can gain his favor as can effective wardens and jailors, those who protect civilized people from criminals and monsters. Blessings and spells often seem to be "unlocked" inside the recipient's mind while magic items often appear when the recipient opens or unlocks a container or door.

BLESSINGS

Door Warden. This blessing allows the recipient to cast the *arcane lock* or *knock* spells (once per day each) without the need for components.

Lock Whisperer. This blessing grants you advantage on checks using thieves' tools made to pick or otherwise manipulate locks.

MAGIC ITEMS

The following item may be presented as a boon from Ninkash. In addition, Ogun sometimes rewards his most faithful followers with the following items: *burglar's lock and key*, chime of opening, dimensional shackles, iron bands of binding, seneschal's gloves*,* and *skeleton key*.*
(*) see *Vault of Magic.*

INFINITY KEY

Wondrous Item, Very Rare (Requires Attunement by a Follower of Ogun)

This key can take various forms, from an old key threaded with verdigris to a shiny new one, but its abilities remain the same regardless of its appearance. While attuned to the key, you can use an action to insert the key into any door lock and "pair" the key to that door.

If you later use an action to insert the key into a different door lock on the same plane of existence as the paired door, the current door will open to the location the paired door led to instead of its usual destination. This effect lasts for an hour. Any creature or object that passes through the door will end up where the original, paired door led. After the hour is finished, the key will not operate until the next dawn.

SPELLS

Ogun often grants his clerics access to the *arcane lock* and *knock* spells and sometimes to the *door of the far traveler* spell (see *Tome of Heroes*).

Rava

Rava is already known for rewarding her faithful by making them into gearforged, but she also rewards her other devout followers.

BLESSINGS

Spark of Creation (Usable by Gearforged Only). While typically Rava oversees new creations, some of that same creative power can be used to repair damaged gearforged. As a gearforged with this blessing, you can use

a bonus action to immediately regain 50 hit points of damage. This blessing is usually a one-time use.

MAGIC ITEMS

The following item may be presented as a boon from Rava. In addition, Rava has also been known to reward followers with items such as the *clockwork mace of divinity** or other clockwork magic items as well as the *loom of fate** and *quill of scribing**.

(*) see *Vault of Magic*.

ARIADNE'S TOOLS

Wondrous Item, Very Rare (Requires Attunement by a Worshipper of Rava)

These tools are identical to a set of weaver's tools except that they are of a higher quality and resistant to rust and wear. When you use these to make an ability check, you have advantage on that check.

While attuned to the tools, when you complete a long rest, you can roll a d20 and write down the result. Once before your next long rest, you can substitute that number for one ability check roll, attack roll, or saving throw roll. If you use this number on an ability check made with the tools, you can also double your proficiency bonus for the check.

SPELLS

In addition to the *soulforging* spell itself (see *Midgard Heroes Handbook*), Rava also can reward her followers with a variety of clockwork spells if they don't have access to those already.

Sabateus

Sabateus typically rewards his followers who recover hidden and ancient lore or who teach the knowledge of the stars and constellations to others. In addition to clerics, druids of the Circle of Stars also honor Sabateus and may be rewarded for their service.

BLESSINGS

Child of the Night. This blessing grants the following abilities:

- When traveling at night, your travel pace is doubled.
- You can always tell which way is north at night
- You gain darkvision to a range of 60 feet.
- You have advantage on Wisdom (Perception) checks when the moon or stars are visible.

MAGIC ITEMS

Sabateus sometimes rewards his faithful followers with magic items such as the *ring of shooting stars* or *robe of stars*.

SPELLS

The following spells are sometimes granted to Sabateus's most devoted clerics: *guiding star**, *shield of starlight**, *starburst**, *starfall**, *star's heart**, and *summon star**.

(*) see *Deep Magic*.

CLOISTERS OF OUTER DARKNESS: THE INEVITABILITY OF RAGNAROK

by Wolfgang Baur

The roots of Yggdrasil grow deep in the void between the stars, and always they suffer from the gnawing of the ancient void dragon Nidhogg. By this ancient wyrm's side stand the scribes of the satarre, taking down the words that will unravel creation and end the foolish work of the gods. In each utterance from the void, these seekers encrypt arcane power over death and destruction, gaining new tools to hammer home the utter inevitability of the void.

Writing down the words of Nidhogg is only the first step in the work of the void cults. Once this dark lore is faithfully written out, it is swiftly conveyed to the Cloisters of Outer Darkness in the Shadow Realm, to its scriptorium in Soriglass, the city of shades and wraiths. There the most potent elements are copied out and sent to the priests of the dark gods: followers of Chernobog, Vardesain, and the Hunter, as well as the White Goddess and Mot, the Lord of Death. Slowly, corruption seeps and spreads from the scaly lips of the void dragon to the widest reaches of the multiverse.

This is the wellspring of the arcane school of void magic (first revealed in *Midgard Worldbook*, expanded further in *Deep Magic*, and continued here for the corruption and education of Warlock patrons).

Hidden Cults of the Doomridden Void

Void cultists are a secretive lot. They seek to destroy all life and all creation, so naturally they make few friends. And yet, controlling such apocalyptic power is thrilling, and the forces of negation, destruction, and death are powerful ones to wield for anyone seeking dominion over the existing world. So who are these destroyers, and where are their efforts focused? Little is known about most of them, though four groups seem to have lasted longer than most. They seem to fall into many mutually suspicious groups, all occasionally allies but more often rivals.

DOOMBRINGERS

As fallen paladins and their allies, the Doombringers are a force for primal destruction—they smash, kill, burn, and destroy. Their goals are to burn cities, wipe out villages, and end the reign of living things by the slow, purposeful murder of anyone and everyone who is not a void cultist. They are known for their use of soul-killing weapons, shields that disintegrate what they touch, and other items and techniques considered abominable by most warrior creeds (such as plague weapons, undead foot soldiers, and the destruction of harvests, wells, and granaries).

Their leaders change rapidly. Since most Doombringers are led by charismatic individuals intent on immediate carnage, their time as "First Among the Doombringers" tends to be short. They operate in small groups throughout the planes, gathering zealous followers through promises of riches, power, and the sheer sadistic joy of tearing down what others have built and grown over years or centuries. Demons and devils are frequently their allies or even servants.

FOLLOWERS OF THE PURE VOID

A rather esoteric group of largely human, satarre, and dwarven mystics, mostly men, these bookish cultists are among those who seek to use knowledge in the pursuit of Ragnarok—or other apocalyptic end times. This often culminates in summoning a cosmic horror or a major fiend, such as a **spawn of Hriggala** (see *Tome of Beasts 2*) or a simple **voidling** (see *Tome of Beasts*). They haunt the libraries of major cities, infiltrating wizard's collegiums and guilds, with an eye toward locked rooms of forbidden manuscripts, and they go adventuring to recover lost or buried works of significance to the void, always seeking to unlock the great blasphemous secrets that will unmake the world. In particular, they seek the bones and relics of void saints and godlings (such as the *bones of the holy Myegathar* and the *Crimson Scepter*, see below), and they often visit the Void itself or dredge it with *mooncatcher's nets* bought at some expense from the shadow goblins of Fandeval. (For more on *mooncatcher's nets*, see *Book of Ebon Tides*, noting that memories can be harvested normally in the Void only on the Ever River. Using the nets throughout the greater Void has only a 20% chance of recovering 1d2 memories since the memories are more dispersed—though those found can have a unique piquancy from their time in the Void.)

The Followers of the Pure Void deny having a leader, as such, but their eldest and most respected figures are two rivals who seem to enjoy one another's company, though their followers always proclaim the greatness of one or the other. The elder is the red-robed Toothless Crumble, a venerable dwarven wizard with a thin white beard and an incredibly keen memory for void lore and symbols. Toothless is said to live on a drifting tower of pure force anchored in the Plane of Stars (more often called the Astral Plane). Equally ancient and learned is Chuptar alz-Faragh, a satarre cleric and scholar whose understanding of Void Speech and the various dark gods is wide-ranging. He often writes short tracts speaking out against monarchies, guilds, and judges—his dream is a world without laws or rulers, where might always makes right and the altars of the dark gods are always bloodstained. He is said to live on a drifting mountaintop where a bridge woven of Yggdrasil's branches serves as a gateway to the multiverse.

SCRIBES OF THE BLACK STAR

This tiny order of satarre and humans visit Nidhogg and transcribe its baleful utterances into Void Speech scrolls that expand the power of the void cults. Most senior members of the cult are older and bookish, though not all. The blackguard Plaguebringer, an enormous bald human, protects Elder Jesparga Lavide, the high priest of Hrigalla, at the roots of Yggdrasil and ensures that the satarre and selang who carry Lavide's scrolls to the Shadow Realm travel quickly and safely. Elder Lavide himself wears a *Mantle of the Void Lord* and carries a dozen potent scrolls for defense. He retains a retinue of void cultists and satarre mystics. Some of these zealots are invariably eaten when the great Nidhogg hungers, but Plaguebringer always brings more eager servants when the supply runs low.

Most of the other scribes of the order do their work secretly, hidden in small scriptoria and back rooms in shrines to other gods. A few work openly in lands where the dark lords are worshipped, and the will of the peasants is bent to gathering quills, making parchment, and

boiling walnut gall for ink. These scribes know each other through a small black star tattoo, typically marked on the wrist of the writing hand or on an ankle.

SISTERHOOD OF THE OUTER DARKNESS

A clerical order devoted to the Void seems a contradiction, but the sisterhood worships the Void with intense fervor and is granted divine power from the darkest side of the cosmos. They see Chernobog, Alquam, Fenris, the Hunter, Hriggala, and the White Goddess as manifestations of the urge for death and chaos, and they consider them prophets or lesser manifestations of the True Void, a being whose purpose is to end the world. Their cloisters in the Shadow Realm receive the writings of the Scribes of the Black Star (their partners who traffic in delivering the translated visions of Elder Lavide).

The cloisters themselves allow only female visitors beyond the First Courtyard, and the order guards its secrets well. Many void saints and Doombringers are said to have been laid to rest in its crypts, and others have been raised from the dead many times—at least until their work brings about the ultimate realization of the Void or their physical bodies fall apart entirely. The main temple is said to contain a living *sphere of annihilation* for sacrificing unbelievers and to be secured by **chained angels** (see *Tome of Beasts*) and **voidlings** (see *Tome of Beasts*), singing a chorus of maledictions.

Their leader is a human with a round face, auburn hair, and a wicked smile: Mother Boslara the Sweet, a practical, manipulative, and extremely dangerous high priestess of the

Dark Pantheon. She is said to be accompanied at all times by a **voidling** bodyguard, and outside of the cloisters themselves, she is most often found riding an **adult boreal dragon** (see *Tome of Beasts 2*) named Frostheart.

Magic Items from the Void

Though followers of the Void seek the destruction of all things, they still find tools useful. Their magic items are quite distinctly made to destroy and to negate life, health, and creation itself.

AMULET OF THE OUTER DARKNESS

Wondrous Item, Common
(Requires Attunement)

This deep-blue sapphire is carved with a single eye surrounded by tentacles or wavy rays. The object is always cool to the touch. You gain the ability to understand and speak Void Speech. In addition, you do not need to breathe when in an airless space (but you are still affected by gas or air effects when in an atmosphere).

BONES OF THE HOLY MYEGATHAR

Wondrous Item, Rare (Requires Attunement by a Wizard or Cleric)

The bones of a void saint are dangerous tools, often a dark-purplish color with ends or joints of pale blue, imbued with the unholy power of the Void. While holding them, you gain the ability to cast the *conjure minor voidborn* spell (see *Deep Magic*) once per day. The conjured creatures obey you so long as they are addressed using Void Speech and will remain nearby for up to 1 hour, fighting for you, guarding a location, or undertaking other tasks. In addition, you are resistant to radiant damage.

CLOAK OF THE VOID

Wondrous Item, Rare (Requires Attunement)

This cloak resembles a field of scattered stars and comets, sometimes shining with color and often in motion. While wearing this cloak, you are immune to spells of 1st to 3rd level, both beneficial and harmful spells. Spells targeting you simply seem to be absorbed and disappear into its fabric.

CRIMSON SCEPTER

Wand, Legendary (Requires Attunement by a Bard, Cleric, or Wizard)

This ancient emblem of the void takes the form of a red-gold scepter with a winding serpent along its length, worked in black opal, and topped with the skull of a void dragon wyrmling, wrapped in a black mist. Some followers of the Doombringers and the Scribes of the Black Star believe this scepter was once used by a dead god or a saint such as Myegathar, and certainly it contains vast amounts of energy.

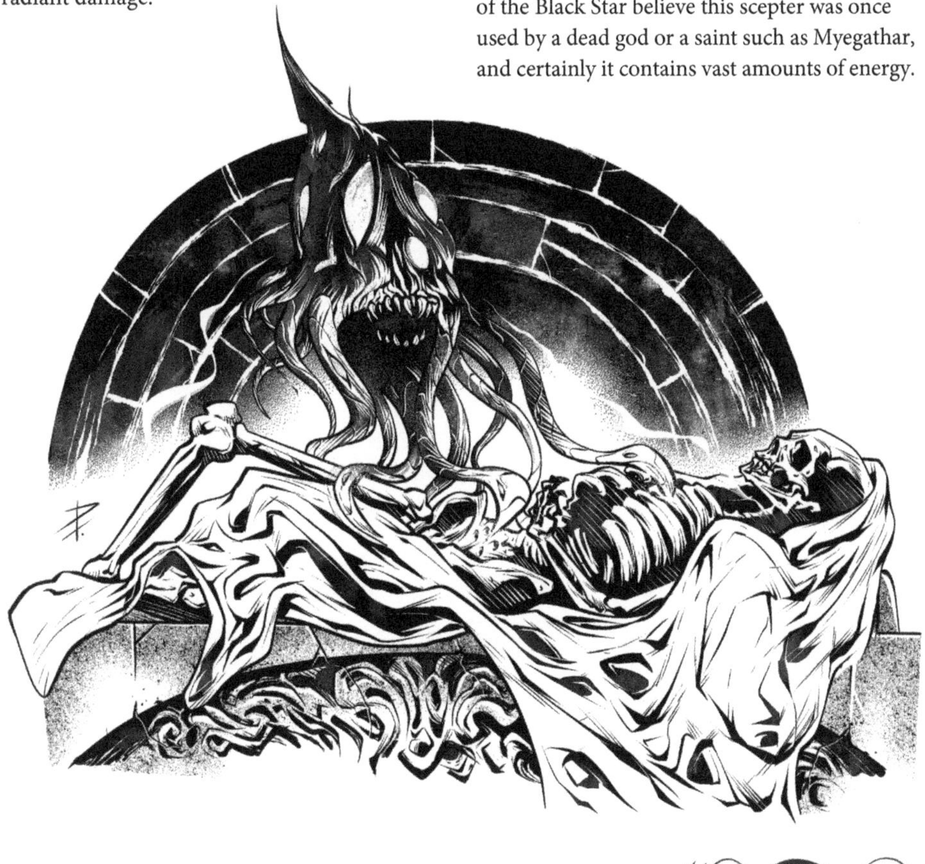

This scepter has 12 charges for the following properties. It regains 1d8 + 1 expended charges daily at dawn. If you expend the scepter's last charge, roll a d20. On a 1, the scepter crumbles into ash and is destroyed.

Anyone holding the scepter and speaking its command word in Void Speech can perform the following actions:

- *Doom Weapon.* By expending 1 charge, any melee weapons you hold while also wielding the *Crimson Scepter* are immediately empowered with an unholy red glow, and you gain a bonus action to make a melee attack, dealing an extra 2d12 necrotic damage on a hit. If the attack fails, the glow and its charged necrotic damage remain so long as you hold the *Crimson Scepter* and the weapon. If either is dropped, the necrotic damage vanishes.

- *Voidstorm.* By expending 3 charges, you may generate three rays of void energy and throw them at one or more targets within 60 feet. Roll a ranged spell attack for each ray. If it hits, the target takes 1d12 necrotic damage. You can spend additional charges to increase the damage by 1d12 per additional charge spent.

- *Unspeakable Utterance.* By expending 6 charges, you can speak an unholy word that affects all creatures within 60 feet of you. This powerful sonic attack strikes fear into the hearts of those affected and damages their sensitive tissues, causing shortness of breath, bleeding from the eyes and ears, and temporary blindness and deafness. Those within the area must make a DC 16 Constitution saving throw, taking 12d6 necrotic or psychic damage (your choice) and being blinded and deafened for 1 minute on a failed save or half that damage and no additional effects on a successful one.

Whenever 4 or more charges are expended at once, you gain 1 point of void taint. (Void taint is an optional rule from the *Midgard Worldbook*.)

DAGGER OF VOID STRIKING
Weapon (Dagger), Uncommon

While holding this dagger, you can speak the command word to gather writhing darkness around your hand. You can then make a ranged spell attack as a bonus action to unleash a bolt of darkness at a creature within 30 feet. If the target is in dim light or darkness, you have advantage on the roll. On a hit, the target takes 5d8 necrotic damage and is frightened until the start of your next turn.

The dagger's property can't be used again until the next dawn. In the meantime, the dagger can still be used as a magic weapon.

DOOMBRINGER'S BLADE
Weapon (Any Ax, Halberd, Sword, or Dagger), Rare (Requires Attunement)

This magic weapon resembles a slice of pure black energy surrounded by a purple or blue nimbus. You gain a +1 bonus to attack and damage rolls made with it. You can choose as a bonus action to change the damage dealt by an attack made with this weapon to necrotic.

In addition, you can use a *doombringer's blade* to tear a hole in reality, ripping open the planar fabric to show the void and shadow just beyond the threshold. You must slice the blade across an unoccupied area as an action, creating a 5-foot cube filled with a dark rift to the Void. Air and water immediately begin to move through the rift, and creatures adjacent to this space must immediately make a DC 14 Strength saving throw while in air or a DC 18 Strength saving throw while in water. On a successful save, they maintain their position. On a failed save, they are drawn into the space containing the rift and take 2d12 force damage. Moving out of the space is treated as moving through difficult terrain. The rift remains until it has consumed either a sentient being or enough solid material to fill a 10-foot cube. This property can't be used again until after a long rest.

EMPYREAN HALO

Wondrous Item, Very Rare
(Requires Attunement)

This open-faced deep-azure helmet is set with bands of bright mithral and generates a solid black, disk-like halo around your head as a protective mark of the dark gods. While wearing the helm, you gain a +1 bonus to armor class and resistance to fire and radiant damage.

FIGURINE OF WONDROUS POWER, MALACHITE SELANG

Wondrous Item, Rare

A *figurine of wondrous power* is a statuette of a beast, small enough to fit in a pocket. If you use an action to speak the command word and throw the figurine to a point on the ground within 60 feet of you, the figurine becomes a living creature. If the space where the creature would appear is occupied by other creatures or objects or if there isn't enough space for the creature, the figurine doesn't become a creature.

The creature is friendly to you and your companions. It understands your languages and obeys your spoken commands. If you issue no commands, the creature defends itself but takes no other actions.

The creature exists for a duration specific to each figurine. At the end of the duration, the creature reverts to its figurine form. It reverts to a figurine early if it drops to 0 hit points or if you use an action to speak the command word again while touching it. When the creature becomes a figurine again, its property can't be used again until a certain amount of time has passed, as specified in the figurine's description.

Malachite Selang. This malachite statuette is of a selang, prancing and playing a pan flute. It can become a **selang** (see *Tome of Beasts*) and play its alien pipes for up to 1 hour. All creatures within 60 feet that can hear it must make a successful DC 14 Wisdom saving throw or be affected by the *hideous laughter* spell. On a successful save, a creature is immune to the piping for 24 hours. Once it has been used, it can't be used again until 3 days have passed.

FROZEN STARRY HALF PLATE

Armor (Half Plate), Legendary
(Requires Attunement)

Said to be crafted by imbuing the hide of a void dragon with null matter and binding it with shadow, this black armor seems to contain stars, comets, and wispy, void-like veils of purple, red, and blue. You gain a +1 bonus to AC while you wear this armor. In addition, the wielder of any manufactured weapon that successfully hits you must make a DC 15 Constitution saving throw. On a failed save, the weapon deals damage normally, and if it's nonmagical, it then crumbles to dust and is destroyed, but if it's magical, it instead is sapped of all magical properties until after the wielder takes a short or long rest (though it is still considered magical, such as for overcoming damage resistance). Creatures that hit you with natural weapons, must also make the saving throw, dealing damage normally but then taking 1d12 necrotic damage on a failed save.

GRIMOIRE OF THE ELDEST

Wondrous Item, Very Rare
(Requires Attunement)

Anyone who reads this volume detailing the foundations of the cult of the void, said to be bound in leather made from human skin, gains 1 point of void taint. It contains all spells with the **void** or **mythos** keyword (see also *Deep Magic*) and can be used to learn any and all of them. It also functions as a direct portal to the purest essence of the Void, a source of alien wisdom that answers questions and prophesizes the future with frightening accuracy.

You can pose a question to the *grimoire of the eldest*, making a DC 16 Charisma saving throw. On a successful save, you know the answer, as if a *commune* or a *legend lore* spell had been cast successfully. On a failed save, you gain 1 point of void taint. This property can't be used again until after a long rest.

(Void taint is an optional rule from the *Midgard Worldbook*.)

HELMET OF NULLIFICATION

Wondrous Item, Very Rare
  (Requires Attunement)

This helmet, covered in rust and verdigris, features glowing inlays in Void Speech. The helm has 3 charges. While wearing the helm, as an action, you can expend 1 charge to surround yourself with a 10-foot-radius invisible antimagic field, cutting you off from the magic imbuing the universe. Within the area, spells can't be cast, summoned creatures disappear, and even magic items become mundane. The effect moves with you, centered on you, and ends after 10 rounds or when you speak the command word. Wizards and clerics wearing the helmet may expend 3 charges and maintain concentration to extend the duration up to an hour. The helm regains all its charges 24 hours after its last charge is expended.

KEY OF THE STARFIELD

Wondrous Item, Rare

While you hold this item, you can propel yourself and up to four other willing creatures safely through the emptiness of the Void, with an effective flying speed of 120 feet.

MANTLE OF THE VOID LORD

Wondrous Item, Legendary
  (Requires Attunement by a Cleric, Sorcerer,
  Warlock, or Wizard)

This luminous garment is made from rich purple cloth stitched with spirals, runes, and comets in golden thread. It has a long hood of black, trimmed in white dragon scales.

You gain the following benefits while wearing the robe:

- Creatures of the Void will not attack you while you wear the robe.

- If you aren't wearing armor, your base armor class is 14 + your Dexterity modifier.

- You can speak and understand Void Speech.

- Your spell save DC and spell attack bonus each increase by 1 for spells with the **void** keyword (see also *Deep Magic*). Targets have disadvantage on saving throws against these spells.

POTION OF VOID SURVIVAL

Potion, Rare

For 1 hour after you drink this potion, you are immune to cold and necrotic damage, and you do not require air if you are a breathing creature.

SCARLET KEY

Wondrous Item, Legendary (Requires
  Attunement by a Bard, Cleric, or Wizard)

When you speak the command word and turn the key while pointing it at foe wearing metallic armor, this item turns the armor molten. The wearer of any metallic armor that is targeted by the *Scarlet Key* must make a DC 15 Dexterity saving throw. On a failed save, the armor, if it's nonmagical, melts and is destroyed, and the target takes 6d6 fire damage, but if the armor's magical, the wearer still suffers the damage, and the armor is not destroyed but instead sapped of all magical properties until after the wearer takes a short or long rest (though it is still considered magical).

If combined with the *Crimson Scepter*, the *Scarlet Key* unlocks an eternal blue flame that dances atop the scepter, which now regains all expended charges each day at dawn, instead of its usual 1d8 + 1.

SHIELD OF ANNIHILATION

Armor (Shield), Very Rare

This entirely black shield resembles a hole in the multiverse. No light that touches it seems to escape. While you are wielding the shield, any weapon attack that misses you by 1 or 2 points on the roll means the weapon is blocked and annihilated. (Wielders of magical weapons are entitled to a DC 14 Dexterity saving throw to avoid the weapon's annihilation.) Artifacts are unaffected by the shield. Creatures whose natural weapons miss you by 1 or 2 points on the roll are not annihilated, but they must succeed on a DC 14 Dexterity saving throw or take 4d10 force damage.

Deliberately touching an object to annihilate it works as expected, destroying up to 2 cubic feet of material each round. However, the shield begins to glow red and purple after each single object destroyed or every 8-cubic-foot portion of a larger object it consumes. After the third object is consumed or after 24 cubic feet of matter are annihilated before taking a long rest, the shield's enchantment overloads, and the shield crumbles to dust.

SHIELD OF INFINITY

Armor (Shield), Rare (Requires Attunement)

The shield has 3 charges, and it regains 1d3 expended charges daily at dawn. If you are holding the shield, you can target a creature within 5 feet as an action. The target must succeed on a DC 15 Dexterity saving throw or be sucked into the airless void within the shield itself and be teleported 60 feet to an unoccupied space of your choice.

STAFF OF RUIN

Staff, Very Rare
  (Requires Attunement by Cleric)

This staff can be wielded as a magic quarterstaff that grants a +2 bonus to attack and damage rolls made with it.

This staff has 9 charges for the following properties. It regains 1d6 + 3 expended charges daily at dawn. If you expend the staff's last charge, roll a d20. On a 1, the staff is destroyed in a fiery burst of brimstone.

Spells. While holding the staff, you can use an action to expend 1 or more of its charges to cast one of the following spells from it, using your spell save DC: *black hole* (9 charges, see *Deep Magic*), *hellfire blitz* (2 charges, see *Deep Magic*), or *insect plague* (5 charges).

Voice of Ruin. While holding the staff, you can use an action and expend 1 charge to empower your weapon and spell attacks. For 1 minute, all successful attacks you make against objects and constructs are treated as critical hits.

STAFF OF THE STARRY ABYSS

Staff, Very Rare (Requires Attunement by a
  Druid, Sorcerer, Warlock, or Wizard)

You have resistance to necrotic damage while you hold this staff.

The staff has 10 charges. It regains 1d6 + 4 charges daily at dawn. If you expend the last charge, roll a d20. On a 1, the staff crumbles to ash and is destroyed.

Spells. While holding the staff, you can use an action to expend 1 or more of its charges to cast one of the following spells from it, using your spell save DC: *conjure minor voidborn* (5 charges, see *Deep Magic*), *doom of the endless void* (5 charges, see below), *dust and ashes* (4 charges, see below), or *tooth of the wyrm* (1 charge, see below).

STAFF OF UNRAVELING

Wand, Rare (Requires Attunement by a Bard,
  Cleric, Druid, Sorcerer, Warlock, or Wizard)

This staff has 7 charges for the following properties. It regains 1d6 + 1 expended charges daily at dawn. If you expend the staff's last charge, roll a d20. On a 1, the staff crumbles to ash and is destroyed.

VOID CULT WARRIORS

Warriors of the various void cults are a strange lot, often armed poorly and led by fanatics. However, some of the more capable and trusted veterans are often given *shields of annihilation* to use against their foes. These items are enchanted fairly quickly and are quite potent but can be easily overloaded if a foe knows their weak points or simply avoids striking the shield.

Spells. While holding the staff, you can use an action to expend 1 or more of its charges to cast one of the following spells from it, using your spell save DC: *banishment* (5 charges) or *dispel magic* (2 charges).

Unravel Matter. With this staff, you can disintegrate any non-magical object weighing less than 1 pound by expending a charge and speaking the command word.

Unravel Creature. By expending 2 charges and speaking the command word, you can choose a creature that you can see within 30 feet. The creature must make a Constitution saving throw. The DC for this saving throw equals 8 + your Constitution modifier + your proficiency bonus. A creature that fails the saving throw must use its action each turn to repeat the saving throw as it attempts to keep itself in one piece. On a successful save, the effect ends on the target. Once you use this feature, you cannot do so again until you complete a long rest.

Spells from the Void

Void magic in its purest form—those spells with the **void** keyword—is the domain of wizards only (see also *Deep Magic*) due to the intense focus and study demanded. However, thanks to the work of the collective cloisters of the Outer Darkness, much of what has been learned from the Void has been greatly distilled and made accessible to a wider variety of spellcasters, bringing the end of things that much closer by ensuring more curious fingers have access to the Void's influence.

For most casters, these spells must be found, rather than known automatically when gaining a level. Void Speech is required to cast them, and the GM may also require that a caster either have the Void Channeler or Void Scribe feat or be a member of a void cult or the Void Savant subclass (see *Midgard Worldbook* for these feats and subclasses).

DOOM OF DESTINY

2nd-Level Enchantment (Cleric, Wizard)
Casting Time: 1 action
Range: 30 feet
Components: V, S, M (a cracked mirror)
Duration: Concentration, up to 1 minute

Up to three creatures of your choice that you can see within range must make Charisma saving throws. Whenever a target that fails this saving throw makes an attack roll or a saving throw before the spell ends, the target rolls with disadvantage.

At Higher Levels. When you cast this spell using a spell slot of 3rd level or higher, you can target one additional creature for each slot level above 2nd.

DOOM OF FOOLS

1st-Level Necromancy (Bard, Wizard)
Casting Time: 1 action
Range: Self (10-foot radius)
Components: V, S, M (a small bell)
Duration: Concentration, up to 1 minute

All creatures within 10 feet of you must make a Wisdom saving throw. You must also make

BLOOD & DOOM MAGIC

The magics of blood and doom—these two styles of magic are often considered related, but their practitioners and their methods are quite distinct. Blood magic draws on blood sacrifices and empowers spells using the vitality of living creatures, and usually the number of creatures affected is quite small. Doom magic, on the other hand, uses the apocalyptic power of the Void to affect multiple creatures with destructive or harmful effect, usually including the caster as a target (for doom is unavoidable).

this save. On a failed save, targets become inept for the duration of the spell. When you cast this spell, choose one of the following:

- Choose one ability score. While doomed, the target has disadvantage on ability checks and saving throws made with that ability score.
- While doomed, the target falls prone at the start of each round, and its speed is halved.
- While doomed, the target must make a Wisdom saving throw at the start of each of its turns. If it fails, it wastes its action that turn, doing nothing.

At Higher Levels. When you cast this spell using a spell slot of 2nd level or higher, the duration is up to 10 minutes. If you use a spell slot of 3rd level or higher, the duration is up to 8 hours. Using a spell slot of 4th level or higher grants a duration that doesn't require concentration.

DOOM OF LAUGHTER

3rd-Level Enchantment (Bard, Wizard)
Casting Time: 1 action
Range: Self (10-foot radius)
Components: V, S, M (a chicken doll)
Duration: Concentration, up to 1 minute

All creatures within range (including you) perceive everything as hilariously funny and fall into fits of laughter if this spell affects them. The targets must make a Wisdom saving throw. You must also make this save. On a failed save, targets fall prone, becoming incapacitated and unable to stand up for the duration. Creatures with an Intelligence score of 4 or less are not affected. At the end of each of its turns, and each time it takes damage, a target can make another Wisdom saving throw. The target has advantage on the saving throw if it's triggered by damage. On a success, the spell's effect ends.

DOOM OF NIGHT

6th-Level Conjuration (Wizard)
Casting Time: 1 action
Range: 120 feet
Components: V, S, M (a vial of shadow dust)
Duration: Concentration, up to 10 minutes

You create a 30-foot-radius sphere of pulsing, luminous purple mist centered on a point you choose within range. This area is heavily obscured. When a creature enters the spell's area for the first time on a turn or starts its turn there, that creature must make a Constitution saving throw, taking 5d12 necrotic damage on a failed save or half as much damage on a successful one. Creatures are affected even if they hold their breath or don't need to breathe. After leaving the mist, the creature takes 5 points of necrotic damage per round until it succeeds on a Constitution saving throw or dies.

At Higher Levels. When you cast this spell using a spell slot of 7th level or higher, the damage increases by 1d12 for each slot level above 6th. The follow-on damage increases by 1 point for each slot level above 6th.

DOOM OF THE BLACK RIVER

4th-Level Transmutation (Druid, Wizard)
Casting Time: 1 action
Range: Self (10-foot radius)
Components: V, S, M (marsh water)
Duration: Instantaneous

You speak a word of unmaking that devours all wood and leather in the area, destroying leather armor, shield straps, spear shafts, arrows, bows, staves, clubs, and so forth, including your own items. Objects made of other materials, such as linen, wool, glass, and metals, are unaffected. Items that are worn or held gain a collective Dexterity saving throw by the wearer. On a successful save, none of that wearer's items are affected. Magical items are never affected by this spell.

DOOM OF THE ENDLESS VOID

6th-Level Transmutation (Void) (Wizard)
Casting Time: 1 action
Range: Self
Components: V, S, M (iron filings and a vial of acid)
Duration: Concentration

You open a rift into the Void itself, tearing apart reality around you. All creatures within 20 feet of you must make a Constitution saving throw. You must also make this save. On a failed save, the target takes 6d6 + 20 force damage. If this damage reduces the target to 0 hit points, it is disintegrated. A disintegrated creature and everything it is wearing and carrying, except magic items, are reduced to a pile of fine gray dust. The creature can be restored to life only by means of a *true resurrection* or *wish* spell. This spell automatically disintegrates a Large or smaller nonmagical object or a creation of magical force. If the target is a Huge or larger object or creation of force, this spell disintegrates a 10-foot-cube portion of it each round. A magic item is unaffected by this spell.

If you maintain concentration on the spell, the same saving throw is required again on your next turn—you must make your saving throw before any target creatures do. If the spell kills you, the effect ends immediately.

DUST AND ASHES

4th-Level Transmutation (Wizard)
Casting Time: 1 action
Range: 30 feet
Components: V, S, M (a ball of crumbly dirt)
Duration: Instantaneous

A thin green ray springs from your pointing finger to a target that you can see within range. The target can be any nonmagical physical object, to a maximum size of 10 feet on a side. If the target is held by a creature, that creature must make a Dexterity saving throw. On a failed save, the disintegrated object is reduced to a pile of fine gray dust. This spell automatically and completely disintegrates

a Large or smaller nonmagical
object or a creation of
magical force. If the target
is a Huge or larger object
or creation of force, this
spell disintegrates a
10-foot-cube portion
of it. A magic item is
unaffected by this spell.

At Higher Levels. When
you cast this spell using
a spell slot of 5th level
or higher, the object size
increases by another
10-foot-cube for each
slot level above 4th.

LAST STRIKE

1st-Level Abjuration (Cleric, Paladin, Wizard)

Casting Time: 1 reaction, which you take
  when you drop to 0 hit points as a result of
  taking damage
Range: Self
Components: V, S
Duration: 1 round

You grant yourself a last burst of energy when
deeply wounded. Before you fall unconscious,
you gain one action. Any roll you make,
such as for an ability check or attack, has
advantage. You automatically fail your first
death saving throw.

NIDHOGG'S BLESSING

*3rd-Level Transmutation
  (Bard, Cleric, Druid, Sorcerer, Wizard)*

Casting Time: 1 action
Range: 60 feet
Components: V, S, M (plate of satarre chitin)
Duration: Concentration, up to 1 hour

This spell transforms a creature that you can
see within range into a new form beloved of
the Void. An unwilling creature must make
a Wisdom saving throw to avoid the effect. A
shapechanger automatically succeeds on this
saving throw. The transformation lasts for

the duration or until the target drops to 0 hit points or dies. If the target is willing, it can retain the new form for 1 day. The new form can be either a **satarre destroyer** (see *Tome of Beast 2*), **satarre mystic** (see *Tome of Beast 2*), for a creature with spells or spell-like abilities, or a **selang** (see *Tome of Beast*), for a creature that already knows Void Speech. The target's statistics, including mental ability scores and hit points, are replaced by the statistics of the chosen creature. The target retains its alignment and personality.

When it reverts to its original form, the creature returns to the number of hit points it had before it transformed. If it reverts as a result of dropping to 0 hit points, any excess damage carries over to its normal form. As long as the excess damage doesn't reduce the creature's normal form to 0 hit points, it isn't knocked unconscious. The creature is limited in the actions it can perform by the nature of its new form, and it can't speak, except for Void Speech, or cast spells, except those with the **void** keyword. The target's gear melds into the new form, so the creature can't activate, use, wield, or otherwise benefit from any of its equipment.

SHADOW SHIELD

2nd-Level Abjuration (Sorcerer, Wizard)
Casting Time: 1 reaction, which you take when you are hit by an attack or targeted by the *magic missile* spell
Range: Self
Components: V, S
Duration: 1 round

A misty black barrier of magical force appears and protects you. Until the start of your next turn, you have a +8 bonus to AC, including against the triggering attack, and you are immune to force and radiant damage.

STAR DRAGON'S RADIANCE

3rd-Level Abjuration (Cleric, Wizard)
Casting Time: 1 action
Range: Self
Components: V, S, M (a scale from a void dragon)
Duration: Concentration, up to 1 minute

While you invoke this spell, it creates an aura in a 10-foot radius centered on you. You and all creatures friendly to you in the aura have advantage on Wisdom saving throws.

TOOTH OF THE WYRM

2nd-Level Necromancy (Cleric, Wizard)
Casting Time: 1 action
Range: Touch
Components: V, S, M (a dragon's tooth)
Duration: Concentration, up to 1 minute

You make a melee attack to touch a target creature with the material component, and a tiny wound appears that grows larger each round. The target takes 1 necrotic damage when touched, and if you maintain concentration, the target must make a Constitution saving throw each turn thereafter. If the save fails, the creature takes double the damage of the prior round (2 damage in the 2nd round, then 4, 8, 16, 32, and so on up to 512 after 1 minute and nine failed saving throws).

The effect can be removed with *lesser restoration*.

TRUTH OF THE VOID

1st-Level Illusion (Bard, Cleric, Sorcerer, Wizard)
Casting Time: 1 action
Range: 120 feet
Components: V, S, M (an empty eggshell)
Duration: Instantaneous

You display a vision of the void and project feelings of hopelessness and despair. The target must succeed on a Wisdom saving throw or become frightened of you, drop whatever it is holding, and take the Dash action to move away from you by the safest available route on its turn, unless there is nowhere to move.

WIND OF THE OUTER VOID

4th-Level Evocation (Cleric, Wizard)
Casting Time: 1 action
Range: Self
Components: V, S, M (a fragment of a meteor or a piece of meteoric iron or stone)
Duration: Concentration, up to 1 minute

You call forth a chilling presence from beyond the mortal world, forming it into a wall of frozen horror. You can make either a straight wall up to 60 feet long, 10 feet high, and 10 feet wide or a ringed wall up to 20 feet in diameter, 10 feet high, and 5 feet thick. The wall provides half cover to creatures behind it, and its space is difficult terrain. When a creature enters the wall's area for the first time on a turn or starts its turn there, the creature must make a Dexterity saving throw. On a failed save, the creature takes 3d10 cold damage and is frightened of you until the end of its next turn. On a successful save, the creature takes half as much damage and is not frightened.

WORD OF UNMAKING

Transmutation Cantrip
  (Bard, Cleric, Druid, Sorcerer, Wizard)
Casting Time: 1 minute
Range: Touch
Components: V, S, M (a chisel)
Duration: Instantaneous

This spell destroys a single small object you touch, such as a key, a dagger, or a wineskin. The object must weigh less than 2 pounds and be no larger than 1 foot in any dimension. This spell has no effect on magical items or items of mithral or adamantine and has no effect on objects held by another creature.

IT CAME FROM THE VOID: SPELLS FROM BEYOND

by Kelly Pawlik

The tainted mass of the Void can be manipulated by only the most depraved and determined of individuals. Those few who meet these criteria find a limitless and flexible source of power, so long as their aims lead to corruption and ruin. The spells presented herein are intended to supplement those presented in *Deep Magic* and follow all of the rules presented in that book, including being available only to wizards.

Void Magic

All spells with the **void** keyword have a verbal component and must be uttered in Void Speech, which cannot be precluded by use of any other feat, feature, or spell.

ABILITY LEECH

3rd-Level Necromancy (Void) (Wizard)

Casting Time: 1 action
Range: 30 feet
Components: V, S, M (a speck of dust from a meteorite)
Duration: Instantaneous

Choose a creature you can see within range. Your target must succeed on a Wisdom saving throw or expend one use of one of its features of its choice that recharges after a short or long rest. The target gains no benefit or effect of expending the feature.

If the target expends uses from a pool of points that recover after a short or long rest, such a Sorcery Points or Superiority Dice, they expend 1d4 points from the pool. Features expended through the effects of this spell are recovered through rest as normal.

AMORPHOUS FORM

4th-Level Transmutation (Void) (Wizard)

Casting Time: 1 action
Range: Touch
Components: V, S, M (a drop of ooze)
Duration: Concentration, up to 10 minutes

A Large or smaller creature you touch becomes a gray ooze. An unwilling target can make a Constitution saving throw at the end of each of its turns to end the effect and resume its normal form. A willing target can choose to become unwilling at any point of the duration and can make a saving throw at the end of its next turn after becoming unwilling. While under the effect of this spell, a creature retains its size, general shape, and alignment and its Intelligence, Wisdom, and Charisma ability scores but otherwise has the statistics of a gray ooze. If the spell ends because the duration elapses, the target is permanently transformed into a **gray ooze**.

At Higher Levels. If you cast this spell using a 6th-level slot, the target transforms into

your choice of a **gelatinous cube** or an **ochre jelly** instead of a gray ooze. If cast using an 8th-level slot, the target becomes a **black pudding** instead of a gray ooze.

BODY OF RUIN

8th-Level Evocation (Void) (Wizard)
Casting Time: 1 action
Range: 60 feet
Components: V, S, M (a fingerprint pressed onto iron)
Duration: Concentration, up to 1 minute

Choose a humanoid you can see within range. The target must make a Constitution saving throw or become infused with a shard of the Void. For the duration, at the beginning of each of the target's turns, it must choose to internalize the wave of energy rising within it or to release it. If the energy is internalized, the target takes 4d10 force damage. If the target chooses to instead release the energy, it takes no damage, but all creatures within 10 feet of it must make a Constitution saving throw, taking 4d10 force damage on a failed save or half as much damage on a successful one.

If a creature is reduced to 0 hit points by this spell, it is disintegrated.

At Higher Levels.
If you cast this spell using a 9th-level slot, no concentration is required.

CLUTCH OF DESOLATION

2nd-Level Necromancy (Void) (Wizard)
Casting Time: 1 action
Range: 30 feet
Components: V, S, M (a burned wishbone)
Duration: Concentration, up to 1 minute

A flexible beam of dead black energy erupts from you, seeking to tether to you a creature you can see within range. The target must succeed on a Strength saving throw or become tethered and unable to move farther than 30 feet away from you. While tethered to a target, you have advantage on any ability check, attack roll, and saving throw involving the target. At the end of each of its turns, an affected creature can make a new saving throw to break the tether.

CORRUPTING SHEATHE

2nd-Level Conjuration (Void) (Wizard)
Casting Time: 1 bonus action
Range: Self
Components: V, S
Duration: 1 minute

Your body is slicked with caustic slime. A creature that hits you with a melee weapon attack or an unarmed strike takes 2d6 acid damage. In addition, while under the effects of this spell, a creature that makes a melee attack against you with a nonmagical manufactured weapon that rolls a natural 1 on an attack roll loses that weapon as it decays and is destroyed.

DECAY OBJECT

Transmutation Cantrip (Void) (Wizard)
Casting Time: 1 action
Range: 10 feet
Components: V, S
Duration: Instantaneous

You cause an object to quickly erode. Choose one unattended, nonmagical object that can fit into a 1-foot cube within range that you can see. The object takes on a slimy texture and becomes pitted and unusable.

An unattended object is one that is not being carried or wielded by another creature. Complex objects made of multiple moving pieces cannot be targeted by this cantrip, nor can small pieces that are part of a larger whole. For example, this cantrip can affect an unattended dagger but has no effect on a lock.

DRAIN VITALITY

1st-Level Necromancy (Void) (Wizard)
Casting Time: 1 action
Range: 60 feet
Components: V, S, M (a drop of blood)
Duration: Instantaneous

You sap a creature's ability to refresh itself through rest. Choose one humanoid you can see within range. The target must succeed on a Constitution saving throw or lose one Hit Die. A target of this spell that has no Hit Dice instead gains one level of exhaustion on a failed save. A target cannot gain more than one level of exhaustion in a day as a result of being targeted by this spell. The target that loses Hit Dice regains them at the usual rate upon finishing a long rest.

At Higher Levels. The target loses an additional Hit Die for each slot level above 1st used to cast this spell. A creature cannot lose Hit Dice and gain levels of exhaustion with the same casting of this spell.

ECLIPSE SIGHT

1st-Level Necromancy (Void) (Wizard)
Casting Time: 1 reaction, which you take in response to being damaged by a creature within 60 feet of you that you can see
Range: 60 feet
Components: V
Duration: Instantaneous

You snarl a curse in Void Speech at the creature that damaged you, shrouding its sight using the Void. The creature makes a Constitution saving throw. If it fails, it is blinded until the end of its next turn.

At Higher Levels. If you cast this spell using a 2nd-level or higher slot, the blindness persists until the end of your next turn.

EMPTY RAIN

5th-Level Conjuration (Void) (Wizard)
Casting Time: 1 action
Range: 60 feet
Components: V, S, M (a raindrop)
Duration: Concentration, up to 1 minute

A frigid, draining rain falls in a 10-foot-radius, 40-foot-high cylinder centered on a point you specify within range. Each creature that starts its turn in the area or enters the area for the first time on its turn must make a Constitution saving throw, taking 3d8 cold and 3d8 necrotic damage on a failed save and half as much damage on a successful one. A creature that fails its saving throw is also prohibited from casting spells while it is

within the area and until the beginning of its next turn after leaving the area.

At Higher Levels. If you cast this with a slot of 6th-level or higher, you deal an extra 2d8 cold or necrotic damage (your choice) for each slot level above 5th.

EVENT HORIZON

7th-Level Evocation (Void) (Wizard)

Casting Time: 1 action
Range: 90 feet
Components: V, S, M (shard of meteoric iron)
Duration: Concentration, up to 1 minute

You form a mild gravity well around a creature. Choose a Large or smaller creature you can see within range. All creatures of your choice within 15 feet of the target must succeed on a Strength saving throw or be restrained. A restrained creature that starts its turn within 15 feet of the target can use its action on its turn to make a Strength check against your spell save DC to stop being restrained and move away from the target.

If the target moves, all restrained creatures within 15 feet of it move as well, maintaining the same distance and position from the target if possible. If an object or creature already occupies that space, the creature moves to the nearest empty space to it. Restrained creatures that move as a result of the target's movement are considered to use their own movement and draw opportunity attacks as normal.

A creature that is restrained by the target at the end of its turn ages 1 year. The target ages 1 year per creature restrained by it at the time the spell ends.

FLASH FREEZE

6th-Level Evocation (Void) (Wizard)

Casting Time: 1 action
Range: 60 feet
Components: V, S
Duration: Instantaneous

You expose all creatures within 10 feet of a point you choose that you can see within range to the frigid heart of the Void. A creature in the area must make a Dexterity saving throw, taking 3d6 cold and 2d6 necrotic damage on a successful save. On a failed save, the creature takes the same amount of damage and is restrained in a block of slimy black ice. A creature that is restrained in ice cannot breathe and must hold its breath or begin to suffocate. It can make a Strength check against your spell save DC to break free of the ice, or it can be broken out. An ice block has AC 13, 27 hit points, is vulnerable to fire damage, and immune to cold, necrotic, poison, and psychic damage.

At Higher Levels. If cast using a 7th-level or higher slot, you deal an extra 2d6 cold damage for each slot level above 6th.

HEART OF THE DEAD STAR

9th-Level Transmutation (Void) (Wizard)

Casting Time: 1 action
Range: 120 feet
Components: V, S, M (a 1 lb. chunk of iron ore that is not consumed in the casting)
Duration: Concentration, up to 1 minute

You form a gravity well around a creature. Choose a Large or smaller creature you can see within range. All creatures within 5 feet of the target, and other creatures of your choice within 20 feet of the target, must make a Strength saving throw or move to within 5 feet of the target. If there are no empty spaces within 5 feet of the target, the creature must move within 5 feet of a creature that is within 5 feet of the target. A creature that starts its turn within 10 feet of the target is restrained and takes 3d12 bludgeoning damage. It can use its action to make a Strength check against your spell save DC to stop being restrained and move away from the target.

When the spell ends, all creatures within 10 feet of the target are shoved 20 feet away from it and fall prone. A creature standing in the path of a shoved creature or in the space it lands in must make a Dexterity saving throw or take 2d6 bludgeoning damage and

be knocked prone. A shoved creature that strikes another creature or object takes 2d6 bludgeoning damage.

KING OF NOTHING

6th-Level Enchantment (Void) (Wizard)

Casting Time: 1 action

Range: 60 feet

Components: V, S, M (a vial of a humanoid's breath)

Duration: Concentration, up to 1 minute

You steal a creature's sense of self. Choose a humanoid you can see within range. At the beginning of each of its turns, the target must make a Charisma saving throw, taking 4d6 psychic damage on a failed saving throw or half as much damage on a successful one.

If the target's hit points are reduced below half its maximum, it becomes insubstantial and hazy. Nonmagical weapon attacks made against it have disadvantage, and it cannot make weapon attacks against other creatures.

If the target dies while under the effects of this spell, it fades away to nothingness and cannot be restored to life by any means short of a *wish* spell or direct intercession of a deity.

PERSONAL CANNIBAL

4th-Level Transmutation (Void) (Wizard)

Casting Time: 1 action

Range: Self

Components: V, S, M (desiccated blackberry)

Duration: 1 minute

You empower your intellect at the expense of your body and personal charm. For the duration, whenever you make an Intelligence check, Intelligence saving throw, or spell attack, roll 1d8 and add the result to your total. You also add the result of a 1d8 roll to your spell save DCs.

Conversely, for the duration, and for 1d4 hours following the end of the spell, whenever you make a Strength, Dexterity, or Charisma check or saving throw, roll 1d6 and deduct the result from your total.

At Higher Levels. If cast using a 6th-level slot, you can add 1d10 to your Intelligence checks, Intelligence saving throws, spell attacks, and spell save DCs, instead of 1d8. If you cast this spell using an 8th-level slot, increase the die to 1d12 instead of 1d8.

SIGIL IN YELLOW

8th-Level Enchantment (Ritual, Void) (Wizard)

Casting Time: 1 hour

Range: Touch

Components: V, S, M (ochre paint, and powdered adamantine worth at least 500 gp)

Duration: Until dispelled or triggered

When you cast this spell, you paint a sigil either upon a surface (such as on a wall or an object) or within an object that can be closed (such as in a book, treasure chest, or cabinet) to conceal the sigil. Regardless of where it is placed, the sigil must be a minimum of 6 inches in diameter and can be no larger than 10 feet in diameter.

A humanoid that gazes upon the sigil must succeed on a Wisdom saving throw or be forced to stare at it for 1 minute. If you are on the same plane of existence as the creature gazing at the sigil, you are alerted to their attention and can choose to do one of the following things:

- Perceive the target's surroundings using its senses.

- Read the target's surface thoughts and determine what was on its mind the moment before its attention was seized by the sigil. On subsequent rounds, you can dig deeper into the target's mind and gain insight into its emotional state and one item that looms large in its mind. If you choose this latter option, the target can make a new Wisdom saving throw, freeing itself of your influence on a success.

- Take total and precise control of the target. On its turn, the target takes only the actions you choose and doesn't do anything you don't allow it to do. Each

time the target takes damage, it makes a new saving throw, freeing itself of your influence on a success.

- You can use your action on each of your turns to change the effect the sigil has on the target. You remain connected to the target for 1 week or until it frees itself of your influence.

UNFATHOMABLE EMPTINESS

9th-Level Divination (Void) (Wizard)
Casting Time: 1 action
Range: 30 feet
Components: V, S, M (bead from an abacus)
Duration: Instantaneous

You force a creature to consider its insignificance. You impart all the mathematical and statistical information regarding the distance between the target's home world and all celestial bodies within the Void. This information is then multiplied by the mass of all of those celestial bodies, divided by the size of the Void, and compared to the size and mass of the target. The target must make an Intelligence saving throw, becoming blinded, frightened, incapacitated, poisoned, and stunned on a failed save or simply stunned on a successful one. As an action, the target can make a Charisma saving throw to regain some of its sense of equilibrium and shed itself of one of the conditions imparted by the spell.

WEIGHTY RESTRAINTS

5th-Level Conjuration (Void) (Wizard)
Casting Time: 1 action
Range: Touch
Components: V, S, M (a pair of manacles that are not consumed in the casting)
Duration: 8 hours

You infuse a pair of manacles that a creature is wearing with the mass and empty magnitude of the Void. The creature wearing the manacles gains four levels of exhaustion while restrained by them. A creature restrained by the manacles cannot gain more levels of exhaustion, and it cannot lose levels of exhaustion by finishing a long rest. The manacles can be removed by making a Dexterity (thieves' tools) check against your spell save DC. If the tools are not magical, the check is made with disadvantage. A creature can only be affected by one pair of manacles enchanted by this spell at a time.

VOIDSHIPS: TO THE VOID AND BACK

by Brian Suskind and Ben McFarland

Aerial vessels such as the flying cities of the Sikkim, the dwarven balloons, and even the questionable kobold-crafted ships, while certainly not common, generate excited commentary in taverns and market squares across Midgard. Even rarer though are the crafts that soar above these atmospheric constructs to venture into the Void (called also Ginnungagap), where the glittering planar spheres hang in the branches of Yggdrasil.

Sailing the Void

When the war ended and the gods stood victorious over the body of their progenitor, Aurgelmir, the final breath of the first giant drifted into the Void. As the breath reflected from the planes and danced among the leaves of the World Tree, it fractured into long, flowing currents between various locations, swirling and eddying unexpectedly in others.

Known as Ymir's Rattle, these "winds" function like swiftly moving rivers of air in the Void, allowing ships equipped with arcane voidhelms to travel at great speed. The strongest currents push objects away from their routes, leaving their course free from natural obstacles. Apart from the currents, patterns of wind revolve around the World Tree and the planes, providing enough propulsion for voidships to function like seafaring vessels.

Midgard's Sphere. Seen from the outside, Midgard hangs from the World Tree like a glittering crystal ornament. Inside the membranous planar barrier, Midgard's planar sphere contains the disk of the world itself and the sun, eight moons, and five planets that orbit it.

Conditions in the Void. The Void is not a vacuum of absolute zero temperatures (unlike space around our own world). The conditions of Ginnungagap are more like those atop the highest mountains. While there is breathable air, it is very thin and not enough to support humanoid life, and cold weather gear must be used to fend off the frigidness that averages around −30 degrees Fahrenheit.

There is no real gravity in this Realm Beyond. Large objects, planes, and the World Tree itself all generate their own gravitational fields. Gravity extends 1 mile from the outer surface of an object without an atmosphere, such as an asteroid, or 5 miles from the edge of the atmosphere of a planet or object possessing an atmosphere.

Though dark, the Void is by no means a lightless space. The World Tree glows with an eternal radiance. The planar spheres reflect this luminescence like crystal ornaments, and the **living stars** (see *Creature Codex*) wander the dark, providing their own brilliance. Illumination similar to a night with a half-moon is typical.

Voidsails. Traditional sails provide the actual propulsion for a voidship. Within an atmosphere, the sails use terrestrial winds, and outside of an atmosphere, they catch Ymir's Rattle. Either way, a ship's forward speed and maneuverability is the same regardless of what winds the sails use. The exception to this rule is when traveling at voidspeed (see below).

Arcane Helms. The vessels that sail the black use magical ships' helms to guide them through air and space. When placed aboard a ship, an arcane voidhelm generates a bubble of artificial gravity and breathable air around that ship. Moreover, the helm allows the ship to levitate and travel at a special movement rate called voidspeed.

Voidspeed Navigation and Travel Time. This magically faster-than-light travel allows a vessel to move at the unimaginable speed of the swiftly moving currents of the Void winds. When traveling at voidspeed, a vessel follows the course of the wind's current, abstractly rendered as a straight line, and can't maneuver. Voidships must drop to normal speed to make any course change before resuming a journey at voidspeed. Thus, a chart of a vessel traveling at voidspeed resembles a series of long straight lines, interspersed by course changes at normal speed.

Captains and navigators typically use Midgard's cardinal directions (north, east, west, and south) with the World Tree as the center of the compass. Traveling up the trunk is called crownward while down

VOIDHELMS

Though there are many varieties with greater or lesser abilities, a basic magical ship's helm is described below.

ARCANE VOIDHELM

Wondrous Item, Rare (Requires Attunement)

This ornate ship's wheel or tiller is fashioned of glyph-inscribed wood with crystal inlays, and it functions to provide levitation and maneuverability for a vessel in the Void.

Passive Properties. The following properties of the helm come into play even when no creature is attuned to it:

- When placed aboard a vessel, the helm generates a bubble of breathable air and gravity around the ship. This bubble extends from the hull in all directions out to a distance equal to the length of the ship. The temperature within the bubble is comfortable and life sustaining. Creatures and objects that fall overboard bob in the bubble as if it were water. While underway, the area between the hull and the edge of the bubble is subject to the relative speed of the vessel (to a maximum equal to the ship's normal maximum speed) and is shielded from any effects of traveling at voidspeed.

Active Properties. While attuned to the helm, you have the sensation of a harmless electrical charge running over your skin. You gain the following abilities when you grasp the helm:

- You can use the helm to levitate the ship (moving upward or downward relative to the current orientation of the vessel) at a rate equal to the ship's normal speed.
- You can steer the vessel in much the same way as the tiller or wheel can maneuver a seafaring ship.
- As an action, you can bring the vessel to voidspeed as long as it is outside of a gravity well. You can use another action to drop out of voidspeed and resume normal momentum. When a vessel drops out of voidspeed, it begins the turn traveling at its normal maximum speed. A vessel moving at voidspeed that enters a gravity well uncontrollably drops to normal speed. All creatures on the vessel must make a DC 15 Constitution saving throw, suffering 10d10 force damage on a failed saving throw or half as much damage on a successful one.

the trunk is rootward. Notable sites act as navigational markers, like the prominent ratatosk community of Grenstad or the massive black-iron spike and its fluttering rope fragment where Wotan hung to gain the knowledge of runes.

The time to travel the millions of miles at voidspeed is swift but not instantaneous since the wind currents change course as they ebb and flow. A vessel's travel time depends on whether it sails within a planar sphere or outside of one:

- Within a planar sphere (but outside a gravity well), travel from one celestial object to another takes 1d3 days with 1d2 − 1 stops at normal speed to maneuver.
- Outside of a planar sphere, travel takes 1d20 + 3 days to travel from one planar location to another with 1d6 − 1 stops at normal speed to maneuver.

PSYCHIC BEACON

Wondrous Item, Rare

A silver bell set with a series of eight removable stones, this item comes with a small, padded mallet. Stones are attuned to the bell and can be detached and given away. When the mallet is used to strike the bell, a ringing is heard from all detached stones when they're held to your ear. This ringing is audible across any distance and even to other planes of existence and persists until the stone is brought back to the bell and placed in its setting. If you hold a stone and concentrate for a full round, you discern the general direction and distance from your stone to the bell. You may also, once per long rest, use a sending effect, transmitting your message to the bell and other stones.

Voidship captains often give a stone to other ship captains in their flotillas or to leaders of groups sent ashore, allowing them to find and communicate with the ship if separated or in trouble.

Brave travelers through the Void often come into conflict with the voidships and flotillas of the folk of Leng or the spiders of Leng, dispatching from driftworlds splintered from Yggdrasil or launching into the black from the arachnid hivewebs, or worse, the techno-organic spheres of the ahu-nixta. Below are examples of each.

Voidships of the Arachni

The arachnoid voidships of the spiders of Leng all feature long, chitinous leg-masts adorned with spidersilk sails. The websteel hulls are constructed around the admonae, a living spider at the heart of the ship, using a process that renders the silk as hard as steel.

ARACHNO-CARRACK

Light and nimble, this spider-like vessel features a wheel on the raised forecastle and a large main deck. Two arachnoid arms stretch forward from the hull, and four other legs, hung with silken sails, curve backward.

ARACHNO-CARRACK

Gargantuan Vehicle (200 ft. by 40 ft.), Organic
Creature Capacity 15 crew, 100 passengers
Cargo Capacity 250 tons
Travel Pace 5 miles per hour (120 miles per day), voidspeed

STR	DEX	CON	INT	WIS	CHA
20 (+5)	7 (−2)	17 (+3)	1 (−8)	1 (−8)	1 (−8)

Damage Immunities poison, psychic
Condition Immunities blinded, charmed, deafened, exhaustion, frightened, incapacitated, paralyzed, petrified, poisoned, prone, stunned, unconscious

Grasping Arms. The forward-facing arms of the ship shoot a pair of webbing tendrils to grapple objects. The tendrils can be attacked (AC 20; 20 hp; immunity to poison and psychic damage). Destroying a tendril deals no damage to the ship. A tendril can also be broken if a creature uses an action to break it (DC 20 Strength check).

On its turn, the ship can take three actions, choosing from the options below. It can take only two actions if it has fewer than 20 crew and only one action if it has fewer than 10 crew. It can't take these actions if it has fewer than three crew.

Fire Ballista. The ship can fire its Ballista.

Fire Webbing Grappler. The ship can fire its Webbing Grappler.

Reel in Grappler. The ship can haul in the Webbing Grappler.

Sudden Move. The ship can use its helm to move with its sails.

HULL

Armor Class 15

Hit Points 300 (damage threshold 15)

CONTROL: VOIDHELM

Armor Class 18

Hit Points 50

Move up to the ship's speed, with up to two 60-degree turns. If the helm is destroyed, the ship can't turn.

MOVEMENT: SAILS

Armor Class 12

Hit Points 100; −5 ft. speed per 25 damage taken

Speed 50 ft.; 20 ft. while sailing into the wind; 65 ft. while sailing with the wind

WEAPON: BALLISTA (×3)

Armor Class 15

Hit Points 50

Ranged Weapon Attack: +6 to hit, range 120/480 ft., one target. *Hit:* 16 (3d10) piercing damage.

WEAPON: WEBBING GRAPPLER

Armor Class 15

Hit Points 50

Ranged Weapon Attack: +6 to hit, range 200/800 ft. (can't hit targets within 60 ft. of it), one target. *Hit:* The target vessel is restrained and must succeed on a DC 14 Strength saving throw, or it can't move away from the carrack. The vessel may spend actions to pull vessels restrained by its Webbing Grappler up to 100 feet straight toward it.

Voidships of the Folk of Leng

Lengfolk voidships are swift galleys constructed of rare woods and richly appointed amenities, well suited to their roles as dimensional merchants. While fast vessels, they do not maneuver as well as the ships of other races.

LENGFOLK BRIGANTINE

The long, angular black hull is fitted with split, lateen-rigged masts and orange sails. The decks of the vessel are sheltered by closely set metal fabric canopies.

LENGFOLK BRIGANTINE

Gargantuan Vehicle (130 ft. by 20 ft.), Inorganic

Creature Capacity 80 crew, 40 passengers

Cargo Capacity 150 tons

Travel Pace 6 miles per hour (144 miles per day), voidspeed

STR	DEX	CON	INT	WIS	CHA
24 (+7)	4 (−3)	20 (+5)	0	0	0

Damage Immunities poison, psychic

Condition Immunities blinded, charmed, deafened, exhaustion, frightened, incapacitated, paralyzed, petrified, poisoned, prone, stunned, unconscious

Unseen Passage. When not actively in motion and not moored at a dock, the Lengfolk voidship blends in with its surroundings. Any Wisdom (Perception) check made to spot a stationary Lengfolk voidship at a distance of more than 30 feet have disadvantage. Pilots attempting to fly a voidship stealthily have advantage on checks made to remain unnoticed.

ACTIONS

On its turn, the ship can take three actions, choosing from the options below. It can take only two actions if it has fewer than 40 crew and only one action if it has fewer than 20. It can't take these actions if it has fewer than three crew.

Fire Etheric Ballista. The ship can fire its Ballista.

Slumbering Mangonel. The ship can fire its Mangonel.

Sudden Move. The ship can use its helm to move with its sails.

HULL

Armor Class 15

Hit Points 500 (damage threshold 20)

CONTROL: VOIDHELM

Armor Class 16

Hit Points 50

Move up to the ship's speed with one 90-degree turn. If the helm is destroyed, the ship can't turn.

MOVEMENT: SAILS

Armor Class 12

Hit Points 100; −10 ft. speed per 25 damage taken

Speed 60 ft.; 30 ft. while sailing into the wind; 75 ft. while sailing with the wind

WEAPON: ETHERIC BALLISTA (×2)

Armor Class 15

Hit Points 50

Ranged Weapon Attack: +8 to hit, range 120/480 ft., one target. *Hit:* 20 (4d10) necrotic damage. Armor and damage threshold has no effect against the attack roll of the Etheric Ballista, and only the Dexterity modifier factored into the target's AC is considered.

WEAPON: SLUMBERING MANGONEL (×2)

Armor Class 15

Hit Points 50

Ranged Weapon Attack: +8 to hit, range 200/800 ft. (can't hit targets within 60 ft. of it), one target. *Hit:* 27 (5d10) bludgeoning damage. Creatures within 5 feet of the target must make a DC 14 Constitution save or fall asleep for 1d4 minutes. They may make a new saving throw if another creature attempts to wake them.

Voidships of the Ahu-Nixta

The techno-organic spheres of the Ahu-nixta strike fear in the hearts of most planar travelers. Slow and ponderous, they are heavily armed and possess self-healing properties. The spheres have no sails but can move in any direction without losing speed, thanks to their unique magic helms.

AHU-NIXTA DREADORB

Gargantuan Vehicle (70-foot-radius sphere), Techno-Organic

Creature Capacity 40 crew, 50 passengers

Cargo Capacity 75 tons

Travel Pace 4 miles per hour (96 miles per day), voidspeed

STR	DEX	CON	INT	WIS	CHA
20 (+5)	6 (−2)	17 (+3)	0	0	0

Damage Immunities poison, psychic

Condition Immunities blinded, charmed, deafened, exhaustion, frightened, incapacitated, paralyzed, petrified, poisoned, prone, stunned, unconscious

Clockwork Regeneration. The orb regains 15 hit points at the start of its turn. If the ship takes acid or fire damage, this trait doesn't function at the start of the ship's next turn. If the ship drops to 0 hit points, this trait stops functioning.

ACTIONS

On its turn, the ship can take three actions, choosing from the options below. It can take only two actions if it has fewer than 20 crew and only one action if it has fewer than 10. It can't take these actions if it has fewer than three crew.

Fire Arcane Cannon. The ship can fire its Arcane Cannon.

Fire Sonic Disruptor. The ship can fire its Sonic Disruptor.

Fire Cascade Artillery. The ship can fire its Cascade Artillery.

Sudden Move. The ship can use its helm to move.

HULL

Armor Class 16

Hit Points 400 (damage threshold 15); −5 ft. speed per 25 damage taken

Speed 45 ft; movement not affected by wind

CONTROL: VOIDHELM

Armor Class 20

Hit Points 100

Move up to the ship's speed with two 45-degree turns. If the helm is destroyed, the ship can't turn.

WEAPON: ARCANE CANNON (×4)

Armor Class 19

Hit Points 75

Ranged Weapon Attack: +6 to hit, range 600/2,400 ft., one target. *Hit:* 9 (2d8) bludgeoning damage and 9 (2d8) force damage.

WEAPON: SONIC DISRUPTOR

Armor Class 15

Hit Points 50

Ranged Weapon Attack: +6 to hit, range 120/480 ft., one target. *Hit:* 33 (6d10) thunder damage. Creatures within 10 feet of the target (including the target if it is a creature) must make a DC 15 Constitution saving throw or be stunned until the start of the orb's next turn. On a successful saving throw, the targets take half as much damage and are deafened instead of stunned.

WEAPON: CASCADE ARTILLERY

Armor Class 15

Hit Points 100

Ranged Weapon Attack: +5 to hit, range 200/800 ft. (can't hit targets within 60 feet of it), one target. *Hit:* 5 (1d10) bludgeoning damage and 4 (1d8) fire damage. Three bolts then leap from that target to as many as three creatures within 30 feet. Each of those creatures must make a DC 15 Dexterity saving throw, suffering the same damage as the first target on a failed saving throw or half as much damage on a successful one.

Each time a creature fails a saving throw, three more bolts leap out from that target as described above. The chained damage ends when there are no more failed saving throws against the artillery's effect.

Story Seeds

How might adventurers encounter vessels from Ginnungagap, other than across the horizon and docked in trading ports?

Questionable Cargo. As the party travels overland, the sentry on watch sees a shooting star whistle overhead and hears a distant thundering with its impact. Difficult travel to the site takes several hours, but a plume of smoke guides them. Upon arrival, the party finds a crashed voidship, its Lengfolk crew dead with many torn to pieces. Something lurks in the wreckage and cargo bay, and if the characters don't stop the creature, it may go on to massacre a nearby logging camp and its delivery caravan. Once the threat is ended, the adventurers have the option of performing the minor repairs necessary to the ship's hull and taking to the skies themselves. But what will happen when the Lengfolk rescuers' ships arrive, answering the last crew's dying distress call?

Take Out Order. The city is in chaos as an arachni voidship arrives. Several enormous spiders of Leng disembark and begin hunting, seizing dozens of prized steeds that were grazing in the reserved pastures. An arachni queen recently gained a taste for horseflesh after consuming the poor mount of a knight from a group of failed attackers. The queen sent these raiders to fetch her next meal, offering one craven adventurer mercy if they guided the ship. The guide escapes and explains the danger if the party can defeat the guide's pursuer. This exploratory ship may prove to be the first of many such expeditions, but only if it returns. Will the adventurers rise to the occasion and enter the spiders' silken vessel, defeat the invaders, and rescue the mounts?

Some Party. After a night of extreme celebrations, the PCs awake in unfamiliar settings as a dying wizard releases them from cells. It seems they were captured and now find themselves aboard an ahu-nixta vessel. Separated from their gear by a wall of force, the party must find a way to lure a drone into the area, reacquire their equipment, and ascertain just what happened. Amazingly, they find they are no longer on Midgard but en route to an Ahu-Nixta scouting post on the moon Selles, hidden in an old temple. They must decide whether they attempt to overwhelm the crew, discover a way off this vessel before they find themselves surrounded by more of the aberrations, or wait to land and explore the ancient structure.

FABLED ELVISH MAGIC ITEMS

by Jeremy Hochhalter

Elves have left their mark across the history of the world as empires rose, fell, and disappeared. Throughout the centuries, elven heroes and leaders etched their legends into the annals of time. There are legendary elves whose names are spoken of in reverence—and sometimes in fear—even to this day. Objects crafted for or by those elves still linger in the mortal realm, left behind during the Great Retreat.

Bands of Infernal Favor

This armband is made of two blood-red metal bands, which cross over one another three times. Between the gaps, crystals are set in place, hollow yet surprisingly durable.

To date, only a few of the *Bands of Infernal Favor* have been found, though their current locations are kept a mystery. Long before the rise of the magocracies—when there was still some trust between the elves and the humans—humans gifted the bands to various elven patrons: mages, druids, and paladins. Ostensibly, the bands were created to boost the wearer's connection with a familiar, companion, or steed. Highly valued by those who received them, it was unknown that the true purpose of the strange, twisted metal was the corruption of elvenkind.

Those who passed them along to the elves were devout worshippers of infernal powers who wished to harness the magics wielded by elves. They sought ways to bend elven wills to their favor, granting them access to the shadow roads.

The elves were wary of the purpose that seemed to lurk within the bands, twisting their companions into fiendish forms. Casting them aside, the bands were hidden away from those who might cause harm. A few, however, have remained unaccounted for.

BANDS OF INFERNAL FAVOR

Wondrous Item, Fabled (5th-Level and Higher Properties Require Attunement by a Paladin, Ranger, Sorcerer, Warlock, or Wizard)

While you are both conscious, you and your familiar, animal companion, or steed can't be surprised while you are within 30 feet of each other.

Infernal Favor (Requires Attunement). As your level increases, you gain the following benefits while using this item. During attunement, and then at dawn of each day, the bands' spikes press into your flesh, draining blood that fills the crystals held in place by the red metal. This process empowers the bands and drains one Hit Die from you. Hit Dice drained in this manner can be recuperated as normal. If this process is not completed, the bands' abilities do not function for that day.

5th Level. You and your familiar, animal companion, or steed both gain advantage on attacks against a creature if you are both within 5 feet of the creature and neither of you is incapacitated.

Additionally, your familiar, animal companion, or steed's hit points increase by the average of your class Hit Die when you increase in level from now on, including multiclass levels.

9th Level. You gain a +2 bonus to initiative as long as your familiar, animal companion, or steed is within 30 feet of you.

Additionally, your familiar, animal companion, or steed does not die or disappear when they are reduced to 0 hit points. Instead, they are dying and may make death saving throws. You may use an action to spend an available Hit Die to stabilize and heal them for the amount of your Hit Die + your spellcasting modifier.

As a bonus action, you can spend available Hit Dice to heal your familiar, animal companion, or steed.

13th Level. You cause your familiar, animal companion, or steed to magically change into a specific fiend of CR 5 or lower. The target's statistics are replaced by the statistics of the chosen fiend, though it retains its alignment and Intelligence, Wisdom, and Charisma scores. It also retains all its skill and saving throw proficiencies, in addition to gaining those of the fiend. (The fiend is an average example of the chosen fiend, without any class levels or the Spellcasting trait. The target can't use any legendary actions or lair actions of the new form.)

The target assumes the hit points and Hit Dice of the new form. When it reverts to its normal form, it returns to the number of hit points it had before it was transformed. If it reverts as a result of dropping to 0 hit points, any excess damage carries over to its normal form. As long as the excess damage doesn't reduce its normal form to 0 hit points, it isn't knocked unconscious.

The target can't use any special senses its normal form has unless the fiend has that sense. If the fiend can speak, the target can speak and understand any language known by you.

Any equipment carried by either form falls to the ground when the change occurs unless both forms could hold the equipment.

Once used, the armband can't be used in this way again until the next dawn.

17th Level. Your familiar, animal companion, or steed gain the fiend type, if it does not already have it, as it takes on fiendish features, such as black eyes, horns, or a fiendish hue. It becomes immune to fire and poison damage and can't be poisoned.

As a bonus action, you can spend available Hit Dice to remove hit points from your companion in order to heal yourself. If your companion has changed shape, those hit points are temporary and last for 1 hour or until they are lost from taking damage.

The Price of Attunement. While attuned to the armband, you have disadvantage on Wisdom (Insight) checks as well as Wisdom and Charisma saving throws against fiends. Charisma (Deception) checks made by you against fiends always fail. At any time, a fiend on your plane within 10 miles of you or your companion may use a bonus action to view what you or your companion see and hear.

Crown of the Eagle Emperor

This golden circlet is crafted in realistic detail as if feathers lie atop one another. Despite its age, there is no sign of damage or tarnish.

The Eagle Emperor, his true name now lost to history, ruled at the High Court of Liadmura in the Ironcrags during a time of expansion and military dominance. Though his empire is now gone, his winged emblem can still be found in the canton. The stories of his heroics and combat prowess are legendary, and woven within them are, what some sages say, hints that the Eagle Emperor was in fact a lycanthrope of some form.

The truth is equally as interesting though. The elven war god, Valeresh, looked favorably upon the Eagle Emperor, bestowing great power upon him. One such boon was lain upon the emperor's crown, allowing the conqueror to change shape into one of the massive golden eagles favored by his people and even allowing his elven form to take on the attributes of such a creature.

Whether Valeresh abandoned the Eagle Emperor or it was simply a matter of fate, no one knows, but during a terrific battle, the elven lord flew high above the armies that battled on the ground, dueling with riders of other winged beasts. Though the tide of battle was in his favor, the Eagle Emperor was suddenly struck down, the magic that sustained his transformation eradicated. His fall took him away from the battle but not before his army saw his plummeting form. Disheartened, the elven troops retreated to find their fallen

lord, of which they found no sign. It is said by some that a soldier in that army found and spirited away the *Crown of the Eagle Emperor,* either to keep it safe or to use for their own purposes. Other legends state that the crown was nowhere to be found, taken back by Valeresh for the Eagle Emperor's failure. This may be true, as their loss as this battle marked the beginning of the fall of the empire.

CROWN OF THE EAGLE EMPEROR

Wondrous Item, Fabled (5th-Level and Higher Properties Require Attunement)

While wearing the crown of the Eagle Emperor, you have advantage on Wisdom (Perception) checks that require sight.

The Eagle Incarnate (Requires Attunement). As your level increases, you gain the following benefits while using this item.

5th Level. Using an action, golden eagle wings appear from your back, granting you a flying speed of 60 feet. Once used, the crown can't be used in this way again until the next dawn.

9th Level. You gain +10 to initiative and can't be surprised.

13th Level. You can use your action to polymorph into an eagle-humanoid hybrid or into an eagle or back into your true form. Your statistics, other than your AC, are the same in each form. You choose whether your equipment falls to the ground, merges into your new form, or is worn by it. Worn equipment functions as normal, but the GM decides whether it is practical for the new form to wear a particular piece of equipment, based on the creature's shape and size. Your equipment doesn't change size or shape to match the new form, and any equipment the new form can't wear must either fall to the ground or merge with you. Equipment that merges with you has no effect until you leave the form. Your hybrid form has wings that grant you a flying speed of 60 feet, and you can hover.

While in the hybrid form, you gain two natural weapon attacks which you are proficient with: Talons, which deal 2d6 + your Strength modifier slashing damage, and Beak, which deals 1d6 + your Strength modifier piercing damage. This damage is magical.

In addition, you are resistant to bludgeoning, piercing, and slashing weapons from nonmagical weapons that aren't silvered.

Once used, the crown can't be used in this way again until the next dawn, except to revert to your true form

17th Level. You are immune to damage from nonmagical weapons. In addition, you may use the 5th-level and 13th-level abilities of the crown twice per day. You also gain the Piercing Cry action below.

Piercing Cry (Recharge 6). You can release a screeching cry in a 30-foot cone. Creatures within this cone must succeed on a DC 18 Constitution saving throw or take 8d6 thunder damage and be deafened. Creatures that succeed on the saving throw take half the amount of damage and are not deafened.

Gorget of the Explorer

This dark-leather gorget is finely worked with a beautiful compass rose. Vines and various flowers decorate the compass.

Scholars argue whether this gorget was created by Emperor Xindrical or if it was made for the ruler that was commonly referred to as the Explorer. In any case, legend tells that Xindrical, ruler of the first elven capital on Midgard, used the gorget's magic to travel fantastic distances in the blink of an eye. What's more, when he traveled on foot, he was able to fend off dangers that left others in dire straits.

After the expansion of the elven empires across the face of Midgard, the gorget was lost to time, though vague references to heroes and villains with similar abilities pop up in scholarly texts. Then again, such tales are often the stuff of chapbooks and bard songs, so it is difficult to

assess if and where the gorget actually appears since being lost to the Explorer Emperor.

GORGET OF THE EXPLORER

Wondrous Item, Fabled (5th-Level and Higher Properties Require Attunement)

You recall any regions you've traveled and can't get lost in those places unless the area has changed excessively or is hidden by magic. Spending 1 minute in deliberation, you can always determine which direction is north.

World Walker (Requires Attunement). As your level increases, you gain the following benefits while using this item.

5th Level. You have advantage on Wisdom (Survival) checks. Spending 1 minute, you can determine how far away the closest ley line is and in which direction it lies.

9th Level. You are not affected by difficult terrain.

As a bonus action, you can activate the gorget to begin creating difficult terrain in your wake for up to 600 feet. This may appear as ice, vines, loose rubble, or similar, but it does not deal damage. Once used, the gorget can't be used in this way again until the next dawn.

13th Level. While at a ley line, you can attune the gorget to that point by spending 1 minute focusing. You may only have one attuned point at a time.

You can teleport yourself and up to eight willing creatures to an attuned point. Once used, the gorget can't be used in this way again until the next dawn.

17th Level. Once per day, you can use an action to choose an elemental type: acid, cold, fire, lightning, poison, or thunder. Aligning the gorget to that type alters the coloring of the decorative bits on the gorget and grants you immunity to that damage type. At dawn of the next day, this immunity fades and must be reactivated.

Sarastra's Baubles

The baubles are a set of four glass globes, fragile in appearance, which hang from a small brass fixture. Other bits of gems, beads, and glass decorate the fine strings from which the baubles dangle. The brass plate has an oblong hole from which a leather strap or strong twine may be laced, allowing the baubles to be hung from a staff or belt loop.

Long before she was the Queen of Night and Magic, Sarastra dabbled in magic that others might label as questionable. The daughter of High Queen Lelliana of Thorn experimented with and created many magic devices before she was banished, though most were confiscated and destroyed. One object that slipped past the watchful eyes of her mother and those sent to scour the lands for such magic were a set of ornaments. Called *Sarastra's Baubles* by those who know of their existence, they are highly sought by scholars, mages, and adventurers alike. Separated from the baubles when she was exiled, Sarastra herself would like to regain possession of these horrid trinkets.

Created by a younger yet no-less cruel Sarastra, one should not be shocked to find out that the future goddess and ruler of the dark fey formed these baubles to torment those who guarded her. Or when necessary, the baubles were used to capture those who learned Sarastra's devious plots, potential snitches that were never heard from or seen again.

SARASTA'S BAUBLES

Wondrous Item, Fabled (5th-Level and Higher Properties Require Attunement)

You have advantage on Charisma-based ability checks.

Will of the Mistress (Requires Attunement). As your level increases, you gain the following benefits while using this item.

5th Level. Through the baubles, you are able to cast each of the following spells once per day (saving throw DC 15): *calm emotions, charm monster, confusion, fear.*

9th Level. As an action, you can use a bauble to send one creature within 60 feet that you can see to a demiplane within the bauble. The creature must succeed on a DC 17 Charisma saving throw or be banished. While in the harmless demiplane, the target is incapacitated. Though aware of what is going on outside the bauble, the creature can't communicate beyond its confines. The creature does not hunger, thirst, or age. Poisons and diseases and other damaging effects that affect it are suspended while the creature is banished. A creature that succeeds on its saving throw is immune to the banishing effect of the baubles for the next 24 hours.

A bauble can hold one creature at a time. You can release a banished creature as a bonus action, at which time the creature reappears in the space it left or in the nearest unoccupied space if that space is occupied. If the creature's original space is no longer within 60 feet of the bauble, it appears in a random space within 60 feet of the bauble's location.

A bauble has AC 12, 10 hits points, and will release a banished creature if broken. Broken baubles reform after 1d4 days.

13th Level. You can incite fear in a creature that is being held within a bauble. As an action, you can force the creature to make a DC 18 Charisma saving throw. If it fails, the creature is haunted by formless terrors for 1 minute. During this time, you can use its fear to heal yourself. As a bonus action, you cause the creature to suffer 3d12 psychic damage, and you regain an equal amount of hit points. If a creature is reduced to 0 hit points within a bauble, it falls unconscious for 1d4 hours but is stable.

17th Level. Time spent in a bauble warps a creature's perceptions about you, making it malleable to your orders. Even though you can't make a creature not dislike or hate you, a creature you release can be forced to do your bidding for 1 hour. During that time, the creature is charmed and can't take actions to harm you. If instructed to do something that it would not typically do, such as harm a loved one, it may make a DC 17 Charisma saving throw to refuse, though it remains charmed by you. A charmed creature can't be forced to harm itself or put itself into situations that would cause its death, such as jumping off a cliff.

To recapture a creature, you impinge your will as an action, and the creature must make a DC 17 Charisma saving throw. If it fails, the creature is once again banished within a bauble. If it succeeds though, the creature breaks free of the spell and is immune to the banishing effect of the baubles for the next 24 hours.

PLAYER

TICK TICK BOOM: THE KOBOLD TRAPSMITH

by Sarah Madsen

Kobolds are particularly fond of traps. And they've a sure knack at crafting bizarre contraptions and deadly devices to confuse and confound even the most skilled of adversaries. Feel free to come in and browse our glorious offerings—just watch your step.

Character Options

Presented here are numerus potential traps, spells, feats, and weapons for characters looking to raise their trapsmithing game. Though one does not need to be a kobold to utilize these features, kobold players will certainly want to take a look.

KOBOLD TRAPS

Never content with a basic foothold trap or simple tripwire, kobolds pride themselves on their particularly tricky and elaborate traps. While often these traps are made more complex than necessary, with seemingly unnecessary mechanisms and needlessly complicated triggers, many of them are subtle, sneaky, and deadly. A kobold trap that isn't comedically obvious and convoluted is a dangerous threat indeed.

Alley-Oop. The alley-oop is a classic spring trap laid beneath a 5-foot-square portion of a floor. A creature who steps on the trapped area must make a DC 16 Dexterity saving throw.

On a failure, the alley-oop springs upward, throwing the creature 15 feet in a random direction where they land prone, taking 2d6 bludgeoning damage. On a success, the character leaps clear as the trap triggers, landing on their feet in a space within 5 feet of the trap and taking no damage. Once the alley-oop has been triggered, it must be manually reset, requiring an action.

Noticing an alley-oop requires a successful DC 16 Intelligence (Investigation) or Wisdom (Perception) check, though an alley-oop hidden beneath a rug or other camouflage might be harder to spot. Disarming it requires a successful DC 8 Dexterity (thieves' tools or tinker's tools) check.

Crafting an alley-oop requires the necessary materials, 25 hours of crafting time, and a DC 8 Dexterity check using tinker's tools.

Book Binding. A book-binding trap involves the use of a hollow book, tightly wound springs, and a folded, wire net. When the book is opened, the net springs outward and engulfs one creature within 10 feet in front of it. The target must succeed on a DC 18 Dexterity saving throw or be trapped by the net and restrained. A restrained creature can make a DC 17 Strength check at the end of their turn, breaking free of the net on a success.

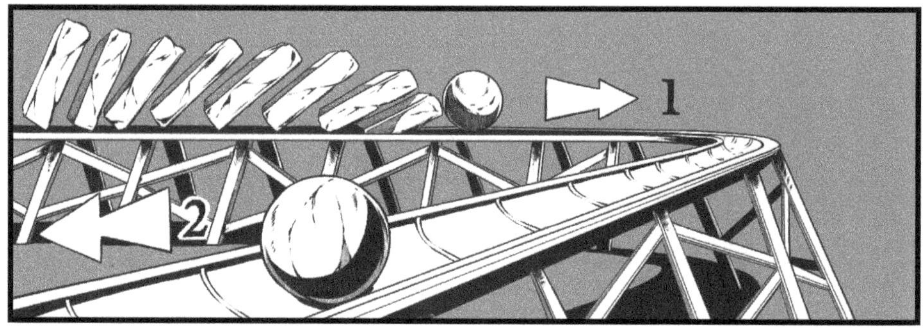

1
2

3
4

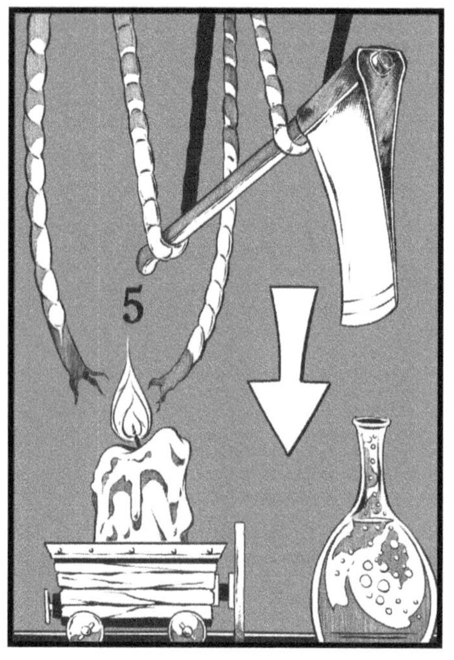

5

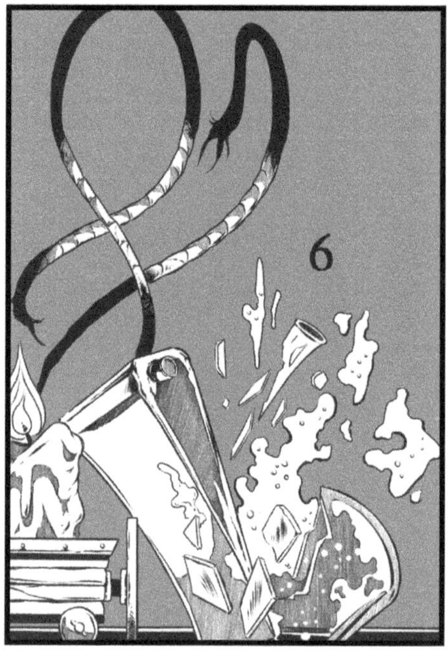

6

A successful DC 18 Intelligence (Investigation) or Wisdom (Perception) check notices the trap, and a successful DC 15 Dexterity (thieves' tools or tinker's tools) check is needed to disconnect the net from the springs and disarm the trap. If the result of the Dexterity check is a 5 or lower, it triggers the trap, targeting the character attempting to disarm it.

A character may craft a book binding with the appropriate materials, 10 hours of crafting time, and a successful DC 12 Dexterity or Intelligence check using tinker's tools. More elaborate versions can be found or crafted, including those with spiked nets, dealing 5d6 piercing damage on a failed Dexterity save, or an electrified version that deals 2d4 lightning damage at the start of every round the creature is restrained. Crafting a more complicated version requires the appropriate materials, 20 hours of crafting time, and a successful DC 15 Dexterity or Intelligence check using tinker's tools.

No Soliciting. Kobolds who require their privacy may make use of a no-soliciting trap on their home. This trap consists of a bulb of hallucinatory gas triggered by the door's knocker. When triggered, a dose of gas is released from the bulb (typically hidden within the frame of the door or behind decorative foliage) and fills a 15-foot cone. Any creatures within the area must make a DC 13 Constitution saving throw. On a failure, they become frightened as their mind is filled with visions of horrible monsters, and they must use their full movement and the Dash action to move as far away from the door as possible by the safest available route on each of their turns. This effect lasts for 1 minute. A creature who starts their turn in the cone must repeat the saving throw. An affected creature may repeat the saving throw at the end of their turn, ending the effect on a success.

Discovering the no-soliciting trap requires a successful DC 12 Intelligence (Investigation) or Wisdom (Perception) check. Disarming the trap requires a successful DC 11 Dexterity (thieves' tools or tinker's tools) check.

Crafting a no-soliciting trap requires a bulb of hallucinatory gas, which can be purchased for 10 gp or created with 2 gp worth of materials and a successful DC 15 Intelligence check

using alchemist's supplies. Each bulb contains six uses of gas before it must be replaced. To install the bulb and rig the tripwire, a character must succeed on a DC 12 Dexterity check using tinker's tools.

Triple Threat. The triple threat is a devious kobold creation, involving three traps in one. Often, a creature will disarm or trigger the first trap only to trip the second trap without a thought. Not to be outdone though, the triple threat involves a third—and often more potent—trap, just for good measure (and for the amusement of the trapmaker).

An item or area trapped with a triple threat can be triggered three separate times, and each individual trap must be disarmed in sequence. When a character discovers the trap with an Intelligence (Investigation) or Wisdom (Perception) check, the exact result determines how many they find: the first trap is detected on a result of 11–13, the first and second are detected with a result of 14–17, and all three traps are detected on a result of 18 or higher.

Similarly, disarming the traps requires three successive Dexterity (thieves' tools) checks, and the difficulty increases with each. Failing one disarm attempt resets all three traps (meaning a character must start over from the beginning). A character cannot disarm a trap they did not find though, so unless all three traps were discovered, one or more will inevitably be triggered. To disarm the first trap, a character must succeed on a DC 12 Dexterity (thieves' tools or tinker's tools) check. The DC for the second trap is 15, and the DC for the third is 17.

For example, a chest trapped with a triple threat may feature a poisoned needle, acid spray, and an explosive canister. The poison needle is triggered the first time a character attempts to pick the lock, the acid spray is triggered the second time a character attempts to pick the lock, and the explosive canister detonates when the lid is opened. Pressing on a hidden button on the side of the chest (DC 17 to locate) disarms the traps long enough to unlock and open the lid, though they reset

with a soft click when the lid is closed again. A character who triggers the poison needle must succeed on a DC 13 Dexterity saving throw or take 2d4 poison damage, and a character who triggers the acid spray must make a DC 15 Dexterity saving throw, taking 2d8 acid damage on a failure and half as much on a success. If the explosive canister is triggered, every creature within 10 feet of the chest must make a DC 18 Dexterity saving throw, taking 5d6 fire damage on a failure and half as much on a success.

Crafting a triple threat is not an easy feat and requires the necessary materials, 30 hours of crafting time, and three separate Dexterity checks using tinker's tools. Each check takes place after 10 hours of crafting, and a failure on one means a total loss on the project, requiring the character to start over from the beginning. The DC for the first check is 8, the DC for the second check is 11, and the DC for the third is 14.

TRAPSMITH SPELLS

Though much of a kobold's skill comes from tools and tinkering, the enterprising kobold trapsmith may go so far as to utilize magic to infuse and bolster their trapmaking.

ANALYZE DEVICE

2nd-Level Divination | Bard, Sorcerer, Warlock, Wizard

Casting Time: 10 minutes
Range: Touch
Components: V, S, M (a pinch of graphite)
Duration: Instantaneous

You spend 10 minutes magically inspecting a nonmagical device, weapon, or other piece of gear, gaining insight into its inner workings without the need to disassemble it. You learn how to use the device, how it functions, and identify any hidden traps or triggers.

If you attempt to recreate the device within the next 48 hours, you can roll 1d8 and add the result to your crafting ability check.

DISMANTLE

3rd-Level Transmutation | Bard, Wizard

Casting Time: 1 action
Range: 30 feet
Components: V, S
Duration: Instantaneous

You target one nonmagical trap you can see within range and harmlessly disassemble it into its component parts, which hover in the air briefly before arranging themselves neatly on the ground in front of you. This disarms the trap without triggering it, though it does not allow elements of the trap to pass through solid barriers. For example, if a portion of the trap is hidden behind a stone wall, that portion remains in place or falls harmlessly to the ground, but it would not pass through the wall to get to you.

At Higher Levels. When you cast this spell using a spell slot of 5th level or higher, you can dismantle one additional trap for every two slot levels above 3rd (so two traps at 5th, three at 7th, and four at 9th).

INFUSE TRIGGER

2nd-Level Evocation | Sorcerer, Warlock, Wizard
Casting Time: 1 minute
Range: Touch
Components: V, S
Duration: Until dispelled or triggered

You infuse a mundane trap with arcane power, causing it to deal devastating magical damage. You can cast this spell on a non-magical trap that deals slashing, bludgeoning, or piercing damage. When you cast this spell, choose a damage type from the following: cold, fire, force, lightning, necrotic, or psychic. The trap deals an additional 2d4 damage of that type when triggered.

At Higher Levels. When you cast this spell using a spell slot of 3rd level or higher, the damage increases by 1d4 for each slot level above 2nd.

THIRD HAND

2nd-Level Transmutation | Bard, Druid, Sorcerer, Warlock, Wizard
Casting Time: 1 action
Range: Self
Components: V, M (a dried spider)
Duration: 1 hour

You grow a third arm and hand, gaining all the benefits that entails. The arm grows from your torso, though the exact placement is up to you. For the duration, the arm and hand function just like one of your own, and you can do anything with it you can do with your others, including carry items, activate items, or wield a weapon or shield, though the extra arm does not grant you any additional attacks or actions on your turn. Additionally, for the duration, you have a +4 modifier to all Dexterity checks made with artisan's tools.

TRAPSMITH FEATS

Feats available to kobold crafters.

EXPERT TRAPSMITH

Prerequisite: Kobold with Proficiency in Alchemist's Supplies, Thieves' Tools, Tinker's Tools, or Smith's Tools

When you make either a Dexterity or Intelligence check or saving throw using tools to craft or disarm a trap, you can add both your Dexterity and Intelligence modifiers to the roll.

NIMBLE

Prerequisite: Kobold

You are adept at avoiding explosions—especially those you cause. When making a Dexterity saving throw to avoid fiery explosions (like that caused by *fireball*), you double your Dexterity modifier for the saving throw.

TINKERED WEAPONS AND GEAR

Kobolds have a particular flair for the dramatic and the deadly—and that definitely extends to their weapons as well. Though many kobolds will use whatever is at hand, be it a sharp stick, a large rock, or a bag of stinging insects, kobold artificers and tinkers are constantly creating new weapons that are both terrifying and unpredictable.

Blademill Cycle. Crafted by some crazed kobold weaponsmith, the blademill cycle combines a pedal-powered cart, a propeller… and swords. Sized to fit a Small creature, the blademill cycle features a seat with three wheels, pedals, and a horizontal, windmill-like fan made of eight longswords. When you operate the blademill cycle, you can use your action to pedal at a speed of up to 35 feet while the blades above you spin at a terrifying speed. Any creatures within 5 feet of you at the end of your turn must make a DC 14 Dexterity saving throw, taking 4d6 slashing damage on a failure or half as much damage on a success. If you are proficient in land vehicles, the DC for the saving throw increases to 16.

BOOM BOX SIZES

SIZE	AREA (RADIUS)	SAVE DC	DAMAGE	CRAFTING TIME	MATERIAL COST	CRAFTING DC
Tiny	10 feet	13	4d4 fire + 2d4 bludgeoning	5 days	50 gp	10
Small	20 feet	15	4d6 fire + 4d4 bludgeoning	10 days	100 gp	12
Medium	30 feet	18	6d8 fire + 4d6 bludgeoning	20 days	200 gp	14

A lever secured beside the seat allows you to brake while still spinning the bladed propeller or to deactivate and collapse the fan to use the cycle as a vehicle without using it as a weapon.

Crafting a blademill cycle requires 200 gp worth of materials, 15 days of crafting time, and a successful DC 8 Dexterity or Intelligence check using smith's tools or tinker's tools.

Boom Box. The boom box is an ingeniously simple (by kobold standards, anyway) contraption made of clockwork and filled with gunpowder. As an action, you wind the crank handle on the side to prime the box, and you can use a bonus action to set the notch-and-key timer up to 2 minutes (to a minimum of 1 second). Once the box is wound and the timer set, the gears inside tick down until the set time, at which point a flint-and-tinder mechanism inside sets the contents of the box alight, causing it to explode. When the box explodes, all creatures within the affected area must make a Dexterity saving throw, as determined by the **Boom Box Sizes** table, taking the bludgeoning and fire damage listed on a failed save or half as much damage on a successful one.

Some particularly maniacal kobold tinkers have taken to adding music box components to the boom box, so the mechanism plays a tinkling tune before it explodes.

Crafting a boom box requires gold, crafting time, and a successful Intelligence or Dexterity check using tinker's tools.

Kobold's Breath. Though kobolds lack the breath weapons of many of their draconic kin, a few daring kobold tinkers have crafted the next best thing. Roughly the size of a heavy crossbow, this two-handed weapon is a jumble of soldered metal, errant tubing, and glass bulbs. When fired, it sprays a 15-foot-long line of fire. Creatures in the line must succeed on a DC 14 Dexterity saving throw, taking 4d8 fire damage on a failed save or half as much on a successful one.

This weapon, while powerful, is not without its risks. When you use it, roll a d12 and consult the **Kobold's Breath Failure Chance** table.

Crafting a kobold's breath weapon requires 75 gp worth of material, 30 days of crafting time, and a successful DC 17 Dexterity or Intelligence check using tinker's tools.

Various alternative versions of this weapon exist that deal acid or poison damage instead of fire.

KOBOLD'S BREATH FAILURE CHANCE

d12	RESULT
1	The weapon explodes in your hand and is destroyed. You take 8d6 damage of the weapon's type.
2–5	Weapon functions but a piece falls off. Must be repaired (using an action) before it's functional again.
6–12	Weapon functions as normal.

TRAPS FOR ALL: KOBOLD CLASS TRAPS

by Victoria Jaczko

Kobolds tend to utilize their natural dexterity, small size, and capacity for diabolically complex thinking when dealing with their enemies. Generally, this plays out as trapping the living daylights out of everything they can.

Typically, the kobold trapsmith works within a warren to trap it for the defense of their kin, protecting their homes and power base from intruders. Conversely, most adventuring parties can only make use of simple traps since life on the road doesn't lend itself well to making (or needing) complicated trap design. Some hunting traps, snares, or magical alarms and glyphs are usually the most a party needs, thus denying kobold adventurers some of their crafty expertise.

Well, not anymore! Below, each class receives a modification to one of their base features (or has it swapped out) in favor of a kobold-variant trap, incorporating the techniques or magic of that class. While these traps can be refitted for any game or for use by any character, they are intentionally given a kobold-flavored "charm" to them for kobold PCs and NPCs to add their characteristic deviousness to their class features.

Class Traps

Each class replaces one of their class features (or uses of one of their class features) with a custom, kobold-oriented trap. These are optional variant features and are subject to GM approval.

BARBARIAN

Kobold barbarians may not be as refined or complicated as their more urbane kin, but they retain a streak of draconic cunning and feral opportunism. The traps they devise may lack sophistication but are quick to craft, take advantage of natural terrain, and tend to hurt. A lot.

At 2nd level, instead of a barbarian's Reckless Attack feature, you can choose to take the Reckless Trap feature.

Reckless Trap. You can produce a trap incorporating scrounged or improvised materials appropriate to the terrain. Sample traps are falling logs, pits, snares, and rockfalls. It requires 10 minutes to set the trap, or 5 minutes if you rush (granting advantage on saving throws to avoid the trap).

Your traps are concealed within natural terrain and use local materials, giving other creatures disadvantage on Wisdom (Perception) checks to spot them. Your traps'

save DC is equal to 8 + your Dexterity modifier
+ your proficiency bonus, made against an
appropriate saving throw for the type of trap,
usually Dexterity or Constitution.

Your trap deals the damage customary
for a trap of its kind plus an additional
1d8 of damage (even if it wouldn't
normally cause damage). The
extra damage increases by 1d8 at
6th, 10th, and 14th levels to a
maximum of an additional 4d8
damage. You can choose for
the trap to deal no damage if it
wouldn't normally.

BARD

Kobold bards set traps with
the intention of proving
their sophistry and wit, caring
less about damaging a foe than
crippling the ego or proving a point.
The bard is well-aware of the stereotypes
and expectations other folk have about
kobolds and use these misconceptions
against them.

At 2nd level, instead of a bard's Song of Rest
feature, you can choose to take the Mocking
Song feature.

Mocking Song. As an action, you can conjure
an illusion of a simple trap, such as a bear
trap, trip wire, or a small glyph. The trap's
illusory nature is revealed by effects that pierce
illusions, such as *true seeing*, and it disappears
if dispelled. Otherwise, setting off the trap or
attempting to disarm it causes it to vanish and
triggers a "song" of high-pitched yips and yaps
that fill the area within 30 feet of the trap. A
creature within the area of effect that can hear
must succeed on a Constitution saving throw
against your spell save DC or be deafened for
1 minute. Once you have used this feature,
you must complete a short or long rest to use
it again.

Starting at 11th level, any creature who fails
its saving throw is also confused, as *confusion*,
for 1 round.

CLERIC

Kobold clerics call upon their deities to
safeguard just about anything they don't want
anyone poking at. The small divine glyphs they
conjure cause pain to those unwise enough to
intrude upon their warren or tamper with their
favorite pickaxe.

At 2nd level, instead of Channel Divinity:
Turn Undead and Destroy Undead, you gain
the Channel Divinity: Minor Glyph Trap and
Major Glyph Trap features.

Channel Divinity: Minor Glyph Trap. As
an action, you present your holy symbol and
speak a prayer of protection over a nonmagical
item no larger than 5 feet by 5 feet. This must

be a specific item. You cannot target a section or floor or wall, but you can target a door or a window of an appropriate size. A glyph in the shape of your holy symbol glows on the item before fading, but it remains visible for those looking for it or with a successful DC 10 Wisdom (Perception) check.

The glyph trap does not trigger if you touch or interact with the item, nor for up to five other creatures you designate when you set the trap. Any other creature who triggers the trap must make a Wisdom saving throw against your spell save DC, taking 1d10 + your cleric level of radiant damage on a failed save or half as much damage on a successful one.

The glyph trap does not harm the item it is on. It fades once triggered and must be reapplied at the next dawn, or it deactivates.

Major Glyph Trap. Starting at 5th level, your Minor Glyph Trap feature deals an additional 2d10 points of radiant damage when triggered. Additionally, when a creature fails its saving throw against your glyph trap, it is instantly blinded for 1 minute, and you are automatically alerted that the trap was triggered as a mental *alarm*, as long as you are on the same plane of existence.

DRUID

Kobolds are used to being overlooked and treated as lesser folk, so they're always ready to flip the tables. Druids kobolds, with their cunning and shapeshifting magic, can trap areas, attuning them to slithery and scaly things and laying low arrogant trespassers.

At 2nd level, instead of two uses of your Wild Shape feature, you gain one use of Wild Shape and the Baleful Marker feature.

Baleful Marker. You can spend a minute creating a marker out of natural materials, such as bone, wood, and feathers, and infusing it with magic. When placing the marker, you can designate a number of similar tokens, like feathers, stones, or carved items, in your possession to be keyed to the ward, granting immunity to creatures that possess one.

Creatures who enter within 20 feet of the ward and do not have a key token must make a Wisdom saving throw. On a failure, they are transformed into a Tiny beast, such as a lizard, rat, or poisonous snake (your choice, set when you place the marker) as the *polymorph* spell for a number of minutes equal to half your druid level (rounded down). If such a polymorphed creature assumes their natural form while within the warded area, they do not have to make the save again, but they do if they leave and reenter. Beasts are immune to the marker's effects.

You can only have one Baleful Marker active at a time. If you construct and place a new one, your old marker is deactivated.

FIGHTER

Kobold fighters set few of their own traps, but they excel when surrounded by traps, whether set by kin, companions, or others.

At 1st level, instead of Second Wind, you gain the Spring Trap feature.

Spring Trap. As a bonus action, you can set off a trap within 5 feet of a creature you are currently engaging in melee and force them to be the target of the trap. You must be aware of the trap's existence in order to set it off. If the trap affects an area that you are within, you are also affected by springing the trap but have advantage on any saving throws it requires.

Once you use this feature, you must finish a short or long rest before you can use it again. You can use this ability twice between rests starting at 5th level, and three times between rests starting at 13th level.

MONK

Kobold monks focus less on spite in their traps, preferring to use their enemies' aggression against them. If reacted to calmly, a monk's trap is mostly harmless. Struggling against their trap, however, makes foes ever more ensnared.

Instead of the Step of the Wind Ki feature ability, you learn Calm Quicksand Trap.

Calm Quicksand Trap. You can spend 1 ki point to channel your energy into an area no larger than a 5-foot cube, creating an invisible space of quicksand-like energy that lasts until the beginning of your next turn. Moving at normal speed or slower through the space does not trigger the trap. Running, casting a spell, making an attack, or taking similar actions within (or through) the space, however, activates the trap. The target must make a Wisdom saving throw against your save DC or be affected by the *slow* spell as the placid energy resists their aggression. The effect persists until the target takes no aggressive or hurried action for 1 round, or after a minute, whichever comes first.

PALADIN

The rare kobold paladin prefers to use traps to punish the truly wicked and unworthy, not to harass or injure simple interlopers. Drawing on their divine connection and heritage (as dragons are the ultimate symbol of judgment), the paladin ensnares enemies with a draconic sense of righteous fury.

At 2nd level, instead of the Divine Smite feature, you gain the Draconic Jaws feature.

Draconic Jaws. You can expend one paladin spell slot to lay a magical snare in an unoccupied space within 5 feet of you. This snare resembles a hunting trap but is obviously magical, bristling with energy and large teeth.

A creature stepping into the trap must succeed on a Dexterity saving throw against your spell save DC or take 1d8 piercing damage and 2d8 damage of one of the following: acid, cold, fire, lightning, or poison. The trap deals an additional 1d8 damage of the chosen energy type for each spell level higher than 1st, to a maximum of 5d8. Undead and fiends have disadvantage on their saving throw.

Creatures who fail their saving throw are also restrained. Freeing itself from the Draconic Jaws requires a successful Strength saving throw against your spell save DC.

The trap persists until a creature breaks free, the trapped creature dies, or until you complete a short or long rest, whichever comes first.

RANGER

Kobold rangers combine their natural affinity for cunning traps with a hunting acumen and adeptness within their preferred terrain. In favored environs, their traps are hard to find,

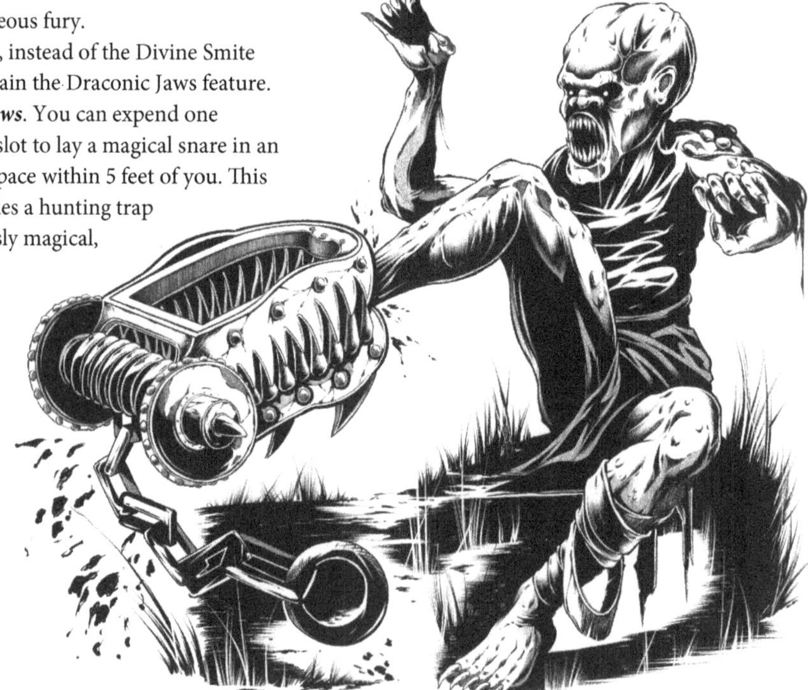

harder to disable, and even harder to escape.

At 1st level, instead of the Favored Enemy feature, you gain the Favored Quarry feature.

Favored Quarry. You are particularly adept at creating and setting traps within your favored terrain and even more so at trapping particular types of foes. When you choose a favored terrain from your Natural Explorer feature, also choose a type of favored quarry: aberrations, beasts, celestials, constructs, dragons, elementals, fey, fiends, giants, monstrosities, oozes, plants, or undead, or, alternatively, select two races of humanoid (such as gnolls and orcs) as your favored quarries. This quarry must be commonly found in your selected favored terrain.

Traps you create or place in your favored terrain impose disadvantage on attempts to spot them with Intelligence (Investigation) or Wisdom (Perception) checks. Additionally, if your favored quarry sets off one of your traps, it has disadvantage on any saving throws made to resist or escape the trap.

If you are within a mile of one of your traps set in your favored terrain, you immediately sense when the trap is triggered, and the type of creature (animal, beast, gnoll, and so on) trapped in it, if any.

ROGUE

Kobold rogues have mastered the art of manufacturing improvised traps with little to no planning and from nothing more than materials at hand. They may be odd-looking and often break after a single use, but the rogue cares little about longevity compared to entangling foes in a snare made from a belt, scavenged wire, or the chain from a broken chandelier.

At 2nd level, instead of the Cunning Action feature, you can choose Cunning Traps.

Cunning Traps. You can take an action to create an impromptu trap of simple design: a hunting trap, snare, trip wire, and so on. As a bonus action, you can set a trap you've created in an appropriate unoccupied space within 5 feet of you. You can set the trigger for when the trap is contacted, when a specific space is entered or stepped on, or when a certain amount of time has passed (no more than a minute).

The DC to spot, disable, or break out of your Cunning Traps is DC 8 + your Dexterity modifier + your proficiency bonus, and each trap has a saving throw appropriate to the trap's design (often a Dexterity saving throw).

Choose one of the following as the trap's effect: deal 1d6 + your rogue level in either bludgeoning, piercing, or slashing damage (appropriate to the trap) or cause the target to be grappled, prone, or restrained until the end of their next turn.

Complex traps, traps requiring significant preparation, or very large traps, like a huge, swinging blade, cannot be made with Cunning Traps. Likewise, at GM's discretion, a situation may render trapmaking impossible, like being completely naked in a totally empty room.

The trap breaks once triggered.

SORCERER

Kobold sorcerers empower traps with the magic of their own blood. A means of flexing their sorcerous mastery, their traps are personalized blood sigils used to ward walls, doors, and objects.

At 2nd level, you can spend your sorcery points to create a Blood Sigil.

Blood Sigil. As an action, you deal 1 piercing or slashing damage to yourself and draw blood to scrawl a sigil on a door, wall, floor, window, or item large enough to contain the sigil. You determine the sigil's appearance, and it radiates magic of the evocation school if targeted with an effect like *detect magic*.

Creatures who step on or over a sigil, touch it directly, step through a portal containing one, or pick up an item containing one trigger it. When triggered, the sigil erupts with magical energy. The creature that triggered it must make a Dexterity saving throw, taking 2d8

acid, cold, fire, lightning, or thunder damage on a failed saving throw (your choice when you create the sigil) or half as much damage on a successful one. Once triggered, this sigil ends.

This sigil's damage increases by 1d8 when you reach 5th level (3d8), 11th level (4d8), and 17th level (5d8). Sigils crumble away after your next long rest unless you continue to invest sorcery points to keep them active.

WARLOCK

Kobold warlocks' patrons are fully aware of their affinity for baubles and cleverness. Warlocks can create pretty little trinkets with their magic and use them to lure the unwary into a trap.

At 2nd level, you do not gain Eldritch Invocations (instead learning your first invocation at 5th level) and gain the Invocation of Greed feature.

Invocation of Greed. As an action, you conjure a small bauble, such as a gem or a piece of jewelry no larger than your hand, infused with your magic. The bauble is fragile and likely to shatter if dropped or handled roughly, and it dissolves into smoke at the next dawn.

The magic of the bauble is inert while in your possession or held by you. Once it is either set down, taken from you, or given away, its magic activates. A humanoid creature within 30 feet who sees an unattended bauble must succeed on a Wisdom saving throw or use their action to move to the bauble and pick it up or, if they already hold the bauble, to examine it. The bauble then turns to smoke and clouds the target's mind, stunning them until the end of their next turn. On a successful save, the bauble simply turns to smoke.

WIZARD

Kobold wizards have plenty of magical options for traps and seldom resort to the mechanical variety their less erudite kin might employ. That said, their deviousness runs just as strong as any kobold, creating an interest in puzzle and riddle traps.

Instead of gaining the Savant feature as part of your Arcane Tradition at 2nd level, gain the Riddle Savant feature instead. (If your Arcane Tradition does not have a Savant feature, work out an appropriate feature replacement with the GM.)

Riddle Savant. Your crafty magic and fondness for complex riddles and puzzles can befuddle an opponent's mind. As an action, you can choose to speak a riddle aloud or to have a *minor illusion* of your voice recite or explain some manner of riddle or puzzle to a location you can see (including remotely, as with the *scrying* spell).

As long as the target is sufficiently intelligent and can understand you, it must make a Wisdom saving throw. On a failure, the creature is convinced it cannot perform an intended action (such as attacking you or opening a door or chest) unless it correctly answers the riddle, and it is compelled to spend each of its actions attempting to solve it. The creature makes an additional saving throw at the end of each of its turns. On a success, the creature is not compelled to answer and does not feel hindered from taking actions, though it may still choose to solve the riddle if it desires.

A creature attempting to solve your riddle or puzzle makes an Intelligence (Investigation) check against your spell save DC. If it succeeds, you can give it another riddle, and the creature will continue to attempt to solve it until it succeeds at its saving throw. Correctly answering a riddle grants the creature advantage on its next saving throw.

The compulsion ends 1 round after you leave the vicinity or stop responding to the target's attempts to solve the riddle or if you or your allies attack the target or cast a spell on it.

This feature automatically fails on creatures with an Intelligence of 4 or lower or who are immune to charm.

SPRIG GNOMES: AT HOME IN THE WASTES

by Mike Welham

While many of the gnomes of Niemheim escaped Baba Yaga's wrath by brokering infernal bargains that forever marked them, a few fled the promised annihilation. A small group took grave risk and traveled to where they'd hoped to always remain out of her reach: the Western Wastes. They knew mere survival would be a challenge, but they preferred that to Grandmother's cruel whims. The first of them quickly learned to distance themselves from dust goblins and eked out an existence in the least-inhabited areas. Early generations had high mortality rates due to hunger, thirst, and the dangerous environment and terrifying abominations. However, they persevered, and word of their success spread among other gnomes seeking refuge. Sprig gnome expeditions to obtain resources also drew more displaced gnomes to this frontier land. They welcome non-gnomes as well into their communities—once ensuring they share the desire to reclaim the Wastes.

Sprig gnomes (occasionally called reclamation gnomes in jest) spend their lives tending to thickets of hardy plants and shepherding animals that can survive the inhospitable conditions of the Wastes. The gnomes even encourage the growth of mutated flora and fauna, celebrating them as specimens that have thrived against all odds. Ultimately, the various sprig gnome clans hope to reverse the devastation wrought by the Great Mage Wars.

Since the sprig gnomes have no shortage of foes in the Wastes, they make alliances with neighboring creatures wherever they can. Notably, the gnomes are on friendly terms with burrowlings (see *Tome of Beasts* for more on burrowlings), applying their hard-earned skills at cultivation to help them, and some burrowlings have relocated near the gnomes' homesteads and act as defenders and an early warning system.

Though many sprig gnome adventurers confine their travels to the Wastes, some venture with parties to regions beyond, so they can reverse the dangerous effects of unchecked magic and pollution in other areas. These wanderers avoid areas controlled by gnomes aligned with the shadow fey or the infernal gnomes of Niemheim. However, they inform independent gnomes they meet about the haven they have built, offering an alternative.

These hardy gnomes typically have some physical trait that marks their birth in the Wastes: a shock of white (or otherwise discolored) hair, bleached skin, or more severe changes. The gnomes don't conceal any of their unique features, making them easily recognizable as sprig gnomes.

Sprig Gnome Names

The gnomes who settled in the Wastes quickly eschewed nicknames and gave their offspring shorter names with harsh syllables to more quickly alert gnome children to dangers. They also adopted clan names based on the features of their homes in defiance of the conditions they fought against. As sprig gnomes have grown more accustomed to the land, some of these rules have relaxed, and members of the youngest generation sport whimsical nicknames again.

Male Names: Gart, Hak, Mip, Stot, Vorg

Female Names: Bez, Ika, Keet, Pix, Tam

Clan Names: Bloodsoil, Hollowbone, Ironthistle, Poxbloom, Shoveleater

Sprig Gnome Traits

You have adapted to life in the Wastes, impacting your longevity but granting you protection from its most immediate dangers.

Ability Score Increase. Your Constitution score increases by 1.

Age. As one of the downsides of an upbringing in the Wastes, the natural lifespans of sprig gnomes have decreased. They live somewhere between 150 and 200 years, even if they spend most of their adult lives outside of the Wastes.

Alignment. Aware of the inherent hostility of the land they inhabit and wishing to provide a contrast to it, sprig gnomes are more good-natured than their counterparts in other regions of Midgard.

Magic Stabilizer. Meditation techniques and arcane training allow you to reduce the chaotic effects of spellcasting in locations where magic has been warped. Any creature within 30 feet of you that casts a spell halves the percentage chance of a random effect. (If this chance is represented by a 1 on a die, the effect occurs 50 percent of the time after rolling a 1.) The distance increases by 10 feet for every 2 levels you gain (to a maximum of 120 feet). A creature can attempt to override this stabilization aura for 1 hour by succeeding on a Charisma saving throw (DC 10 or your spell save DC, whichever is higher).

Unspoiled Repasts. Edible food and untainted water are difficult to obtain in the Wastes, but as you gain experience, you learn how to remove contaminants. When you reach 3rd level, you can cast the *purify food and drink* spell with this trait. Once you cast this spell with this trait, you can't do so again until you finish a long rest. Intelligence is your spellcasting ability for this spell. Every 5 levels thereafter, you can use this ability one additional time between long rests.

Waste-Inured. You were raised in the Western Wastes and miraculously avoided the worst of what it can throw at someone. You have advantage on all saving throws and ability checks against effects generated by the Wastes or the Dread Walkers dotting the land.

Languages. The constant threat of dust goblins has required you to learn when they lurk about. You can speak, read, and write Goblin.

New Feats

The following feats expand on the sprig gnomes' features.

ABERRANT FOE

Most of your hostile encounters involve the many aberrations that spawn in the Western Wastes. You gain the following benefits:

- Increase your Constitution score by 1, to a maximum of 20.
- Whenever you make an Intelligence (Arcana) check related to the origins of an aberration, you are considered proficient in the Arcana skill and add double your proficiency bonus to the check, instead of your normal proficiency bonus.
- You have advantage on attempts to escape grapples from a creature grappling you with a tentacle or similar appendage.
- You have advantage on saving throws against effects from an aberration that inflicts a condition on you. This does not apply to the aberration's spellcasting.

GREEN THUMB

Prerequisite: The ability to cast at least one spell beneficial to plants

You are very knowledgeable about plants and their care. You gain the following benefits:

- Increase your Wisdom score by 1, to a maximum of 20.
- If you cast a spell or use an ability that conjures or creates a plant creature, the creature has 50% more hit points, and it gains a +1 bonus to AC.
- Plants you grow are considered magical for the purposes of effects targeting them.
- Whenever you make an Intelligence (Nature) check related to the origins of a plant, you are considered proficient in the Nature skill and add double your proficiency bonus to the check, instead of your normal proficiency bonus.

TURN ABERRATION

Prerequisite: The ability to turn a type of creature, such as through Channel Divinity.

You make yourself anathema to aberrations. As an action, you perform the same ability that you already use to turn creatures, but you instead target aberrations. Each aberration within 30 feet that can see or hear you must make a Wisdom saving throw. If the creature fails its saving throw, it is turned for 1 minute or until it takes any damage.

A turned creature must spend its turns trying to move as far away from you as it can, and it can't willingly move to a space within 30 feet of you. It also can't take reactions. For its action, it can use only the Dash action or try to escape from an effect that prevents it from moving. If there's nowhere to move, the creature can use the Dodge action.

WASTE WALKER

Your upbringing in the wastelands has given you a sixth sense regarding its dangers. You gain the following benefits:

- Increase your Dexterity score by 1, to a maximum of 20.

- You are unaffected by natural difficult terrain in badlands and similar regions.
- You have advantage on checks to determine whether a plant or beast is safe to eat, and you have advantage on Survival checks to find drinkable water or shelter from storms.
- You have advantage on saving throws against effects that give you the poisoned condition.

School of Preservation

Sprig gnomes have learned to combine arcane magic with the nature magic of druids. Willing teachers of this new arcane tradition, the gnomes have ensured its lessons have spread beyond their clans. Some gnomes who risk retribution from dark-aligned gnomes have made the journey to the Magocracy of Allain, where their nascent school has gained a modicum of acceptance, drawing curiosity from dilettantes and a few serious practitioners. Its blending of two distinct types of magic, however, have raised eyebrows among the arcane purists within the colleges of magic.

As a preservationist, you seek spells that protect the natural order or that remove harmful effects that impede or threaten life. In pursuit of these goals, you also disdain necromantic magic that makes a mockery of life.

PRESERVATION SAVANT

Beginning when you select this school at 2nd level, you can add druid spells to your spellbook. At 2nd level when you add two spells to your spellbook for free, you can add druid spells rather than wizard spells. At 3rd level and higher, you can replace only one wizard spell with a druid spell. Additionally, you no longer cast necromancy spells. Finally, the gold and time you must spend to copy a druid spell into your spellbook is halved.

SEEDLING

Starting at 2nd level, when you select this school, you sprout a seedling from your hand, neck, or other part of your body that receives regular exposure to the sun. You can use your action to encourage the seedling to produce berries, which provides as much sustenance as a meal or provides oxygen to you for an hour, keeping you from choking or suffocating. Once you use this feature of the seedling, you can't use it again until you either finish a long rest or cast a 1st-level or higher spell that conjures or grows plants.

If the seedling is severed from your body, a new one grows in its place in 1 minute.

OVERCOME THE UNNATURAL

Starting at 6th level, when you target an aberration, ooze, or undead with a spell, that creature has disadvantage on its saving throw. Additionally, if the spell deals damage, the creature is treated as if it has vulnerability to the damage type if it doesn't already have that vulnerability. If it already has that vulnerability, the spell deals the maximum possible damage.

NATURE'S RESILIENCE

Beginning at 10th level, any beast or plant that you conjure or transmute gains resistance to acid, fire, and slashing damage for the spell's duration. If the creature already has resistance to a damage type, it instead gains immunity to that damage type.

MATURED TREE

Beginning at 14th level, you can use your action to command your seedling to detach from you and grow into an **awakened tree**. You can use your action to return the tree to its seedling form. It can remain in tree form for up to 8 hours, after which it reverts to a seedling. You must then complete a long rest before you can transform it into a tree again. You can use another action to encourage the tree to produce enough fruit to feed up to 8 creatures or to create enough oxygen for up to 8 creatures to breathe for an hour. You can use this feature with the same frequency as the seedling's feature. Finally, you can use your action to grow the tree to prodigious size, becoming a treant for 10 minutes. Once you use this feature of the Matured Tree, you can't use it again until you finish a long rest.

If the tree is destroyed, a new seedling sprouts from you in 1 minute, but you can't grow it into a tree again until you complete a long rest.

New Spells

Sprig gnomes developed the following spells to minimize the Wastes' deleterious effects and enjoy greater attunement to nature. They happily share these spells with others to expand their efforts to reclaim despoiled lands.

CONJURE PLANTS

4th-Level Conjuration | Druid
Casting Time: 1 action
Range: 60 feet
Components: V, S, M (an ounce of soil)
Duration: Concentration, up to 1 hour

You summon fey spirits that take the form of plants and appear in unoccupied spaces that you can see within range. Choose one of the following options for what appears:

- One plant of challenge rating 2 or lower
- Two plants of challenge rating 1 or lower
- Four plants of challenge rating 1/2 or lower
- Eight plants of challenge rating 1/4 or lower

Each plant is also considered fey, and it disappears when it drops to 0 hit points or when the spell ends.

The summoned creatures are friendly to you and your companions. Roll initiative for the summoned creatures as a group, which has its own turns. They obey any verbal commands that you issue to them (no action required by you). If you don't issue any commands to them, they defend themselves from hostile creatures but otherwise take no actions.

At Higher Levels. When you cast this spell using certain higher-level spell slots, you choose one of the summoning options above, and more creatures appear: twice as many with a 6th-level slot and three times as many with an 8th-level slot.

DAMPEN REACTION

2nd-Level Transmutation | Druid, Wizard

Casting Time: 1 action or 1 reaction, which
you take when a creature within 60 feet of
you is the target of an alchemical attack or
breath weapon

Range: 60 feet

Components: V, S

Duration: 8 hours or instantaneous

When you cast this spell, you impede the
catalyst for an alchemical or acidic concoction.
If you cast this spell using an action, you can
choose up to 10 cubic feet of material (such as
a pool of acid or alchemical fire), which deals 2
fewer dice of damage from contact with it. This
reduction in damage lasts for the duration.

If you cast this spell using a reaction, each
creature in a 10-foot-radius sphere centered
on a point within range takes 2 fewer dice of
damage from an alchemical source (such as
a vial of acid or alchemist's fire) or from an
effect that deals acid damage (such as a black
dragon's breath weapon or the *acid splash*
spell). If the damage is reduced to 0 as a result
of casting this spell, any effect that deals
ongoing damage no longer applies (such as
that produced by alchemist's fire).

At Higher Levels. When you cast this spell
using a spell slot of 3rd level or higher, you
reduce the damage dealt by 2 dice for each
slot level above 2nd. Instead of reducing the
damage, you can choose to increase the area by
10 cubic feet for a slot level when you cast this
spell as an action.

FORTIFY PLANTS

3rd-Level Abjuration | Druid

Casting Time: 1 action or 8 hours

Range: 120 feet

Components: V, S

Duration: Concentration, up to 10 minutes or
instantaneous

With this spell, you can improve a single plant's
ability to withstand damage, or you grant
lasting protection to ordinary plants in an area.

If you cast this spell using 1 action, you target
a single plant within range. The plant gains a
+2 bonus to AC as you toughen its epidermal
layer. Additionally, you can choose one of
the following damage types: acid, cold, fire,
necrotic, poison, or slashing. The plant gains
resistance to the chosen damage type.

If you cast this spell over the course of 8
hours, you enhance all plants in a 100-foot
radius centered on a point within range. The
plants are treated as magical plants for 1 year.
Additionally, you can choose one of the above
damage types. The plants have advantage
on saving throws against spells and effects
that deal the chosen damage type and have
resistance to the damage type.

At Higher Levels. When you cast this spell
using a spell slot of 4th level or higher, you can
grant the plant(s) resistance to an additional
damage type for each slot level above 3rd. The
bonus to AC increases by +1 for every two slot
levels above 3rd.

PLANT LEY LINE HUB

9th-Level Conjuration | Wizard

Casting Time: 8 hours

Range: Touch

Components: V, S, M (a rose that has
remained in bloom for at least 1 year and
planted on a ley line for at least 1 month)

Duration: Instantaneous

You plant the rose in a location without ley
lines while you cast this spell. Afterward, the
flower stays in bloom permanently. It has
hit points equal to your hit point maximum
at the time of casting the spell, and it has
immunity to all damage types except necrotic.
The rose has a telepathic bond with you that
lets you know if the rose is under attack or is
damaged. This bond persists even if you are on
a different plane.

If you sacrifice a spell slot of 8th level (or
2 spell slots of 6th level or higher, or 4 spell
slots of 4th level or higher) when you cast this
spell, such that you permanently lose access
to those spell slots, you can teleport yourself

and up to eight creatures who are within
60 feet of you to the rose's location as an
action. This teleportation transcends planar
distances. Additionally, you have advantage
on all attack rolls and saving throws when
defending the flower.

Once per month, the rose creates a smaller
version within 60 feet of itself, or of another
secondary rose, to extend a ley line through
itself and the second plant. This smaller
rose has resistance to all damage
types except necrotic and half
the original rose's hit
points. If the smaller

rose is destroyed, the established ley line fades
away after 24 hours. When you cast the spell,
you can set the parameters for the spread of
the ley lines (either one line up to a certain
length and then another line or radiating out
in a starburst pattern from the original). If you
don't set up the path for the ley lines produced,
the original rose spreads its ley lines out
alternating along each cardinal direction.

WINDRUNNER ELVES

by Robert Fairbanks

Elusive, eccentric, and unpredictable, windrunner elves have quietly traversed Midgard's vast central grasslands for millennia. These diminutive nomads roaming the steppes and plains are thought to originally hail from the elven capital of Sephaya, long since abandoned during the Great Retreat. When the Sephayan nobility withdrew, they fled to the Arbonesse along the fey roads. However, legends hint some were denied sanctuary, and those numbers, with households and retinues in tow, continued onward, disappearing into the then-uncharted east. Whether this second migration was by force or by choice remains a mystery. Many scholars suggest windrunners are the descendants of those unsettled elven expatriates. Less popular lines of research have led experts to suggest windrunners may have origins nearer to the mountains of Beldestan or points even farther east. Aggressively autonomous, the windrunner clans have little love for the remnants of the scattered elves. The notion of owing allegiance to the elves of the west is considered offensive, and outright hostility can result at the mere suggestion of fidelity to the Imperatrix of the Grand Duchy or the River Lords of the Arbonesse.

After the Great Retreat. Several windrunner traditions claim that sometime after the Great Retreat and their expulsion from the Arbonesse, another series of schisms formed among the fleeing Sephayan refugees. Some academics cite treachery and scandal among a still panicky, opportunistic Sephayan nobility. Others speculate the approach to Demon Mountain as somehow a magical or psychic initiator to the four migrations. Even in those times, the mountain was an ill-omened place. From far afield, the great Sephayan sorcerers and wizards could sense the mountain as a place of vast and tumultuous energies, which only added to the elven nobilities' foreboding and unrest. In either case, a third elven dispersal had begun in the shadow of what would later be called Demon Mountain.

The Windrunner Clans. Four great houses now parted ways. Some skirted the Wormwood, disappearing northeast of the Demon Mountain. The majority turned south, toward wide, rolling, coastal plains and gentler climes. Four elven bloodlines, who over centuries would divide, survive, and remerge, ultimately "stabilized" into the eight windrunner clans that today roam the windy plains and trackless steppe-lands.

For nearly all windrunners, primary subsistence is derived from nomadic herding. With the aid of trained herding and hunting dogs, the clans cohabitate and tend to antelope, musk ox, and bison. Windrunner societies are self-governing tribal confederacies, built on ancestral ties and political alliances. They are a fiercely self-reliant people: passionate, territorial, and ardently devoted to their post-exodus way of life.

The clans build no fences and do not believe in the ownership of land. They do, however, fiercely defend sacred sites and hunting grounds, even from one another. Long-standing feuds occur often over water, grazing, and wintering rights.

Characteristics. Windrunners are slight even by elven standards, and individuals reaching a height of 5 feet are rare. They keep their hair braided, knotted, pinned, or even shorn off to withstand the relentless winds. Windrunner attire usually consists of tanned and dyed hides and furs. They adore tattoos and piercings and make intricate fetishes to denote clan and status.

Elves Aloft

While the windrunners' use of kites is noteworthy, it is somewhat overwrought in the minds of many. Travelers' tales, however, keep getting more elaborate with each telling.

Typical kite use for the clans is to cross chasms and other treacherous land, launching from horseback or descending from precipices. They also use them for competitive events and for herding livestock and marking land for grazing and water. They are storied for sending aloft tethered lookouts via kite. Distant clusters of kites can often be seen fluttering above their herds.

Their rain wagons, or water wains, one of the few wheeled conveyances used by windrunners, are fitted with a cunning channeling system for the collection, storage, and distribution of rainwater.

Equipment of the Windrunners

The windrunners have developed many tools for hunting on the planes.

Birding Shaft. These short, thick-shafted arrows have blunted, weighted tips. Instead of damage, a creature hit by one must make a Constitution saving throw with a DC 8 + your proficiency bonus + your Dexterity modifier. On a failed save, the creature is stunned until the end of its next turn.

Lasso. The target of a successful lasso attack is grappled and restrained. While the grapple persists, you may pull the target by 5 feet per turn as a bonus action or dismount a mounted target, knocking it prone. The lasso has a 15-foot reach.

A creature can use its action to make a Strength (Athletics) or Dexterity (Acrobatics) check (target's choice) contested by your Strength (Athletics) or Dexterity (Acrobatics) check (your choice), freeing itself or another creature within its reach on a success. Dealing 5 slashing damage to the lasso (AC 10) also frees the creature without harming it, ending the effect and destroying the lasso.

Windrunner Bolas. When a creature is hit by a ranged weapon attack made with bolas, it must make a Strength or Dexterity saving throw (target's choice) with a DC 8 + your proficiency bonus + your Strength or Dexterity modifier (your choice). On a failed save, the creature is restrained until the bolas are removed. On a successful save, the creature takes damage but is not entangled.

A creature can use its action to make a DC 12 Strength (Athletics) or Dexterity (Acrobatics) check, freeing itself or another creature within its reach on a success. Dealing 5 slashing damage to the bolas (AC 10) also frees the creature without harming it, ending the effect and destroying the bolas.

Windrunner Boomerang. A boomerang thrown within its short range returns to you after it is thrown. If you have a Dexterity

NAME	COST	DAMAGE	WEIGHT	PROPERTIES
Martial Melee Weapons				
Lasso	5 gp	—	6 lb.	Finesse, reach (15 feet), special (see below)
Martial Ranged Weapons				
Windrunner Bolas	25 gp	1d4 bludgeoning	3 lb.	Finesse, light, thrown (range 30/60), special (see below)
Windrunner Boomerang	15 gp (standard)/ 25 gp (bladed)	1d4 bludgeoning (standard)/1d4 slashing (bladed)	3 lb. (standard)/ 4 lb. (bladed)	Finesse, light, special (see below), thrown (range 100/300)

score of 15 or higher, you automatically catch the returning boomerang. If not, you must make a DC 15 Dexterity saving throw to catch it. On a failed save, the boomerang lands at your feet. If you fail the save by 5 or more, the boomerang strikes you, dealing 1d4 bludgeoning damage (or slashing damage if it is a bladed boomerang).

Magic Items of the Windrunners

The windrunners favor magic items that are especially useful on the Rothenian Plane.

CEDARSKIN CUIRASS

Armor (Studded Leather), Very Rare
  (Requires Attunement)

This lightweight, fragrant piece is finely crafted of doeskin and reinforced with strips of woven cedar bark and rawhide. The armor is treated as *+1 studded leather*. In addition, while you wear it, you have advantage on any saving throws related to poison and disease, and difficult terrain doesn't impede your movement.

SAIGA HELM

Wondrous Item, Very Rare
  (Requires Attunement)

This antelope skull is fashioned as a helm and engraved with druidic sigils. While wearing it, you gain a +1 bonus to armor class and are immune to the stunned condition.

Additionally, you can headbutt an opponent. On a hit, the target takes 7 (2d6) bludgeoning damage and must succeed on a DC 15 Strength saving throw or be knocked prone.

SNOWSHOE RABBIT SNOWBOOTS

Wondrous Item, Very Rare
  (Requires Attunement)

These low, soft boots are fashioned of enchanted snowshoe rabbit pelts and have wide, overlong soles. Icy terrain doesn't impede your movement, and you have advantage on Dexterity (Stealth) checks made to hide in snow.

Additionally, on speaking the command word, you gain +15 feet of movement, plus your jump distance is tripled. When this property has been used for a total of 1 hour, the magic ceases to function until you finish a short or long rest.

WIND KUKRI

Weapon (Dagger), Rare (Requires Attunement)

You gain a +1 bonus to attack and damage rolls with this magic weapon.

If wielding a pair of *wind kukri*, you gain a +2 bonus to attack and damage rolls made with each weapon. In addition, you gain the following abilities while wielding the pair:

- Once per turn per kukri, when used as a thrown weapon, it flies back to your hand safely after each attack roll. If you don't have a hand free, the weapon lands safely at your feet.

- When you score a critical hit with a kukri, the target takes an additional 2 (1d4) thunder damage.
- A target hit by both kukris in the same round must succeed on a DC 13 Strength saving throw or be pushed back 5 feet and deafened until the end of their next turn.

Spells of the Windrunners

While windrunner elves certainly acknowledge the existence of other peoples' deities, they worship none, though they do have a rich druidic tradition and sorcerers are not uncommon.

BREEZE WALKER

2nd-Level Transmutation | Druid

Casting Time: 1 action
Range: Self
Components: V, S, M (a pheasant feather)
Duration: Concentration, up to 1 hour

Choosing a direction, you summon a strong, steady breeze to swirl beneath your feet and propel you. You levitate to a sustained height of 3 feet for the duration, and travel in the chosen direction is at 150% of your movement. Travel in any other direction is at 50% of your movement.

While mounted, your mount's movement is affected as well.

WINDBLOWN

4th-Level Evocation | Sorcerer

Casting Time: 1 action
Range: Touch
Components: V, S, M
(a pinch of quail down)
Duration: Concentration,
up to 1 minute

You cause a column of air to swiftly launch the target creature or object up to 100 feet straight up. A creature can make a Dexterity saving throw to grab onto a fixed object it can reach, thus avoiding being launched. If some solid object (such as a ceiling) is encountered on the way up, the target strikes it just as if they had fallen the same distance. Once at its apex, the target remains buoyant, bobbing in midair, and will be blown along with the prevailing wind. When the spell ends, the target falls to the ground. This spell has no effect on flying creatures.

Windrunner NPCs

Silent figures appear all around you in a heartbeat. Dozens rise from the tall savannah grass like ghosts. These small, hide-clad elves seem to bristle at your approach, heavy bone knives clenched in their tattooed fists.

Medium Humanoid (Elf), Any Non-Lawful Alignment

Armor Class 15 (studded leather)
Hit Points 52 (8d8 +16)
Speed 30 ft.

STR	DEX	CON	INT	WIS	CHA
12 (+1)	17 (+3)	14 (+2)	11 (+0)	14 (+2)	9 (−1)

Skills Animal Handling +4, Perception +4, Stealth +5, Survival +4
Senses darkvision 60 ft., passive Perception 14
Languages Common, Elvish
Challenge 2 (450 XP)   **Proficiency Bonus** +2

Fey Ancestry. The elf has advantage on saving throws against being charmed, and magic can't put them to sleep.

Keen Hearing and Sight. The elf has advantage on Wisdom (Perception) checks that rely on hearing or sight.

Pack Tactics. The elf has advantage on an attack roll against a creature if at least one of their allies is within 5 ft. of the creature and the ally isn't Incapacitated.

ACTIONS

Multiattack. The elf makes two Bone Knives attacks or one Bone Knives and one Lasso attack.

Bone Knives. *Melee Weapon Attack*: +5 to hit, reach 5 ft., one target. *Hit*: 5 (1d4 + 3) slashing damage.

Lasso. *Melee Weapon Attack*: +5 to hit, reach 15 ft., one target. *Hit*: Target is grappled (escape DC 14). While the grapple persists, the target is restrained. The elf can use a bonus action to pull a grappled target up to 5 feet or to dismount a mounted target, knocking it prone.

Boomerang. *Ranged Weapon Attack*: +5 to hit, range 100/300, one target. *Hit*: 5 (1d4 + 3) bludgeoning damage.

BONUS ACTIONS

Fast Hands. If the elf hits the same target with two Bone Knives attacks in the same round, they can make an additional two Bone Knives attacks against the same target.

ELF, WINDRUNNER SKIRMISHER

Medium Humanoid (Elf), Any Non-Lawful Alignment

Armor Class 16 (studded leather)
Hit Points 112 (15d8 + 45)
Speed 30 ft.

STR	DEX	CON	INT	WIS	CHA
14 (+2)	18 (+4)	16 (+3)	11 (+0)	14 (+2)	12 (+1)

Saving Throws Dex +7, Wis +5
Skills Animal Handling +5, Perception +5, Stealth +7, Survival +5
Senses darkvision 60 ft., passive Perception 15
Languages Common, Elvish
Challenge 5 (1,800 XP) **Proficiency Bonus** +3

Fey Ancestry. The elf has advantage on saving throws against being charmed, and magic can't put them to sleep.

Keen Hearing and Sight. The elf has advantage on Wisdom (Perception) checks that rely on hearing or sight.

Mounted Warrior. When mounted, the elf has advantage on attacks against unmounted creatures smaller than its mount. If the elf's mount is subjected to an effect that allows it to take half damage with a successful Dexterity saving throw, the mount instead takes no damage if it succeeds on the saving throw and half damage if it fails.

Pack Tactics. The elf has advantage on an attack roll against a creature if at least one of their allies is within 5 ft. of the creature and the ally isn't Incapacitated.

Precision Shot. When the elf attacks with a ranged or thrown melee weapon, their attacks ignore half cover and don't have disadvantage at long range.

ACTIONS

Multiattack. The elf makes three Obsidian Scimitar attacks or three Shortbow attacks.

Obsidian Scimitar. *Melee Weapon Attack*: +7 to hit, reach 5 ft., one target. *Hit*: 7 (1d6 + 4) slashing damage. For each hit a target takes from this attack, the target takes an additional cumulative +1 slashing damage at the start of each of its turns, so for example, three hits on a target would mean an additional +3 slashing damage per turn. Any amount of magical healing or a DC 13 Wisdom (Medicine) check stops this extra damage (and resets the count). Constructs and undead are immune to this extra damage.

Bolas. *Ranged Weapon Attack*: +7 to hit, range 30/60, one target. *Hit*: 6 (1d4 + 4) bludgeoning damage, and the target must succeed on a DC 15 Strength or Dexterity saving throw (target's choice) or be restrained. A restrained target is freed with a successful DC 12 Strength (Athletics) or Dexterity (Acrobatics) check or by dealing 5 slashing damage to the bolas (AC 10).

Shortbow. *Ranged Weapon Attack*: +7 to hit, range 80/320, one target. *Hit*: 7 (1d6 + 4) piercing damage.

Spellcasting. The elf casts one of the following spells, using Intelligence as the spellcasting ability (spell save DC 11):

- 2/day each: *hunter's mark, waft**
- 1/day each: *pass without trace, thunderous charge**

    (* See *Deep Magic*.)

SERVANTS TO THE GODS: FAITH IN THE CROSSROADS

by Sebastian Rombach

From Ariadne, the Clockwork Oracle, to Wotan, the All-Father, the gods of Midgard are as majestic as they are varied. But as legendary as the myths of the gods are, their gospels carry little weight without servants to spread their dogma. Among the common folk of Midgard, worship is as often a collective experience as it is a solitary one, steeped in generations of practice, service, and tradition. Let's look at a few of these servants, how they congregate, and how their piety affects those around them.

Polytheism in Midgard

Midgard is a world where polytheism is the primary way mortals view divinity. Pantheons are separated by region, godly individuals by their focus, and nearly all of them are worshipped by most mortals. From the gods' perspective, who is receiving worship from whom is obscured by the use of masks (see *Midgard Worldbook*). But the vast majority of folks remain largely unaware of such deceptions. Instead, mortals worship the gods they believe in, in their own way regardless of what lies behind the heavenly curtain.

To address how characters might express reverence and piety, you can look to the actual practices of polytheism. Though the study of any theology can be a lifelong pursuit, there are two schools of polytheistic thought—hard polytheism and soft polytheism—that can be used as launching points for lending nuance and verisimilitude to characters.

Hard Polytheism. Hard polytheism is defined by the solid belief that each deity is separate and distinct. Hard, or steadfast, polytheists are defined by their belief and conviction in what the gods are, what they want, and what they offer.

Characters that subscribe to hard polytheism regularly seek others of like mind to congregate with, attempt to win over those who are undecided, and shun those who oppose their views. When a steadfast polytheist's beliefs are destabilized, such as a debunked miracle or a religious leader revealed for a fraud, their reactions are often dramatic and occasionally extreme.

Soft Polytheism. Soft polytheism is, in contrast, somewhat easygoing. Individuals who practice this type of faith believe that the divine beings fill more archetypal roles in accordance with mortal conditions or beliefs rather than rigid definitions. Soft, or flexible, polytheists are only a few leaps of logic away from understanding how the gods use masks to achieve their goals, or they would if they believed that the gods were actual beings. The pitfall of soft polytheism is its tendency toward reductivism. Soft polytheism comes with an inbuilt assumption of agnosticism or even atheism that is diametrically opposed to the will of the gods themselves. Characters who subscribe to this theology are more open-minded and sometimes more thoughtful, reverent even, but much less pious than characters at the opposing end of the spectrum. At their worst, soft polytheists are implacable skeptics who, no matter the evidence, will always seek to explain away miracles and divine experiences.

Religion in the Crossroads

The Crossroads region is aptly named where gods and their worshippers are concerned. No community here is inured to the genesis of new faiths or the exodus of the obsolete. Hard and soft polytheism, pantheism, atheism, and agnosticism abound in equal measure.

This revolving door of divinity means no end of confusion and conflict where religious beliefs are concerned. But rather than engage in outright crusades against each other, the major faiths of the Crossroads develop rivalries over attendance and hierarchy while fostering alliances over shared interests.

These faiths know that to gain followers they must continually manifest miracles to establish and reinforce belief. The gods know this too. Consequently, nearly all the gods are more direct with their priests here than elsewhere in Midgard, providing divine power and blessings to captivate hearts and minds.

Keeping the peace is a difficult, multipronged task in this religious landscape. Because of the complexities of interfaith relations, the religious orders of Khors, Lada, Perun, Rava, and Volund periodically meet to address mounting concerns, reassess old accords, and occasionally bury the hatchet. In this way, a quietly organized committee called the Clergy of Carrefour Faiths works from the shadows.

Clergy of Carrefour Faiths

Founded by select representatives from the major religious orders of the Crossroads, the Clergy of Carrefour Faiths is a roundtable sect devoted to caretaking the religious-political balance while maintaining anonymity from the public eye.

The clergy itself is represented by no more than five chapters at any given time, meeting in secret and only once in a season in the Ironcrags, Magdar Kingdom, the Black Hills, Perunalia, and near Zobeck. Only in occasions of dire peril do all the chapters meet at once, when the needs outweigh the risks of exposure. With the clergy spread out across the Crossroads, each chapter is led by five representatives called Clovers—a priest each from the faiths that follow the major gods of the Crossroads Pantheon. In addition to these five seats, each chapter hosts a skeleton crew of spy-priests that gather information and carry out the Clovers' directives.

Members of the clergy recognize each other by a mark, pin, or some other affectation that depicts a three-leaved clover enveloped in a green and copper ribbon. The Clovers of each chapter also wear enchanted brooches in the same style that prevents the wearer from deceiving another brooch-wearing Clover. This enchantment helps to ensure the integrity of the clergy is maintained against personal interests.

With such wide ground to cover and many religious interests present at any given time, the clergy's focus is limited to only a few, albeit vital, tasks. The Clovers and their secret priests verify miracles, dispense justice upon oathbreakers, and silence heresy in their own religions. To ensure that these goals are met with satisfaction by the entire clergy, each Clover is responsible for addressing the violations of members from their own religious orders only and to honestly report their successes and failures to their peer Clovers. The very structure of the Clergy of Carrefour Faiths

was founded to prevent one god's adherents from interfering with the internal conflicts of another. At least, directly.

All members are sworn to secrecy and take solemn, binding oaths. To a member, nothing is more sacred than a kept vow and nothing more profane than a broken one.

OATH DOMAIN (DIVINE DOMAIN)

Vows are not to be made lightly. Seek out and castigate those who would break their word.

Whether by divine mandate, personal devotion, or ministerial duty, you have taken on the solemn burden of holding others to their vows and punishing those who break them. Clerics who take this domain are warily regarded, even feared, as inescapable inquisitors. Some clerics choose this domain to hunt down oath-breaking paladins and bring them to justice, and others might serve religious governments and organizations as inquisitors, lawmakers, or even spies. Regardless of your motivations, you know that while words hold power, vows carry authority.

CLERIC LEVEL	SPELLS
1st	*command, insightful maneuver**
3rd	*hold person, zone of truth*
5th	*compelling fate*, speak with dead*
7th	*banishment, compulsion*
9th	*geas, tongue tied**

(*) see *Deep Magic*.

OATH AND INQUISITION

At 1st level, you gain proficiency in Investigation as well as with whips and warhammers. You also learn one language of your choice.

CHANNEL DIVINITY: VOW OF CONFESSION

Starting at 2nd level, you can use your Channel Divinity to compel others to swear an oath against their actions.

As an action, you can present your holy symbol and speak a phrase of authority. Choose any number of creatures within 30 feet of you equal to your proficiency bonus + your Wisdom modifier (minimum 1). A targeted creature must succeed on a Charisma saving throw or drop what they are holding and spend their reaction reciting a promise, vow, bond, or oath they have made in their lifetime. Any creature that does not share a language with you has advantage on their saving throw. Creatures who do not have a language or have an Intelligence less than 8 are not affected.

CHANNEL DIVINITY: HOLDING WORD

Starting at 6th level, you can use your Channel Divinity to hold someone's actions and words against them. Choose one creature within 60 feet of you that you can see and that can hear you. That creature must make a Wisdom saving throw. On a successful save, the creature's movement speed is halved until the end of its next turn. On a failed save, choose a number of actions equal to your proficiency bonus (Attack, Cast a Spell, Dash, Disengage, Dodge, Help, Hide, Ready, Search, Use An Object). The creature is unable to take those actions for a minute. The creature repeats their saving throw at the end of their turn, ending the effect on a success.

Humanoids who have broken their word or violated an oath within a year and a day have disadvantage on their saving throws against this feature. Creatures who do not have a language or have an Intelligence less than 8 are not affected.

POTENT SPELLCASTING

Starting at 8th level, you add your Wisdom modifier to the damage you deal with cantrips.

THOUGHTS AND PRAYERS

At 17th level, when you are subject to an effect that allows you to make an Intelligence, Wisdom, or Charisma saving throw for half damage, you instead take no damage on a success or half damage on a failure, provided that the effect has a verbal component that you

can hear. Additionally, you can expend a spell slot of 1st to 4th level to gain telepathy to a range of 60 feet for 10 minutes, a slot of 5th to 8th level for 1 hour, or a slot of 9th level for 24 hours.

Order of Unbridled Waves

The Order of Unbridled Waves is a brotherhood of coastal priests and maritime cavaliers who worship Nethus, King of the Sea, and proselytize the bounties of his faith. Commissioned by Ocean Seer Qorette Mardefon, High Priest of Nethus, the order's mandate is as clear as calm waters and follows a hard polytheistic approach. Honor Nethus and the tribulations of his bondage by ensuring liberty and freedom for all.

The order, still in its infancy, indiscriminately accepts membership from any who seek admission. More than a few outsiders voice skepticism of this policy though. The order's detractors point to the lax vetting of prospective members, claiming rotten fish ruin the whole catch. But members of the order rebuke these criticisms. The order requires all initiates to take solemn oaths that echo the pledge Nethus is believed to have made for his freedom.

In addition to these oaths, new members are expected to perform a ceremony called the Vigil of Night Tides, honoring the matrimonial vows Nethus made to Hecate, Queen of Night. The task entails sailing outward amid a full moon, submersing oneself in the night-lit waters, and enduring what comes until dawn's first light concludes the ritual. The especially fortunate are visited by giant seahorses who bear the vigilant persons safely back, a blessing from the Lord of Fish and Whales himself.

The order, while based in Capleon and assisting with the Steps of the Sea's reconstruction, sends its new recruits out across open waters on a pilgrimage of exploration. These priests come from all walks of life, whether they were sailors or gladiators, prisoners or slaves. Every member is welcomed into the order and trusted with the same duty: crusade in the name of freedom, for the good of the innocent and the worthy.

In everyday affairs, laypeople of the order serve as advocates in domestic and maritime disputes, provide refuge for the pursued, and dispense blessings such as the christenings of new sea vessels.

OATH OF TIDES (SACRED OATH)

Break the chains that anchor you in place and pledge your freedom on open waters.

The Oath of Tides calls for paladins to embody the tempestuous majesty of the sea. Like unpredictable ocean currents, paladins who follow this oath tend toward neutral and chaotic alignments. Many of those who take the Oath of Tides suffered under some form of bondage but found freedom and purpose in personifying the uncontainable sea.

TENETS OF TIDES

The Oath of Tides borrows its tenets from sea shanties sung by wistful sailors and warrior-poets compelled by ocean splendors. Paladins who uphold these tenets remember their origins, especially that which held them back, to move past the razor shoals of old history. Tidesworn paladins must strive to keep the wind in their sails as they explore life's deep mysteries and press ever onward. The Oath of Tides asks those who swear it to overcome their obstacles, pursue new avenues, and cut loose whatever weighs them down.

Chase the Horizon. Let my travels follow the stars and honor the moon. Through self-sacrifice, I free my heart to find my fortune.

Cherish Life's Ripples. All of life is a stream, a river, a sea. While I yet breathe, I will revel in and cherish thee.

Douse the Enemy. Let my foes cower behind their walls. I still shall crash upon them, drown them, quash them all.

Keep Unfettered. So long as my heart swells in my breast, let no barrier, chain, or obstacle do me arrest.

OATH SPELLS

You gain oath spells at the paladin levels listed.

PALADIN LEVEL	SPELLS
3rd	*create or destroy water, expeditious retreat*
5th	*find steed, shatter*
7th	*water breathing, water walk*
9th	*control water, freedom of movement*
17th	*conjure elemental* (water only), *exsanguinate**

(*) see *Deep Magic*.

CHANNEL DIVINITY

At 3rd level, you gain the following Channel Divinity options.

Rebuke the Deep. As an action, you present your holy symbol and speak a prayer, censuring sea creatures. Each beast, fey, humanoid, or monstrosity of your choice that can breathe underwater or that has a swim speed within 30 feet of you and can see or hear you must succeed a Wisdom saving throw or be turned for 1 minute or until it takes damage.

A turned creature must spend its turns trying to move as far away from you as it can, and it can't willingly move to a space within 30 feet of you. It also can't take reactions. For its action, it can use only the Dash action or try to escape from an effect that prevents it from moving. If there's nowhere to move, the creature can use the Dodge action.

Torrential Surge. As an action, you present your holy symbol or slam a melee weapon down before you to conjure a surging wave of water that flows away from you in a 20-foot cone. Any creature that is no more than one size category larger than you caught within the cone must make a Strength saving throw or be knocked back 20 feet and fall prone. On a successful saving throw, a creature is only knocked back 10 feet and does not fall prone. Any creature that is knocked into an object, such as a wall or column, takes 1d6 bludgeoning damage for every 5 feet traveled. A target knocked back this way does not incur opportunity attacks.

SLIPSTREAM AURA

Starting at 7th level, you gain a swim speed equal to your movement speed. Additionally, allies within 10 feet of you begin their turn with a swim speed equal to yours and can spend a bonus action to Dash.

At 18th level, the range of this aura increases to 30 feet.

ROLLING TIDES

Starting at 15th level, the waves you create surge and recede like the tides. When you use Torrential Surge, you create a second wave that pulls creatures back toward you, prompting a second saving throw from any creature caught in the effect. If a creature fails both of its saving throws, they are overcome with sea sickness and are poisoned until the end of its next turn.

TYPHOON CHAMPION

At 20th level, you take on aspects of a sea deity. Your skin carries the sheen of seawater, your hair stays damp and flows in thick waves, and your features take on fish-like exaggerations while you are bathed in moonlight.

By using an action, you can summon a swirling typhoon (or a whirlpool if underwater) centered on yourself. The typhoon lasts for

THE PARABLE OF PERUN'S GIFT

For Perun's faithful, it is not enough to simply make war. A common parable called "Perun's Gift" illustrates this.

The parable teaches that when Perun saw that life was stagnant, he "gifted" the plains with lightning storms. These lightning storms in turn caused wildfires, laying waste to everything aground and driving all creatures away. Perun's enemies and allies alike learned to fear him for this. But when the thunderstorms calmed and the ashes dispersed, new plantings budded, and saplings revealed themselves beneath the scorched brush. The new growth in turn attracted hale creatures. Before long the land was renewed with vigor, brighter and more vibrant than ever before.

The moral behind Perun's Gift is that Perun's wrath is actually a blessing and that conflict is necessary for spiritual, and literal, growth.

10 minutes or until you dismiss it (as a bonus action) and follows you around, granting the following benefits:

- As an action, you can target one creature within the typhoon's radius and knock the wind out of them, possibly causing targets to suffocate or drown. The target must make a Constitution saving throw or run out of breath. While breathless, targets are unable to speak or cast spells with verbal components and have disadvantage on attack rolls and skill checks. A breathless target can repeat their saving throw at the end of their turn, ending the effect on a success or by exiting the radius of the typhoon. Constructs, oozes, and undead are unaffected by this effect.
- At the start of each of your turns, you regain 10 hit points.
- Wind and water swirl around you in a 60-foot radius, making the area difficult terrain. Any creatures affected by your Slipstream Aura ignore the difficult terrain.
- Your melee attacks deal an additional 1d8 bludgeoning damage and knock Large and smaller targets back 5 feet. A target knocked back in this way does not incur opportunity attacks.

Once you use this feature, you can't use it again until you finish a long rest.

Servants of the Storm Lords

Among the religions, cults, and secret orders of Midgard, none are as bombastic as those who worship the gods of thunder, lightning, and battle.

Mavros, Thor, and Perun all command similar levels of fanaticism and expect similar rituals and sacrifices. What separates the tempest gods in the eyes of their followers is how they are worshipped and what ideals they value above others.

The Order of Mavros, a regimented and expansive religious organization, preaches foremost on waging war. But partaking in war is not enough for Mavrites. The need to emerge victorious, to do so with honor, and to respect the opponent and the trappings of war itself are recurring themes in the order's sermons and doctrine. To a follower of Mavros, lightning-swift strikes and the thunder of battle are their prayers and hymns.

This focus on war, however, actually contrasts with how the Northlanders exalt Thor. Followers of the Thunderer place higher importance on slaying monsters and earning their glory from personal deeds. So too are Thor's followers more solitary in nature, eschewing large, regularly attended congregations for more intimate offerings to shrines and after hunts, personal moments of piety during storms, and dedications of glory in the face of perilous encounters.

While Mavrites seek to honor their god through their actions, followers of Thor seek to emulate the Thunderer himself, striving to become like him in their own deeds.

And the servants of Perun? Many Perunites seek war and action like the Order of Mavros while others dance and taunt the rain like Thor's followers. And in fact, every priest of each Storm Lord will find cause to practice like the priests of the other. But some servants of Perun prefer to ponder on the duality, the polarity, that Perun symbolizes as the lord of both strife and rebirth.

While understanding the cause and effect of conflict is worthwhile, many Perunites see such studies of harmony as a waste of time. The mainstream Perunite doctrine preaches war as the worthiest of goals. But places like the Thunderbolt Monastery exist for those who are open to Perun's deeper meanings.

THUNDERBOLT MONASTERY

A cloistered hermitage resting on a peak in the northern spur of the White Mountains, not far from the White Wood, nestled on the White Road ley line, the Thunderbolt Monastery functions as a lightning rod for spiritual and climatic activity. Under the leadership of

Grandmaster Hymolt, monks here spend their lives studying the monastery's extensive library of historical and religious writings. Adhering to a flexible polytheistic approach, the monks chiefly worship Perun but also the various aspects of divinity as it manifests in war, thunder, and lightning. It's believed that the monastery keeps a one-of-a-kind copy of the *Annals of Mavros*, an apocryphal scripture supposedly cataloging prophecies that predicted all of Mavros's Great Saints and the coming of many more, though none at the monastery choose to confirm this rumor.

The monastery itself is actually a system of three buildings interconnected by roughhewn mountainous tunnels. Reaching the monastery requires a steep hike through scree, charred trees, and winding switchbacks, often through the mudslide-inducing rainstorms that frequent the locale.

Despite being devout worshippers of the gods of thunder and war, the monks are ill-regarded by members of the House of Swords for their differing approaches to piety. The House of Swords sees the monastery as a place of cowardice, bordering on heresy, for the latter's unwillingness to get directly involved with countrywide conflicts. Truthfully, the monastery holds no policy against violence or war. They simply consider their responsibility to keep wartime records a higher priority.

Privately, many high-ranking priests and political leaders from the Seven Cities and the Crossroads journey to the monastery seeking insight or to report wartime developments for the monastery's scribes.

While waiting for these clandestine visits to conclude, the visitors' entourages are invited to observe a rare treat. In addition to their historical duties, the monks of Thunderbolt Monastery practice a unique form of martial art, manifesting primal forces through their very bodies. Witnessing these fervent practices, more than one visiting warrior has stayed behind to exchange battle knowledge. So too do plenty of monks accompany dignitaries when their visits conclude, hoping to see the wider world of Midgard and gain first-hand accounts from battlefronts and war rooms.

Grandmaster Hymolt. Hymolt Goslarrsen is a man of deep thought and outspoken opinion. Unlike his predecessor, Vicello Falderan, who preferred to maintain a certain political balance, Hymolt is a man who brashly says what he thinks, no matter who or what the subject might be. Though his thick accent betrays his non-nativity to the region, his bombastic persona has earned him unwavering devotion from his fellow monks and the begrudging respect of the Seven Cities' numerous war leaders. His most noteworthy work is the *Chronica Tonitrum*, a compiled history of the Seven Cities' many conflicts and their religious significance. Though treated as scripture by Hymolt's monks, the account is oft-maligned (typically by those it critiques) for its scathing annotations that point out political missteps and military blunders. A fierce and disciplined combatant, both in debate and in combat, Hymolt is unforgiving of those who choose to hide their mistakes rather than own them.

WAY OF THE STORM (MONASTIC TRADITION)

Gather yourself like a cloud on the horizon and strike with the sudden fury of the heavens.

Monks who practice the Way of the Storm are living fonts of storm energy, tapping into the wellsprings within themselves to conjure powers attributed to deities of tempests and battle fury. What mages spend lifetimes of studying esoterica to achieve, storm monks learn to do through intensive contemplation, religious study, and rigorous training.

Their doctrine holds that the ki within us all is a measure of divinity, and it is up to the individual to learn to access it. Monks who practice this tradition seek to transcend the limits of their mortal coil to become living lightning rods, scouring the battlefield with fistfuls of lightning while leaving charred foes and sonic booms in their wake.

BONUS PROFICIENCIES

At 3rd level, you gain proficiency in Religion. You also gain proficiency with calligrapher's supplies.

SPARKING STRIKES

Starting at 3rd level, you learn to draw upon the storm inside you to empower your blows. Whenever you expend ki, your attacks deal additional lightning or thunder damage (your choice) equal to your proficiency bonus until the beginning of your next turn. Any creature within 5 feet of a target you hit with this feature also takes the additional lightning or thunder damage.

STORM'S DISCIPLE

Starting at 6th level, your connection to your inner storm swells as you gain new ways to expend ki.

Discharging Rebuke. When a creature hits you with a melee attack, you can spend 1 or more ki points as a reaction, forcing that creature to make a Dexterity saving throw. On a failed save, the target takes lightning damage equal to the result of your martial arts die per point of ki expended. On a successful save, the target takes half as much damage. You can never spend more ki points than your proficiency bonus in this way.

Lightning Reach. You can expend 2 ki points as part of a ranged weapon attack to double the weapon's range. Unless the weapon is ammunition, broken, or held by another creature, it returns to your hand at the beginning of your next turn.

VOLTAIC SOUL

At 11th level, you've learned how to move with the storm and how to let it move through you, mastering the pain to recharge your spirit. Whenever you take lightning damage, you regain 1 ki point. Whenever you take thunder damage, you can immediately use your reaction to use your Step of the Wind feature at no ki cost.

TURBULENT STEP

At 17th level, whenever you use your full movement on your turn, you can take an action to expend 4 ki points and create a 30-foot cone of thunderous force aimed behind you. The cone originates after you have come to a stop. All creatures caught within the cone must make a Constitution saving throw, taking 8d8 thunder damage and being deafened until the end of their next turn on a failed save or half as much damage and no additional effects on a successful one.

Rites of the Crossroads

Each god is honored with rituals and sacrifices according to their own principles, yet many of the faithful in the Crossroads share common ground in religious rites and rituals.

BLESS FEAST

Prerequisite: Requires a Holy Symbol and a Pound of Fresh Food per Person

Fellowship takes many forms: spending time together in public prayer when Khors has hidden the sun behind overcast skies for too many weeks, Volund-worshipping friars basking in the heat from a roaring forge and quenching a still red-hot blade in their sweat, dwarves passed out from a night of merriment and ale, "gone to visit Ninkash." What makes a feast so sacred is that it is a shared act, not a solitary one. For travelers who frequent the Sultan's Road, a blessed meal holds the most significance.

Characters that share a fresh meal (rations are unfit as a sacred offering) benefit from a blessing called Volund's Sjelevarme, which lasts for 24 hours. While under the effect of this blessing, a character has advantage on death saving throws and saving throws against fear, provided they are within at least 60 feet of someone else with whom they shared the meal.

Prerequisite: Requires Proficiency in Religion and a Holy Symbol

When Turn Undead or the *dispel evil and good* spell are unavailable or inadequate, other measures may be required to end a possession. To do so, a character must make a series of checks with a DC determined by how tenacious the possession is.

The character makes three checks: Intelligence (Religion), Wisdom (Religion), and a special Charisma check that has a bonus equal to a roll of the character's largest Hit Die (this roll doesn't spend that die). The DC for each of the checks is determined by the possessing creature's CR + 1d6 + 10. Generate a separate DC for each one.

If the character succeeds on two or more checks, the possession ends, and any spirit present is driven out and away as if by a cleric's Turn Undead. If the character fails on two or more, the possession becomes entrenched, and any further attempts to expel the possessing spirit automatically fail for the next 24 hours. Allies can use the Help action to assist, but they may have to contend with any complications. Intimate knowledge of the possessing spirit or demon, such as a true name or hidden secret, could potentially provide advantage on one of the checks.

Complications. Possessions are challenging under the best of circumstances. A creature that doesn't want to give up its host will most likely retaliate against those performing the ritual as well as anyone else present. After each check is made, roll a d6 and consult the **Possession Complications** table to see what complications characters might have to deal with. If a complication calls for a saving throw or skill check, the DC is the same as the previous check.

POSSESSION COMPLICATIONS

d6	COMPLICATION
1	Doors and windows slam open and shut while furniture and other loose items fly around the area.
2	Candles, torches, and any other open flames or flammable materials flare with intense heat, catching fire and potentially spreading.
3	Every creature present, including the possessed creature, if any, must make a Constitution saving throw or gain one level of exhaustion.
4	One present character at random must make a Wisdom saving throw or fall under the effect of a *bestow curse* spell. The curse lasts for a week or until re-moved by *remove curse* or similar magic.
5	The possession moves to another crea-ture or area and requires a successful Wisdom (Perception) check to locate.
6	No complication.

SANCTIFY LAND

*Prerequisite: Requires the Ability to Cast
Divine Spells*

With intense prayer and devotion, a place
or thing can be sanctified. This becomes a
regular duty for those priests charged with
the caretaking of holy sites, shrines, and
temple sanctuaries. Altars, mausoleums, and
sepulchers are also frequent targets, especially
if intrusion or unholy resurrection is a risk.

While not as powerful as higher-level divine
magic, a divine spellcaster can spend a short
rest in prayer and the preparation of material
sacrifice to achieve a similar magical effect.

After spending a short rest in prayer, roll percentile dice. If you roll a number equal to or lower than your character level, you are successful, and any items you sacrificed are used up. You may then choose one secondary effect from the *hallow* spell, which then stays in effect for a week or until dispelled. For every 10 gp you spend in sacrificed material you add 5 to your character level for the purpose of this rite.

Holy Orders

Holy orders are typically a temple's official recognition of a paladin's oath, a priest or cleric's ordination, the crowning of royalty, or the marking of an important event. Holy orders differ greatly based on the deity of the religious persons conducting them. Here are holy order rituals you might bear witness to while in the Crossroads.

Khorsicans. The most common holy orders for Khors's faithful are the ones received when being knighted in the Order of the Undying Sun. Oaths taken in this ceremony are recited from the *Book of the Sun* as a high-ranking member of the church, or in a few cases, Queen Dorytta herself taps the shoulders and head of the prospective knight with their own sword.

Ladites. Followers of Lada always carry out their holy orders at dawn and always from a high point, such as a cliff, hill, or even a roof if necessary. After scripture from the *Golden Book of Ruby Laughter* is quoted, a procession is led to the nearest clinic or infirmary where the newly ordained spend the rest of their day fasting as they work to heal the sick.

Perunites. In order to satisfy Perun, his priests only conduct their holy orders during stormy weather, preferably as close to thunder and lightning as possible. A bull is slaughtered, and its blood is used to anoint whoever is receiving the holy orders. Then ritualistic combat to first blood is held. If the newly anointed loses the fight, they are excommunicated for their failure and must seek penance.

Ravanites. Serving the patron deity of industry, Rava's priests conduct holy orders for new businesses and temple-approved inventions. More christening than ordainment, bottles of sacred wine, or beer if the proper obeisance has been made to Ninkash, are broken upon new foundations, ribbons are cut, and vows of responsible trade are made.

Vaer. To followers of Ninkash, community and responsibility are prime virtues, and this reflects in their holy orders. When a dwarf enters the Vaer, they undergo a test to demonstrate their wisdom and worth. The prospective priest must go to every witness present and get them drunk, though not so drunk as to become irresponsible, harmful to themselves or others, or too incoherent to join in the final drinking song of the night. Only once a dwarf has successfully done this are they admitted into the Vaer.

Volundites. Holy orders devoted to Volund differ by region and by who is leading them. The dwarves of the Free Cantons hold a call and response ceremony, hammering tools down on anvils in rhythm and syncopation to concerted chanting. The Khazzaki of the Rothenian Plain, however, wear beautiful, multicolored vestments decorated with Volund's symbols, and they dance and sing well into the night.

INDEX

Tony DiTerlizzi